IN THE CHILLING AFTERMATH OF WAR,
THEIR FIERY PASSIONS BLAZED ACROSS THE
BATTLE-SCARRED LAND . . .

Anna Kelley Terrified of losing the man she loved, she kept a desperate secret from him—until it was almost too late. . . .

Nate Foster Sworn to uphold justice in a war-torn land, he dared to desire the one woman whose devastating deception could cost him his life. . . .

Fran Rogers Driven by demons of hate and jealousy, she burned for revenge against the Northern butchers who'd murdered her husband—and the traitorous woman who'd stolen her love. . . .

Darryl Kelley Destroyed by a war that had ravaged his mind and corrupted his soul, he wanted revenge for the pain he'd suffered—but he couldn't forget the lady who tormented his dreams. . . .

Embers of the Heart

Bantam Books by Rosanne Bittner

MONTANA WOMAN

EMBERS OF THE HEART

Embers
of
the
Heart

Rosanne Bittner

Bantam Books
NEW YORK • TORONTO • LONDON • SYDNEY • AUCKLAND

EMBERS OF THE HEART
A BANTAM BOOK / SEPTEMBER 1990

ISBN 0-553-28599-8

Published simultaneously in the United States and Canada

Bantam Books are published by Bantam Books, a division of Bantam
Doubleday Dell Publishing Group, Inc. Its trademark, consisting of
the words "Bantam Books" and the portrayal of a rooster, is
Registered in U.S. Patent and Trademark Office and in other
countries. Marca Registrada. Bantam Books, 666 Fifth Avenue, New
York, New York 10103

PRINTED IN THE UNITED STATES OF AMERICA

OPM   0 9 8 7 6 5 4 3 2 1

They will hammer their swords into plows
and their spears into pruning knives.
Nations will never again go to war,
never prepare for battle again.

—Isaiah 2:4

Foreword

In the years preceding the Civil War, a private war had already started in territories that had not yet declared whether they were for or against slavery, for or against states' rights. This tension spawned the infamous border wars between Kansas and Missouri, led by men like John Brown and William Quantrill. The abolitionists came to be called jayhawkers; those in favor of slavery and states' rights, bushwhackers.

During the War Between the States, most such men joined either the Union or the Confederacy, but a few remained behind to create havoc for innocent civilians in Kansas and Missouri. When the war was over, many of these men had lost track of their original causes. Plunder and murder had become a way of life, something men like Quantrill and "Bloody" Bill Anderson could no longer control. Men who had been fighting for what they believed was a good cause used their knowledge of guerrilla warfare to become flagrant highwaymen and bank robbers, with names as famous as Jesse and Frank James.

Some men returned from the war completely changed by

its horrors and the hatred it bred in their hearts. And for many of their women, the fires of love were doused by bitterness and vengeance, leaving only a few, small, dying embers in their hearts.

Most of the major historical episodes in this novel, such as the raid at Centralia, Missouri, are true; however, the characters and their personal stories are purely fictitious and a product of the author's imagination. Any resemblance to characters bearing the same names who might have existed during this time period is purely coincidental.

I'll remember you the way you were,
Before our hearts were ravaged, dear,
By war's cruel sword that cuts so deep
And leaves but embers, and a tear . . .

—*Rosanne Bittner*

Chapter 1

1860

Anna stopped packing for a moment and touched the pearl necklace that graced her slender neck, the little golden heart at its center representing Darryl's love for her. He had given it to her on their wedding day, hardly a year ago. It had been a year of blissful love for them, but life had not been so blissful on the streets of Lawrence, Kansas.

Her heart ached for Darryl and the way he had been treated just because he came from a plantation family in Georgia. Sometimes it seemed all of Kansas was ready to explode. She was sick of all the hatred, the fighting that seemed to go on daily in the streets between those for or against slavery and states' rights. Border wars with Missouri between bushwhackers and jayhawkers had devastated the countryside and had taken many lives needlessly.

"I feel like this is my fault, Darryl," she told her husband.

She heard a deep sigh, and in the next moment his strong, gentle hands were on her shoulders. He nuzzled her thick, strawberry-blond hair, then wrapped his arms around her from behind.

"Don't be ridiculous," he answered. He spoke with the

heavy Southern drawl that she had learned to love. "It's the prejudice of all the ignorant people in this town. Lawrence is full of jayhawkers, and I'm from Georgia. My parents own slaves. Most of these people can't see past that."

"It isn't fair," Anna answered, turning to look into his soft brown eyes. Darryl was a sturdy but slender man, always immaculately dressed, his dark hair neatly combed. She had been attracted to him the moment he had come to Lawrence, a new, young doctor, ready to devote his services to the Kansas frontier, where doctors were scarce. That was two years ago, and she had only been sixteen. Darryl was twenty-six then. Why did two years suddenly seem like ten? So much had happened, so many hurts and insults to a man who had come here out of a sincere desire to help.

"You tried so hard, Darryl. You've done nothing against any of these people. You've never taken sides—"

He put his fingers to her lips. "There's no sense going over it again and again, Anna." He studied her lovely blue eyes, loving the feel of her perfectly curved body against his own. She was only eighteen, but there was nothing childish about her, except her innocent virginity when he had married her. Anna was a strong young woman, raised in a rough frontier town, a creature of amazing grace and beauty that he had never expected to find when he came here to set up his practice. He had hoped there would be a child by now, but he never mentioned it to her. He knew that deep inside it worried her that she still had not conceived.

"I'm not going to stay here and continue to see you suffer insults because of me," he continued. "Let alone the danger to your very life. That burning torch thrown through the window two nights ago is as far as I'm going to let this go. I'm worried something will happen to you just because you married a Southern man."

"But I don't think of you that way. You're just my husband, a fine doctor who could have helped this community."

"It doesn't matter what you think. Right now this whole country is full of hatred, Anna, and you and I can't do anything about it."

Her eyes teared, and she wrapped her arms around him,

resting her head against his chest. "I'll miss my sister, and Father, even though right now I'm so angry with them. I hate all these hard feelings. Joline and I were always so close when we were growing up, especially after Mother died."

"I know. Someday this will all be over, and you'll be close to your family again. In the meantime, your pa and your sister will be all right. They're both strong and stubborn." He smiled to himself. "Like you," he teased. He petted her hair. "I would have liked to get along better with your pa, Anna. When I first came here, we seemed to do just fine. Then Greg Masters came along," he added, referring to Joline's new husband. "He started up with all that antislavery talk, still starts an argument every time we're with them."

He let go of her. "I can't make them understand, Anna. My folks don't whip their slaves and tear their families apart and all the other things most Northerners think. I know those things go on, but not on my folks' plantation." He let go of her, running a hand through his dark hair. "Hell, without slave labor, my folks couldn't keep the place going."

Anna dropped her eyes, her emotions mixed. She didn't want to tell him that she also could not fully understand the concept of slavery. Even if the slaves were well treated, it still didn't seem quite right to "own" human beings. Sometimes when Darryl talked about them, it seemed almost as though he didn't really think of them as human at all. But because of the true compassion he seemed to show for his own race, his desire to be able to help and heal, she didn't want to believe he could think differently about Negroes. After all, here was a man who could have chosen to stay on that plantation and live off his wealthy parents. But he had chosen to be a doctor, had chosen to come to the frontier, where doctors were so badly needed. His parents had sent him money when he told them of his marriage to Anna, but he had put that in a savings account—"For our children," he had told her. She worried now whether she would be able to give him any.

Darryl came closer, touching her chin and leaning down to kiss her cheek. "Someday, when all this is over, I'll take you to Georgia, Anna. You can see for yourself the kind of people my folks are. You'd love it there. The plantation is beautiful. Somehow we'll get through all this." He ran his fingers over the pearl necklace. "You just remember who gave you this necklace and what it represents. You hang on to it, no matter what happens."

She met his eyes, frowning. "I don't like the way you said that. We're just going to Missouri to live with a friend of yours, right? I mean, if this country ends up in war, you wouldn't go off and leave me, would you?"

She saw pride and anger glitter in his dark eyes, and her heart tightened with dread. "It's a possibility, Anna."

"Darryl—"

"Anna, it's becoming more and more obvious the Union is jealous of our Southern wealth and our free labor. They want to crush us. The big factory owners in the North are out to destroy us—to destroy our whole way of life! My father and his father before him worked all their lives to build what they have. If the Union had its way, the South would be changed forever. My parents and others like them are about to face the possibility of losing everything they live for! Do you think I could sit by and let that happen?"

Her eyes widened with a mixture of astonishment and near disappointment. "I thought . . . I thought we felt the same way about all this hatred, all this ridiculous rivalry between North and South. I thought we were both neutral in our feelings—that we just wanted to live our lives apart from all of it."

He stepped back, voicing an odd snicker of surprise. "Anna, what kind of fantasy world are you living in? I would *love* it if we could do that. But this is getting too big for both of us. It's going to be impossible not to get involved eventually." He threw up his hands. "Hell, I'm not saying I'd march off to war tomorrow. I'm just asking you to remember who I am, where I come from, what all this means to my family."

"But . . . you're a *doctor*. You *save* lives. You don't destroy them."

He nodded. "And I hope to keep it that way. If war should come, and if I decided to do my part in defending the South and states' rights, I would volunteer as a doctor. That's all, Anna. I'd help the ones who get hurt."

She swallowed back a lump in her throat. "But . . . you'd still be in danger. You could still get killed."

He pulled her against him again. "Anna, it hasn't even come to that yet, and it might *never* come to that. I'm just trying to explain the worst possibilities. I want you to be ready, and I want you to understand and to support my beliefs."

She loved him, trusted him. What did slavery and states' rights and possible war have to do with their personal needs and passions? In fact, right now, what did her own doubts about slavery matter? She just wanted her husband to stay close to her. She didn't want him to go away or get hurt, and right now she didn't want to make matters worse by admitting she couldn't quite agree with his beliefs.

"I'll try to understand, Darryl. And I do support you, because I love you so much. I just . . . I don't know. Ever since that torch came through our front window, I've begun to realize how serious this is. It frightens me."

He rubbed her back. "Well, it just so happens that it frightens me, too. Things will be better in Columbia. Missouri is having its own battle between jayhawkers and bushwhackers, but there the sympathy is for the South, at least for the moment. We'll live with Fran and Mark for a while, Anna, just till we see if this all comes to war, and see how dangerous things are. We'll be safer that way. After a while, if things calm down, we'll find our own place."

"I hope it's soon. You know how much I enjoy having my own home, fixing things my own way."

"I know. I just figured Missouri was a reasonable compromise right now. You won't be so far from your pa that you lose touch. I'll be with an old friend from Georgia and from school. We'll just kind of wait things out in Missouri—see what happens. For the moment I don't think it's wise to go any farther east, either north or south."

She looked up at him. "Do you think Fran Rogers will like me?"

He grinned. "How could she *not* like you? You're beautiful and sweet and you get along with anyone."

She ran her hands along his upper arms, lowering her eyes. "You said you and Fran were close once."

"We were very young, and we lived near each other. It was a childish fling, that's all. Fran's father was an overseer on the plantation. Fran and I used to go riding together sometimes, and one summer when we were only about sixteen, I kissed her. I went off to school that year, and that was the end of it. The next summer we both realized it was just a childish thing. That's about all there was to it."

She met his eyes again. "Maybe she didn't take it all that lightly. Maybe she loved you more than you think—the handsome young son of her father's boss. She might still have feelings for you." She ran her fingers over the thin scar on his left cheek, put there at an early age by a riding accident.

Darryl chuckled. "She's married to Mark, Anna. I brought him home one summer from school and introduced them, long after I had broken things off with Fran. By the next summer Fran and Mark were married. End of story." He leaned closer then, touching his nose to hers. "Besides, she didn't turn into the beautiful woman you are. Fran took after her father, who was a big, mean sort of fellow. I'm not saying she took after him in personality, just physically. She's tall and strong and could probably outdo some men; and right now I don't want to talk about her."

He met her mouth tenderly. Tensions had been so high, it had been a while since they had made love. Darryl had made it beautiful for her on their wedding night, and she had quickly learned that lovemaking was something to be enjoyed, not dreaded. The kiss became deeper, warmer, both of them expressing a need to put aside anxieties and talk of war, and just enjoy their love.

He picked her up in his arms and carried her into the bedroom, neither of them caring that she had already stripped the bed and packed the blankets. For the moment she would forget about the hatred in Lawrence, forget that she was being forced to leave this lovely house Darryl had rented for them and that they had sold the lovely furnishings he had bought for her. He had promised her a new home and new furnishings when they got settled in Columbia.

Darryl had always taken good care of her. He had money from his family, and he was capable of earning good money himself as a doctor. Perhaps in Missouri he would do even better. After they were married he had insisted she buy the best furniture, the finest clothing, and he had even hired a woman to help with cooking and cleaning.

Anna Barker Kelley had not asked for any of it, nor had she married Darryl because of his wealth. She simply loved him. She had been raised on a farm outside of Lawrence, the daughter of Tom Barker, a man who came from hardy stock in Illinois. Anna and her sister, Joline, had helped their father with the farm all their lives, Anna taking her mother's place inside the farmhouse and with general farm chores expected of a farm wife, Joline helping with the heavier chores. Their father had often teased that Joline was the "son he never had," and both sisters worked hard.

Anna was accustomed to living without the luxuries Darryl offered her. But Darryl had insisted. For him the finest things were a way of life. Darryl Kelley came from another world, a world of wealth and slaves and a gracious, gentler way of living. Anna was learning to accept and enjoy the kind of life he wanted for her. And as she became lost in his lovemaking, she gave no thought to the possibility that one day soon she might have to draw on the rugged Barker strength that had been bred into her.

1861

The new home in Columbia never came to be. Missouri was as full of strife and bloodshed as Kansas, and Darryl insisted it was safer to continue to live with Mark and Fran. He never even got around to setting up a practice. Instead, they both helped with the Main Street Inn, the restaurant the Rogerses owned. Fran and Mark had moved to Missouri to be closer to Fran's mother, who had come here to live with a sister in Centralia after Fran's father died. Mark had set up his business here in Columbia because it was a bigger town, only a short train ride from Centralia. The couple had done well. Mark had studied business in college, and he loved to cook. He had combined that love with his education and had created a successful restaurant. But lately they had lost a few customers because they were "Confederates from Georgia."

Anna wondered now how a whole year had slipped by so quickly. And when and how, during that year, she and Darryl had lost the seemingly perfect love they had shared back in Lawrence for that first year of marriage.

She was packing again, this time for an even more heartbreaking reason than having to flee Lawrence and come to Missouri. This time she was packing a few things for Darryl, who was going off to war with Mark Rogers. He had told her so matter-of-factly, as though she had no choice in the decision, with a look in his eyes telling her not to argue the issue. Three months ago the Confederates, as the citizens of the Southern secessionist states called themselves, had fired on Fort Sumter. Union soldiers had answered the shots. The United States was at war, and Darryl could not ignore his Southern pride. The Union was already moving into Southern territory, threatening his family's very way of life.

It seemed incredible to Anna that any state would want to secede from the Union, but several already had, including Georgia. A barrage of political game playing and a test of Federal versus state control had culminated in a dreaded war, with slavery emerging as the apparent key issue. Anna knew it went much deeper than that, but things had happened so fast, and there were so many misunderstandings and confused rumors and newspaper stories, that how and where the ugly mess had truly begun seemed vague now. She sensed this was fast becoming a war of pride, like children wanting to have their own way.

"I wish you would stay right here," she told Darryl, keeping her voice low, since Fran and Mark were still in the house. The house itself had already been sold. Fran and Anna were to take rooms at a boarding house not far from the restaurant Mark and Fran owned. Fran was to use the money from the sale of the house however she needed while Mark was gone.

"This should only take a few weeks," Mark had said at the dinner table last night. "Then again it could take a lot longer. You women will be a lot safer in a place where there are more people, and you won't have so far to walk to the restaurant, so you won't have to worry about thugs and outlaws."

"God knows there is enough fighting right here in Missouri," Anna continued aloud as she continued packing.

"We're needed a lot worse in other places," Darryl answered. "There are too many pro-Union forces here. Missouri is already a lost cause, as far as I'm concerned. You know what happened at Boonville. Governor Jackson has already retreated to the southern end of the state. I'll probably go to Georgia and check on my folks, then go on to Richmond and formally volunteer my services."

"You'll just volunteer as a doctor, won't you?" she urged. "You won't get involved in the fighting?"

Their eyes held as he buttoned his shirt. "I'll do my best, Anna. It all depends on how ugly this war gets."

She turned away. "You're only doing this because of Fran and Mark. They're both so . . . so adamant that the South is right . . . already so devoted to the Confederacy. Mark talked you into this. He railed and ranted about going off to fight for the South, and he infected you with his patriotism. A disease, that's what it is. It's like an ugly disease that is festering and spreading." Her voice choked, and she could hardly see what she was doing for the tears in her eyes.

Darryl moved to the bed and sat down, pulling her down beside him. "It isn't that way, Anna. It's a matter of standing up for what a man believes is right."

"But what if you're *not* right?" she gasped, tears running down her cheeks as she faced him. For the first time since she had known Darryl Kelley, she saw a flash of anger in his eyes.

"Do *you* think I'm wrong? Do you think the *South* is wrong?"

She looked at her lap. "I don't know what I think about anything anymore. I only know that I love you and I don't want you to go away. Missouri is exploding with gangs and thugs, jayhawkers and bushwhackers. The home we were going to have here never came to be. And the quiet happiness we shared when we first got married disappeared so quickly. I'm so sick of talk of war and states' rights and slavery, of Union and Confederate causes." She met his eyes again. "I just want to be with you, Darryl. I want our own home, my own kitchen, an office for you in one wing. I want my wonderful physician husband here, helping people get well, sitting at our own supper table every night. I can't stand the thought of not knowing where you are or if you're all right."

He grasped her arms as she broke into tears. He drew her against him, letting her cry. "I'll write, Anna. And if I volunteer as a doctor, I'll be behind the lines. I'll be all right. As long as you take a room at that boarding house and stay close to the restaurant, you'll be all right too, while you wait for me. I suppose there are safer places you could go, but there isn't time to decide where, and I need to know exactly where I can find you when I come back. Besides, I promised Mark you'd stay here and help Fran at the restaurant."

"Fran doesn't like me." She turned away and rose, wiping at her eyes with a handkerchief she took from a pocket on her blue cotton dress.

"That's nonsense."

"You know that it isn't," Anna answered, her voice stronger. "She knows my father and Jo's husband are pro-Union, that they've already left to volunteer. You saw how she shunned them when they stopped here to see me; you know how she has behaved toward me ever since. She looks at me as though I'm the enemy. And if it was just that, it wouldn't be so bad. But she was unfriendly even before that. She's always acted almost jealous of me, ever since we first came here, as though I've interfered with the friendship she and Mark shared with you."

Darryl watched her as he slowly rose. "Anna, that's all in your imagination. I've told you that before. You feel out of place because Fran and Mark are from my past, from my home; and because we're all Confederate sympathizers."

"It's not my imagination." She closed her eyes and turned away. Darryl studied his wife's beautiful form, always surprised at how well she carried herself in spite of coming from a Kansas farm. She had all the grace and elegance of the most refined Southern belle.

"Darryl," she said softly. "I don't want *you* to think of me as an enemy. I want you to understand that I don't take *anyone's* side in this war. I detest the fighting, on both sides. And I simply . . . love you. I want us to get back to the life we planned when we first got married."

He walked over to her, putting his hand on her waist. "We will, Anna. It might take a few more months, but it will happen. I can understand how hard it might be for you to stand behind the Confederacy, but I *do* need you to stand behind *me.* I need your support, Anna. I need you to understand the part of me that compels me to do this. This is for my family, for a whole way of life, for Georgia."

She turned and met his eyes, realizing that for the moment Georgia and his family came before his love for her. To know that made her realize just how important this was to him. "Just come back to me, Darryl," she said in a near whisper. "We've had . . . so little time."

He drew her into his arms, and they embraced deeply, desperately. "I'll come back, Anna. That's a promise."

They clung together, and Anna wept bitterly. Darryl wove his fingers into the cascading waves of her hair, wondering how long it would be before he held her this way again, wondering for a moment if leaving was right—but only for a moment. The thought of losing the plantation, of the Union dictating how the Southern states should conduct their business, was all he needed to revitalize his determination.

"We've got to finish packing," he told her then.

There was a knock on the door to their room. "Mark is ready," came Fran's voice. Anna detected the excitement in the few words. Fran Rogers seemed almost elated that her husband was going off to war. She was a staunch Confederate, declaring one night that any Southern man who didn't volunteer to fight for the "cause" was little more than a coward and a traitor. She had even said she'd go and fight herself if she could, and Anna didn't doubt she would do just as well as any man. Fran fit Darryl's description. She was a big woman, tall and dark and domineering, not beautiful, but not really unpleasant to look at. Big and plain, that was how Anna thought of her.

"We'll be right out," Darryl called to the woman.

Anna pulled away from Darryl, blowing her nose and wiping at her eyes. She shoved her handkerchief back into the pocket of her dress, realizing there was no use prolonging the agony. Darryl and Mark were leaving today, and that was that. It was time to be strong, for Darryl's sake.

"Anna—"

She waved him off and proceeded to finish packing his bag. She realized this would all have been a little easier if she could have gotten closer to Fran—if she could talk to the woman, share her feelings. But there was a cold cloud around Fran Rogers that Anna had been unable to penetrate. She seemed at times almost emotionless—all business when it came to the restaurant, a near dictator to those around her; a woman who operated on exact schedules and who seemed uninterested in feminine pastimes, such as piano playing or embroidery or joining a quilting club. She almost seemed more man than woman in personality, and Anna could picture her commanding an army. She wondered sometimes what Darryl had ever seen in her, but perhaps she had been different when she was younger.

It mattered little now. The fact remained she would have to continue putting up with the woman until Darryl returned. At least the boarding house where they would room was the same place where Claudine Marquis lived. Claudine was the new cook Mark had hired to take his place. Claudine was from New Orleans, originally from France. She was an older woman, and extremely friendly. She had warmed to Anna right away, taking Anna under her wing like a mother hen. Fran always frowned darkly and ordered Claudine back to work whenever she caught the woman chatting with Anna. At least now, in the evenings after the restaurant was closed, Anna could go and visit Claudine whenever she wanted. With Darryl gone, there would be no one else to talk to in this town where few could be trusted.

She thought for a moment about her sister, Joline, alone on the farm now, their father and Jo's husband gone off to war. She knew that she was not alone in her agony. Hundreds, probably thousands of women would be going through this grief in the coming months. She worried about Joline, wondered if she should go to her. But there were still too many hard feelings over the way Darryl had been treated. When Greg and her father had come to see her before going off to volunteer for the Union, they wouldn't even speak to Darryl. War was not going to heal the wounds. It would only make things worse.

"Everything is ready," she told Darryl, her voice sounding far away. Darryl fussed with his jacket, having chosen to wear a plain, inexpensive suit.

"No sense wearing my Sunday best," he told her rather sheepishly when she turned to look at him. "Before long I'll be wearing a Confederate uniform and won't need civilian clothes at all."

Her eyes met his. "I love you, Darryl," she said softly.

His own dark gaze moved over her. "And I love you."

"I wish . . . I wish I could have given you a child. Maybe then you would have stayed."

He shook his head. "No, Anna. I would only have had more reason to fight—to preserve his inheritance. In a way I'm doing this for the children we haven't had yet—but will have, when I come back."

If you come back, she thought. She kept the words to herself. There was nothing more to say, and no time to make love again. They had done all that last night, then had fallen asleep in each other's arms. She prayed that someday soon Darryl Kelley would again be able to hold her that way. "Please write as often as possible," she told him.

"I will. And I'll give you an address where you can write back. They'll find me, wherever I am." He picked up his bag and wrapped an arm around her shoulders. "And don't let Fran upset you. Fran is just Fran. She's got nothing against you personally. While we're gone, you two will need each other."

Anna didn't reply. There was no sense trying to convince him of what she was sure Fran's feelings were toward her. They walked out of the room, and Anna suddenly felt as though she couldn't breathe. Dread welled up in her soul like a vise, squeezing at her heart, her ribs, constricting her throat. The moment had come to say good-bye.

They made their way downstairs and to the porch outside, where Fran, hardly smaller than Mark, who was a slender, fair man of medium height, was embracing her husband. There were no tears in her eyes, only a sparkling excitement. "It's about time," she told Darryl when she spotted them. She let go of Mark and rushed over to embrace Darryl. "Come back to us," she told him. A look came into her eyes that Anna had noticed before, something deeper than friendship. Anna's womanly instincts told her that Fran had never really lost her affection and passion for Darryl. She kissed him on the lips, then turned back to Mark.

"You two take care of each other. Try to get into the same regiment, or whatever they call it."

"We will," Mark said with a smile. "Ol' Darryl and I have been looking out for each other ever since school."

Anna could hardly believe how joyous both Mark and Fran seemed. It was like an exciting new game to them. Didn't they realize how serious this was? Didn't Fran realize her husband could be killed? She watched the woman grasp a hand of each man, squeezing them, her face showing pure pride and conviction. "This is for Georgia, my love, my friend—for the South and all she stands for. Kill those Yankees and get it over with."

Anna felt her stomach turn. The woman was talking about Anna's own father, her own brother-in-law. She suddenly realized Mark and Darryl would be fighting against them! Newspaper headlines about brother fighting against brother had significance for her in a way they never had before. And she knew that Fran Rogers most certainly considered her a Yankee enemy, even if the woman didn't say it in so many words. The next few months were going to be hell.

"We'll do our best," Mark was saying. He kissed his wife once more, and Darryl returned to embrace Anna, giving her a long, gentle kiss of good-bye.

"I love you," he whispered.

"I love you, too. Come back as soon as you can, Darryl."

"You know I will. I miss you already."

She caught a trace of tears in his eyes as he took the bag from her and stepped off the porch. He mounted a sturdy black gelding, and Mark mounted his Appaloosa. For a brief moment Darryl looked as though he were considering changing his mind. Then he turned his horse and rode off, refusing to look back. Mark followed.

Both women watched, and Anna wondered if Fran's chest and throat hurt as badly as her own.

"They look wonderful," Fran said. "The South is going to win this war, Anna. You'll see. Your Union can't force us to live under a dictatorship."

Anna didn't answer. For the moment she didn't feel like getting into an argument with the woman.

Fran took a deep breath. "We'd better go open the restaurant."

Anna looked into the woman's dark, commanding eyes. "Today? Can't you leave it closed for today?"

"Why should I?" Fran answered, giving Anna a familiar look of disdain. "Might as well keep busy."

"But we . . . we have to pack to go to the boarding house. The new owners of this place are moving in in two days."

"We'll pack tonight. They bought the furniture with the house, even some of the china. There isn't that much to take." She folded her arms. "I hope you aren't going to be all down in the mouth about this, Anna. Our husbands have gone off to fight for a worthy cause. You should be proud." Her eyes narrowed. "But then I suppose you're rooting for the Union. I hope you realize that's traitorous to your husband."

"I don't call it being a traitor, Fran. I love him, and I don't want him to get hurt, that's all. I take no sides in this war."

"Of course you do. Everyone does. And I have no doubt which side you are on." She dropped her arms, forcing a light smile. "But never mind. You'll come around in time, and you'll see that the South is right in everything they're doing. Right now we have to think about survival while Mark and Darryl are gone. The more business we can do at the restaurant, the less we'll have to draw on the reserve money our husbands left us. Darryl promised Mark you would stay and help me with the restaurant. You will, won't you? You should respect the friendship Darryl and Mark share—the friendship Darryl and *I* shared."

Anna drew on inner reserves to keep from crumbling. Darryl had just ridden out of her life, perhaps never to return, and Fran stood there talking about opening the restaurant, as though nothing had changed.

"I respect Darryl and *Mark's* friendship," she answered, seeing the flash of anger in Fran's eyes at her answer. "I said I would help, and I will. I want to be your friend too, Fran. We need each other now."

"Oh, but we *are* friends," the woman answered in her Southern drawl. Her lips twisted into a sneer, and she turned and walked into the house. Anna had never felt more alone, but she was determined to be strong and put up with Fran. After all, she had to stay in Columbia. She had promised to be here when Darryl came back. And he *would* come back. He had to.

She turned to see if she could still see him, but he was already out of sight, heading east. A chill moved through her, a terrible premonition that she could not even name.

Chapter 2

1863

The stagecoach bounced and lurched over the rough dirt road, heading back to Columbia. Anna squinted against the dust, pulling a leather shade down over the window nearest her. Outside, an August sun beat down on countryside farms, some of them sitting in black ruin because of the devastating border wars that still raged between Kansas and Missouri.

Anna knew the trip she had just made to Lawrence had been dangerous, but she could not afford to take the train, and patching things up with her sister had been important to her. It was becoming more and more evident that Joline might be all she had. A year ago their father had been killed, and two months later Jo's husband, Greg.

Another year gone by, a year of sorrow knowing how Joline was suffering, sadly aware that neither of them would ever see their father again, that Jo's husband was never coming home. Having to put up with Fran's coldness had not made things any easier.

Worst of all, Anna had not heard from Darryl in over a year. The letters had come fairly regularly at first, until he had written and told her he was being allowed to go and check on his family again. That was the last she had heard from Darryl, who had been gone two whole years now. All she had was his picture and his letters, a wedding ring . . . and the pearl necklace.

Life had become an agonizing waiting game, her only pleasure being her visits with Claudine in the evenings. She wasn't quite sure she would have kept her sanity without the woman's kind attention and support. Fran grew more distant by the day, as the war seemed to be taking a turn for the worse for the South. She had not heard from Mark for several months. He and Darryl had become separated, so even in Mark's last letter there was no mention of Darryl, if he was dead or alive, sick or healthy.

Now she at least had the comforting feeling of knowing there were no more hard feelings between herself and Joline. She had felt some apprehension about seeing her sister, but the moment they had set eyes on each other, all the love and friendship they had always shared returned. Both women had suffered losses, and both had realized they could not let this ugly war destroy their own relationship. Anna had contemplated staying at the farm, but she kept telling herself that Darryl could return any day now, that she had to be in Columbia waiting for him. Surely he would come soon, as he had promised.

Her two-week visit with Joline had been pleasant and melancholy. She would have liked to stay even longer, but she had already been gone too long and knew she was needed at the restaurant.

Anna was amazed at how well Jo had kept the farm going all by herself, but her sister was like that, pretty and small, but a hard worker, with a strength that belied her size. Anna feared Jo was in trouble financially, but her sister had insisted everything was fine.

Anna wished she could help, at least financially, but her own resources were dwindling. She had not bought one new dress since Darryl had left, nor anything but the most basic necessities. She looked down to brush dust from her dark blue linen day dress, and she noticed that one of the embroidered flowers looked frayed, as did the hemline. The leather of her high-top shoes was getting thinner. Even the luggage she had brought along was looking worn. But she refused to spend one penny more than necessary, admitting with secret dread that the money Darryl had left might be all she had left to support herself. If something happened to Darryl . . .

She shivered, telling herself she must not think that way. Darryl would be all right. He was coming home soon. She just had to be patient and pray. One thing she knew for certain—if he didn't return soon, she would have to find another means of making money than working for Fran, who was becoming more unbearable every day. The only reason Anna continued to help was because Darryl had promised Mark she would do so. She wondered if Darryl would be angry if she went back on that promise. If only he understood how horribly Fran treated her, how awful she had become since Darryl and Mark had left, especially since it appeared the North was going to win this hideous war.

The coach rocked and creaked, and she peeked out the window to see Columbia on the distant horizon. She breathed a sigh of relief that she had completed the dangerous trip without an attack by raiders. She opened her handbag and took Darryl's last letter from it. She carried it with her all the time, had read it more times than she could count, trying to decide from it what condition Darryl might have been in at the time he wrote it; trying to glean something from between the lines that would explain why she had heard nothing more from him in over a year.

There was a simple "I love you" at the end, but none of the passion and the flowing lines expressing how he loved her and missed her that there had been in the other letters. He had only written about how ugly the war was getting, how horrible the wounds, how the South was losing. The letter was full of bitterness and hate, desire for revenge upon the "damn Yankees." He didn't even know Greg and her father were dead, and she wondered now if he would even care. She shivered at the realization that something in him had changed, that her husband might be losing the compassion and gentleness he once possessed, qualities that had made her love him so much.

She folded the letter and slipped it back into her purse as the coach clattered into Columbia and up to the stage depot. Anna was the only passenger since the last stop. She climbed out, grateful to stand on solid ground. She ached from the long ride and looked forward to getting to her room and taking a long bath.

The driver unloaded her bags for her, and Anna shoved a small brocade bag under her arm, then picked up the two bigger ones and began walking. The boarding house was not far up the street, and she would pass the restaurant on the way. She tried to decide whether she should stop and see how things were going at the inn, but Fran would probably put her to work immediately, and she was so tired that everything seemed to hurt.

She forced her feet to move and walked a full block to the restaurant, noticing with surprise that it was closed. Fran never closed the establishment for any reason. Anna frowned, wondering if somehow Fran had lost all her help, but that seemed unlikely. The women who worked for her were all women whose husbands had gone off to war and who needed the money. They wouldn't quit. Perhaps Fran herself was sick, but that too was unlikely. Fran was as strong as a horse. Anna had never known her to be sick or to even mention a minor headache or any other kind of ailment.

She walked past the restaurant and headed for the boarding house another block away. As she came closer, she noticed a black curtain nailed to the outside of Fran's second-story window.

"Dear God," Anna murmured. Her blood chilled as her pace quickened. She climbed the steps to the double front doors of the boarding house, her legs feeling more and more like lead, every step an effort. She set down one bag and opened a door, hurrying into the cool entranceway of the neatly kept house. She set her bags down and sunlight filtered softly through the frosted glass of the oak door as she closed it.

She removed her gloves and Claudine appeared at the top of the broad oak stairway. "Anna," she exclaimed. She hurried down the stairs as quickly as her stout, aging frame would carry her. "Oh, Anna, it is so good you have come back!" The words were spoken in Claudine's heavy French accent. "It is so terrible. Poor Francine! She just got the news yesterday!"

Anna's eyes teared as the two women embraced. "It's Mark, isn't it? Is he dead?"

"Oui," Claudine replied, patting her back and releasing her hold. "You must see if you can comfort her, Anna. *Rien ne peut adoucir sa peine!* I cannot console her. She was so bitter before. Now it is worse."

Anna closed her eyes and sighed. "I'll go right up, but I'm not sure seeing me will help any."

"I am getting some fresh water for her. And we must try to get her to eat. She has not had one bite since the news. And perhaps now that you are back, we can open the restaurant and keep it going until she feels ready to work again, *oui?*"

Anna nodded, looking up the stairway when she answered. "Yes, I suppose we could do that. Fran can't afford to let it be closed for too long. None of us can." She looked at Claudine, hope in her eyes. "I don't suppose there has been any news about Darryl?"

Claudine shook her head, gray streaks showing in the pale brown hair pulled into a tight bun. "I am sorry, *ma chérie.*"

Anna set her gloves atop one of her bags and walked to the stairway. "Give me a few minutes alone with her before you bring the water," she told Claudine. She climbed the stairs, dreading what was to come, but feeling an obligation to do what she could to help, if Fran would even accept her condolences. The temporary reprieve from horror and death and from Fran's arrogant, accusing eyes that Anna had enjoyed during her two weeks back at the old farm were over. It was time to face reality, and she wasn't sure she could handle this. Mark's death came too close, reminding her that Darryl could also be dead. What other reason could there be for not hearing from him in so long? She struggled against tears for poor Mark, hoping he had not suffered a slow death. She told herself to be strong. She didn't want to break down in front of Fran and make things worse.

She opened the door to Fran's room quietly, noticing the woman sat in a rocker near the window where the black curtains hung, open just enough to see out. "Come in, Anna," the woman said dully.

Anna quietly closed the door. "How did you know it was me?" she asked.

"I saw you walk past, and who could help but hear Claudine's chatter? That woman can be such a nuisance sometimes. If she wasn't such a good cook, I'd get rid of her."

The words were spoken with no emotion. Anna ignored the remark, certain that right now Fran must hate the whole world and everyone in it.

"I don't know what to say, Fran. At times like this, it seems that expressing one's sympathy isn't enough. I feel the loss, too. Darryl and Mark were such good friends. This will be very hard on Darryl."

"You don't know the half," Fran answered. "I notice you said it would be hard on Darryl, but not on you." She continued to stare out the window, rocking quietly for a moment. "You never liked either one of us because we were special to Darryl."

Anna closed her eyes, reminding herself to stay in control. Fran was grieving and bitter. "That isn't true, Fran. I was very fond of Mark, and I wanted very much to have a closer friendship with you, but you didn't seem to want that at all. You have always treated me like an enemy, and I'm sorry if I did something to make you feel that way."

A strange sound came from the woman's lips. "Darryl always did like the cute little blond girls," she said with a sneer. "Did he ever tell you he was the first man to make love to me?"

Anna paled. "What?"

Fran kept rocking, refusing to look at her. "We were only sixteen. It was really more of an experiment than anything else. At least I realized later that's what it was for Darryl. It meant a lot more than that to me. Then he went off to college, and I wasn't finished growing. I blossomed into this mannish shape, and he was off east courting pretty little things like you. When he brought Mark home that summer when I was nineteen, for some reason Mark was attracted to me. I knew my love for Darryl was hopeless, and I thought maybe I'd make him jealous or something by going with Mark. It didn't work. When Mark asked me to marry him, I figured why not? Who else would marry me?"

"Fran, that's ridiculous."

"No, it isn't. I married Mark, and I learned to love him— and now he's gone, the only man who will ever really love me. Killed by *Yankees,* people like your father and brother-in-law."

Anna felt the ugly pain in her stomach. "They're dead, too. There have been terrible losses on both sides, Fran." Her voice choked. "The pain is the same for all of us. For all I know, Darryl is dead, too!"

The rocker squeaked as the woman continued rocking and staring out the window. "Yes . . . Darryl," she said. "That would be the worst loss."

The affection in her voice was obvious. Anna wanted to scream at Fran for telling her about Darryl making love to her, for talking about him at all when it was her own husband she was supposed to be mourning. Why had she told Anna now, and why hadn't Darryl ever told her the truth? Did he think he was protecting her? Or had it truly been such a game for him that he had thought no more about it? Her emotions were torn between sympathy and hatred, and she wondered if Fran had just made up the story to be cruel.

She breathed deeply for self-control, angry that Fran always seemed to find a way to try to break her, even now in her time of grief. "I came in here to see if I could comfort you," she said then. "Apparently you don't want my comfort, or my friendship. I'm terribly sorry about Mark, Fran. I truly am."

"I suppose you are," the woman answered. She slowly rose, turning to face Anna, strands of hair hanging about her face where they had fallen from the bun at the top of her head. Her dark eyes looked almost wild, and there were dark circles under them. Her appearance was almost frightening, and Anna struggled not to show the literal fear the woman put into her at that moment. "Don't be so surprised that I'm not crying," she told Anna. "I stopped crying years ago. My father beat all the tears out of me by the time I was twelve or so. I never told anyone the things my father used to do to me, not even Darryl."

Anna looked shocked. "Your father?"

Fran stepped closer, her black taffeta dress rustling with her walk. "That's why Darryl meant so much to me, and later Mark. They showed me that a man could be kind. I never knew that when I was growing up. My mother suffered plenty, too. That's why I urged Mark to move here after Father died and Mother came up here to live with her sister. The things we suffered together had created a special bond between us, and I wanted to remain close to her." She turned away again, walking back to the window.

"In those growing-up years Darryl was my best friend," she continued absently. "If I don't seem to like you, it's because you have interfered with that friendship. Until Darryl married you, I could imagine he belonged to me, even though I was married to Mark. In a way, he still does belong to me, because we share something you can never share with him—a past, our first experience at lovemaking, and a love for the South you could never understand. You're a Yankee at heart, Anna, and when Darryl comes back, you'll have problems."

"I've told you I take no sides in this war."

"You've just come back from visiting your *Yankee* sister whose *Yankee* husband and *Yankee* father were killed fighting for the Union. Don't tell me you take no sides in this war, Anna." She turned to face her again. "And if Darryl's family loses everything in this war, they aren't going to have much use for Darryl's *Yankee* wife. In fact, Darryl himself might not have much use for you when he gets back."

"Our love is stronger than that," Anna answered furiously.

"Is it? We'll see."

Anna shook her head. "You're a bitter, angry woman, Fran. God knows, in some respects you have a right to be. I am terribly sorry about Mark, and I say that with all sincerity." She turned toward the door. "Claudine and I are going to open the restaurant in the morning. You take as long as you need for mourning."

She opened the door, and Fran called out to her. "I'll be there myself in the morning," Fran told her. "The restaurant is all I have left of Mark. He would want me to keep it going."

Anna felt the lump in her throat. Poor Mark. He was truly a good man. Had he known his wife still carried a torch for Darryl? What would he think about Fran talking about Darryl while still mourning Mark? "Yes, he probably would," she answered. She walked out and hurried to her room, closing the door, suppressing an urge to scream. Darryl and Fran. What an ugly, shocking thing to tell her, and what an odd time Fran had picked to tell it. Why had Fran told her at all? Just to hurt her because she hated her so much?

It wasn't that it was any kind of threat to her marriage. After all, it had been years ago, and it apparently had meant nothing to Darryl. Yet now, with the South losing the war, how would Darryl feel about his own wife when he returned? Would Fran take on a sudden, new importance to him, just because she understood him better?

She took several deep breaths, telling herself that exhaustion and the sudden shock of learning of Mark's death was taking its toll on her mental stability. She must not let Fran get to her this way. So what if she had had a childhood fling with Darryl? That was all in the past, and Darryl loved her. She again touched the pearl necklace, which she wore every day, no matter what dress she had on. Touching it brought a kind of relief. She had promised to always wear it as a symbol of their love.

She sat down on the bed and closed her eyes, remembering their last night together, the promises of love, Darryl's promise to come back to her. Nothing could change that love. Nothing. Fran was just a jealous, bitter, grieving woman who had tried to relieve her grief by lashing out at someone else. That had to explain why she had chosen this moment to tell Anna about Darryl and her. Darryl might even be angry with her for telling.

She rolled on her side, dreaming of the day Darryl would come back and they would leave this place, leave Fran Rogers. He would set up a practice in a bigger city, and they would have the home they had dreamed about. She would give him children, and everything would be the way it was supposed to be before this terrible war had taken so much away from them. Weariness and grief overcame her, and in moments she fell into a much-needed sleep.

Anna awoke to someone gently shaking her. "Anna, I am sorry, *ma chérie,* but you must wake up."

Anna groaned, rolling onto her back and slowly sitting up, her mind foggy.

"I brought up your bags, child. I would have let you sleep, but I have heard something I think you should know about," Claudine was saying. "Something terrible has happened at Lawrence, Kansas, and since your sister lives there, I thought you would want to know."

Anna rubbed at her eyes, reality gradually returning again. Mark was dead. Now something had happened at Lawrence? Nothing seemed real. "What?" she asked. She looked at Claudine, who stood near her, her eyes full of sympathy.

"I am so sorry to bring you more bad news. I was outside cutting some roses to put in Fran's room. I thought it would make her feel better to have some flowers. I heard some men talking. They said they heard that awful raider Quantrill attacked Lawrence, Kansas, and burned down half the town. Many were killed!"

Anna just stared at her a moment, letting the news sink in. Quantrill was one of the most notorious of the border outlaws. "Joline," she suddenly exclaimed, jumping up. "I'd better get to the telegraph office and see if I can find out if she's all right!" She glanced in the mirror, lightly powdering her face and hoping it helped hide the circles under her eyes. She had fallen asleep completely dressed. Even her straw hat was still perched on her head, but slightly crooked. She repinned it and grabbed her handbag.

"Thank you for waking me, Claudine." Her eyes met Claudine's. "I don't know how much more bad news I can take. If only Darryl would come home. Everything will be all right then, won't it?"

"*Oui.* He will come soon, I am sure. Or you will get a

letter." The woman patted her arm. "I am sorry to bring you such news, especially today.

Anna closed her eyes. "I'm beginning to get used to bad news," she said wearily. She opened the door to her room. "Darryl is my last hope, Claudine. And Joline. I pray nothing has happened to her."

"At least you had a visit with her, and you became close again, no?"

Anna nodded. "Yes. It was a wonderful visit. We put all the hard feelings behind us. We were just sisters again, like it used to be. I don't know what I'll do if something has happened to her now."

Claudine put a hand on her arm. "You will go on, because you are strong and brave."

Anna smiled weakly. "I'm not so sure about that."

"Would you like me to come with you?"

Anna shook her head. "No. I'll be all right. You stay with Fran."

She hurried out, still so tired that she felt numb. Everything seemed fuzzy and unreal. She even wondered if she had just dreamed the things Fran had told her. What an ugly past the woman had had, suffering her father's beatings, believing she was unattractive and unwanted. No wonder she had thought the world of Darryl. Anna could not bring herself to hate the woman, in spite of how hard Fran seemed to be trying to *make* her hate her.

Right now it didn't matter. Fran was not about to share her grief with anyone. It was possible that for the moment Joline needed her much more than Fran. She hurried to the crowded telegraph office, waiting in line for her turn. When she reached the telegrapher, she was relieved to find there was already a message waiting for her from Joline. She quickly scanned it.

"Am all right," it read. "Farmhouse burned, crops destroyed. Have help. Don't worry. Will write in more detail soon. Stay in Columbia. Too dangerous for travel. Love, Joline."

She sighed and folded the message, feeling a new loneliness. The old farmhouse where she and Joline had shared so many happy early years had been destroyed. Father gone,

Mother long dead, Greg dead, now the old farm—and Darryl missing, perhaps dead himself. It was as though someone were out to rob her of her past, rob her of her identity.

She wondered how anyone could attack and murder innocent people, destroy what people had worked their whole lives to build. She felt a growing hatred in her heart for the raiders and wished they would all be caught and hanged, whether jayhawkers or bushwhackers.

"Afternoon, Marshal." The telegrapher spoke up then.

Anna, who had been lost in thought, felt a commanding presence beside her. "Hello, Newt," came a low voice. "Got any more messages from Lawrence?"

"Not yet, sir. You picked a good time to be in Missouri, seems like. Think the trial in St. Louis will take long?"

"I hope not. I'd feel better if I could go to Lawrence and help out. I feel like a traitor to my own state not being there for a thing like this. I'll get some of those bastards—" He hesitated, looking down at Anna. "Excuse my language, ma'am, but I'm pretty upset over this thing with Quantrill."

Anna looked up at him, and her natural womanly appreciation for a fine-looking man was stirred at the sight of him. The marshal was a tall, handsome man with wide-set gray eyes and dark hair, a neatly trimmed mustache following the perfect line of his upper lip. His brawniness seemed to fill the small office, and he wore a marshal's badge on a leather vest over a shirt that matched his eyes.

"It's all right. I feel the same way about the raiders," she told him. "My sister lives in Lawrence. I've just received a telegram from her."

The marshal pushed back his hat a little, letting a few dark curls escape from under it and revealing suntanned skin. Anna guessed him to be perhaps in his late twenties or early thirties. "I hope she's all right," he said.

His eyes had a way of holding hers as they spoke, and he seemed to be searching her own. She supposed it was the detective in him, that he was the kind of man who was always asking questions and summing people up. "Yes. She's fine. But our old farmhouse was burned." She finally managed to tear her eyes away from his. "It gives me chills to think I was just there visiting, and the coach that brought me back must have gone right through country where Quantrill and his men were riding."

"Well, you're a very lucky woman. I'm glad your sister is all right. I know you must be concerned, but I wouldn't go running back there if I were you. You can see now what dangerous country it is between here and central Kansas. If I have my way I'll find some of those men and put them behind bars where they belong. I've experienced their form of justice firsthand, and they're ruthless outlaws, plain and simple. What they do has nothing to do with the war."

"I have thought the same way." She glanced up at him once more and his soft gray eyes brought sensations to her insides she had not felt in a long, long time.

"I'm glad you're on my side. A lot of people are fool enough to think what these men do is all right." He nodded. "I hope your sister will be fine." He turned to the telegrapher then. "I'll check back once more before I get on the train, Newt. Someone might call me back to Kansas, but with that trial coming up and all, I don't have much choice but to go to St. Louis. See you later." He turned and touched his hat to Anna. "Good luck to you and your sister, ma'am."

"Thank you."

The man left, standing head and shoulders above most of the men outside as he walked away. Anna turned to the telegrapher. "Who was that, Newt?"

"Marshal Nate Foster, from over Kansas way. He's on his way to testify against a bad hombre who robbed a bank in Kansas and one in St. Louis. He was caught once and escaped. If he's the same man, he'll be tried and sentenced in St. Louis and then Foster will take him back to Kansas to finish out his term up at Leavenworth. Foster does a lot of picking up and delivering of offenders, especially between Kansas and Missouri. He's been by here before. Always checks for messages from headquarters."

"I didn't ask for his life history, Newt. I just asked his name. I like to know to whom I've been talking when a stranger speaks to me."

Newt grinned. "I understand. Your sister's all right, then?"

"According to this telegram, but I really can't tell much from it."

"How's Francine doing? The word about her husband came through yesterday."

Anna's heart tightened at the memory of her conversation with Fran. "She's holding up just fine," she answered. She rubbed at her eyes again. "So far this has been one of the worst days of my life, except for the day my husband rode off to war."

"Well, today could have been worse," the man answered as another telegram began coming in. "You could have been attacked by Quantrill and his men. I expect if you were, you wouldn't be standing here talking to me right now." He shook his head. "I just wish I'd get a hopeful message from your husband. That would help brighten your day. Sorry you came back to so much bad news."

"It's all right, Newt. Maybe Darryl will surprise me and come riding back in person before too long. I just hope he wasn't with Mark Rogers."

"Yes, so do I."

Anna left, glad to know Joline was all right but wondering what had been left out of the telegram. She noticed Marshal Foster talking to the local sheriff outside. It seemed that everywhere tongues were wagging about the news of Lawrence. The marshal glanced at her and nodded, and to Anna's astonishment, she again felt the stirring of long-absent womanly attraction and longings. She reddened slightly and hurried away, supposing the feelings came from her loneliness, her longing for Darryl and her need to let someone else be strong.

She admired Jo's strength and courage. Her sister had told her she was just as strong. "Pa raised us that way," she had said. "Ever since Mother died, we've known we had to be strong. And since we've been apart and Darryl and Greg went off to war, we've had only ourselves."

It was not a comforting thought at the moment. She longed for Darryl, longed for a man to hold her at night, to make the decisions for them, to come and tell her everything was going to be all right.

She hurried back to the boarding house, little realizing

that Marshal Nate Foster was watching her, thinking what a fine-looking woman she was. He felt sorry for the pretty young woman who the sheriff had just told him was waiting faithfully for a husband gone over two years, a husband from whom she had heard nothing in the past year.

"Kind of hard on a man, knowing all these women are walking around waiting for their men to come back, isn't it," the sheriff told Nate. "Makes a man want to help relieve their loneliness."

Foster grinned. "Speak for yourself, Clyde."

The sheriff chuckled. "Well, it doesn't make much difference with ones like Mrs. Kelley. She's a strong, faithful woman. She's not about to take comfort in some other man as long as there's a chance her husband is still alive. That one will wait five, six more years, if she has to."

Nate tore his eyes from Anna Kelley. "Wouldn't mind having a woman who'd wait that long for me," he answered with a grin.

"Hell, you're out riding the plains and borders too much to keep a woman, Nate, you know that."

Foster laughed. "I suppose you're right." He could not help one more glance at Anna, his manly instincts appreciating her lovely form and graceful walk, surprised that he found himself wondering what kind of personal hell Anna Kelley must live in—a sister in danger in Lawrence, a husband missing. He brushed away the thought. Anna Kelley was just one of thousands, and there was nothing he could do to help any of them. He hated this war with a passion. Most of all, he hated the border raiders, who had all but destroyed his own family.

Chapter 3

September 1864

Anna approached the train, ignoring the crowd on the platform. In these times, one never knew who could be trusted, who might be offended by the wrong comment. Besides, she was so consumed with her own aching loneliness that she hardly noticed people anymore. Every move was mechanical, every day a test of her patience and strength.

Three and a half years had gone by since Darryl had ridden out of her life; and it had been two years since that last, bitter letter. She kept clinging to the hope that any day he would appear at the boarding house, or at the restaurant. Because of that precious hope, she continued to put up with Fran's belligerence and bitter attitude. She had considered finding other work, but she couldn't help feeling obligated to help the woman; and she knew that when Darryl came back, if he came back, the restaurant was the first place he would come. With the South obviously losing the war, things were going to be enough of a strain between herself and Darryl, without him thinking she had deserted Mark's wife, and his old friend.

Her feelings about Darryl were becoming mixed now. She was twenty-two years old already. She wanted a home, children, a husband at her side. Had she really been only sixteen when she met Darryl, seventeen when she married him? It all seemed like a lifetime ago. She still loved him dearly, still waited faithfully. But not knowing what had happened to him was worse than hearing he was dead. At least to know for certain would mean she could get on with her life, horrible as the thought of his death might be.

She wondered sometimes if he was so badly hurt that he wouldn't come to her because he was afraid she wouldn't want him anymore. Surely he had more faith in her love than that. Surely he knew she just wanted him home, no matter what kind of injuries he might have.

She almost envied Joline and Fran, who at least knew the truth about their husbands. Joline's letters had brought Anna her few moments of joy over the past year. Rugged, spirited Joline had left Lawrence and had headed west, for a place called Montana, to start a new life and settle under the Homestead Act. She wanted to get away from places that brought painful memories. Everything in Lawrence was gone now, even Jo.

It was obvious from Jo's letters that she had fallen in love with Clint Reeves, the mountain man she had hired to guide her. Anna was glad for her, and had not been surprised when her adventurous, independent sister had told her she was heading west. She worried about the dangers her sister would face, but Jo probably welcomed the adventure. It would help her overcome her grief.

The crowd pressed around Anna. The train platform was filled with all sorts of people, including several Union soldiers on leave. They began boarding the train, while a few Confederate sympathizers in the crowd jeered them. Anna thought how she too would like to get away from all this agony and ugliness. She had the same Barker spirit and strength as Jo did. But she was forced by Darryl's silence to stay here in Columbia, where she was beginning to feel like a prisoner.

Joline had been able to put the past behind her, or at least it seemed so in her letters. That was something Anna wished Fran could do, but the woman was buried in the past and could not seem to get out of it, becoming more and more withdrawn and gloomy every day.

Anna had welcomed this trip to Centralia and a chance to be away from Fran. She hoped that this favor she was doing for Fran would help ease the tension between them. Fran's aunt had died, and Fran's mother, who had been living with the woman, was getting too old to live alone. She wanted to come and live with Fran. It was a busy time of year, and Anna had offered to go to Centralia to accompany the woman back to Columbia, since Fran didn't want her traveling alone in such troubled times. Anna's fondest hope was that having her mother around would improve Fran's disposition.

Now the pressing crowd forced Anna to mount the steps to the back of the passenger car. A conductor took her arm and helped her up. She walked into the car, then hesitated a moment, realizing this was the car which many of the Union soldiers had boarded. She felt suddenly awkward surrounded by those whom Darryl would have regarded as the enemy, even though she personally still felt a loyalty to the Union. To sit down inside a train car packed with bluecoats made her feel almost traitorous to her husband, who could be lying dead from a Union soldier's bullet.

"Let's go, lady," someone behind her complained. "The train's about to leave."

Before Anna could take a seat the train lurched, and a heavy body nudged her accidentally from behind, causing her to stumble forward. Her bag went sliding ahead of her, and a strong hand grasped her arm, stopping what would have been an embarrassing fall into the aisle.

"I'm awful sorry, ma'am," a deep voice said.

Anna turned, her face red, her hat knocked cockeyed. The tall man looking down at her had a hard time suppressing an urge to laugh at her disheveled appearance, for it was obvious she was a woman who insisted on being primly proper in her attire, every hair in place.

"I didn't mean to bump into you like that," the man told her.

Anna stared into gray eyes set into a handsome, tanned

face. The man wore a marshal's badge. Suddenly each recognized the other, and Anna could not stop the color that came into her cheeks, nor could she deny the unexpected warm, safe feeling that came over her. She wondered if he noticed her joy at seeing him, or if he detected her own surprise at that joy.

"Marshal Foster! Why, it's been over a year since I saw you at the telegraph office."

He smiled that unnerving smile. "You're the woman with the sister in Lawrence."

"Not anymore. She's gone to Montana."

"Montana!"

"Lady, will you please find a seat?" The same heckler who had called out to her a moment earlier was getting angry.

"We'd better get you out of the aisle," the marshal told her. He took hold of her arm again and gently urged her into the closest seat. "I'll get your bag." He walked forward, picking up her carpetbag and fighting his way around more passengers as he came back to sit down across from her, taking an aisle seat. He set her bag in the aisle seat beside her so that both outside seats were occupied.

Anna hoped that no one would bother to step over him to sit in the first seat directly across from her. She realized the man's size would inhibit others. Even in a bent position his long legs sprawled awkwardly, his knees reaching nearly to the opposite seat, creating a barrier. Anna sensed he had deliberately chosen the seat and had set her bag in the other seat to discourage bothersome strangers. Whether it was on his own behalf or hers, she was not certain.

"You all right now?" he asked.

"Yes, I'm fine. Thank you so much."

The train lurched again, and the soldiers toward the front of the car laughed and began chanting a song about "going home." It was obvious they were going to be somewhat rowdy, but Anna didn't doubt they deserved to let off some steam. God only knew where they had been, what they had seen.

Anna couldn't help noticing how young they were; many of them appeared to be only sixteen or seventeen. She watched them, suddenly too shy and embarrassed to meet the eyes of Marshal Foster, who she sensed was watching her from under the hat he had pulled farther down over his forehead.

She did not realize just how closely he really was watching her. Marshal Foster was thinking that Anna was exceedingly beautiful, her yellow hair and blue eyes reminding him of someone he had loved once. She was all lady, he was sure of that. He had not expected to see her again, and the encounter had awakened notions he had no right having.

He thought how her lips had a pretty curve to them, and the rest of her body had its own lovely curves. His investigative mind made him wonder where she was going, why she was boarding the train alone. Besides the sister who had been a victim of the raid in Lawrence a year ago, how else had she been affected by the bloody civil war that had torn the nation in two? Had she ever heard from her husband? He realized he didn't even know if the man had gone off to fight for the North or the South. The sheriff of Columbia had never mentioned it.

What was her name again? Anna? He couldn't remember the last name. He noticed the way she watched the Union soldiers, as though she were a little bit afraid of them, yet she didn't speak like someone from the South, and she was originally from Lawrence, a town made up almost solely of Union sympathizers.

The train let off a roll of steam and made a rumbling sound, then groaned to a start, slowly moving away from Columbia. Anna turned to look out the window, watching the sea of faces at the depot. Most of the men in the crowd were very old or very young. There were few healthy men in their prime left in the peaceful areas. Moments later, a conductor entered the passenger car asking for tickets.

Anna searched her handbag for her ticket, while Foster shifted in his seat, reaching into his back pocket. Anna glanced at him, noticing he wore a wide gunbelt filled with bullets, and a six-gun rested at his side, its holster strapped around his right thigh. He was so tall and broad that it was obvious the seating arrangement was going to be cramped for him. He had to stand up finally to get the ticket out of his back pocket.

"How long before we reach Moberly?" he asked the conductor.

"Oh, maybe an hour and a half. Depends on whether we stop at Centralia. Don't know for sure if there's passengers there to be picked up. For some reason we couldn't get through to them from Columbia. Probably a line down someplace. You picking up a prisoner, Marshal?"

"That's about the size of it."

"Well, I reckon keeping the peace among civilians has to be taken care of, war or no war. Kind of strange, you having to go around haulin' in criminals, while men can be out there shooting each other down legally in the name of war, isn't it?"

"It certainly is." The marshal handed the man his ticket and sat back down. Anna handed her ticket to the conductor then.

"How about Centralia?" she asked the man. "When will we get there?"

"Oh, Centralia isn't far. Forty-five minutes or so."

"Well, the train will *have* to stop there, because that's where I'm getting off."

"Well, then, I reckon we *will* stop there." The man laughed. "Have a nice trip, ma'am."

"Thank you." Anna could not help looking at the marshal then, feeling as though it would be rude to deliberately look away. "Thank you for keeping me from the total embarrassment of falling into the aisle," she told him.

Nate grinned, and his gray eyes filled with warmth and sparkle. "Just part of a day's work," he told her. He pushed back his hat. "By the way, how did you know my name?"

Anna reddened again, trying to think of a good answer. It would seem too bold to tell him she had asked. "I . . . heard the telegrapher talking about you to someone else after you left—that day I saw you in the telegraph office—remember?"

How could I forget? he felt like answering. He grinned. "Yeah, old Newt likes to gossip. Trouble is, now you know my name, but I don't know yours." How could he tell her he had asked the sheriff? She might be offended to realize he had asked about her.

Anna smiled. "Anna. Anna Kelley."

Yes, now I remember. "You live in Columbia, then?" he asked aloud. He wouldn't tell her he already knew her husband had been missing. It seemed too awkward now to ask her if the man had ever shown up.

"Yes," she answered, "but I'm originally from Lawrence."

"I figured that, since your sister was there. Is it true—she went to Montana?"

Anna laughed lightly. How good it felt to talk and laugh. "Yes. If you knew Joline, you wouldn't be too surprised. She's a brave one, and daring, and quite an independent woman."

He loved watching her eyes, watching her lips move. "I'll bet you're just like her."

Her smile faded slightly. "Oh, in some ways we're a lot alike, but not in looks. Joline has dark hair and brown eyes. As far as being independent—" He saw sorrow come into her eyes. "Well, I might find out soon enough just how independent I am—or I should say how independent circumstances will force me to be."

I'll bet she still hasn't heard from her husband, he thought. *It must be a couple of years by now.*

"Joline left because of bad memories," Anna explained. "Our father and her husband were killed at Shiloh. Father died right away. Jo's husband died a couple of months later. That was the hardest part for Jo. She didn't know he had been hurt, or she would have gone to him." Her eyes shone with tears and she looked away again. "At any rate, I think Jo just wanted to get as far away from this war as possible."

Nate nodded. "I can't blame her there. A lot of us would like to get away from it."

Anna turned to look out the window, sobering. "How true. It wouldn't be so bad around here if it weren't for the constant fear of raiders." The conversation was more personal than she would have liked, yet for some reason she found Nate Foster easy to talk to.

Nate frowned. "Someday all those men will be behind bars or hanging at the end of a noose, if I have anything to do with it. They're outlaws, pure and simple. I don't care how much they holler about doing what they do in the name of states' rights or even abolition."

Anna put a hand self-consciously to her hair, wondering if any had come loose from under her hat when she got bumped. "I agree they're nothing but outlaws," she answered.

Nate removed his hat and ran a hand through his own thick hair, then put the hat back on. "Trouble is, Quantrill has spawned a whole new breed of men—men who have learned to enjoy what they do and will probably go right on doing it after the war is over. One of the worst is Bill Anderson."

Anna shuddered, meeting his eyes again. "The one they call Bloody Bill?"

"Yes." A strange mixture of sadness and anger passed through Nate Foster's eyes then. "It's men like Quantrill and Anderson that caused me to put on this badge."

Anna wondered about the remark but was afraid of appearing too nosy if she asked for details. "Well, like the conductor said, someone has to stay here and make sure civilians don't turn into animals while the war is raging farther south," she told him. "I believe someone said that day at the telegraph office that you were actually from Kansas territory?"

He grinned again, and she suddenly blushed when she realized she had as much as admitted she remembered everything about that day. "Yes, ma'am, just like you. I operate out of Topeka. I'm on my way to pick up a couple of men who are suspected of murder and robbery in the Topeka area."

Anna took another quick glance at his virile physique, the gun at his side. "Your job must be very dangerous."

"Not as dangerous as being a pretty young woman traveling alone." He enjoyed the pink that came to her cheeks, and he wished she wasn't wearing gloves so he could see if she still wore a wedding band. "What sends you to Centralia? You have family there?"

Anna suddenly felt self-conscious and a little guilty. She still loved Darryl, and she was waiting faithfully for his return. But Nate Foster had a way of making a person feel completely at ease, and she wondered if she was talking too much or perhaps giving him the wrong impression.

Foster noticed her sudden uneasiness. "I'm sorry. You'll have to excuse my nosy questions. It's the detective in me, I guess. I'm used to asking people a lot of questions. It's really none of my business."

"No, it's quite all right," Anna answered. She realized how much she missed Darryl, how starved she had become for a man's attention. Plenty of men had gawked at her and flirted with her at the restaurant, but none made her feel as warm and alive as Nate Foster had made her feel in just these few minutes. She noticed how strong his arms looked, and she thought about other young men she had seen return from the war, with limbs missing, men scarred for life, both mentally and physically. How she prayed Darryl would return the same handsome, gentle, caring man he had been when he left. She sensed that was the kind of man Nate Foster was, and in that respect he reminded her of Darryl.

She felt her hat and realized it was still out of place. She quickly adjusted it as she answered him. "I work at a restaurant in Columbia," she volunteered. "The owner, Francine Rogers, has kept it going on her own since learning a year ago that her husband was killed. Fran's mother lives in Centralia. The woman's sister recently died, and Fran wants her mother to come and live with her. She's quite old and Fran didn't want her to make the trip alone. I'm going to get her while Fran keeps the restaurant going."

Nate watched the way her lips moved when she talked. Her rose-pink velvet dress fitted her bodice in a way that made a man uncomfortable, the front of the dress sporting tiny, velvet-covered buttons that ran from the soft curve of her throat down past the fitted waist. The high neck of the dress was outlined with delicate lace, and her small velvet hat matched the dress. She appeared to be a woman of elegance, but the dress looked well worn, as though lately her funds had run short, something most people had experienced since the war.

"That's nice of you," he told her. "And I'm sorry you lost your father at Shiloh. He a Union man?"

Anna glanced at the car full of soldiers, and Nate detected

a new uneasiness. "Yes. He and Joline's husband both fought for the Union." She removed her gloves, suddenly feeling too warm.

Nate noticed the gold band on her left hand. He met her eyes then and realized she had caught his curious stare. Anna turned her gaze back out the window, and the sudden silence between them was almost embarrassing to her. She felt her defenses rising, and she turned back to face Nate Foster's discerning eyes, wondering why on earth she cared what he thought about anything.

"My husband is from Georgia," she told him, holding her chin proudly. "I have never really taken sides in this war, Marshal Foster. I met Darryl before the country got into this mess. He's a doctor, and a fine man. I didn't care about North or South or slavery. We tried to live our own private life, but people in Lawrence wouldn't let us. We were finally forced to leave just because Darryl was from Georgia and his parents owned a plantation. No one cared what a fine man he was, what a good doctor he was. They didn't want any 'Southern butcher' touching them, and they accused Darryl of being a spy for bushwhackers. My husband finally felt a responsibility to do what he could for the—"

She hesitated, glancing at the soldiers again. They were all talking and laughing and paying little attention. The few who were quiet were wounded men who were sleeping.

"—for the Confederacy," she finished. "But he's not fighting and killing men. He's a doctor, and I don't doubt he has helped Union prisoners as well as Confederate men. Darryl is a very gentle, caring man."

Nate smiled sympathetically. "You don't need to defend him, Mrs. Kelley." He took a thin cigar from a shirt pocket. "Do you mind?"

"No. Go right ahead."

He lit the cigar, wondering why he felt so disappointed to know her husband was apparently still alive, a Confederate man, no less. He puffed on the cigar for a moment. "You didn't have to tell me any of that," he finally told her. "Like I said, it's none of my business."

"I know. But I saw you look at my ring, and I knew you were wondering."

He smoked quietly a moment longer. "Word is Sherman is raking through Georgia right now. Won't be long before the war is over."

"I hope you're right. God only knows what has happened to Darryl's home and family . . . or to Darryl, for that matter. I haven't heard from him for quite some time now. Every day I think maybe today he'll come walking through the door and we can finally live the life we intended to live before all this horror started."

Nate realized his guess had been right. The man was still missing. "Well, I hope it works out that way for you, Mrs. Kelley. But you have to remember that war can do a lot of things to a man. Changes some men forever. It will take your husband some time to get back to that nice life you've got pictured for yourselves. He probably won't seem like the same man who left."

Anna looked back out the window. "I'll help him through whatever problems he brings home with him. I just want him to come back in one piece." She felt tears stinging her eyes. She sometimes had trouble remembering what it was like to be with Darryl, even had trouble picturing his face. Would he seem like a stranger when he returned? Three years was a long time.

The sign creaked on one hinge, hanging limply after the other hinge had been shot off by the drunken bushwhacker. CENTRALIA DEPOT, the sign read.

"Hey, Doc, you sure that telegraph ain't workin'?" someone shouted.

Darryl Kelley, bearded and in dire need of a bath, emerged from the depot, leaving behind the telegraph operator, who was out cold after Darryl's pistol-whipping. "Don't worry," he shouted. "The line is cut, and that operator won't be sending any messages for a while."

"Yahoo!" The other man shot off his gun, adding to the almost-continuous shooting around the depot and throughout the little town of Centralia. Bloody Bill Anderson and nearly one hundred fifty of his raiders had taken over the town, robbing, shooting, and having a grand time terrorizing Centralia's citizens. A barrel of whiskey stored at the depot had been broken open, and the outlaws were feeling their alcohol, as well as forcing some of the innocent bystanders to join them in their little party.

Darryl laughed as he watched one of his friends push a woman to the ground and pull off her boot. He dragged the woman toward the barrel and dunked her boot into the whiskey, then pushed her back down and forced the whiskey into her mouth, most of it spilling over her face. He leaned down and kissed her with great gusto, while she screamed and struggled. When her husband grabbed her assailant in an effort to help his wife, the raider landed a hard fist into the husband's belly, then proceeded to beat the poor man nearly to death while the wife ran off.

Darryl thought about Anna as he watched the woman run. A little pain pierced his heart at the thought, but there was no room in his life now for someone like Anna. There was room only for vengeance.

He looked around at the pandemonium. Children were wandering and crying, women were screaming and either running or cowering with their children. Those men who tried to fight were soundly beaten, even shot. Other men just ran. Some of the citizens were drunk, after whiskey had been forced down their throats by the marauders.

"Serves them right," Darryl muttered. Most of Centralia's citizens were pro-Union. Most were supportive of Sherman's march through the South. Of course there was nothing more Sherman could do to Darryl's family and home. Both had already been destroyed. Darryl would never forget what he had seen. It would burn in his gut forever, and he knew he would never stop hating. It would be impossible to go back to Anna now. Besides, there was a kind of power in riding with a man like Bill Anderson. Wherever they went, people shivered in their shoes. He had tried being kind and gentle once, and all he got in return was to be chased out of Lawrence like some kind of criminal.

Someday, he thought. *Someday I'll be the one in charge. People will remember Crazy Doc in the same way they'll remember Quantrill and Anderson.* He didn't mind being called crazy.

Lord knew the head wound he had suffered had taken its toll. He couldn't remember things well enough to return to practicing medicine. There were times when he could hardly remember his own name, times when he forgot all about Anna. Whiskey was his friend now. It took away the pain, took away the memories.

Johnny Field came riding hard toward Darryl then, grinning broadly, shooting into the air. "Hey, Doc! Train's coming! Somebody told Bill there might be Union soldiers on it! We're gonna' have us a good time now!"

Darryl walked up to the tracks and watched toward the south, while several other bushwhackers hastily added to a barrier they had put up to stop any train that might come through. Johnny was right. In the distance Darryl could see the trail of smoke from the engine's stack.

He grinned. If it was true Union soldiers were on that train, he would surely soothe some of his need for vengeance today. He hurried to find his horse, while the sky blackened with the dense smoke from buildings the bushwhackers had torched.

"Centralia just ahead," the conductor announced as he walked through the passenger car.

Anna pulled her gloves back on and looked out the window. She couldn't see the station yet. She turned to Marshal Foster. "I'm glad to have met you again, Marshal. I wish you luck in getting your prisoners back to Topeka."

He smiled softly and nodded, reaching over and crushing his cigar in an ashtray mounted to the wall. Anna caught the scent of man and leather, again feeling a little guilty at realizing she found Nate Foster an attractive, likable man.

"And I hope your husband returns safely from the war, Mrs. Kelley, no matter what side he fought with." He straightened in his seat. "Once this war is over it will be time to forget about taking sides and just try to heal the wounds. I'm afraid it will take a long time for that to happen. But you seem like a woman who has a great capacity to forgive and forget."

Anna blushed lightly. "I try, Marshal. Like I said, I never really took a side in this war. I don't believe in slavery, but I have a personal interest in my husband's family, who owned slaves. It's a very difficult situation for me."

She turned to look out the window again, then frowned. "Marshal, look out there! There's some kind of fire!"

Foster leaned over the vacant seat beside him to look out the window. He moved into the seat closest to the window then, turning his back to Anna to see better. "What the hell—"

He could see men now, riding wildly, shooting, people running, a few men fighting. The train braked violently, and Anna's body flew against Nate Foster's back with a jolt. She grabbed at his arm in surprise and Nate turned, helping her back into her seat.

"You all right?" he asked her.

"I . . . I think so. What's happening?"

"I'm not sure."

They could both hear shooting and screaming outside then. A bullet shattered the window ahead of them. Nate grabbed Anna and forced her to bend low in her seat. "Get on the floor," he told her. "It must be raiders!"

Anna's heart pounded with fear. What on earth was going on outside?

"Stay down there," Nate was telling her. "I'll—"

His words were cut off when several men barged into both ends of the passenger car. "Everybody off this train!" one of them shouted.

Nate was still bent over Anna. She felt him push something against her arm. "Put this in your handbag," he whispered. She took it, realizing it was his badge. She quickly hid it in her bag.

Chapter 4

"Come on! Let's go!" One of the outlaws waved a gun at Anna and Nate. Anna felt a gentle hand on her arm. "Stay close to me, Mrs. Kelley," Nate Foster told her quietly. He rose, helping her up. Anna's ears rang with curses as men with guns stormed up the aisle, herding the Union soldiers off the car, calling them every name they could think of, beating on some of them before they could get off the train. Anna shivered at the cruelty of the raiders, as one soldier cried out when he was yanked from his seat by his wounded arm.

"Well, well!" a man behind her said gruffly, grabbing her arm and yanking her around. "What do we have here? You the wife of one of them bluecoats?"

Anna stood speechless as the man laid the barrel of his pistol at her throat.

"Leave the lady alone," Nate Foster told the man. "Her husband is a doctor in the Confederate army."

The man gave Anna a shove back into a seat, pulling back the hammer of his revolver and pointing it at Nate Foster's face. "Well, ain't that lucky for her now?" The man looked

Nate over, and Anna could smell his perspiration. "Unloose that gun, mister, and I might let you live."

Nate hesitated.

"Please do what he says," Anna told him, terrified that Nate Foster would be gunned down before her eyes.

Nate glanced at her, realizing that to cause a skirmish here could get her hurt, which was why he had hidden his badge. These men were looking for excuses to kill, and in this situation, he didn't have a chance against them.

Nate slowly and reluctantly unbuckled his gunbelt, seething inside. He had taken on men like this before, jailed plenty of them. To have to knuckle under to their kind made his blood boil.

The rest of the car was nearly empty. All the soldiers had been herded out the other end. Anna heard someone just under her window shout, "Please, don't shoot!" A shot quickly followed, and she felt a thud against the car.

Anna wanted to scream. It was like some unholy nightmare. Nate dropped his gunbelt and reached over to take Anna's arm. Just as he leaned over, his assailant's pistol came down hard across the side of Nate's head and Nate literally fell into Anna's lap.

Anna screamed, grabbing at Nate as he started to roll off her lap onto the floor of the car.

"Let's go, lady!" Nate's assailant ordered Anna. "Get off the train. And it's a damn good thing you're on the Confederate side."

Anna looked up at the man, enraged. "You didn't need to hit him. He did what you asked! And my husband may have fought for the Confederacy, but that doesn't mean I support the likes of you!"

The man jammed his pistol against her breast. "You watch your mouth, woman. We ain't killed any women yet, but you sure do tempt me. Now get off this train!"

Nate groaned and grasped at the arm of her seat. Blood poured over the side of his face as he managed to sit up, and Anna grasped his arm. "Come on, Mar—I mean, Mr. Foster. Let me help you."

Nate was only vaguely aware of rising, of leaning on the small shoulders of a woman as someone shoved at them

from behind, jabbing a pistol painfully into his ribs. Nate
and Anna half fell down the steps of the train onto the
platform, stumbling into a cloud of dust raised by the
horses of the raiders as some of them rode around and
around the train, shooting and cursing and continuing to
order everyone else off the train.

"Over here!" Anna told Nate, coaxing him through a
crowd of onlookers. Nate grabbed hold of a post that supported the porch roof surrounding the depot and took a
handkerchief from his pocket, wiping at blood that kept
getting into his left eye.

"I'm so sorry, Marshal. I don't think he would have hit
you if it hadn't been for my presence," Anna told him. Her
nose stung with the acrid smell of smoke coming from the
burning buildings not far away.

Nate blinked, feeling confused at first, then recognizing
her. "Mrs. Kelley?"

"Yes." She reached up and took the handkerchief from his
hand and pressed it against an ugly cut at the side of his
head. "Right here. Hold it here. Press tight."

Nate did as she told him. "Did he hurt you?" he asked.

"No, I—" Anna had turned her gaze to the train, and her
words caught in her throat. "My God!" she muttered.

Nate followed her gaze to see the Union soldiers all lined
up against the train, some of them already naked, others
removing their clothes at the order of the raiders.

Anna clung to Nate's arm. "Marshal, what in God's name
are they doing?"

Nate watched as the raiders rode back and forth in front
of the soldiers, shouting orders, laughing, drinking.

"You're too damned slow," one of the bushwhackers said
to a young soldier who was crying as he struggled to get off
his long johns while half the town of Centralia watched in
stupefied horror. The raider shot, and an ugly hole opened
up in the top of the young man's head. He fell forward to
the ground, his long johns half off.

"Bastards!" Foster muttered. "Murdering bastards! I'll
hunt down every one of them!"

Anna stared in shock as the soldiers, many of them only
in their teens, stood naked then against the train car. Some

of them were crying, some begged for their lives, others just stood staring in horror, speechless.

"What do we do now, boss?" someone asked.

A man on a buckskin horse rode through the crowd in front of Anna and Nate, scattering some of the onlookers. The man rode forward then, facing the soldiers.

"It's Bill Anderson," Nate said quietly, revulsion in his voice.

Anna felt a sickening chill at the words. She had heard terrible things about the man. Never did she dream she would actually set eyes on him.

"You are to be killed and sent to hell!" Anderson shouted to the trembling soldiers. He turned then to a very young man who rode beside him. "Archie, muster them out."

The young man dismounted and walked toward the soldiers. He pulled his pistol and began shooting at random. The naked, unarmed soldiers began falling. In moments more of the bushwhackers joined in the melee, yelling and laughing as they poured bullets into the frightened, pleading young men.

Just in front of her Anna saw the spotted rump of an Appaloosa, saw a man seated on the horse take aim and deliberately shoot down one of the naked men. The man on the horse laughed and rode off. Anna shivered at the familiar sound of his laugh, but it didn't register that she could possibly know the vicious killer.

She covered her face then, unable to watch any longer. She turned away as soldier after soldier collapsed in a bloody heap. She felt an arm come around her then, and she leaned against Nate Foster, weeping at the hideous sight she knew at that moment she would not forget for the rest of her life.

People were screaming, other women were weeping. Not far from Anna and Nate a man vomited.

"Down with the Union!" a raider shouted as he rode past.

Anna pulled away from Nate, suddenly embarrassed that she had leaned on him and let him hold her.

"You all right, Mrs. Kelley?"

Anna just shook her head and wiped at her eyes. "I don't think I ever will be," she sobbed.

Nate led her to a bench. "Sit down here." He winced as pain shot through his skull from the blow he had taken. He sat down beside Anna, leaning close to her. "The best thing you can do for yourself is sit quietly and don't draw any attention to yourself. When men are this riled and out of control, there's no telling what they'll do. I'm just damned sorry I couldn't do something about all this."

Anna wiped at her eyes and looked up at him. "Marshal, there must be over a hundred of them. The depot is full of them, and there are obviously more in town. You saw the buildings burning when the train pulled in."

"That's why I had you take my badge. I was afraid you'd get hurt if they saw it. If there weren't so many I'd try to stop them, but there's nothing I can do." He winced with pain again. "Give me my badge. I'll put it in my pocket."

Anna obeyed. All around them people groaned and wept. One woman stumbled past them, her clothes torn and her hair tumbled. Anna suddenly realized that in the shock of what had just happened, she had forgotten all about Fran's mother.

"Henrietta!" she exclaimed, jumping to her feet. "I've got to find her! She's old and alone!"

"You'd better stay right here, Mrs. Kelley," Foster warned.

"No. How could I face Francine if something happened to her mother because I wasn't with her? She has already lost a husband."

"Wait!"

Anna hurried off without any thought to her own safety. Nate started after her, but dizziness suddenly overwhelmed him and he sank to his knees while the raiders continued to charge through the streets and around the depot, celebrating their "kill."

Anna searched the small crowds of terrified, weeping citizens around the depot. No one had gone to see if any of the soldiers were left alive, everyone afraid that if they tried to help, they too would be shot. A few men lay sprawled on the ground, badly beaten, some of them shot. Anna could hardly believe the things she was seeing. This was not war. This was something much more evil.

She walked blindly up a street then, thinking perhaps Fran's mother might have run from the marauders at the train station and had headed back toward town. She sensed a horse riding down on her from behind then, and she turned to see someone riding hard toward her.

She shivered with terror and began running, but the rider quickly caught up and brushed by her so closely that she fell. She got back to her feet, anger now taking over her fear as she brushed herself off and cast a bold look at the rider, his horse just ahead of her. She saw the spotted rump again, heard the familiar laugh. She stood her ground, eyeing the man squarely as he turned his horse and headed back toward her.

Suddenly Anna felt as though all life was flowing out of her fingers and toes onto the ground. She realized in an instant why the laugh was familiar.

"Darryl!" she gasped.

The man's smile faded as he came very close to her. He just stared at her, saying nothing, a look of shock on his face.

Anna struggled to keep her sudden light-headedness from making her pass out. The man was dirty, and he needed a shave. But she knew his blue eyes. And there was the thin scar on his left cheek. No two men could have a scar exactly alike. And the way he looked at her now, the sudden recognition, told her all she needed to know.

"Darryl, what are you doing? Why?" She shivered as the truth sank into her. This was the same man she had seen shoot down one of the young soldiers in cold blood.

He suddenly burst into laughter again, his eyes looking wild. Then he pulled his wedding ring from his finger, his eyes growing sinister as he sobered. He threw the ring to the ground in front of Anna. "Go to hell!" He whirled his horse and rode off.

Anna stood staring after him in shock. Black smoke swooped into her face with a sudden change in the wind, and she began coughing, realizing she was indeed awake and this was all real. It really was her own husband she had seen on the Appaloosa, her own husband who had shot down one of the defenseless young soldiers in cold blood.

She looked down into the dusty street, then stooped down to pick up the ring Darryl had discarded. She held it with a shaking hand, staring at it in disbelief. *"Go to hell!"* The words stung her ears. Why! She had done nothing but wait faithfully for him. What had happened to her gentle physician husband? What had happened to the man she had loved so much before he went off to war? How could someone like Darryl be mixed up with men like Bloody Bill Anderson and why had he never told her he was back, that he was alive?

She remained in a stooped position, feeling sick. "Darryl," she groaned. Her mind reeled, full of unanswered questions. Her dreams of welcoming Darryl home with open arms, of starting a new, peaceful life together, were suddenly shattered in one moment, one look. She squeezed the ring into the palm of her hand, then opened her handbag and dropped it inside.

"Mrs. Kelley!"

She heard the marshal's voice behind her. In moments the man was helping her to her feet, but her legs felt rubbery.

"Mrs. Kelley, you shouldn't have run off like that! My God, woman, these men are crazy right now." He helped her to a boardwalk and Anna did not object. She was still stunned by what she had seen. "I think they're finally leaving town," she heard Nate Foster tell her. His voice sounded so far away, almost like an echo.

"I . . . have to find . . . Mrs. Sloan," she murmured. She clutched her handbag, desperately afraid Nate Foster would find the ring inside, would ask her about it. Already shame was replacing her horrible disappointment and grief. How she wished someone had come and told her Darryl Kelley had been killed in the war instead of having to discover what he had become. How could she tell Nate Foster, or anyone, that she was the wife of a murderer, an outlaw? And that was surely the only label one could give to Darryl Kelley now.

Again the reality of it brought a sickening nausea to her stomach, and she fought an urge to vomit. She felt ashamed, embarrassed, cheated. She could have handled

Darryl coming home with a limb missing or some other hideous wound. She had even prepared herself all this time to face the fact that he might be dead. But this . . . this was the worst situation she could ever be forced to face. Nothing had prepared her for this.

"Mrs. Kelley, you're white as a ghost. This has all been too much for you," Nate said.

For the moment she was grateful for his strong arm, which kept her from collapsing. He led her into an alley.

"We'll just stay here until they're gone," he told her.

Anna said nothing. She simply closed her eyes and leaned against Nate, hardly aware that she was again taking comfort in a near stranger, allowing him to hold her. She needed to hang on to something strong, or she feared she would scream and thrash and behave like a madwoman.

Nate Foster gladly held her, almost angry with himself for enjoying it. He couldn't quite understand why he felt such a keen sympathy for Anna Kelley, why he felt so drawn to this woman he hardly knew, so responsible for her welfare. Her situation was a strange one—a woman whose father and brother-in-law had fought for the Union, but whose husband was off fighting for the South. The war had created painful personal trauma for so many, including himself. He was suffering his own remembered horror at the moment, fighting memories of the screams of his own loved ones who had died at the hands of bushwhackers. What he had seen today only made him vow more deeply to hunt down men like Bill Anderson.

Several minutes later the shooting stopped. Some people walked around as though in a daze while others screamed and wept. Some were running around calling out the names of loved ones, while others gathered together to try to stop the fires. Nate gently pushed Anna away, keeping hold of her arms.

"I'll help you look for your friend's mother," he told her. "What's her name?"

Anna wiped at her eyes. "Henrietta. Henrietta Sloan. She's just a frail little woman."

"All right. I'll help you find her, and then you stay with her while I go back to the train and get your bag and my gun. My horse and saddlebags are in a boxcar on the train. I'll get all my belongings and come back to you and see that you get on another train back to Columbia. You're all right now, Mrs. Kelley. They're gone."

I'll never be all right, she wanted to scream. *One of them was my husband!*

Nate kept an arm around her as he led her up the street. They searched faces but Anna did not see Henrietta. Finally they approached a woman lying near a hitching post. Nate knelt down and turned her over, and Anna gasped and turned away, breaking into new tears.

Nate sighed, inspecting the body. "Looks like she took quite a blow to the head. Someone must have ridden her down and made her fall against the hitching post," he told Anna. He took the old woman's shawl from around her shoulders and covered her face with it. "I'm afraid she's dead, Mrs. Kelley."

"Dear God," Anna wept. "How can this be? How can this be?"

Nate rose, putting a hand on her shoulder. "War has a way of creating monsters out of ordinary men."

How well she knew.

"I want you to stay right here. Will you promise me?"

Anna nodded.

"I'm going to run back to the depot and get my things. It will only take me a few minutes."

Foster squeezed her shoulder, then left her. Anna turned and sat down on the boardwalk near Henrietta Sloan's body. She didn't know the woman well, but she had met her a couple of times. Having to tell Fran that her mother was dead was going to be the hardest thing Anna would ever have to do. But then she realized there was one thing that would be even harder to do, and that was to admit that her own husband had been among the bushwhackers who had caused all this havoc and death. She wished she could just melt into the dusty street and no one would ever find her.

Anna was hardly aware of what was going on around her as she stared at poor Henrietta's body. Farther up the street men battled fires, and people ran about in confused rage.

Anna had no idea how much time passed before Nate Foster came riding back to where she sat, her carpetbag hooked over his saddle horn. He had wrapped a piece of gauze around his head, and already it was bloodstained. Dried blood caked the side of his face and his neck. He dismounted, helping Anna to her feet.

"We got the telegraph working again," he told her. "The Thirty-ninth Missouri Infantry is headed this way. They were tracking Anderson and his gang." He touched her shoulder. "I'll see if I can find the undertaker. I expect he's going to be a busy man for a while, but if he's got anyone to help him, we can get Mrs. Sloan taken care of and get a coffin made for her. You can take her body back to Columbia with you and let her daughter bury her there. I don't know how else to handle this."

"You don't have to do any of this, Marshal," Anna told him, her voice flat.

"I can't leave you alone in this situation, ma'am. Now I want you to get up on my horse. I'll carry Mrs. Sloan and we'll go back to the train station and I'll get you some help. The fires are spreading and you might be in danger here."

"It doesn't matter," Anna said absently.

"What?" Nate frowned and studied her a moment. "You're all right. It's over now. I know what you've seen has been a shock, but you couldn't have done anything about any of it, including what happened to your friend's mother. Were you very close to Mrs. Sloan?"

Anna looked up at him as though she didn't even know what he was talking about. "Mrs. Sloan? Henrietta? Not really."

Nate searched her lovely blue eyes, seeing a terrible grief there.

"What is it, Mrs. Kelley?"

Anna turned away. How could she tell him? How could she tell anyone—ever? "It's just . . . those poor young soldiers . . . and poor Henrietta, and Fran," she muttered, needing an excuse for her horrible grief. She felt like mourning Darryl the same as if he had been killed. In her mind and heart, he had been.

Nate felt sorry for her. He helped her onto his horse,

then picked up Henrietta Sloan's dead body. Ordinarily a woman as small as Mrs. Sloan would be no problem for a man of his strength, but his head wound and loss of blood had weakened him, and by the time he got the woman's stiffening body to the depot he was perspiring and felt light-headed again.

He gently laid the dead woman on a grassy area beneath a tree near the depot and helped Anna down from his horse. Their eyes held for a moment as he lowered her, and he saw a certain loneliness deep in her wide blue eyes. He felt a sudden desire to hold her close, to kiss her tears away.

"Tell me, Marshal," she said quietly. "Why have you been left so unaffected by the war?"

Nate studied her curiously. "How do you know that I am?"

"Because you're still a decent man."

He sighed deeply, letting go of her and taking the reins of his horse. "I'm not unaffected, ma'am. I have suffered my own losses. Like I told you earlier, the war and things that happened before the war are part of the reason I'm a marshal. Some men turn to outlaw ways, others decide to go after them. I'm the one who goes after them, and I carry my own scars."

"Yes. Don't we all?"

Foster pushed back his hat. "Ma'am, I can't help feeling that something happened when you ran off on me. You've acted strange ever since I found you. Did someone say something to you, do something?"

She looked down at her handbag. "No. I've just . . . never seen such horror as I witnessed today. The more it settles in, the more ill it makes me feel."

He touched her arm. "Time will take care of a lot of it, Mrs. Kelley. Like I said, if I could have stopped it, I would have tried. But I knew it was hopeless. If it helps any, you can be sure soldiers will be tracking Anderson and his men. I wish I didn't have other assignments or I'd form a posse and go after them myself. But this is Missouri. I've got no jurisdiction here. If they set foot in Kansas, they're going to regret it."

You would be hunting down my own husband, she felt like

telling him. But the shame of it prevented her from saying the words. "I . . . don't know how to thank you for what you're doing," she told him. "You need to see a doctor yourself, Marshal Foster."

"I'll get to myself later. You sit down here in the grass. This could take some time. Are you hungry?"

"No." Anna sat down wearily. "My stomach is too upset to think about eating. But I could use a drink of water."

Foster took a canteen from his horse and handed it to her. "Keep this with you. I'll be back in a while."

"Thank you."

Anna clutched the canteen and Nate tied his horse nearby. He walked off to get help, and Anna looked down at her dress, noticing for the first time that Nate Foster's blood had stained the skirt. The sight of the blood brought back the horror of the murders she had witnessed, and to recall that Darryl had been a part of it was a shattering awakening.

She rolled to her side and wept bitterly, groaning Darryl's name, wondering how she could ever pick up the pieces of her life and her marriage. Through tears she angrily and furiously dug a hole in a soft spot of earth near the tree under which she sat. She tore through her handbag, finding the gold ring inside, then just looked at it for a moment before putting it into the hole and covering it up. To her, Darryl Kelley was as dead as if his body had been returned to her. If she could not bury the man, she would bury the symbol of their union.

With dirt-stained fingers, she touched the pearl necklace she had worn faithfully. She quickly unclasped it and shoved it into her handbag. In her shock, humiliation, and anger, she could only think for the moment of how to hurt Darryl as he had hurt her today. She vowed never to wear the necklace again.

"I'll *sell* it," she hissed through gritted teeth.

Chapter 5

Anna rode back to Columbia in a daze. She could not get the horror of Centralia out of her mind, nor could she shake the vision of Darryl's wild eyes, or forget his hideous laugh and his cruel, shouted words—"Go to hell!" How could Darryl of all people shoot an unarmed man and laugh about it? Darryl, her gentle, kind, caring physician husband!

Never had her heart been so torn. He was still her husband, the man she had once loved with great passion. But the Darryl she had seen at Centralia was a complete stranger. What was her duty to that man? And what were his own intentions? Did he mean just to ride out of her life and never return, to continue the life of an outlaw? Where did that leave her? She was a married woman with no husband at her side. Her situation was worse than if Darryl had been killed; and her shame was total and devastating.

She had said nothing to Nate Foster, and already she was determined to say nothing to anyone about what she had seen. The last thing she wanted was to be known as the wife of a murdering, insane outlaw. She would be in great danger if Northern sympathizers in Columbia knew. More than that, her own shame would be unbearable.

What would Nate Foster think if he knew? The sudden thought irritated her. What difference did it make what the man thought? Their brief encounter after a whole year was just that—a brief encounter, a coincidence. Still, she wondered now what on earth she would have done at Centralia without him. He had been badly hurt trying to defend her. And without his guidance and help after the sordid massacre, she would have been lost and terrified. He had even held her. Yes, he had held her. She remembered now, remembered the comfort of his arms, the arms of a man she hardly knew, while her own husband was one of those wreaking all the bloodshed and terror. Now, in her sorrow and lingering terror, she almost wished Nate Foster was still here with her.

She could not imagine a worse situation than her own present predicament. What was she supposed to tell poor Fran? That the very bushwhackers Fran supported had been the cause of her own mother's death? How awful for Fran, who would be waiting expectantly, happily at the train station for her mother, only to be met with a coffin. Perhaps she already knew about the massacre. After all, the telegraph had been fixed, and it had taken hours to get the coffin for Henrietta. It would be dark by the time Anna got back to Columbia. Surely Fran already knew something had gone wrong. Still, she wouldn't be expecting a coffin.

The train rumbled into Columbia. Yes, people knew. There was a crowd waiting at the station. The train finally came to a stop, and as people from Centralia disembarked. Expectant friends and relatives greeted them enthusiastically, relieved to see they were all right. The depot was almost instantly alive with hugs and tears and talk of the massacre. Anna watched them through the window, wishing she could just stay on the train and never leave it, wishing it could take her far away from all of this horror.

She rose from her seat after the car was empty and walked to the rear platform of the car, searching the crowd for Fran. She finally spotted her watching anxiously. She made her way through the crowd, and when Fran saw her standing there alone, her eyes widened in horror. Anna moved closer.

"I'm sorry, Fran. I've never seen anything so horrible, and I hope never to see such a thing again." She struggled to keep her composure. "By the time I got to the station, the outlaws were already creating havoc for the townspeople. Your mother was nowhere to be seen. I was so stunned . . . I didn't know what to do at first. I saw them . . . shoot down those poor, unarmed soldiers, right in front of my eyes. If it weren't for a marshal who happened to help me, I'm not sure what I would have done. We . . . looked for your mother, found her in town." Her heart pounded with grief at the look in Fran's eyes. "She . . . she must have been running, probably from one of the bushwhackers, and fell and hit her head." She closed her eyes and bowed her head.

"My mother is dead," Fran said coolly, more as a statement than a question.

Anna met her eyes again. "Yes. The marshal . . . he helped me find an undertaker, got him to make a coffin to bring her back in. You . . . might want something nicer to bury her in. The one she's in now is just a plain wooden box."

Fran closed her eyes and sighed deeply. "All she had to do was tell them she was from Georgia. That's all she had to do."

"What?"

"The bushwhackers. If one of them was chasing her down, she should have just told him she was from Georgia and he would have helped her, not hurt her. It wasn't their fault. Mother was just too old. She didn't understand what was happening—didn't understand the bushwhackers were her friends."

Anna stared at her in disbelief. "Friends! Fran, did you hear what *happened* today? Those men forced young, unarmed Union soldiers from the train, some of them wounded! They made them strip naked in front of all the townspeople, and they shot them down in cold blood!"

Fran met her gaze, and a chill swept through Anna at the realization that those eyes didn't seem much different from the eyes of some of the outlaws who had killed the soldiers. "They did what they had to do," she told Anna. "This is war, Anna, remember? But then I forget. *You're* a Yankee. This is really their fault. They started this damn war! Why couldn't they just have let the South mind its own business? And you—you should have been with my mother! *You* should have been killed, not her!"

Anna's eyes widened in shock at the words, and she paled slightly, but she refused to flinch as she glared right back at Fran. "Maybe I should have," she answered, her eyes blazing. "But that isn't the way it happened, and I risked my life trying to find your mother in town. She wasn't at the depot where she was supposed to be, and it's probably a good thing. You weren't there, Fran. You don't know the horrible things I witnessed today! At least your mother didn't have to see it."

The Barker pride welled in her soul, making her furious at Fran's remark, and furious with Darryl for being a part of the raid at Centralia. "You call what happened at Centralia *war,* Fran? I call it cold-blooded *murder!* It's one thing to wear a uniform and shoot at an enemy when he is shooting back at you! But to be wearing civilian clothes and to gun down unarmed men on peaceful leave is in my mind a hanging offense! Those men aren't fighting for the South. They're wild, unruly outlaws who are using the war as an excuse to murder and rob and rape! How can you stand there and defend them, when your own mother is dead *because* of them!"

"She's dead because of *Yankees!*" Fran towered over her, her dark eyes frightening. For a moment Anna wondered whether the woman might kill her if they were alone. Fran stiffened and backed away then. "I can't help thinking you could have done something. But then as you say, I wasn't there. I suppose I should thank you for at least seeing the body was taken care of. I'll go talk to the conductor and find someone to get Mother to a funeral home where I can arrange for a proper burial."

Anna realized the woman had no idea of the horror of Centralia. If she did, it didn't bother her. Not being able to share it made the hurt and horror of it even worse, and to think Fran actually thought it was partly her fault brought on an agonizing loneliness.

"Do what you have to do," Anna answered. "The coffin is in the third car. It's marked. You clearly don't want any more help from me." She held the woman's eyes boldly. "I'm sorry for you, Fran. Not because of Mark or your mother. I'm sorry for what this war is doing to you. You're using it to release all the bitterness inside of you because of your past."

She turned away and left the woman standing at the depot. She knew she should tell Fran she had seen Darryl, that he was alive. Fran would be overjoyed to know, and she would probably be happy to learn Darryl had been a part of the bloody massacre. She would say he was doing his job right. But Anna was not about to let the woman celebrate Darryl's hideous change. Anna could not consider him anything but a murderer, and she realized now that even if he came back to her, she could never look at him in the same way again.

And what if he *did* come back! What if he wanted her to be a wife to him again? Perhaps he would force her to join him and those with whom he rode. Or perhaps the law would find out who he was—who *she* was! She could be arrested!

She was hardly aware of the people around her. Her mind swam with mixed emotions and indecision. She wanted to love Darryl. He was her husband. It would have been difficult enough to pick up their marriage again after being apart for more than three years, without even any letters over the last two years. But to return to the bed of a man who murdered wantonly, savagely, seemed ludicrous, impossible.

How she hated this war! How she hated the way it hardened people, and turned ordinarily decent people into animals. She even found her own heart hardening—putting up a defense against Darryl's hurt. She was already becoming more calculating, having already decided to forget the sentimental value of the pearl necklace and sell it for money she was going to need to survive. After all, she had just as surely lost her husband as if he had been killed.

She buried her needs and heartache. She knew she had to

for the time being or go insane. She didn't want to feel anything. If Darryl truly wanted her to go to hell, he had certainly picked the right way to send her there, for her present predicament was a *living* hell. Her marriage had become a prison, and Darryl Kelley held the key to her cell.

Anna attended Henrietta's funeral. Fran shed no tears. She stood as stalwart as a tree, staring at her mother's grave with a blank look in her dark eyes. In many ways Anna still felt sorry for the woman and wished there was some way she could help her; but it was obvious Fran hated her more than ever.

Anna walked away after the last hymn was sung. Claudine walked beside her, keeping an arm around her, little knowing that Anna's sorrow was not for Fran or even for Henrietta. It was for what the war had done to Darryl. She could not bring herself to tell Claudine the truth, and keeping it all inside made her feel so ill that she could not even find the strength the next day to get out of bed and go to the restaurant. Claudine had told her the latest news—the Union soldiers who had gone after the Centralia raiders had been surrounded and bushwhacked. Every last soldier had been murdered, many bodies horribly mutilated.

"What are we coming to?" Claudine moaned. "White men who are no better than the savage Indians, and to their own kind! When I came to this country I never believed such a thing could happen."

The news was devastating. Anna knew Darryl had probably been with the men who committed the horrible deed. Darryl, her Darryl—the kind, gentle, caring man she had married. Every time she closed her eyes she could see the naked, bloody bodies of those young men at Centralia. She could hear some of them begging and crying.

After three days of sedatives and rest, Anna felt her pride and determination take hold. She had to do something. Somehow she had to survive this and make a life for herself. A Barker didn't just lie down and wither away when faced with a problem, monumental as this one might be. Again the calculating, practical side took over. The first thing she realized she had to do was leave the restaurant. She could not keep submitting herself to Fran's hatred and emotional battering day after day.

She rose and bathed and put on the dark blue linen dress she had worn coming home from Lawrence. The hem was becoming even more frayed, but there was nothing she could do about it. Few people in the streets dressed in immaculate new clothes now. Money was too scarce.

She left her room and spent the day searching for work, not an easy task in a time when there was little work to be found, and too many women like herself trying to survive until their husbands returned. At least those other women had that hope. In her own case, she no longer looked forward to her husband returning at all.

At noon she stopped at a jeweler's shop to sell the pearl necklace. Again she deliberately buried her emotions. The jeweler examined the necklace, little realizing the sweet love it had once represented, having no idea what torture she suffered handing it over. It was like cutting out a piece of her heart and holding it out to him for sale. The man gave her fifty dollars. She had no idea if that was enough, but fifty dollars was fifty dollars. She took the money and left, letting out a little gasp and nearly breaking down outside the door.

She breathed deeply and held her chin higher, marching on up the street. She felt branded, as though she wore a huge sign that said her husband was a murdering outlaw. Yet people around her acted the same, spoke to her in a friendly way, unaware of her personal agony.

By the end of the day her feet ached, but she had found a job working for an old woman named Liz Tidewell, an aging widow who had kept the large home she and her husband had once shared with their several children, and had turned it into a boarding house because she was lonely. The woman could no longer keep up with the big house and needed help.

Anna took the job, which didn't pay as well as working for Fran, but part of her pay was a free room on the second floor. In these times of danger for women alone, not having to walk the streets to go to work was a benefit she could not ignore, and just being out from under Fran's angry looks would be worth the lower wages.

Anna left then and headed for the restaurant, resolving to be strong and determined. It was time to ignore the promise she had made to Darryl, who had so blatantly and cruelly ignored his own promises. She no longer owed any loyalty to Fran Rogers. She knocked on the front door of the restaurant, which was now closed. One of the hired help let her inside, and she walked briskly to the back room, where she knew she would find Fran sorting through her receipts for the day.

She opened the door and went inside, where Fran sat at a desk, one lamp dimly lit. The woman looked up at her with the dark, burning look Anna had grown used to seeing. "So," the woman said coolly, "you finally got out of bed. Darryl should have married someone stronger."

She looked back down at her paperwork. "You might be surprised at how strong I really am," Anna answered, just as coldly. "There are some things you don't even know about me, Fran, but that doesn't matter now. I've come to tell you I'm leaving my employment here. I've found other work."

Fran continued sorting through papers for a moment, letting the air in the close room hang silent. Anna wanted to scream and lash out at her, but she knew the woman was deliberately showing no surprise.

"You owe me some back pay," Anna continued. "I'd like to collect it."

Fran sighed deeply and leaned back in her chair, looking up at her again. "Will you still be in Columbia?"

"For the time being."

"What about Darryl? When he comes back, he'll come here looking for you. Where should I tell him you are, or don't you care about your own husband, who might be badly wounded somewhere?"

Again Anna was tempted to tell the woman the truth but refused. She not only did not care to see Fran's approval of what Darryl had become, but the woman might spread word in town, making things very dangerous for Anna. It was not uncommon for the deserted wives of suspected outlaws to be attacked in the streets.

"I'll be at Liz's Boarding House, on Fifteenth Street." Anna's thoughts raced. What if Darryl *did* come to Columbia? Did he dare? Was his face becoming known? How on earth would she handle such a situation? She could never live with the man he had become. *Don't think about it now,* she told herself. *You can only take a day at a time.*

"You going to live there?"

"Yes," Anna answered. "A free room is part of my pay. I'll be helping Liz Tidewell. She's getting too old to keep the place up by herself. I think it's best to leave, Fran—best we don't run into each other in the evenings at the boarding house where we live now. After all that has happened, there isn't much reason for me to stay on here."

A sneer moved over Fran's mouth. "No, I suppose not. I half expected this. In fact, I was thinking of letting you go. I only kept you on here because of Darryl." She opened a side drawer of her desk. "But then there isn't much hope that he's still alive, is there?" Her voice actually choked slightly on the words. She took out some paper money.

"I'd rather be paid in coins," Anna told her. "In these times, I don't put much trust in greenbacks."

Fran's eyebrows arched in surprise at Anna's firm voice and rather determined nature. "You'll have to come back tomorrow then, after I've gone to the bank. I don't keep gold and silver here."

"Fine. I'll come at eleven."

Fran rose, their eyes holding. "Will you let me know if you hear something from Darryl?"

Darryl Kelley is a murdering raider who rides with Bill Anderson, Anna wanted to scream. "Yes," she answered aloud. "But I'm sure that if he comes back to Columbia himself, he would contact you."

Fran smiled, a victorious look on her face. "Of course he would. Darryl is a loyal friend, which is more than I can say for you."

"Or for yourself," Anna answered. "But then we were never friends to begin with, so neither one of us has to worry about loyalty, do we?"

Fran's dark eyes narrowed. "No. I suppose not. Just

promise me you'll tell me if Darryl writes you or contacts you in any other way."

Now Anna felt somewhat victorious, horrible as her secret was. "I'll tell you, as long as I get my back pay."

"You'll get it."

"Fine. Good-bye, Fran. In spite of the way you have treated me, I appreciate having had work here." Anna quickly turned and left. She could almost feel a knife turning in her back, and she was glad to get out of the room.

Claudine helped Anna move to Liz Tidewell's house, all the while saying how terrible it was that Anna felt she had to leave the restaurant and how much she was going to miss her.

"You can come visit me any time you want, Claudine," Anna assured the woman. "I don't want this to interfere with our friendship. Sometimes I think you're the only genuinely sweet, loyal, caring person left in this world."

"Oh, you must not think such a thing, Anna. Do not let all of the ugliness around you spoil your own sweet nature. And do not give up your trust in the goodness of others, in spite of what you saw at Centralia, and in spite of that nasty-tempered Fran. Soon Darryl will come home," the woman assured Anna again. "I am sure. Everything will be all right when your husband is back."

Oh, how I wish that could be true, Anna thought. *He's already back, Claudine, and everything will never be all right again.*

It seemed the world was crumbling around her, and she felt helpless to stop it. Was there really any goodness left in anyone? The only other good person she could think of right now was Joline, but Jo was clear out in Montana, and Anna was sure her sister had plenty of troubles and challenges of her own. She was not about to burden Jo with a letter filled with her own woes.

There was one other good person she could think of—Nate Foster. Yes, Nate was a fine man, the kind of man Darryl used to be. Now Darryl had become the kind of man who would be hunted by men like Marshal Foster. She felt a little guilty that the thought of Nate always brought her comfort, but right now, just like Claudine said, she needed to remember there were good people left in the world, and Nate was one of them. Still, what did it matter? Their two encounters had been quite by chance and meant nothing.

When the last piece of baggage was carried into Liz's house, Anna embraced Claudine, a woman who had suffered her own losses at a young age and understood what Anna was going through. Claudine's own husband had been killed in the French revolution of '48. Claudine had come with her sister to America, settling in New Orleans. Her sister eventually married, after which Claudine came north with a friend. The friend had died, but Claudine stayed on. She was a marvelous cook, but more than that, she had become Anna's best friend. Even so, Anna had still not been able to tell the woman the truth about Darryl.

"Claudine, I'm not going to be here for long. I'm tired of working for others. I want something of my own. Maybe if I can save up enough, I can open my own restaurant. I've learned a lot working for Fran. If I ever get my own place, I'll steal you away from Fran and pay you more to cook for me."

Claudine pulled away and smiled. "I would love to come and cook for you, *ma chérie,*" she answered. "But as I say, your husband will come, and you will go off with him. He will make the money, and you will stay home and raise the babies, no?"

No, Claudine. I don't think so. "I have to think about survival right now, Claudine," Anna answered, "and the very real possibility that Darryl is never coming back."

Claudine clicked her tongue and shook her head. "Oh, such a sorry predicament for one so young and beautiful."

"Well, I can't sit around forever worrying about it. I've got to get on with my life, Claudine."

The woman clucked and mothered and helped get Anna settled into her room before finally leaving. Anna felt weary, but she also felt as though a great weight had been lifted from her shoulders. She no longer had to live under the dark cloud of Fran Rogers. At least that part of her burden had been lifted. She walked to a window, pushing back a lacy curtain to stare out the back side of the house into open country.

"Where are you, Darryl?" she said softly. "Why are you doing this? What should I do about our marriage?"

She was desperate to get beyond the anger and bitterness. Old memories of the love they once shared nudged her again, making her want to find excuses for what Darryl had become, making her tell herself she must continue waiting for him, for she had made sacred vows the day she married him. "For better or for worse." Little had she known just how "worse" things were going to become.

Anna poured coffee for one of Liz's male patrons.

"You hear the Federals caught seventy or eighty of Quantrill's men?" the man she served asked another at the table.

Anna set the coffeepot on the buffet and listened, taking a deep breath to keep her hands from shaking as she sat down at the table herself. All the food had been served, and she decided to have her own meal now so she could hear the news.

"That's what I heard over at the post office this morning," the second man answered. "Killed quite a few of them too, including that Bill Anderson. I guess with a name like Bloody Bill, he deserved to die."

"Shot in the back of the head, they say."

Anna looked down at her food, struggling to show no emotion. Oh, how glad she was, glad a man like Bloody Bill Anderson was dead! She wondered if Nate Foster knew. But of course he must. Men like that knew such things before anyone else. Afraid of being discovered and questioned if she appeared too interested, she didn't dare ask any questions herself. She quietly sipped her coffee, letting the men's conversation give her all the information she needed. She knew both men, Andrew Taft, a traveling salesman, and Ted Corning, an ex-Union soldier from Columbia who still limped from a wound suffered at Gettysburg.

"Took most of the prisoners up to Leavenworth," Taft was saying. "I hope they hang all of them. I know there's a lot of people in this town who think what they did at Centralia and later to those Union soldiers who went after them is all right, long as it was done to Union men. But in my book, no man deserves that."

"I agree." Corning swallowed a piece of bacon. "With the South all but surrendered, I reckon this will pretty much put an end to the raiding. That leaves Quantrill, but I hear he's faded into the shadows—hiding out someplace farther south. I expect after losing some of his top men, he'll lay low now."

"Let's hope so. What I worry about is all those men who rode with him. Some of them won't be able to quit that kind of life, you know. There's a couple brothers with the last name of James that still do some raiding, I'm told. And some other one they call Crazy Doc—he's got himself a gang, too."

Crazy Doc, Anna thought. She had no doubt who the man was. Her stomach turned.

"Well, maybe the James boys and the Doc were among the ones who got sent to Leavenworth."

"Let's hope so. I was talking to the sheriff just the other day about that. He said sometimes killing just gets in a man's blood once he's done enough of it, and he just doesn't know how to stop once he's started. I don't doubt the hills and woods all over this territory will be full of robbers and murderers for some time to come." Taft glanced at Anna. "Sorry, ma'am, for such talk. I kind of forgot you were sitting there."

"It's all right, Mr. Taft. A person would be hard put to avoid such talk anyplace in town. It seems to be all that is on anyone's mind." Little did they know that her mind was whirling with the possibility that her own husband could be among the dead or those who had been taken to Leavenworth.

The man studied her beauty, finding it disappointing that she was married, as did most available men in Columbia. He couldn't help wondering just how lonely she was, if she might be especially vulnerable. But there was an air of propriety about Mrs. Darryl Kelley that made a man keep his distance. He was not ignorant of the fact someone as young and beautiful as Anna Kelley would not look twice at a middle-aged, potbellied man like himself. Ted Corning had the same thoughts, but he knew he was homely, and he was ashamed of the scars he carried on his leg and side. For him, women like Anna Kelley were untouchable, something to be admired but not approached. Besides, she was a married woman. Both men felt sorry that she had no idea what had happened to her husband.

Anna quietly finished her meal, then excused herself to the kitchen, where she found Liz Tidewell scrubbing at a pan. She felt sorry for the old woman, all her children scattered, two sons killed in the war. Liz was another rare example that such losses didn't always have to make a person bitter and gloomy. Liz was a cheerful, hard-working woman for whom Anna enjoyed working.

"Let me do that for you, Mrs. Tidewell," she told the woman.

"Oh, it's all right. I must say, having you here is a big help, Anna. I just can't seem to keep up anymore."

Anna set her dishes on the kitchen table and took a deep breath for courage. "Mrs. Tidewell, I hate to ask this of you, since I've only been here a couple of months. I know how much you need my help."

The woman stopped scrubbing and looked at her, eyebrows arched. "You're not leaving already, are you?"

"No. It isn't that. However . . . I do have to go away, but only for a week or so, I promise."

"Well, child, what is it that takes you away? You aren't leaving Columbia, are you? It's dangerous out there for a woman alone, you know."

"I know. But this is important. I'll take the risk."

"My dear, have you forgotten Centralia?"

Anna closed her eyes and turned away. "No. I will never forget Centralia. But Mr. Taft and Mr. Corning said this morning that some of the worst leaders of those outlaws have been killed or captured, including the one who led the raid at Centralia. I don't think something like that is going to happen again."

"Well, where on earth are you going, honey?"

Anna turned to look at the woman's heavily wrinkled face and gray hair going white. "I'm afraid it's personal. But I'll be back, I promise. I'd like to leave this afternoon, if I can find a train going in the right direction."

The old woman sighed deeply. "If you must. But I think it's dangerous. Does it have something to do with your husband?"

Anna struggled to show no emotion. "No. I'd really rather not say."

Mrs. Tidewell shook her head. "If it's so important, then go. And God be with you."

"Thank you. I'm sorry to leave you like this."

"Oh, I've been doing this work for a lot of years now, and staying busy keeps me from thinking about things better forgotten."

"I know exactly what you mean." Anna hurriedly cleared the table when the men were through, and she washed and put away the dishes. She removed her apron and hurried to her room, quickly packing. She had to have some answers. Much as she hated the thought of having to face Darryl, she could not go on this way, not knowing what had happened to him, what he wanted to do about their marriage, how he felt about her—about anything. With the life he led now, she had no idea how to contact him. Hearing about the arrests was the first clue she'd had about how she might find him.

Perhaps he was at Leavenworth, or at least perhaps someone there would know if he was dead or alive. The thought of going there, of facing some of those desperate men clawed at her stomach so that it pained her, but she had to know. She would go to Leavenworth and find out what had happened to Darryl Kelley.

Chapter 6

Anna noticed several men in Union blues waiting at the depot at the town of Leavenworth. She stepped down from the train and watched them begin to unload supplies from one of the boxcars. On her journey here she had contemplated how she should ask about Darryl without giving away the fact that she was his wife, or any kind of relative at all. She had decided to pose as someone who hated him. Her heart pounded with dread and indecision as she wondered how she should behave or what she should say if she discovered Darryl really was at Leavenworth. Once he recognized her, the Union soldiers would know who she was and she could be arrested, but it was a chance she would have to take. She had to know whether or not she still had a husband and what was going to happen to him.

She drew a deep breath for courage and approached the soldiers. They gladly stopped their work to drink in the sight of the beautiful young woman with the pretty blue eyes and sun-bright hair, who today wore a blue-flowered calico dress that matched her eyes, with a small, round straw bonnet on her head that was decorated with ribbon that matched the dress. She carried an expensive Paisley shawl, since the weather had grown cooler. The shawl was one of the few expensive garments she had left that still did not look worn.

One of the men stood up after setting down a carton and grinned. "Hello, ma'am. Anything we can do for you?"

"I would like to go to Fort Leavenworth and speak with the commander there," she told them. "Can you help me?"

"You men get back to work!" A man with stripes on the sleeves of his jacket barked the order and approached Anna, removing his hat when he came closer. The others returned to unloading the boxcar, but kept glancing at Anna. "What is it you want, ma'am?"

"I . . . I'd like to go to Fort Leavenworth and talk to the commander."

The man looked her over. "I'm Sergeant Hillary. These men and I are from the fort." He put out his hand and Anna shook it.

"My name is Anna Wade," she lied. "*Miss* Anna Wade." She had left her wedding ring behind. "I am trying to find out about the bushwhackers who were brought to Leavenworth—the ones who rode with Bill Anderson?"

The man frowned. "Don't tell me a pretty thing like you is involved with men like that."

"Oh, no!" She struggled to appear sincere. "I . . . I was at Centralia, sir. I lost a brother, and a very dear friend was badly hurt. I've come to make sure these men are properly punished for that horrible day. And one man in particular—I believe I heard his men call him Doc. I saw him shoot down my brother. I am wondering if this . . . this Doc was among those killed or captured. It's possible his real name is Kelley . . . something like that. I think someone shouted out that name, also. It was a confusing, horrible day, but every part of it stays vividly in my mind, and I remember every word spoken, or I should say, shouted."

Real tears came to her eyes then at the renewed realization that Darryl was a part of the massacre. The tears were convincing enough for the sergeant. "I'm sorry, ma'am, that you witnessed that. We're all mighty angry about it, and we want justice done also—especially after what was done to Major Johnston and his men when they went after those da—Those bushwhackers."

"Yes, I heard about that. Can you help me?"

The man toyed with his hat. "Well, ma'am, I'm afraid most of the prisoners have been sent on up to the Union prison at Rock Island. I can at least find out about the one called Doc, search the records for the name of Kelley."

"I would appreciate it very much."

He put his hat back on his head. "My men will be through here shortly. Why don't you wait at the Melody House. It's a nice diner just up on the main street of town. I'll see what I can find out and come back to let you know. No sense in you having to stand around a fort full of men."

"No, I . . . I'd rather go along. I want to see the men who are still here. I'll never forget the face of the one called Doc. He . . . he might lie about his name or something. I want to see for myself." She dropped her eyes. "Besides, if he is there, I want to see him face to face. I want to be able to tell him what I think of him, and to tell him myself I hope he hangs for what he did."

The sergeant frowned. "Ma'am, you don't want to get close to a man like that. Nothing you say is going to change him. I wouldn't—"

"I must see him! Maybe it won't mean anything to him, but it will to me," she answered, her eyes filling with tears.

The man sighed and nodded, little knowing the real reason for her tears. "If you insist, ma'am."

Anna dabbed at her eyes with a handkerchief. "You're very kind, Sergeant."

The man smiled sympathetically. "Anything for a pretty young lady like yourself, especially when she's been a victim of bushwhackers."

The sergeant couldn't help wondering if perhaps she had been raped by bushwhackers and that might be the reason for her insistence on seeing one man in particular. He interpreted her tears as tears of shame and vengeance. He ordered his men to hurry up with the unloading so that they could take Anna Wade to the fort. The thought of getting to look at the woman all the way back put energy into the men, and they finished the job in another half hour.

A pall of loneliness and a sense of terrible dread engulfed Anna as she climbed up onto the wagon seat, assisted by Sergeant Hillary. The rest of the men jumped onto the back of the wagon, sitting on crates. Anna prayed she could calmly handle anything she might discover at Leavenworth as the wagon bounced uncomfortably over a dusty road.

"Have you seen battle, Sergeant Hillary?" she asked.

"Oh, yes, ma'am. I was at Shiloh."

"Oh, how terrible." A lump rose in her throat. "My father and a brother-in-law were killed at Shiloh."

"I'm right sorry, ma'am. What were their names? Maybe I knew them."

She couldn't tell him her father's real name, which had to be the same as her own. "Tom Wade," she lied. "My brother-in-law was Greg Masters." At least she could tell the truth about Greg.

Hillary shook his head. "Don't know either name," he answered.

"Are you married, Sergeant?"

"Yes, ma'am. Got a wife and three kids in Ohio. Soon as this war is done with, I'll be out of the army and can go home to them."

"Well, I'm glad for you—glad you weren't hurt at Shiloh." Anna thought how lucky the sergeant's wife was. He would come home to her a whole and decent man. She took a little more hope in humanity at the realization that here was a man who had seen one of the bloodiest battles of the war, and had not let it destroy him.

She hung on to her straw hat as the wagon jolted its way over a hill and through a heavily wooded area. She thought about the stories she heard and read daily about outlaws hiding out in places like this, realized how dangerous the train trip and now this wagon journey were. But nothing mattered now except finding out about Darryl. It took nearly an hour to reach the fort, and her heartbeat quickened at the sight of it, her stomach churning at the possibility of seeing Darryl face to face.

The wagon clattered through the huge parade ground, where men were riding by on horseback, while other men in blue coats were marching in drills, and still others shouted orders. Anna wondered what they would all think if they knew her husband was a Confederate, if they knew he had been one of those who participated in killing the unarmed Union soldiers at Centralia.

They passed a huge cannon, and rode on past a long row of two-story buildings. "Those are the barracks for the enlisted men," Hillary told her. "They're called the Syracuse Houses. That one up ahead, with the pillars, that's the Rookery. That's where the officers live. I'll take you to headquarters."

"Where are the prisoners held?" Anna asked him.

"Those left are over in a block building on the other side of the parade ground." He pointed to a long building with barred windows. Soldiers stood guarding the doorway. Anna shivered to think that a man like Darryl could end up imprisoned in such a place. How could it happen, and why? Should she love and forgive him, or hate and shun him? She realized she could probably do neither. She was walking a middle road that for the moment had no end.

The sergeant pulled up in front of headquarters and helped Anna down, instructing one of the other men to take the wagon to the supply post. The men all smiled and tipped their hats to Anna, who nodded to them before climbing the steps to headquarters, her legs shaky. The sergeant ushered her inside.

"I'll take you to Lieutenant Asher. He's been in charge of the prisoners brought in after Anderson was shot. He knows more about those men than anybody here."

Hillary led her through the freshly painted frame building, along the polished wood floor of a hallway to a door with a sign that read Asher. He knocked on the door. "Sergeant Hillary, sir. There's a lady here who wants to talk to you."

"Come in."

Hillary opened the door and led Anna inside, saluting the lieutenant, whose eyes showed an appreciation for Anna's beauty. He returned Hillary's salute, then offered a chair to Anna.

"I picked her up in Leavenworth, sir," Hillary explained. "She was looking for someone to bring her here. I figured she'd be safest with us. I tried to tell her to stay in town, told her I'd get the information she wants, but she insisted on coming herself."

Asher frowned. "Oh?" He looked at Anna. "And what information is that?"

Anna swallowed, hoping she would not give herself away. "I'm looking for someone . . . among the prisoners," she replied. "My name is Miss Anna Wade. My father was a Union man. He was killed at Shiloh."

"I'm sorry to hear that."

"Yes, well . . . that doesn't really have much to do with why I'm here. I was . . . present at Centralia when Bill Anderson and his men raided the town and the depot."

Asher glanced at Hillary, both men suspecting the worst. "You can go now, Sergeant," Asher told the man. "Did you get those supplies off the train?"

"Yes, sir. I've got to get to my men and make sure they store them where they're supposed to. I'll be around if and when you want me to take Miss Wade back to Leavenworth."

"Fine." The two men saluted again and Hillary left. Asher sat down behind his desk. "So, Miss Wade, you were at Centralia. That must have been a terrible experience."

Anna reddened, certain what he might be thinking. She decided to let him think it, as long as she might be allowed to view the prisoners. "It was," she answered. "My brother was killed, and a close friend of his badly injured. I . . . I was also injured." She cleared her throat and dabbed at her eyes again. "When I heard a number of those men had been captured, I wanted to see for myself if one in particular had been caught—or killed, I hope. He's the one who shot my brother. I heard someone call him Doc. It seems I also heard the name Kelley, but I'm not certain."

"Doc? You mean the one they call Crazy Doc?"

"I believe he might be the same one," she answered. "I wanted to be sure justice was done. I don't feel he should just spend time in prison. He should hang."

Asher sighed and leaned forward, resting his elbows on his desk. "I quite agree, and many of those taken up to

Rock Island *will* hang, I assure you. But I know who this Crazy Doc is."

Her heart pounded. He knew it was Darryl?

"What I mean is," he continued, "I know who you're talking about. We were hoping to catch him with the others, but he wasn't with them this time. We've heard from the other prisoners that he has his own gang now and has headed into Indian Territory."

"Indian Territory!" She looked at him in surprise. If that was true, God only knew how long it would be before she ever saw Darryl again. How was she supposed to know if he was dead or alive? How much longer should she go on waiting? Did he plan ever to return? The idea of divorce was beginning to whisper at the back of her mind, but the thought was humiliating and devastating, as though she had somehow failed the marriage, in spite of what Darryl had done.

Time. She just needed a little more time. Somehow this horror would end, wouldn't it? She realized then she needed an explanation for her sudden surprise.

"You mean . . . you let him get away?" she asked. "That murdering outlaw got away?"

"Miss Wade, he wasn't with them to begin with. I'm sorry. I realize how important it must be to you that he be caught, or you wouldn't have come here like this."

"No, you don't know," she answered, genuine tears coming. "You don't know anything about it."

"I'm sorry, Miss Wade."

She drew in her breath and swallowed back the tears. "I want to see the prisoners who are still here. I want to talk to the man who told you this Crazy Doc is in Indian Territory."

"Miss Wade, that isn't a very good—"

"I want to see him," she said louder, rising from her chair. "I want to view the prisoners and make certain this Crazy Doc isn't among them. They could be covering for him."

"I truly doubt it, ma'am. And the building where they're being held—well, those are some pretty desperate, hopeless men. It's dirty in there, and it doesn't smell too good."

"I don't care. Please take me there."

The lieutenant ran a hand through his hair, then rubbed at the back of his neck. "If you insist. I'll go with you." He reached out and took his hat from a rack, perching it on his head. "But you're not going inside that building. I'll have the guards muster the prisoners out and line them up outside for you."

"Fine." Anna wiped at her eyes and held her chin proudly as she followed Asher outside and across the parade grounds. Men stared, and Asher shouted orders to two armed men to accompany him. They followed eagerly, watching Anna's pleasant form as she walked in front of them. When they reached the prisoners' building, Asher ordered the surprised guards to bring the men out and line them up.

Anna's heart pounded so hard her chest hurt as she watched with dreaded anticipation, wondering as each man came out if he might be Darryl. When every man was out, she counted fifteen. The guards lined them up, and she proceeded to walk past each one and study his face. The eyes that stared back at her made her feel sick. Most of them looked at her as though she were prey, and she could see in their eyes the crazed fury of killers. They were dirty and poorly dressed, a few were wounded, all needed a shave. This was the kind of man Darryl had become.

She turned to Asher. "I don't see him," she told the man, wondering how much longer she could stand in front of them and be undressed and raped or murdered in their imaginations. "Where is the one who knew Crazy Doc?"

Asher led her to a man on the left end of the lineup, a thin man with a deep scar across his right eye and his lips. Anna realized that many of them had suffered in the war, but so had others. The war had not turned them into men who robbed and plundered, men who murdered for the thrill of it. She could not accept the war as an excuse.

"You knew Crazy Doc?" she asked the man.

He grinned, showing yellow teeth. "Sure. He just showed up one day—wanted to join up with Anderson and his bunch. I rode with Anderson." His eyes moved over her. "I helped kill those bastard Union soldiers at Centralia." He glanced at Asher and grinned. Asher stood rigid and unemotional, refusing to let the remark bring the reaction the man wanted.

Anna swallowed back her revulsion and breathed deeply before asking the next question. "Do you know who he really is—his real name?"

The man shook his head. "Nobody knows. He never said. Just liked to call himself Doc. Said he really was a doc, but some kind of head wound kept him from practicin'. Left him nervous and loony as a bird knocked silly, know what I mean? That's where he got the nickname *Crazy* Doc. He *is* crazy; real unpredictable, you know?"

So, he was wounded. That at least partly explained his actions, but it didn't change her awkward situation. And why hadn't he come to her? She would have tried to help him. He didn't have to turn to the life he was leading now. Surely he remembered her. After all, he had recognized her that day at Centralia. Crazy. Unpredictable. That made her own situation worse. God only knew when he *might* show up after all, might want her to go away with him, might expect her to be a wife to him in every respect. She had loved the Darryl who had left, but she was afraid of the man he had become. Her only saving grace at the moment was the fact that no one seemed to know his real name. That would help her keep this awful secret.

"You told Lieutenant Asher that this Crazy Doc is in Indian Territory," she told the prisoner. "How can you be sure?"

"I ain't. I'm just almost sure. He left our group just before we was caught—headed south with a few other men, said he was goin' to lay low in Indian Territory till this thing over Centralia and the massacre of Johnston's men blew over. I expect he did just that."

"You swear he wasn't with you when you were caught—wasn't sent up to Rock Island?"

"No, ma'am. What the hell do you care, anyway?" He grinned then. "He get hold of you during a raid? Maybe you liked it and you're lookin' for more."

"That's enough," Asher told the man, taking Anna's arm. She fought the weakness in her legs and nausea at the remark. She turned away with Asher and left the lineup. "I told you it was useless," Asher was telling her. "I had a feeling all you'd get out of this was insults. You should have listened to me, Miss Wade."

Anna hardly heard him. Darryl an outlaw, unpredictable, a rapist, a murderer. Now he was in Indian Territory. He apparently had given no thought to her and the predicament in which he had left her. She was his wife, yet she had no husband. She felt torn by loyalties—to Darryl, to herself. Somehow she had to go on with her life. Was she to wait forever, just because he was her husband and had been wounded? Was there hope that he would get better? If she knew that, it would help her decide what to do.

She walked blindly alongside Asher, her mind racing in confusion. If only Darryl would come back to her, healed, remorseful, explaining that it was the wound that made him do what he did. Yet somehow she suspected he still knew right from wrong, that hate and vengeance had a great deal to do with his actions, and *that* was something she could not forgive. And although the prisoner with whom she had spoken didn't know his real name, someone else, anytime, anywhere, could discover it and tell the law. She felt doomed to a life of loneliness, and possibly a life of shame.

Asher had no idea why she needed his support to walk. The encounter with the prisoners had been too enlightening, for she had faced men who were what Darryl had become. She could hear Darryl's laugh as he shot at the soldiers at Centralia, heard it again as he tried to ride her down, heard his screamed wish that she would "go to hell."

"I'd like to go back to Leavenworth now," she told Asher. "I might still be able to get a train back to Columbia tonight."

"Of course. I'll get a more comfortable buggy for you and take you back myself. I'm sorry you didn't get the answers you came for, ma'am."

I got more answers than you know. So, Darryl was still alive. He had been out of her life now for close to four years, yet she was still bound to him, bound by the wedding band she had left at home. Her wifely instincts told her she must honor that ring, honor her vows, and she wanted more than anything to believe all he had done was because he had been wounded, that he would someday return healed, still loving her. Yet she knew that was a foolish hope.

Indian Territory. Only the most wanted men hid out there. That was what Darryl was now, a wanted man who would no doubt already have a price on his head. Would he emerge from Indian Territory to raid and murder innocent people again? Worse, would he come looking for her? She was no longer certain she wanted him to find her.

She returned to Columbia, and to helping Liz Tidewell. Her future was so unpredictable and undecided that she could not think beyond a day at a time. She was determined to go on with her life and be independent, but how she would accomplish that was impossible to decide.

She still could not bring herself to give serious thought to a legal divorce. It just was not something a woman did, and in spite of all Darryl had done, she still felt traitorous and unfaithful entertaining such thoughts. What would others think? Would they think less of her, divorcing a man who was missing and presumed dead, just for her own convenience? That was how they would view it. The gossip would be cruel and painful.

If only they knew the truth of her situation. She couldn't even divulge that without bringing on a different shame, let alone danger to herself. She was trapped in a horrible nightmare, and the only way she could save face in public was to continue to wear her ring and wait for her poor, missing husband to come home. Still, she couldn't live in this abyss forever. She had to make some kind of decision.

Four months passed. Anna received a letter from her sister telling her she had settled in a lovely valley west of Virginia City, Montana. It sounded like dangerous country and a terribly risky venture. Yet Anna envied her sister's knowledge of what had happened to her husband and her ability to start a new life without him.

She wrote back to Jo, but she did not tell her sister the details about Darryl and what he had become. How could she explain? She couldn't even bring herself to admit it openly to anyone, or to fully face the truth herself. She continued to wait for a miracle, but with every passing, empty day, it became more evident there would be no miracles, no answered prayers. She wrote Jo only that Darryl had returned a changed man and that she was not sure her marriage would survive, telling Jo that perhaps someday when she was more certain what life would hold for her, and when she had healed from the war, she would write in more detail about what had happened.

"I am thinking of leaving Columbia and all things familiar," she wrote. "Perhaps I will go as far west as the Kansas-Pacific will take me. If I leave, I will let you know where I have settled. Maybe I'll come all the way to Montana and join you." It was a happy thought.

Someone knocked on the door of her room then, and she heard Liz's voice. "Anna, there is a nice young gentleman downstairs to see you."

Anna jumped up from her bed and quickly smoothed her plain gray cotton dress. Her heart pounded with apprehension. Was it Darryl? Surely he wouldn't dare ride right into town! But then how many here knew who he was? She went to the door. "Who is it?"

Liz put a wrinkled hand to her mouth and smiled. "He calls himself Nate Foster. Wears a U.S. Marshal's badge." Anna felt her cheeks going crimson and felt her blood warm. "I'll go make some tea," Liz told her.

The old woman left her, and Anna quickly went to a mirror and brushed her hair, which fell in long, golden waves today. She wished she had done more with it, but there wasn't time now. She pinched her cheeks for color, although her own flustered state already brought color enough to her face. Then she chided herself for caring how she looked.

Nate Foster! How had he found her? But that was a silly question. A man like Nate Foster found anyone he wanted to find. He had actually remembered her over these past six months, had chosen to look her up. Wrong as it might be to be happy to see a man, she could not ignore the welcome feeling of knowing someone cared about her, thought about her. She had heard nothing from Fran Rogers since leaving the restaurant, and Claudine had been kept so busy she had been able to visit only once or twice a week.

Anna went down the stairs, careful not to hurry. She noticed a sheepskin coat hanging on a peg in the hallway, and already she picked up the scent of leather and outdoor air, along with the pleasant scent of a man's toilet water. She walked into the parlor to see him standing there, looking more handsome than she had remembered. His soft, gray eyes met her own, and he was clean-shaven, his mustache well manicured. He sported a clean, white shirt and black vest. He held a wide-brimmed felt hat in his hand, and on his hip hung the wide gunbelt and Colt revolver. He smiled, the same, warm smile she remembered.

"Marshal Foster!" She moved closer and put out her hand. "How kind of you to come and see about me. I've thought about you so often since Centralia, wondered if you were all right."

He took her hand and squeezed it lightly. She felt a strength she knew he could use to crush her, yet she enjoyed the wonderful, warm feeling of knowing he was a good, kind man who would never do such a thing. "It's been the same for me," he told her. "I know it's not proper to call on a married woman, but I have no dishonorable intentions, Mrs. Kelley. I just couldn't quite get you off my mind." He let go of her hand.

"Well, I'm glad you thought to look for me. Now I can see that you survived just fine yourself." She noticed a small scar at his left temple, all that was left of his wound at Centralia.

Nate watched her eyes, seeing a distant loneliness, reading tragedy behind their mystic blue. He looked her over, feeling a natural ache at the sight of her, thinking again what a shame it was that she was married. He almost hated himself for bothering to find her, for now his memory was refreshed all over again as to how beautiful, yet unavailable she was. What a fool he was to be unable to stop thinking about her.

Anna in turn felt old, unexpected desires rush through her as she stood in his commanding presence, realizing he was looking at her with a man's appreciation for a woman.

It was evident in one look that Marshal Nate Foster was interested in her as more than a passing friend, and both of them hid their disappointment that this was a situation neither of them could admit to or act on.

"And how about you?" he was saying. "I know it was a terrible day for you, and I remembered you were badly shaken, not to mention the fact that you hadn't heard from your husband in months. I couldn't help being concerned, Mrs. Kelley. I mean, well, what we went through together that day—it kind of left us unintended friends, you know? I felt a responsibility to check back and see if you were all right."

"I know exactly what you mean. Tragedy has a way of drawing strangers together." She looked away and turned to sit down in a chair. "And sometimes it can separate people who were once very close." She glanced up at him. "Sit down, Marshal Foster."

"Call me Nate."

She smiled. "Then you must call me Anna."

He sat down in a loveseat and Liz brought in a tray with a teapot and cups. She smiled at both of them, and Anna could read the curiosity in the old woman's eyes. She thanked Liz for the tea and Liz left the room.

"Would you like some tea?" Anna asked Nate. He nodded, and she poured him a cup. While she wasn't looking he took the opportunity to study her hair, the lovely lines of her small face, her slender arms and hands, the fullness of her breasts that peeked just slightly above the square-cut bodice of her dress. She was even more beautiful than he remembered. "I'll let you put in the sugar and cream, whatever you prefer," she was saying.

He proceeded to spoon in some sugar while she poured her own cup. "What did you mean about tragedy sometimes separating people who were once close?" he asked.

She felt her color rising again, felt the terrible ache. What would a man like Nate Foster think of her if he knew the truth? He was such an honest man, a man who lived by the law. Would he think less of her? She felt as if she were stuck with this shame for the rest of her life.

"The woman I worked for at the restaurant—when she

lost her husband in the war, she grew colder, harder. Then after Centralia—" Anna sighed and sipped some tea. "Well, you know her mother was killed. But she didn't even care how it happened. She said it wasn't the bushwhackers' fault, that if they had known Henrietta was from Georgia, they wouldn't have harmed her. Fran's husband was killed by Union soldiers, so she fully supported what those men did at Centralia. We had an argument about it. I thought she was my friend, but she began looking at me as an enemy, a Yankee. I've never really taken any particular side in this war, Marshal Fos—I mean, Nate. But Fran didn't see it that way. The strain became too much, so I left and came here to work for Mrs. Tidewell."

He drank some tea himself, wrapping his big hand around the entire cup rather than holding it by the handle. "That's too bad. I've suffered my own personal tragedies because of bushwhackers. I guess there aren't many who have been left untouched by all of this. I am surprised that this woman could continue to support them after what happened to her mother."

Anna saw sorrow in his eyes, and she longed to ask him what the personal tragedies were he had mentioned. But she didn't feel she knew him well enough to pry into his private life. And, after all, she couldn't let herself get emotionally involved. She had enough problems of her own without adding to them by letting herself care about a man she could never have.

"Fran is a true Confederate. Since her husband's death, she seems to have become more extreme about it."

He drank more tea and set down his cup, meeting her eyes. "What about your own husband? Any word?" he asked cautiously.

Anna looked down at her tea, amazed at how easy it was becoming for her to lie whenever it was necessary. "No," she answered. "I have no idea what has happened to him." *Oh God, Nate, he was there! He was at Centralia,* she wanted to say. *He's a murderer and an outlaw, and I don't know what to do. Please help me. You're a lawman. Maybe you could find him.* Something told her he would understand, yet she could not bring herself to admit to such an ugly shame.

Even though she had no right to be interested in him, a part of her wanted him to continue seeing her as he saw her now, a proper woman, a grieving war wife—not the wife of a hideous outlaw. And she still feared being arrested, as other bushwhacker wives and relatives had been.

"I'm terribly sorry," he was saying. *And damn disappointed,* he was thinking. He wouldn't wish her the sorrow of death; yet he had not been able to help the tiny wish that he would come here and find she had been widowed. "At least the worst of the raiding is over, with Anderson dead. I have no doubt Quantrill will be found, too. Unfortunately, I'm afraid some of the others will continue with their outlaw ways. One of the worst of them got away—one they call Doc. I have a feeling he's just waiting it out somewhere in Indian Territory, maybe even building his gang, preparing to wreak more havoc on innocent people."

Anna quickly set down her cup, afraid she would drop it. She folded her hands so he wouldn't see them shaking. "That . . . would be terrible."

He rose. "Well, if I have anything to do with it, he won't ride for long. But I cover a lot of territory. One man can't be in ten different places at once. That's the hell of it."

She looked up at him, picturing the devil Darryl had become shooting down a good man like Nate Foster. "Your job must be very dangerous. I'll keep you in my prayers, Nate."

Their eyes met in quiet understanding. "I'll do the same for you, although I'm not very good at praying."

"I'm sure God listens to a man who risks his life upholding the law."

He laughed lightly, embarrassed. "Well, maybe so. I, uh, I'd like to stay longer, but I'm not even supposed to be in Columbia. I had some things to do in Independence, and I figured as long as I was in Missouri, I'd take an extra day or two and come find out how you were. I'm due back in Topeka the day after tomorrow. I don't think I'm going to make it, but I'll find some excuse."

Anna rose, feeling a sudden sadness that he was already leaving, yet realizing neither of them had any right wanting to be together for more than a quick hello. "Thank you so much for coming, Nate. I'm glad you're all right."

His eyes moved over her again. "I'm glad you are too, but I'm sorry about what happened with your friend—and very sorry you still don't know about your husband. It must be hell for you."

She dropped her eyes. "It is."

He sighed deeply. "Anna—" The way he spoke her name made her heart flutter. How she longed to lean on him, to feel his strong arms around her, to have him tell her he cared and that everything would be all right. She raised her eyes to meet his. "I just . . . Are you really okay? I mean, do you have other friends here in Columbia?"

She put on a smile for him. "Yes. I'm fine. I'm sure I'll hear from Darryl soon, and old Mrs. Tidewell is wonderful. She's just like a mother."

"I remember you said your father was killed at Shiloh, but I don't remember if you said anything about your mother."

"She's been dead for years."

"How about the sister who went to Montana?"

Anna laughed lightly. "Joline is settled somewhere near Virginia City. It sounds like she's doing all right, and I think she's in love again." The words made the color come back to her cheeks. He smiled softly.

"Well, that's good." He cleared his throat nervously. "You take care of yourself, Anna. I don't get this far east often, but maybe I'll check on you again in a few months. I hope you hear from your husband."

"Thank you." She walked with him to the hallway, where he pulled on his sheepskin jacket. It was late February 1865, and the air outside was cold and damp. The jacket only accentuated his fine physique. He put on his hat, and again their eyes held, each of them wanting to say more but unable to because of social proprieties.

"Good-bye, Anna. You're a fine, strong woman. I'm sure all your prayers will be answered soon and you'll have your husband back."

My real husband is gone forever. "I hope you're right," she said aloud. "And do be careful, Nate. I'll always remember you, always be grateful to you. I don't know what I would have done that day without your help."

He longed to pull her into his arms. She looked so sad, so vulnerable, so lonely. How terrible it must be for her not to know if her husband was dead or alive. How long would this woman go on being faithful to a memory? "Well, things just sort of happened. I always thought it was kind of strange, us running into each other like that after seeing you that day at the telegraph office. That's been quite a while ago now."

"Well, God works in mysterious ways, they say. Perhaps He made you sit down beside me on the train, knowing I'd need help later."

He smiled again. "Could be." He tipped his hat. "Well, I can't stand here all day. Good-bye again."

"Good-bye, Nate."

He turned and went out the door. She stood with the door ajar a moment and he waved back to her. She waved and watched him mount his horse. It was the same horse he had taken off the train at Centralia, a big buckskin gelding. He nodded once more and rode off.

Anna closed the door. She struggled to keep from thinking the thoughts that moved through her soul at the moment, to keep from feeling the natural needs and desires that had been stirred in her woman's body. She climbed back up the stairs slowly to her room, her whole body feeling like lead, her heart aching to feel again, to love and be loved. Oh, how she wanted to feel like a woman again. Nate Foster had stirred much too much emotion in her, had awakened needs she had no right experiencing. How dearly she wanted her own home again, her own kitchen and hearth, children. All her dreams were shattered now.

She suddenly realized more clearly than ever that she must leave Columbia. She didn't dare let herself see Nate Foster again, and she had a feeling he would come back. She was also afraid now, afraid Darryl would come looking for her, drag her away and force her to be a wife to him, to live the miserable life of an outlaw's wife. She was afraid of her own husband, and also afraid of allowing her feelings for some other man to grow.

"I'll go to Montana," she said quietly to herself. *I've got to get away,* she thought, *away from Darryl and away from Nate Foster. Maybe if I go far enough, I can clear my mind and decide once and for all what I should do. I'll go see Jo. Jo can help me.* Deep inside she knew it was a foolish thought, but she didn't know what else to do to keep herself from doing what she really wanted—to run right into Nate Foster's arms and beg him to hold her and never let go.

Chapter 7

April 1865

Anna watched the changing scenery. The wooded hills of Missouri became more scarce as the train moved across the border into Kansas. She sat nervously twisting a handkerchief, terrified of another incident like Centralia, as the train rumbled through the volatile border towns.

She was glad no one had decided to sit down beside or across from her. She didn't feel like explaining where she was going or why. She did think, though, how pleasant it would be if Nate Foster were sitting across from her again. She had enjoyed talking to him on the two occasions they had met, and she thought what a pity it was they could not have met under different circumstances: if she were single and unscarred by the war; if he wasn't a lawman pursuing the man she still called husband. She wondered what Nate would think when and if he went to see her again, only to discover she was gone.

She gazed out at the wide Kansas prairie and farmland. Yes, Nate had a lot of territory to cover. It was unlikely she would ever run into him again, especially once she headed for Montana.

The train whistle blew, and its mournful wail only added to her feelings of sorrow and loneliness. Never had she felt so disoriented, so homeless and out of place. She realized now those feelings had started clear back when she and Darryl first left Lawrence, and she had first said good-bye to her father, never to see him again, and to Jo, not to see her again until her visit three years later. The war had destroyed all her dreams, all her ideals, all her plans for the future.

The old family life was gone, Jo was gone, the farm was gone, Darryl and the life they had shared were gone. She had never even met his parents. She and Darryl had talked so often of going to Georgia and visiting their plantation. Darryl had described his home as a place of beauty and rich, Southern culture. A palace of a home, with gentle, loving parents who treated their slaves well. Was all that gone now? Were his parents dead?

A terrible pain pierced her heart when the train stopped at Lawrence. The town was partially rebuilt, but she could still see signs of the raid. She was glad she could not see the old farm. She wanted to remember the house the way it had been. And oh, how she wished she could see Joline standing at the train station.

She turned away from the window. An incident in Columbia recently had finally made Anna decide she had to get out. A woman whose husband had admitted to riding with Quantrill had been beaten and raped in an alley. Anna could no longer risk having the truth discovered about her own husband.

Leaving Liz and Claudine had been the hardest part. Finding such good friends was not easy, but if she could reach Montana, she would be with Jo. Her eyes teared at the memory of her parting from Claudine at the depot. She would miss the woman terribly. Claudine had wept and hugged her as though saying good-bye to a daughter. Anna had hoped to fulfill her dream of opening her own restaurant, and hiring Claudine; but that dream would have to wait a while. For now she simply had to get out of Columbia. She needed time to think and plan. She had been sorely tempted to tell Claudine the truth about Darryl, but still she held back. She could not yet bring herself to utter such shame to another human being, not even Claudine.

She shook away the painful memories and took a little notebook and a pencil from her handbag and began doing some figuring, suddenly desperate to stop the flow of memories and to occupy her mind. She wrote down the day's expenses, keeping careful track of the precious little money she had left. She had used up a lot of what Darryl had left her but had managed to save a little also. When she finished, she studied the pencil, marveling at the wonderful new invention that made it possible to carry a writing instrument without having to worry about ink.

She put the pencil back in her handbag. Her stomach growled from hunger, as she had skipped supper at an earlier train stop, figuring she could save a little more by eating less. The train itself was costing a pretty penny. She would have taken a coach, as she had a year and a half ago when she went to visit Jo, but this time she had farther to go, and in early spring it was still quite cold. The train offered more protection and a little more warmth, and it was certainly more comfortable.

Steam poured from the side of the engine ahead, and the train chugged and lurched, taking off again. Anna lost some of her nervousness, since most of the Union soldiers who had originally been on the train at Columbia disembarked at Leavenworth. After what she had seen at Centralia, in her mind soldiers meant trouble. By the time they reached Lawrence, the soldiers were all gone, and now that the train was leaving Lawrence, they were also heading out of the most troublesome border areas. From here on an attack by bushwhackers was much less likely, and since most such raids had stopped, she rested easier.

She stared out her window to the south. Somewhere out there, below the Kansas border with Indian Territory, was Darryl. Was he indeed still alive? What kind of life did he lead now? Would he ever find her, try to explain? How long could she keep waiting and wondering? The questions boiled over in her mind until sometimes she thought she was the one who was going crazy. She put her head back, the conversations behind her becoming a dull mumble. She let the darkening night and the rhythmic rumble of the train lull her to sleep, but it was a troubled sleep, and she kept jumping awake through the night, visions of Centralia, of Darryl's evil grin and chilling laugh haunting her.

This was her second night on the train, and according to the conductor, it would be her last. By the end of tomorrow, they would reach the end of the Kansas-Pacific track. More was being laid, and eventually it would go all the way to central Colorado, but for now, a town called Abilene was the last stop. From there Anna would have to find a stagecoach, and after that probably a wagon train to take her to Montana. How she was going to manage it all, she had no idea, and she was beginning to wonder how Jo had managed.

At least Jo had found a good guide. That was apparently the first priority. Of course, it didn't hurt to be in love with the man, as she knew by now had happened with Joline. She smiled at the thought of Jo falling for a rugged mountain man. She looked forward to meeting him when she reached Montana. She fell asleep imagining what life would be like there.

Anna awoke to a sunrise, and she watched out the window again as the train rocked and rattled past a few farms. She realized that during the night they had passed through Topeka, which Nate Foster had told her was his home base. It seemed strange to pass right through in the middle of the night.

Was he there? A man like Nate could be anywhere. She could only hope she wouldn't accidentally run into him again before she could head farther west. She was not at all sure she could keep going and vow never to see him again if she set eyes on him one more time, and if she saw the same thing in his eyes she thought she had seen when he visited her in Columbia.

Fate was so strange, and sometimes cruel. Why had God brought her together with a man who attracted her so, knowing she could never have him and had no right even giving him a second thought? And how ironic that she had been thrown together with Nate the very same day she discovered Darryl was still alive.

The train stopped in a tiny, unnamed town long enough for people to disembark and eat breakfast. Anna felt grimy. It seemed that even though they were in enclosed passenger cars, the black smoke from the engine's stack managed to find its way through cracks and crevices into the cars behind it. Every time someone opened a door at the front end of the car to go out onto the platform and get some fresh air, more smoke came inside. Anna wished there was a place to go and wash, but there was only a public outhouse behind the train station where passengers could relieve themselves. She ate at a tiny diner, quickly choking down hard biscuits and some kind of tough meat that was not worth the ridiculous price she paid for it. After years of working for Fran, she was keenly aware how badly these towns needed decent restaurants for train passengers.

They boarded the train again. In a few hours they would be at Abilene. The land grew leaner, with few trees and a horizon that stretched for miles. There were fewer farms, fewer towns. This barrenness west of Topeka seemed like remote nothingness to her, yet its loneliness matched her own feelings. Right now she felt that she fit this land. She hoped she could slip into it and vanish, never to be recognized, never to be found by her deranged husband or by the man she knew she dared not see again.

The hours melted into afternoon, and they had gone for miles without seeing anything but the endless telegraph poles that ran alongside the railroad tracks. Anna drifted off to sleep again, only to be awakened by a sudden crash and the breaking of glass in the window behind her. A woman screamed and men swore. Anna sat up straight, hearing gunshots. She looked out the window to see half-naked Indians on painted horses riding alongside the train, hooting and yipping, shooting and throwing rocks at the train windows.

"Everybody get down," a conductor yelled as he ran inside the passenger car, his head bleeding from a tossed rock. He slammed the door. "Down! It's Cheyenne!"

Another window broke and Anna put her head down, her

heart pounding with terror. The conductor was crawling down the aisle. "Don't worry, folks, they can't actually stop the train. This happens every once in a while. The Indians don't like the railroads coming into their land—scares away the buffalo. They usually save their attacks for the train crews building track farther ahead, but sometimes they pick on the trains."

"How long before we reach Abilene?" a man shouted above the yipping and shooting.

"The engineer's steamin' her up to full speed," the conductor answered. Another stone crashed through a window. "We'll make her within the hour. Just stay calm and keep down, away from the windows."

Anna was too terrified to ask any questions. She wondered just how wise she had been to come here. She had to agree with Jo on one thing: this land was wild and exciting and kept a body occupied. But for the moment all she could picture was her hair hanging from some warrior's belt, her body riddled with arrows. Was this to be her end then, with no one to ever know what happened to her? She thought about Nate Foster. How did the man survive, riding alone in country like this?

Men cussed and women continued to scream and weep, and for the moment Anna wondered why she had ever left Columbia. The train whistle blew, and the train swayed and rumbled along the track so fast Anna feared it would jump the track altogether and they would all die in a train wreck. Better to die that way than at the hands of Cheyenne warriors.

After another twenty minutes of the frightful war whoops and gunshots, she realized the noise had stopped. The conductor slowly rose and peeked out a window. "They're gone," he announced. "Must be getting close to town. Sorry about the inconvenience, folks. At least they didn't tear up the track and cause an accident."

"You mean sometimes they do that?" a woman asked.

"It's happened. I didn't mention it because I didn't want to get you all upset and more panicked than you were. We'll be all right now."

Anna sat up and leaned back in her seat, putting a hand

to her heart and breathing deeply in relief. She could not help a grin and a light laugh. What had she gotten herself into? As if she didn't have enough troubles.

The train reached the depot at Abilene. Anna rose and brushed at dust and soot on her dark blue calico dress. She adjusted her straw bonnet and gladly left the train. It felt good to walk around, but once outside, the sensation of swaying remained with her. She grasped a post on the depot platform to keep from stumbling, and she wrinkled her nose at the strong smell of animals and manure in the air. The weather was warmer here, the sun bright, and she removed her shawl, noticing what seemed hundreds of pens and miles of fencing beyond the depot. A few cattle grazed inside some of the pens, but most of them were empty.

"Howdy, ma'am. Welcome to Abilene," a man nearby said. She turned to see a man wearing a wide-brimmed hat and a sheepskin jacket giving her the once-over. He sported a two- or three-day beard and wore a bandana around his neck and a six-gun at his side. His stained, well-worn pants were tucked into knee-high, dusty leather boots.

"Thank you," she said hesitantly, unsure what to think of him, although his smile was sincere and his eyes showed respect.

"What's a pretty lady like you doing in a cow town like this?"

"Cow town?"

"Can't you smell it? Men like me, we think it's a good smell, but I reckon to a lady like you it's a little strong. Me, I herd cattle. Now that the war's about over, and the railroad has come to Abilene, I expect this little place will become one of the biggest cow towns in the country. All them ranchers in Texas will be herding their cattle up here to catch the trains going east." He looked her over again. "Now, you—you look like a lady who's maybe married to one of them rich cattle ranchers, or maybe to a banker. We've got lots of bankers comin' into Abilene, figurin' it's gonna grow fast."

Anna pushed a piece of hair behind her ear. "No, I'm no banker's or rancher's wife. Please, could you tell me where I might find a stagecoach going farther west?"

The man pushed back his hat, glad to carry on a conversation with such a beautiful woman. Compared to the sorry whores in Abilene, she was a welcome sight, but his anticipation waned when she removed her gloves and he saw a wedding band.

"West? How far?"

"I'm thinking of trying to reach my sister. She's in Montana."

"Montana!" He removed his hat and scratched his head. "Ma'am, I don't know what your reasons are, and I expect it's none of my business, but you'd be riskin' your honor and your life by going any farther west than this, let alone to Montana. Ain't you heard about all the Indian trouble?"

"Well, I . . . I don't know much about Indians. But our train was attacked by Cheyenne warriors."

"Ma'am, a train is one thing. A coach, that's somethin' else. The Indians are causin' a lot of trouble, from here to Colorado and up in the Dakotas. Indians attack a coach you're on, you can bet nobody would live. In fact, the stagecoach hasn't been runnin' at all for the past few days. It's just too dangerous—pure suicide for a pretty woman to head any farther west on one. Excuse me, ma'am, but one look at that pretty, white hair of yours, and they'd snatch you up like a ripe strawberry. And if they didn't kill you, you'd be wishin' you was dead."

Anna reddened, turning away to watch her baggage being unloaded.

"I don't mean to be rude, ma'am. I'm just statin' a fact."

She felt the tears wanting to come. If she couldn't go farther west, what was she to do? Stay here, in this wild, dirty, smelly town? Now that she had come this far, she couldn't bear the thought of going back. Unbearable as this place was, it still felt good to be away from Columbia. At least here she guessed people didn't much care about the war back East. They were waging their own war—against the elements and the Indians. She felt herself falling farther and farther into a black hole where she lost all identity.

"I . . . appreciate your advice," she told the stranger. "I will have to think about this. Is there a decent boarding house or hotel in town?" She kept her eyes averted, not wanting him to see the tears in them.

"Yes, ma'am, up at the other end of town there's a boardin' house run by a man and wife name of Hectar and Agnes White. You picked a good time to come. Any later, and you'd not find a room anywhere. In a couple more months this town will be packed with cowboys—men like me who herd cattle. And there will be more cattle out in them pens than you could ever count in a day. Why, there's times when you can't even see any land, just cattle."

"Well, I'll . . . I'll go see about getting a room. Thank you." She hurried away, picking up her bags, shoving one under each arm, then bending to pick up the two bigger ones.

"Ma'am, I'll carry them bags for you. I don't mind." The stranger was beside her again. "Name's Ben Tucker. And I'm always glad to help a fine lady like yourself."

Anna was too tired to argue, and the April day was suddenly growing hot. "If you really don't mind, Mr. Tucker."

Tucker gladly lifted the bags, carrying the three heaviest ones while Anna took a smaller one. "You think about what I said now," he told her. "Whatever reason you got to go to Montana, I'd put it off for a while, ma'am. I wouldn't steer you wrong. The mood the Indians is in, it would go bad for a pretty lady like you if they got their hands on you. You'd best stay in Abilene for a while, or go back where you came from."

"I can't go back. I've come this far, Mr. Tucker, I'm not going all the way back."

"And how far is that? Where'd you come from?"

"I'd rather not say right now. I hardly know you, Mr. Tucker."

"I understand."

She stopped walking and looked up at him, wondering how old he was. He looked like he was in his forties, but his skin was so weathered and lined, she supposed he could be younger, just aged from the elements. "I don't mean to appear rude, Mr. Tucker. I'm just very tired, and very disappointed about the Indians. If I can't get to Montana, I just don't know what I'll do."

"Well, Abilene sure could use somebody with class like you." He glanced at her hand. "What about your husband?"

She turned away. "My husband is . . . He's still not back from the war," she answered. She reasoned that was at least half true, for the war still raged in Darryl's heart. At least telling people she had a husband would help keep men from pestering her.

"I'm right sorry, ma'am. You got family in Montana?"

"A sister."

They walked down a dusty street, and Anna could feel rugged, bearded men staring at her. She was aware of painted women standing here and there, and piano music came from inside saloons. Horses and wagons clopped and clattered up and down the street, and she had to be careful not to step in horse dung. The smell of cattle and manure stung the air everywhere, and for the moment she could not imagine getting used to such an odor. People like Ben Tucker and the others who stood around in the streets seemed unaffected by it. She thought how much worse it must get in the hot summer, when the cattle pens were full.

They reached the boarding house, which was painted white with blue trim, but the white was a grimy gray halfway up the side of the building from dust. It was obvious the owners tried to keep the house looking neat, and there were some budding rosebushes along the front porch. But in a town like Abilene, Anna could already see, it was almost impossible to be completely tidy.

Tucker set her bags down on the porch near the door. "I'm sure they'll have a room, ma'am."

"Thank you so much, Mr. Tucker. I'd like to pay you." She opened her handbag, but the man waved her off.

"No, ma'am, it's not necessary. I consider it a privilege to help a lady like yourself. You just remember what I said. You give it a lot of thought before you go headin' any farther west."

"Yes, I will. Thank you again." She reached out her hand, but Tucker just rubbed his along his chaps.

"Oh, I couldn't shake your hand. Mine are too dirty." He tipped his hat. "You have a nice day now. I sleep out back of the livery, if you need any more advice or help." He gave her a wink and walked away, taking long strides on bowed legs. Anna watched him a moment, wrinkling her nose again at the smell in the air.

Abilene. Was this dusty, rank-smelling cow town to be her final destination? Her eyes teared and her throat ached. She breathed deeply, telling herself that at least this was not Columbia or Centralia or Lawrence. At least here the war seemed far, far away, and that was most important. It was not likely Darryl would find her here any too soon, but at least if he did come looking for her, no one in this town would know him.

She could not help wondering if Nate Foster would find her here. After all, she was in Kansas Territory, his home ground. It looked as though she would have to wait it out for a while in Abilene. She could only hope Nate wouldn't find reason to come here.

It all seemed so unreal. What was she doing here? Landing in a wild cow town had not been in her plans, but then nothing that had happened to her over the past few years had been in her plans. She felt her life being led along by some unknown force that she blindly followed. She seemed no longer to have any control over her own fate.

She straightened her shoulders, reminding herself that at least she had made it this far and she was safe. She knocked at the door, where a sign hung that said Vacancy.

It was July 1865 when Fran took the note from the young boy who had come to the back door of the restaurant. It was addressed to Anna. "Where did you get this, child?" she asked. "There is no Anna here anymore."

"A man outside of town, he paid me a whole nickel to bring it."

Fran studied the shaky writing, an odd sensation coming over her. Was Anna up to some kind of secrecy involving the war? But the war was over now. Why would someone be sending her secret notes? Besides, everyone in Columbia who knew Anna would also know she was no longer here. It would have to be someone who had not seen her in a while.

Her blood rushed as she realized who it must be. Darryl? But why the secrecy? "Thank you," she told the boy. She slipped the note into her apron pocket just as Claudine came into the kitchen. The boy ran out the back door.

"What did that troublemaker want?" Claudine asked.

"Just looking for a handout." Fran stirred some soup. "Claudine, have you heard from Anna?"

Claudine kept her back turned, always suspicious now of Fran. "I have had a couple of letters. She is in Abilene."

Fran glanced her way. "I think it was horrible of her to run off that way, without hearing from Darryl first. How could she do that to him? He might come looking for her, and he won't even know where to find her. I think it's shameful. It only shows that she married him for his money. Now that he's probably broke, maybe even crippled, she doesn't want anything to do with him."

"Oh, I do not think it is that way at all. Anna is not that kind of woman. She has a good heart. I think perhaps she feels her husband is either dead, or he has deserted her. It has been very hard for her. I think she only wanted to get away from familiar things for a little while so she can think more clearly. She was going to go all the way to her sister in Montana, but Indian trouble stopped her. For now she will stay in Abilene, at least until the trouble is over." The woman looked at Fran. "At least she has told us where she can be found. I do not call that running off."

"Well, I do. And I don't expect she'll last long in a wild, dirty town like Abilene. I've heard about it," Fran drawled. "I think she is crazy to go into that kind of country. She should have stayed here and waited for Darryl." She tasted the soup, irritated at what she considered traitorous behavior by Anna. She slipped her hand into her pocket and felt the note. She would read it herself. Perhaps Anna was up to some kind of spying, helping identify some of the bushwhackers who had taken part in the raid at Centralia. Perhaps the note was from some Union man.

Claudine left the kitchen again, and Fran quickly took out the note, ripping open the envelope. Her eyes widened and her body tingled with a mixture of joy and curiosity at its contents. "Meet me in the shed behind the restaurant after closing," it read. "We have to talk. Darryl."

With shaking hands Fran put the note back into her

pocket. Darryl! The way the note read, one would think Anna already knew he was alive, that perhaps they had already been meeting! But they couldn't have been, or Darryl would know Anna was no longer in Columbia. Why didn't he just come here himself? Was he in trouble?

She returned to the soup, adding some salt. Her mind whirled with the possibilities. "Bushwhackers," she whispered. Was Darryl afraid to be seen? Was he a wanted man? Her heart leaped at the thought of it. Continuing the war against the Yankees through raids was the most commendable act she could imagine. The war might be over on paper, but it was not over for men like Darryl, and her heart swelled with pride. Anna would hate such a thing, but Anna didn't understand.

She tasted the soup again. Darryl was still alive! She felt like weeping with joy, and her hand shook with excitement. She had to know for sure the reason for the secrecy, and Darryl couldn't be left waiting and wondering. She would go herself to meet him tonight.

Chapter 8

Anna stood on the porch of the boarding house listening to the wild laughter and piano music in town. It seemed that Abilene never slept, especially in the summer. Men roamed the streets all night, drovers who arrived in town ready to get drunk and sleep with the whores, to gamble and let loose after long weeks, sometimes months, on the trail, facing all kinds of dangers, not the least of which were marauding Indians. Nighttime was a good time for a decent woman to stay off the streets. There had been some killings and numerous fistfights and gunfights. Sometimes drunken drovers rode or walked around shooting into the air just for the hell of it.

Anna had gotten used to the uncivilized town. A local sheriff tried to keep the peace as best he could, but it was not an easy job. In some respects, Anna could hardly blame the drovers, and she did not fear them. She had discovered that when she walked into town by day to do her shopping, most of them treated her with great respect. To them, a proper lady was a rare sight, someone to be treated with honor and near awe.

Word had spread quickly that Anna Kelley's husband had been missing for several years. Anna had not given anyone exact dates. Most who knew only that much surmised her husband must be dead. After all, they reasoned, what man in his right mind would desert a woman like Anna Kelley?

Anna quickly learned that most of the drovers were from Texas, where feelings were strongly Confederate. She at least did not have to face shame and crude remarks just because her husband had worn gray, although there were nightly fights in town between Union and Confederate sympathizers who still carried bad memories from the war. But most of them were trying to put the war behind them. The bigger concern in the frontier towns was Indians. Soldiers already weary from the War Between the States were being sent west to beef up the forts that guarded the various railroads and wagon trails on the frontier.

With more soldiers coming west, more forts being built, more railroad men, Southerners coming west who had lost homes and land from the war, and hundreds of drovers who landed in town every summer, Abilene was booming. The wild shooting and laughter of the night was replaced in the day by the sound of bawling cattle, train whistles, and the pounding of hammers and scraping of saws, as new buildings went up every day. Anna could not help thinking how fast a person could get rich in this town with a good restaurant business. She was working now for the Whites, much as she had worked for Liz Tidewell—cooking for their six boarders.

The Whites were good people, who had lost everything but a small amount of money early in the war and had come west like so many others to get away from bad memories. They were Southerners, but not prejudiced or full of hate like some, in spite of the fact that one of their two sons had been killed early in the war at Fort Sumter. The other son had come west with them and was building his own ranch outside of Abilene.

Anna had resigned herself to staying in Abilene, at least through the winter. The Whites were good to her, and the constant activity of the unorganized, burgeoning town helped ease her personal agony. But she was tired of relying on others for her income. The Barker independence that had sent Joline to Montana also thrived in Anna.

She could not help thinking about starting a good restaurant in this town full of hungry men. And she was not oblivious to the fact that a lot of those men would patronize her establishment just for a look at her. She was not a vain person, but it was impossible to ignore the fact that men practically fell over themselves trying to win her attention. Her heart ached at what she knew was the truth: that she could not consider another man, not legally, and not in her own heart. There was only one man who might send her mind reeling with indecision, and she prayed he would not find her here.

She walked back inside to join the Whites, who sat beside the hearth in their parlor. Because of flies and mosquitoes this time of evening, especially in summer, few sat outside on their porches. A breeze drifted through a screened window, bringing little relief, and also bringing the smell Anna never would have believed she could learn to ignore.

"I'll finish this shirt for you," Anna told Agnes then, picking up some of the woman's mending. The White boarding house was one of the few clean and tidy buildings in Abilene. Agnes fussed constantly because of the endless dust in the air, and her immaculate habits were put to the extreme test in the cattle town.

"Oh, it's not necessary, dear," the woman answered.

"I don't mind. I'm not sleepy enough to go to bed." Anna glanced at Hectar. Her naturally friendly nature, and the fact that her husband had been a Confederate, had quickly won over the Whites, who felt sorry for her predicament. Anna felt she could trust the Whites, and she hoped their friendship was not too new for her to ask what she had in mind.

Hectar sat puffing on a pipe and reading his Bible. He had told Anna once that she reminded him of a young woman his dead son had loved, a young woman who had died from a flu-like ailment. For that reason he had taken a special liking to her, and Anna had long ago stopped calling them Mr. and Mrs. White. It was Agnes and Hectar, at their insistence.

"Hectar," Anna began. "I have a tremendous favor to ask of you. I hope you don't think I'm being too forward, and if you want to say no, please don't worry about offending me."

The man's eyebrows arched. "Now how could I say no to anything you ask?"

Anna smiled, setting the shirt aside. "I wouldn't say yes too quickly."

The man closed his Bible and took his pipe from his mouth. "Well, what is it?"

Anna swallowed her pride. Somehow she had to find a way to be on her own. "I'm wondering if you and Agnes would consider . . . loaning me a little money."

Hectar glanced at his wife. Hectar was a pudgy, short man with bushy gray eyebrows and dark hair that was gray at the temples. He was not the least bit attractive, but he had a kind spirit and gentle brown eyes. Agnes leaned forward, all ears at the request, her dark eyes showing curiosity and a hundred wrinkles forming around them when she smiled. "Whatever for, dear?" the woman asked.

Anna met Agnes's eyes. "I need to have something of my own, a business where I can make my own money. Both of you have been very helpful during these past three months since I arrived, and I appreciate your friendship. I never expected to stay so long here, but I feel more relaxed and settled in Abilene now—I've even gotten used to the smells!"

They all laughed.

"So what kind of business would you get into?" Hectar asked.

"The money my husband left me is almost gone, but with your help I would have enough to open a restaurant. I learned the business back in Columbia, and you already know I can cook well and know how to serve people. In a town like Abilene, there is no doubt a good restaurant would be a big moneymaker. I would only be open for breakfast, lunch, and early suppers. I would close up before dark."

Hectar puffed on his pipe again. "You've made up your mind then not to go to Montana?"

Anna reached over and picked up the shirt. "I think it's too dangerous to go any farther right now. Perhaps in a year or two I'll reconsider. I'm not even sure yet how settled my sister is. I'll have to wait for another letter. I telegraphed the post office at Columbia and gave them a forwarding address. At any rate, if I decide to go, I'm sure the restaurant would be a big enough moneymaker that it would sell easily, or the two of you might want to take it over yourselves. Either way, I wouldn't leave unless things were going well and I had paid back what I owe you. We can even put that in writing if you wish."

Hectar leaned back in his chair, contemplating her request. "We aren't rich people ourselves, Anna. How much would you need?"

Anna hesitated, then decided to get it over with. How she hated asking for money. "Five hundred dollars? I have five hundred of my own left. With a thousand I could get whatever else I need through a bank, have a good-size building built, and be in business in a couple of months. You know how fast they raise a building in this town."

Hectar grinned. "That they do. Of course, we would hate losing you here. You're a big help to Agnes. You don't have to do this, you know. Here you're well paid and you have a free room."

"I know. But I've got to get on with my life, get into something that's just mine so that I don't have to depend on anyone else for my livelihood. In towns like this there is a lot of opportunity, even for women."

"Well, I just hope you find out soon what has happened to your husband. A beautiful young lady like yourself shouldn't be wasting her best years alone."

"Now, Hectar, she feels bad enough," Agnes chided.

Anna wondered what good, decent people like the Whites would think of her if they knew the truth. Even though their son had been a Confederate, they would never approve of what had happened at Centralia.

Hectar tamped out his pipe. "I think I can loan you that much, Anna. But I wouldn't do it for just anyone. And I will do it partly because I think you're right that a good restaurant would be very profitable here."

"I am deeply grateful. I don't like having to ask at all, but I have nowhere else to turn right now. I'll go talk to Mr. Eastman at the bank tomorrow. I have my savings there, and Mr. Eastman has always been helpful. I don't think I'll have a problem."

"Good. Then it's settled. I'll go with you and take care of my share of the loan."

Anna's eyes shone with tears. People had been so good to her—Claudine, Liz Tidewell, the Whites. It hurt so much to have to lie to them. But it seemed the longer she lived the lie, the harder it became to admit the truth. She could only move through life now in her own little prison, hoping she would hear something about Darryl, yet desperately afraid to see him at all; loving the Darryl she once knew, hating the one he had become. She was a widow, with a husband who was still alive.

"Darryl? Are you out here? It's me, Francine." Fran's heart pounded wildly, unsure if it was really Darryl who had sent the note, unsure what she would find. Was it someone who meant Anna harm? She tried to see in the darkness behind the shed. "Darryl, if it's you, it's all right to show yourself. I don't know what your problem is, but Anna is gone, Darryl. Please let me help you."

She gasped then when someone touched her shoulder from behind. A hand came over her mouth for a moment. "Don't scream or anything," came a gruff whisper. "It's me —Darryl. I don't want anybody to know I'm here."

He slowly removed his hand. Fran could smell whiskey and sweat. Darryl kept hold of her arms as he turned her. "Where's Anna?"

"Darryl!" She touched his face. "Oh, Darryl, you don't know how good it is to see you, to know you're alive," she whispered, straining to see him in the dark. "Darryl, my Darryl! Thank God! My God, Darryl, where have you been? I was sure you must be dead. I got word three years ago that Mark had been killed."

"I probably *should* be dead," he answered in a gravelly voice. "Sometimes I wish I was." He let go of her. "I was with Mark when he was killed, Fran."

She stepped back, letting out a little gasp. "He didn't suffer," Darryl added. "It was snipers that got him. I was right beside him when it happened. He took a bullet square in the head, and I took another one—it grazed my skull so that I'm no use as a doctor anymore."

He pulled a small flask from a pocket of his jacket and took a swallow. "I can't control my hands well enough, and I get headaches—real bad headaches. I'm tanked up with laudanum and whiskey most of the time." He began pacing, and as Fran's eyes adjusted to the moonlight she could see his face looked much thinner, and he needed a shave. "This thing with my head makes me do crazy things," he continued. "When I came to, after I was wounded . . . I couldn't even remember for a while who I was."

He took another swallow of whiskey. "Mark and I . . . we had already been separated for a while. Then we were taken prisoners and landed in the same temporary prison camp. We escaped. I guess the regiment we'd been with never knew what happened to us."

"But . . . no one ever told us you had been taken prisoners."

He laughed nervously, continuing to pace. "Hell, the regiment we were with didn't know its ass from a hole in the ground. Things had gotten pretty bad, men missing, troops divided up, officers killed. I'm not surprised nobody reported it. Somebody must have found Mark later, found his papers on him. That's probably how he finally got reported as killed."

He suddenly turned and snickered. "I've got men of my own now, Fran. Some might think this war is over, but not for me . . . not for *me!*" He came closer, his eyes and grin looking wild in the moonlight.

"I don't blame you," Fran answered. "I feel the same way you do, Darryl. There are other ways to get back at the Yankees." She touched his shoulders. "Oh, Darryl, you have no idea how wonderful it is to know you're alive! I haven't been this happy since you rode away with Mark."

He pulled away, as though he hardly heard her. Fran could see he didn't seem able to concentrate on one train of thought for very long. "My men," he told her, pacing again. "They say I'm crazy, but that's good. Makes them afraid of me. Makes them obey me."

Fran had to concentrate to understand him because of the rapidity with which he spoke the words, which also had a slight slur to them. "What men, Darryl?"

"My men, that's all. Hell, Fran, you must know about the bushwhackers—Quantrill and the like. He's given up, but I haven't."

"Oh, Darryl, you *are* a part of the raids. I'm glad."

He took off a hat and ran a hand through his hair. "Yeah, well, I'll bet Anna isn't. I've got to find her, got to know if she's told anybody."

"Told anybody! How could she tell anyone when she doesn't even know if you're alive or dead."

He put his hat back on. "She knows, all right. She saw me at Centralia."

Fran's breath caught in her throat. "Centralia! You were *there?"*

"I was there, all right. Anna never told you about it?"

"Not a word!" Fran put a hand to her cheek. "No wonder she was so upset afterward! And no wonder she left town. She must be afraid people will find out she's the wife of an outlaw."

"Outlaw?" He laughed nervously, still constantly pacing. Fran could see he was a far cry from the calm, educated, gentle man who had left nearly four years ago. "Yeah, I suppose that's what I am now. It didn't start out that way. But after my folks . . . my home—You don't know what I've seen, Fran. And then Mark—shot down right beside me —that bullet I took. It might as well have killed me for all my pain, and . . . and it took away my skills. All I've wanted ever since is to kill Yankees. Now . . . I don't know. It's gotten to be a way of life, only most of those I once rode with have been caught and hanged or shot or put in prison. Even Quantrill. He's dead, too. You hear about Quantrill?"

"Yes. It was in all the papers. Union soldiers shot him. Bushwhacked him is the more likely explanation. The poor man. He'd decided to live a life of peace, and they still killed him—and with the war already over."

"Bastards, all of them! *You* understand, don't you?"

"Yes. Of course I understand. But not Anna. Her heart was never for our side, Darryl. She was terribly upset by Centralia. She kept saying it was horrible what was done to those soldiers, but I didn't think it was. My mother was killed that day, Darryl. Anna had gone there to bring Mother back here to live with me, but she found her dead. Still, I never blamed the bushwhackers, Darryl. It was an accident. She was running and she fell. She didn't know enough to tell them she was from Georgia. I blame the Yankees who started all this hatred, not the men who were a part of the raid."

"Yeah, yeah, you're right there. I'm sorry about your mother. I . . . I remember her some." He took off his hat again. In the moonlight Fran could see the wide, white scar through his scalp. "I never should have married Anna. She knows it now. I threw down my wedding ring when I saw her. But now I'm worried she'll tell somebody who I am. My men, the law, they only know me as Doc. They don't know my real name."

"I don't think she told anyone, Darryl. She never even told me! I can hardly believe it. But the only reason she won't tell, Darryl, is because she's ashamed. She shouldn't be. She should be proud." He finally stopped pacing, and she stepped closer, putting her hands against his chest. "When I first found out about Mark, I wanted to die. Oh, how I've hated the Yankees ever since! I was happy when I heard about Centralia. *Happy!* Anna and I, we hardly talked after that, she was so angry with me." She threw her arms around his neck. "Hold me, Darryl. It's been so long since a man held me."

He put his arms around her hesitantly. Here was a woman who understood him, who believed in continuing the cause. Here was a true Confederate woman, and an old friend from his past.

"I'm so glad it was you," she was saying. "I read the note because Anna was gone. I just knew who it had to be from. It's been so long, Darryl. I thought maybe you were dead, too. So did Anna, but now I know that for almost a year she's known you are alive. How could she keep that from me?" She raised her face, keeping it close to his own. "Oh, Darryl, you never should have married that Yankee woman. She only wanted your money. Now that she knows you've probably lost everything, she doesn't care one whit about you."

He liked the feel of her breasts against his chest. He hadn't been with a decent woman in a long time, not one who smelled fresh and clean like Fran. There had only been whores, and most of them were Indian women. Here was a woman from the good life he had once led, his best friend's wife and the first woman he had made love to. How many years ago had that been? Not that it had meant anything at the time. But now, after all that had happened, after losing the old homestead and his family, it felt good to be near someone from that life, someone who cared about the old Darryl.

He thought about Anna, pretty Anna. He had thought once it could work between them—until the war. Fran was probably right. Anna was probably ashamed of him. Fran wasn't. Fran understood.

"I need a woman, Fran. I need to know somebody cares. And you, you must need to *be* a woman. We could . . . help each other, like when we were kids. If you really support what I'm doing, help me now, Fran."

"Of course I'll help you," she whispered, her lips close to his. "I love you, Darryl. I've always loved you. Don't you know that?"

He covered her mouth with his own in a savage kiss. She felt his beard scratching her chin, but she didn't care. She needed a man. What better man than Darryl, the only man she had ever truly loved. He could belong to her again!

The rage and hatred in her soul welled up to match his own, so that she didn't mind the discomfort of lying on the bare ground while he ripped at the bodice of her dress to get at what he wanted. Darryl was back and he'd been hurt. He needed her.

He raked over her savagely, without an ounce of gentleness or any words of love. He had a need and she intended to fill it, for she needed him just as badly. She felt his mouth at her breasts, his hands yanking at her bloomers. In an instant he was ramming himself into her. Sticks poked at her back, but she paid no heed. More than that, this was Darryl. She had dreamed of this for years. Who cared if he was someone else's husband? Anna didn't deserve him. Anna was not a true and loyal wife. She had gone away, deserted him. And she was a Yankee.

Fran offered herself up to him wildly, crying out with the glory of it. He grasped at her bare hips and groaned as he released his pent-up desires, spilling himself into her, then pulling away and sprawling out on his back, panting.

Fran lay still for a moment, then slowly sat up, searching for her bloomers. She pulled them on over her shoes and knee-high stockings, then straightened the bottom of her dress and crawled to where Darryl lay. She bent over him, her breasts hanging out of the ripped bodice of her dress. "Darryl," she whispered, touching his face.

"I might . . . come back once in a while. I'll send you notes."

"Come back any time you need me. I'll be right here." She lay down beside him, putting her head on his shoulder.

"Where is she, Fran?"

Oh, how she hated Anna, now, more than ever. "I don't know. Truly I don't," she lied. "We argued. She didn't tell me where she was going. But her sister went to Montana. Maybe she went to be with Joline."

"That Yankee husband of Joline's make it through the war, or her father?"

"No. They were both killed at Shiloh."

"Good. Serves them right."

"You going to look for Anna?"

"Yes. I guess I owe it to her to talk to her. Besides, I want to make sure she doesn't intend to tell anybody who I am. She might even suggest the law watch your place, the restaurant. That's why I hid out here and sent the note." He stared at the stars for a moment. "She's still my wife," he said then.

Fran sat up quickly. "What does that mean? You aren't going to do with her what you just did with me, are you? We *belong* together, Darryl, you and I. Our loyalties and memories are the same. Anna doesn't understand you. She doesn't even love you anymore."

"I'll see when I find her. I'm just saying she's got to decide. I never got to talk to her that day at Centralia, never got to explain. And I was . . . I was worse that day. Sometimes my brain doesn't work right, you know? I do crazy things. Maybe I should have grabbed her up and made her come with me instead of throwing my ring at her. I just wanted her to know I'm not the Darryl Kelley she married, that's all. She's got to accept me the way I am or forget about me—and if she's going to forget about me, she's got to keep her mouth shut, tell people I'm dead or something."

"Oh, I have no doubt she'd agree to that. She doesn't want you anymore, Darryl. It's a shame, I know—I think it's traitorous." She leaned over him, kissing him. "But I'd never betray you, Darryl. Never. Tell me you won't go back to her or take her away with you. Promise me you'll come back here to me when you need a woman."

"It's not easy. It's a long way to come, and these parts are too civilized for me now. We run the border now, keep in supplies by robbing stagecoaches, settlers. Planning a bank job soon. Why don't you move your business farther west—like Independence, maybe? It would be easier for me to come to you there. I expect I could show my face on the streets in any of these towns and nobody would know me. But I don't like to take the chance."

"All right, Darryl. I'll see about going to Independence. But that's closer to Leavenworth. There are a lot of Union soldiers there."

"They don't scare me any. Now that the war is over, it's the regular law that will be after men like me. The soldiers are going to be involved with the Indians. They won't bother with outlaws anymore. Handling the law is a whole different thing—easier. It's usually just a posse of civilians who come after you, and most of them don't know how to handle a gun. Besides, me and my men, we've got some good places to hide out down in Indian Territory. The Creeks, Choctaws, Cherokee, they hide us out for a little whiskey and money."

"Take me back with you, Darryl. You could do that, couldn't you? I could sell the restaurant and just go away with you—be there for you whenever you need me."

"I don't know. I'll think about it. Might be able to use you better here or in Independence where you can hear the latest news and all. Do me a favor, Fran."

"Anything you ask."

"Go to the post office tomorrow and see if Anna left a forwarding address."

She sighed. "You'll come back to me, won't you?"

"You know I will. I'll be here tomorrow night. You can tell me what you find out. And bring a blanket. We'll stay out here all night together."

She smiled. "Oh, yes, I'd like that. I'll come out as soon as we close." She sat up straighter. "Do you still love Anna, Darryl?"

He leaned up, then got to his feet and buttoned his pants. "No. Everything is changed now." He put a hand to his head and stumbled slightly. Fran grasped his arm.

"Darryl, what is it?"

"The pain . . . never know when it will hit me." He looked around for the flask of whiskey he had left on the ground. He quickly picked it up and swallowed more. He shoved it back into his pocket and began stumbling around, turning in circles and flinging out his arms. "Damn . . . Yankees," he growled. "Damn, damn Yankees!" He grasped his head and went to his knees.

Fran smiled to herself as she walked over and touched his shoulder. "Anna's a Yankee, too, Darryl. Don't you be forgetting that."

"I won't," he growled, his breathing coming in quick pants. "I won't! I won't! You . . . you find her, find out where she's gone," he said, his words slurring again. Fran touched his head and he flung out an arm, knocking her away. "Don't touch me! Don't touch me when I'm like this! This is when I'd . . . I'd like . . . to kill." He jumped up, turning to look at her and laughing like a crazy man. "Oh, I enjoyed that day at Centralia, Fran. You should have been there!"

She smiled. "I wish I had been. But there will be other Centralias, Darryl."

He grasped his head in both hands. "Yes. Yes, there will be." He stepped back. "You do like I said. You find out about Anna. I'll be here tomorrow night. I'll take care of you . . . like Mark would have done."

"And I'll take care of you, Darryl, the way Anna should have but won't. You can't depend on her anymore, Darryl. She's deserted you. But I'm here. I'll always be here."

He nodded, laughing nervously again, then darted off into the darkness. Fran brushed dirt from her clothes and went inside the restaurant to get a shawl to wrap around her torn dress. Her heart pounded with excitement. Darryl was alive! He was here, and he was hers again! Mark wouldn't mind that she had comforted his old friend. He would be glad. In spite of the pain and rough treatment, she had gloried in sharing herself with Darryl, in celebrating the fact that he was alive, in giving him the comfort Anna would never be willing to give him now.

She frowned at the thought of Anna. Pretty, soft, nice, Yankee Anna. Why should Darryl try to find her? It would do no good. She had already made up her mind she would not tell him Anna was in Abilene. Seeing her would do him no good. It might even get him in trouble. Anna might decide to tell the law who Crazy Doc really was and where he might be found. He needed someone like her now, not Anna. Darryl couldn't think for himself anymore. He needed someone who understood his problem, understood his hatred and his need for vengeance.

She hurried home to the boarding house and up to her room before anyone could see her. She closed and locked the door, then lit a lamp and stood before a mirror, opening her shawl and staring at the marks on her chest and breasts from Darryl's almost brutal use of her. She felt absolutely victorious.

"He's *mine* now," she said to the mirror. "To *hell* with Anna Kelley!"

Chapter 9

September 1865

Business was even better than Anna had anticipated. The days were long and hard, but she loved the work, needed the diversion of the restaurant. She simply called it Anna's Diner, with the words "Breakfast, Lunch, Supper . . . Good Coffee . . . No Liquor" added under the name. Red checked curtains hung at the windows, and Anna had hired one woman to do nothing but keep the floor and tables scrubbed, a constant chore in a place like Abilene.

She had bought the latest in coal-burning cookstoves, a huge contraption that Hectar called a "monster," but a necessity. It had eight burners and three ovens, and all were in use most of the day. Two more local women had been hired three days after Anna opened, one to help cook and the other to wait tables. Anna had thought she could keep up herself, but the very first day she was so busy that Hectar and Agnes had to come over and help. Whenever there was a break between meals, bread dough and other food had to be prepared for the next meal.

Breakfast ran into lunch and lunch into supper, so that some days Anna was hardly aware which meal she should be preparing. Still, it was good therapy. She wanted to be so busy there was no time to think about Darryl and her lonely situation. She wanted to be so tired at night that she fell instantly to sleep without memories of the nights she used to share with a loving husband. And a booming business meant she could pay back Hectar sooner than she thought.

Although it was September, a lot of cattle were still coming in. Outside, the town was as wild and dirty and noisy as ever. But inside Anna's Diner, men knew to be more quiet. They always washed their hands and faces outside first, where Anna kept a tub and towels, insisting no one enter with dirty hands or with cow or horse dung on their boots. A bristly brush was kept at the corner of the building for men to use to scrub their boots before coming inside. On their way inside they were greeted by a sign near the door: Remove Hats. No Shirtless Men. Wash Hands and Clean Boots Before Entering. No Drinking.

Once inside, they passed a table where a sign read: Deposit Guns Here. No Guns Allowed Beyond This Point.

A few men had scowled and left, but most respected the signs. For those who didn't, Hectar would immediately go and get the local sheriff and the unruly customer would be ousted.

Word about a clean, pleasant diner where a man could get the best food for miles around quickly spread, and before long, few men minded all the rules. The good, "woman-cooked" food made it worth washing hands and putting down guns. Besides that, most hoped to catch a glimpse of the owner.

"Prettiest thing in skirts this side of Kansas City," some said.

"What a waste," others said. Rumor had it her husband had gone off to war and had never returned, and she didn't know if he was dead or alive. Confederate or Union, it didn't matter. The fact remained that the pretty Mrs. Anna Kelley was in a sad situation for someone so young and beautiful, and more than a few available men who patronized her restaurant found themselves wishing Anna would get word that her husband was indeed dead. There was a woman worth going after: independent, a hard worker, a survivor. She was the right kind of woman for these parts, and plenty of her customers went to bed with pleasant dreams of the kind of wife she would make.

Anna was forced to hire two more women to help wait tables during the busiest hours. By October she was able to pay back all of the five hundred dollars she had borrowed from Hectar. She was making enough each week by then to make bigger than required payments to the bank, as well as begin to build a substantial savings. What she would ever do with it, she wasn't sure, except that she wanted to build a small house of her own. She was tired of living in boarding houses.

At least now she knew she could take care of herself. But she couldn't help wondering what her customers would think if they knew the truth about her. Were these men like some of those in Columbia? Would they look at her with disgust if they knew her husband was a murderer and a thief? Would she lose all her business?

The fear of what her reputation would be if they knew never left her. No matter how busy or tired she was, she made a point of reading the local paper every night, checking to see if there were any stories about an outlaw called Crazy Doc . . . but there never were.

December came, and only a few herds trickled into town. The biggest drives were over. Business remained good, but Anna found the hours she had to put in more bearable. She began closing on Mondays and Tuesdays so that she could rest. She had grown even thinner, and the local doctor had given her a tonic.

"I have a feeling it's not the work that's getting you down, young lady," the man told her. "It's the worry over your husband."

How right he was, but he had no idea what the true nature of that worry was.

It was on a Sunday in early January that her problems and worries became more complicated. She had been so busy, she had managed to put thoughts of Nate Foster far to the back of her mind. But old feelings and memories were almost painfully awakened when one of her waitresses, young

Sandra Sloan, the daughter of one of the town merchants, came back to the kitchen.

"We have a slight problem, Anna," the girl told her. "Hectar says to ask you."

"What is it, Sandra?" Anna wiped her hands on her apron.

"There's a man out there who says he can't give up his gun. Says in his position, he can't afford to, on account of a marshal never knows when somebody might go gunning for him."

"Marshal?"

"Yes, ma'am. He calls himself Marshal Foster. Wears a badge. Hectar thinks it would be okay—" The girl frowned. "You all right, Anna? You look flushed."

Anna put her hands to her face, wondering how she looked. She had been cooking all morning. She needed to brush her hair, and she wore only a plain brown cotton dress. "I'm . . . I'm fine." Why was she shaking like this? Oh, it irritated her to be so flustered. It was ridiculous and uncalled for, and terribly wrong for her to be excited because Nate Foster was right in the next room! She told herself it didn't matter how she looked. She had no right wanting to impress any man. "I . . . happen to know the marshal. I'll go greet him myself. You go back to your work, Sandra."

"Yes, ma'am." The girl turned away grinning, realizing there must be something special about Nate Foster.

Anna took a deep breath to calm her rapidly beating heart and walked into the dining room. She could not help smiling then at the surprised look on Nate Foster's face as she came closer. His eyes moved over her in the way they had nearly a year ago when he visited her in Columbia. She felt the flush returning to her cheeks and wished she could hide her own joy better, fearing it would be misinterpreted. "Nate!"

He removed his hat. *"You're* the Anna of the famous Anna's Diner?"

She laughed lightly. "Well, I don't know how famous it is, but yes, I'm the Anna."

A few men watched, envying the look Marshal Foster

brought to Anna Kelley's eyes, and wondering how the mysteriously untouchable and unapproachable Anna knew the marshal.

"Well, I'll be damn—I mean, well, this is a real pleasant surprise."

"Come and sit down, Nate. Go ahead and leave your gun on. I don't think you'll cause a ruckus with it, will you?"

He laughed lightly, his gray eyes sparkling with delight. "Only trouble I get into is the kind somebody else starts."

She led him to a table at a corner of the room, near a window. "Now you can see outside in case something is going on you need to know about. You're lucky I had a table. If you had come in summer, you would probably have had to wait in line."

"I don't doubt that from what I've heard," he answered. He removed his sheepskin jacket and hung it on the back of the chair.

"I can hang that up for you if you like," she told him.

Their gazes met, both of them full of questions. "It's fine." He looked around the room. "This is real nice, Anna. Heck, I've heard about this place all the way to Topeka and down in Indian Territory."

Her heart quickened at the words. Indian Territory! Had he heard anything about the one called Crazy Doc? How safe was he, riding in such an unruly land? But why did she care whether or not he was safe?

"Men say it's the best food around," he was saying. His eyes moved over her again. "They also say the owner is the prettiest woman in Kansas. I have to agree with them there. I thought of you when I heard about the place, but I didn't really think it was the Anna I knew who ran it."

She smiled, feeling warm at the compliment. "Well, it *is*. And I don't know if my cooking is all that good. It's possible that it just seems wonderful by the time these men get here. Lord knows when they hit this town they're hungry as bears and sick of camp food. I imagine anything would taste good to them."

"I don't believe that. I believe it's as good as they say." He noticed how thin she was. "Must keep you awfully busy."

"It certainly does. But I'm making good money, and I need to be busy." She handed him a menu. "Why don't you decide what you want, and you can let me know if the rumors about the food were true."

He frowned, lightly brushing her fingers when he took the menu. "Anna, I'm glad for your success and all, and I admire the way you can take care of yourself, but if I may be so blunt, what in the world are you doing here in Abilene?"

She folded her arms self-consciously when his eyes rested on her full bosom for a moment before meeting her eyes again. "Well, I kind of ended up here by accident. I had decided to try to get to my sister in Montana, but I guess I'm a bit of a coward. Everyone here told me it would be suicide for me to make a trip through Indian country right now, and I decided I value my scalp a bit too much to risk it. Maybe it's just vanity, but I don't think I'd look very good bald."

He laughed lightly, but true concern showed in his eyes. "That was a very wise decision. People were right to tell you that. And it isn't just your scalp that would—" He hesitated as she reddened. "Well, anyway, I'm damn glad you didn't try to go." His eyes shone with true delight at seeing her. "So, your sister is still surviving in Montana?"

"Yes. I got a letter not long ago. It was several months old, of course. She wrote it last winter. She said the winters up there are unbelievably cold and that apparently several of the mice in the area decided they were as cold and lonely as she was. They decided to winter it out in her cabin, and she said she was so lonely she quit trying to kill them or chase them out. She said one in particular became kind of a pet."

They both laughed, and Nate thought how disappointing it was that he could never court this lovely woman, never have her for himself. Or could he? He sobered as their eyes met. "May I ask if you've heard from your husband?"

Her heart quickened at the words. She knew the true meaning behind them, knew what he really wanted to know.

No, Nate, I can't start seeing you. I'm so sorry, because in the brief moments I've had with you, I can see what a wonderful man you are—and how lonely. "I don't mind," she said aloud. "I'm afraid nothing has changed. I still don't know what has happened to him. I haven't heard a thing." This man, of all men, was the last one she would want to know that her husband was the notorious Crazy Doc. How much more disgraceful a thing could she admit to him, let alone the fact that she had never told him she knew very well her husband was alive, had seen him that awful day at Centralia? She read the disappointment in his eyes at the words.

"How much longer are you going to go on like this, Anna?"

She brushed at her apron. "I don't know. But I can't talk about it right now. I'm awfully busy in the kitchen." She smiled for him. "I suggest the beef and peppers, with boiled potatoes and my special corn casserole."

He handed her the menu. "I'll take your word for it. And make the coffee hot and black."

"Yes, sir. I'll make sure there's a little more than the normal helping on your plate. And dessert is on me—hot apple pie."

"Sounds good."

She started to turn, and he couldn't help reaching out and grasping her wrist. The feel of his big, strong hand brought forth lovely, long-buried desires. "Anna." She turned and he took his hand away. "Could we talk? I mean, I'll be in Abilene the rest of the day. Could I walk you home after you close? I can't just eat and go after seeing you again. I . . . I would have come back to Columbia to see you again, but I spent a lot of time in Indian Territory this summer, hunting two different gangs without much luck. I don't know, one thing after another came along. I took some time to visit a brother and sister in Topeka. The opportunity to go all the way back to Columbia just never came up. But I thought about you, a lot."

She felt a sudden, ridiculous urge to cry. She smiled nervously to fend off the tears. "Well, I'm flattered." She hugged the menu to her breast. "I suppose it would be all right. I feel the same way. I'd like to talk, too. I mean, something like what we went through at Centralia—I guess that will always make us friends, won't it?"

"That's the way I see it." *But I want to be much more than friends, Anna Kelley,* he wanted to say. "Thanks, Anna. What time do you close?"

"Eight o'clock, before all hell breaks loose in the rest of town." He laughed at the words. "It's not so bad this time of year, but in the summer—" She rolled her eyes. "A person has to dodge wild bullets half the time. It can be pretty crazy here, but I'm getting used to it, and it helps me keep from thinking about things that would probably drive me insane if I had to dwell on them. I'm even getting used to the flies and the smell."

He laughed again. "Now that takes real fortitude in this town. Since the railroad came through, it's never been the same. And with all the Indian trouble, it looks like it will be a while before they can finish the line. Abilene will remain the primary cattle town for a few years yet."

"Well, that's fine with me. It's good for business." She smiled and left him, going into the kitchen and breathing deeply with joy and nervousness. "Sandra," she said. "Make sure you give your best service to Marshal Foster. Take him a good hot cup of coffee right away."

The girl smiled. "Yes, ma'am."

Anna stoked up the stove so it would keep the kitchen warm all night and let the bread dough rise. She quickly brushed her hair and put the brush back in her handbag, wrapping a heavy shawl around her shoulders. It had been a mild winter, and right now there was only a dusting of snow on the ground. The night was cold but still.

She came out into the dining room, where Nate waited. They walked out together, and Anna closed and padlocked the door. "I live in a boarding house at the other end of town, but I'm going to be building my own house soon."

He frowned. "You walk through these streets every night to get home?"

"Most of the men know me. I seem to have earned their respect. They're a wild bunch, but good-hearted. Most of them are decent, just ready for their whiskey and good food and—well, a different kind of woman than I am." She was glad for the darkness so he couldn't see her blush. "Besides, Hectar White, the man who owns the boarding house, usually walks with me. He's a good man—loaned me some money to help get the restaurant started."

"Where is he tonight?"

She shrugged. "He's the man who greeted you at the door earlier. I told him he could go on home. With a marshal to walk with me, I don't think I have much to worry about."

He grinned. "Well, you have a keen understanding of the nature of these men when they hit town after a cattle drive. But don't take too much for granted, Anna. There are still those few who don't have respect for anything with a skirt on, and after months on the trail, a man can have a little trouble distinguishing right from wrong, especially when he sees someone as beautiful as you."

She smiled bashfully. "Well, thank you for the continued compliments. But to tell you the truth, I carry a small revolver in my handbag."

He laughed heartily then. "I have a feeling you don't need me *or* Hectar. And here I thought I was being so chivalrous."

She laughed a bit in return. "You are. Gun or no gun, I still feel much safer and more relaxed with you beside me." *Oh, how good it would feel now to have your arms around me,* she thought, *to be able to lean on you and have you tell me everything will be all right.* "How long will you be here, Nate?"

"Just till morning. That's why I wanted to see you once more before I leave." He stopped in front of a closed livery. Most of the people still moving around town were farther up the street at the saloons. Piano music and laughter could be faintly heard, coming from behind doors now closed because of the cold. An owl hooted somewhere as Nate turned to face her in the moonlight. In the darkness he seemed taller, more provocative. She caught the scent of leather.

He sighed deeply. "Anna, I can't help asking what you intend to do."

"Do?"

"With your life. You're still so young and beautiful. You

can't go on like this, not knowing about your husband. If you want, I could check some records for you—"

"No! I . . . I've already done that," she said quickly, desperately afraid of what he would find. Nate Foster was a marshal, a clever man. And somehow, even if there could never be anything between them, she would be devastated if he found out about Darryl. "There just is no record," she added. "I've tried everything. I'm just going to . . . to wait it out a little longer. Hectar says I should have him declared officially dead. But what if I do, and then I hear from him? I've got to give it more time."

He reached out and touched her shoulders, sending shuddering needs through her veins. "I can understand what you're saying. But it's been years. The best years of your life are being wasted."

"Waiting for your husband isn't a waste. I have no choice, Nate. You must know that."

He felt the pain in her words. He squeezed her shoulders lightly. "Anna, I'm going to keep coming back—not often, mind you. And I won't—I won't press you. But I've got to admit I haven't been able to stop thinking about you, worrying about you. Maybe I've got no right, but at the least, we're good friends now, aren't we?"

She looked down, unable to keep looking into his eyes in the moonlight, unable to bear the temptations being so close to him brought to her body and heart. "Yes. I've thought about you a lot, too. I was happy to see you today, to know you're all right. I often wonder if you're hurt or dead."

"I understand your situation, Anna. I just want your permission to . . . well, to look in on you now and then, walk you home like this when I'm in Abilene. I just want to keep in touch until you find out about your husband. But if you'd rather I didn't—"

"No, it's . . . it's all right. I'd like that." She finally met his eyes again. "There's no sense denying we feel something . . . a little special. And as long as it goes no farther than that, I don't suppose it's so terribly wrong. A woman can have a man friend just as well as woman friends, can't she?"

He grinned. "Sure she can." He let go of her and started

walking again. "The war sure did mess up a lot of lives, didn't it?"

Her heart ached at the words. "It certainly did." She wondered again what his own personal tragedy had been. "Sometimes I wonder if mine will ever be normal again."

"Sure it will. Things have a way of working out." They walked past a couple of saloons. "I'll be gone quite a while again after tonight, back to Topeka. I've got some court matters to take care of, some testifying to do. I've come close a couple of times to catching two outlaw gangs the Federals want real bad. One is led by a Bill Sharp, the other by that one they call Crazy Doc."

Anna felt suddenly light-headed.

"So far they've both eluded me. It's really frustrating. They're both rapists and thieves—and murderers. No one in the outlying areas anywhere in Kansas or Missouri is safe from them. But I'll get them. Sooner or later I'll get them."

She struggled to keep her composure and to keep her rubbery legs from giving way. "I . . . hope you do, Nate. I just pray you won't get hurt doing it."

"Oh, I manage to take care of myself."

"Have you had to kill a lot of men?"

He sighed deeply. "I've killed my share, but it never gets easier. That's the hellish part of the job, but somebody has to do it."

"Of course they do. You say you have a brother in Topeka?"

"Yes. A sister, too. She's only seventeen but she's in a wheelchair. Crippled—thanks to bushwhackers."

Her heart froze at the words. His own sister! Crippled by men like her husband! "I'm so sorry."

"Yeah, well, anytime I get weary and fed up trying to find some of those men, I just think of Christine, and it gives me the strength and incentive to keep going."

They walked on in silence for a few minutes, Anna's thoughts filled with the horror of what he had told her. Maybe it was better if she didn't let him see her anymore, yet she already knew that a part of her could not let him go. "Here's where I live," she said, stopping in front of the boarding house.

He took her arm and led her up the steps to the front door. "Thanks for letting me walk with you, Anna. I'm sorry we didn't have more time, but I'm glad I found you again. The way we keep accidentally running into each other, I can't help thinking maybe we're somehow destined to at least remain friends. I'll make no bones about it. I wish it could be more than that, but I respect your situation, and I won't push."

"I appreciate that." She met his gaze. "If it . . . if it doesn't seem too bold . . . I sometimes find myself wishing the same thing. You're a good man, Nate, and I'll never forget how you helped me at Centralia."

He grasped her arms. "Anna—"

She turned away. "I'd better go inside." She opened the door and he let go of her. She moved inside, keeping the door ajar. "God be with you, Nate. I'll pray for your safety."

He smiled resignedly and nodded. "I appreciate it. See you in a couple of months, then?"

She nodded. "Maybe I'll have some news."

"Maybe."

Their eyes held a moment longer. He turned and walked off into the darkness then. Anna closed the door, leaning against it, shaking with a mixture of renewed passions and horrible dread that he would learn the truth. Now she knew Darryl had not changed at all. He had chosen a path she could never share with him; one that would surely lead him into the sight of Marshal Foster's gun. How long could she keep the awful truth from Nate?

Chapter 10

Anna opened the letter with anticipation and dread. Every time she heard from Claudine, she wondered if it would be to tell her Fran had heard from Darryl, or that Darryl had sneaked into Columbia and asked Fran or Claudine where she was. She frowned with wonder and suspicion at the contents of the letter, sitting down on her bed and turning the lamp higher.

"Dear Anna," it read. "I do not know what has come over Francine. She has sold the restaurant and has simply disappeared. I was let go nearly a month ago, when the new owners took over. They had their own cook and did not wish to have my services. I have been working at a hotel since then, and the address is on my envelope.

"Francine gave no explanation for selling her restaurant and leaving town. Perhaps she has gone back to her home in the South. She did not seem the least bit upset at letting me go and hardly gave me a good-bye. She took most of her clothes from her room at the boarding house, but left a good deal of them, as well as the furnishing that belonged to her, telling the landlady to keep it or sell it. Out of curiosity, I talked to the manager of the bank where I know Francine kept her money, and he told me she took everything out of her savings.

"I wish I could tell you that we have heard something from your husband. I do not know him myself, but I am sure Francine would have told me if she had heard from him. Francine was becoming so mean-spirited, I do not miss her so much after all. I am ready to take your offer to come and work for you. I would have done so sooner, but Francine always would beg me to please not leave her because there were no other good cooks. Then—away she goes! So, my loyalty to her meant nothing, she treated me just as she treated you.

"I need to know if you wish me to leave some kind of message and forwarding address with the new owners of the restaurant in case your husband should try to contact you there. I have said nothing to them because I was not sure of your wishes. Please let me know. I remain your dear friend and I hope you still need another cook. Love from Claudine."

Anna immediately sat down to write back. It was obvious from the letter that Claudine was disappointed and lonely. She missed the woman's friendship, and she could think of nothing more wonderful than to have Claudine come and work for her, as she had wanted the woman to do since the day she opened. She quickly wrote down that she most certainly wanted her to come to Abilene, as soon as possible.

She sat back then to contemplate the news about Francine. It was indeed strange, and Anna could not help wondering if it could have something to do with Francine's pressing need to do something for the rebel cause. But what could she possibly do now? The war was over.

The suspicion that it could have something to do with Darryl gnawed at her insides. Had she heard from him and not told her? If Darryl had gotten in touch with Francine, he would know where she was now. Why didn't he try to contact her? Did he intend to just let her dangle in suspense for the rest of her life, to let her guess just when he might come for her? The thought that he could come and demand that she be a wife to him, that he could try to take her away with him, always put a knot in her stomach and brought a rush of dread to her heart. She could never go with him now. Still, if he tried to contact her, she had to allow it. She had to know what to do, how he felt, what had happened.

"Tell the new owners someone might come by asking about me," she wrote. "Tell them it's all right to let them know where I am, and give them my address. I need to know what has happened to my husband." She wished she could share the grief of the truth about Darryl at least with Claudine, but she had become more determined than ever to keep it a secret. Every time she thought about Nate Foster's sister, she shivered to think Darryl had become the very kind of man who had crippled the girl.

Her thoughts moved to Nate, as they always did, several times a day now, ever since Nate had left nearly three months ago. She found it amazing that after one walk with him, she missed him, and she realized how dangerous her feelings for him were. She realized she would have to be very careful of her heart. She was not free to love . . . not now, maybe never.

She finished her letter to Claudine and put down the pen. Again she thought of Fran and Darryl, then brushed away the thought. It just seemed impossible that if Darryl had been to Columbia, he would not come to see her here in Abilene. His only reason for going to Columbia would have been to find her in the first place. Besides, he surely didn't dare show his face in a place like Columbia. And Nate had already said the man was in Indian Territory. Darryl had apparently buried himself in the outlaw life, and Anna was doomed to wait and wonder.

There came a knock at her door then, and Anna folded the still-unfinished letter. "Who is it?"

"It's me, Agnes," came the reply. "We have heard some bad news, Anna. Hectar thought you should know."

Anna frowned, opening the door to her room. "What is it?"

"It's that Marshal Nate Foster," the woman answered. "Hectar just read it in the newspaper. He's been bad hurt—some kind of shoot-out during a bank robbery in Topeka."

Anna felt her heart pound with dread. She hurried past

Agnes and down the stairs to Hectar's study, where the man looked up at her over spectacles from behind his desk. He quickly set his pipe aside as she came into the room.

"Hectar, what has happened to Nate?"

The man frowned. He had been well aware that Anna had strong feelings for the marshal, in spite of her painful marriage situation. He could hardly blame her, and he felt sorry for her problems. He handed her the newspaper. "Says here he was badly wounded in a shoot-out in Topeka. Happened to be near the bank when it was being robbed. The men ran out, caught him by surprise. He managed to kill one of them, wound another. The one he wounded, folks say, is that there Crazy Doc. It was his gang that robbed the bank and killed one of the customers, a young woman."

Anna felt as though someone were draining the blood from her veins. She quickly sat down. "Dear God," she muttered. She put her head in her hands, and Hectar came from behind his desk to put a hand on her shoulder. "I didn't know the man meant that much to you," he told her. "I mean, I knew you were friends, Anna, but I didn't mean to upset you like this with this news."

How could she explain? It wasn't just Nate. Poor Nate! How badly was he hurt? Still, it wasn't just that. It was Darryl! It had been *Darryl* who robbed the bank, Darryl who shot Nate Foster! He hadn't changed his ways at all, and he had boldly ridden into a heavily populated town and robbed a bank! A woman had been shot dead! How could he do such a thing? And now not only did she have to wonder if her own husband was dead or painfully wounded, but he'd been wounded by Nate, her dear friend, the man she knew good and well she was falling in love with. For whom should she mourn the most? How long was God going to allow her to be torn apart by this agony, allow this unfair torture to her soul?

"Hectar, will you do me a favor and see if Sandra and Berle can keep the restaurant going, maybe with your help? If you can't, just close it for a few days. This is our slowest time of year anyway."

"You're going to Topeka?"

She looked up at him. "Yes," she answered. "It might seem bold and wrong, but I feel I should go to Nate and just let him know I care. I just hope I get there in time."

"Maybe it's not as bad as the paper says," Agnes put in. "They like to exaggerate."

Anna's mind whirled with mixed emotions, her grief over Darryl and what he had become almost unbearable. "I hope you're right, Agnes." She rose, her legs trembling, a strong urge to scream welling up in her soul. Nate could have died, could still die, by her own husband's bullet. In spite of her short association with Nate, she knew she would be grief-stricken if something happened to him. Yet realizing that fact enhanced her guilt at her concern for another man when her own husband was also hurt.

Still, it wasn't her husband who also lay wounded and in pain somewhere. It was a man who had become a stranger, an outlaw who robbed and raped and murdered—even murdered women. No, she would not grieve for such a man. She had already lost her husband, as far as she was concerned. She had already grieved for him, had already wept so many tears she wondered how she could ever produce more. She could weep over the man he used to be, but not for the man he was now.

"Hang on, Doc, just hang on," Fran begged, tears in her dark eyes. She winced when he cried out with pain, while one of his men followed directions from Darryl himself on how to locate the bullet. Using his knowledge of such things, Darryl had refused too much laudanum so that he could direct his man in digging the bullet out of his own body. It was buried deep in his left ribs. His ankles and wrists were tied so that he couldn't thrash around too much and cause the knife to go astray.

Fran dabbed at blood with a shaking hand. Since she had chosen to sell everything and come with Darryl, life had been hard. But for Fran the inconveniences had been worth it. She had willingly let Darryl use some of her money for supplies, and the first couple of months had been peaceful. They had lived in a crude cabin deep in thick woods in western Missouri, while Darryl planned his robbery of the federal bank in Topeka. Fran had used her restaurant skills to cook for Darryl's eight men. They were all ex-Confederates, most of them carrying scars from war wounds, some of them, like Darryl, carrying deeper, unseen scars from the horrors of war.

Like the others, Fran called Darryl Doc. It was his choice, and Fran honored it. He said his old name belonged to his parents and the old life he came from. The others apparently had no idea his real name was Darryl Kelley, and Doc wanted it that way. "The old Darryl Kelley died back there in Georgia when he found his folks dead and his home burned," he had told her once.

There were moments when Fran was a little bit afraid of him, but she remained patient. After all, it wasn't his fault, the way he was. The war had done it to him. He drank too much, but that was because of the headaches. He had spells when he flew into fits, firing off his gun, breaking things. Sometimes when he took her in bed it was more like rape. But she was determined to stick with him and help him. For so long she had wanted to do something to help the cause. Now, even though the war was over, she had found a way. More than that, she was with Darryl, which was all that mattered to her. She would do anything for the man she loved.

Darryl's screams filled the tiny bedroom of the cabin while the bullet was retrieved from his body. He lay panting then, and Fran struggled to keep from crying.

"Damn . . . sonofabitch," Darryl groaned. "Who the hell . . . was it . . . shot me! What happened to Nick?"

"He's dead, Doc. Don't you remember?" Fran held gauze to the still-bleeding wound while Jerry Baskins, the man who had dug for the bullet, plunked it into a pan of water. He stopped to wipe sweat from his brow.

"Doc ain't too good at rememberin' things," Jerry said then. He grinned and shook his head. "That ole' scar on his scalp makes him forget things."

"Yeah, well, I won't forget you digging into my guts," Darryl answered.

"You're the one told me to do it, Doc. Hell, we don't

want to lose our leader. You're lucky. It went deep, but far enough to the side not to do a lot of harm."

"Felt like . . . a lot of harm to me." He grimaced with pain. "How much . . . did we get?" Jerry and Fran began wrapping his middle.

"About eight thousand, Mink says."

"Good. Good. We can . . . go to Mexico, live like kings for a while, huh? Lay low." He looked at Fran. "Would you like that, Fran?"

"Whatever you say we should do, Doc."

Darryl closed his eyes. "I'm . . . coming back, though. After things . . . cool down. I'm coming back . . . find that bastard that shot me . . . and killed Nick. Anybody find out who it was?"

"Mink went back to a little town not far from Topeka," Jerry told him. "He's gonna check the papers, ask around. He'll find out who it was."

"You going to kill him, Doc?" Fran asked.

"You bet I am. I think . . . he wore a marshal's badge. A Yankee, most likely."

They finished wrapping Darryl's wound, and Jerry took the bloodied gauze and rags and the pan of water out of the room. Fran leaned over Darryl, bending down to kiss his cheek. "Doc, before we leave for Mexico, why don't you have a couple of your men spread the word that you died. If the law thinks you're dead, we'll have a much easier trip south. Maybe they won't be hunting quite as hard for us."

"They'd still come after us for the money."

"I suppose. But if that marshal thinks you're dead, at least he'll be left off guard. Then when you come back for him, he won't be expecting you. And if you pull any more jobs, they won't know who to blame, because they'll think you're dead. We could even go away for good. We could go back south and settle."

He moved his eyes to meet her dark ones. Fran was not pretty, not like Anna. But she was good to him. "I've still got a wife."

"We put Anna behind us the first night you came to see me and made love to me. You know you can never go to her now, Doc. She's so uppity and proper and pampered, she'd never accept you as a rebel. And she'd never give up everything to come with you like I've done. I've sacrificed for you, Doc. Anna ran off on you," she reminded him, as she did frequently. "She could be all the way to Montana by now. It's obvious she doesn't care about you anymore. If she did, she would have left a forwarding address so you could find her. If we tell everyone you're dead, she'll get word eventually. Then she can get on with her own life and we can get on with ours."

Fran dreaded the thought of Darryl trying to find Anna. Would he take her with him if he saw her again? She had told him she had no idea where Anna had gone. But she knew Anna was in Abilene. She could only hope Darryl wouldn't find out for himself.

"I suppose . . . I could let her divorce me. She's no use to me . . . anymore. Everything is changed, changed," he said. Fran could see his mind was starting to wander again. "Used to . . . be good. But her heart . . . was never in the cause, was it, Fran?"

"No. And you can't contact her, Darryl. She'll betray you. She'll turn you in. Why should you worry about letting her divorce you? You'd have to contact her for that. Then people would find out about you. She hasn't told anyone yet, as far as we know, but you can't trust her to hold true to that. If she thinks you're dead, she'll forget about it all and get on with her life. It's the safest way."

"What if . . . she marries again?"

Fran suppressed a smile. "So? Let her marry. Who will ever know the difference if we go away?"

"That . . . marshal, when I come back . . . to kill him."

"He'll be dead. If everyone thinks you're dead, no one will be pointing fingers at you for his death—not unless you face him out on a public street in front of others."

He grimaced with pain. "He won't . . . see me. That bastard . . . will never know what hit him. He killed Nick. Nick was a . . . good friend." He closed his eyes. "You tell Jerry . . . have the others send word through the ranks . . . I died from my wounds."

Fran breathed a sigh of relief.

"We'll head south . . . split into two groups . . . meet at the Rio Grande down by Brownsville, Texas. We'll live good for a while, huh? We'll let these . . . bastards up here . . . think we're done. They think the war is over. But not for me . . . not for me. We'll . . . be back. Anna . . . she's no good, is she?"

"No, Doc, she isn't. She wasn't the right woman for a Southern man." Fran had quickly learned that in his mental condition, it was easy for her to steer Darryl in whatever direction she wanted. Whenever he mentioned Anna, she made sure he thought Anna had run off on him, betrayed him. "It's best this way, Doc. You need to rest a good long time after we get to Mexico. Maybe your headaches will even get better. And if everyone thinks you're dead, you'll be free for a while. It will be easy to convince them. A lot of people saw you get shot."

"Yeah. Yeah." His breathing came in deep pants. "I don't think that posse followed us here. The river . . . gives us good cover. We ride along the middle of the river . . . they lose our tracks. This has been a good hiding place. But we've . . . pulled too many jobs. They're going to find us here eventually."

Jerry came back inside then. "How's he doin'?"

"He's getting tired." Fran covered Darryl. Jerry came closer to the bed and leaned over the man. "Mink says it was a Marshal Nate Foster that shot you. You got him too, but he's gonna be all right."

Darryl took a deep breath against pain. "Nate Foster, huh?"

"He's been a marshal for about seven years—trained and got the job after his family was attacked by bushwhackers back in '58."

Darryl swallowed. "That means he's . . . a jayhawker, a Union man."

"Looks that way. And he's good, real good. Folks talk about him like he's some kind of hero to them. I didn't run into too many that had never heard of the man."

Darryl managed a slight grin. "Maybe my . . . first bullet didn't . . . get him, but the next one will." He met Jerry's eyes. "Give me a couple of days. Then we ride south.

But we won't forget . . . that name . . . Nate Foster. If
he's . . . such an all-fired . . . good marshal . . . he'll
still be around when we come back." He looked at Fran.
"You remember . . . what I told you. Tell the others. And
. . . fix the boys something to eat, will you? Then you
. . . ride into the nearest town with Jerry . . . make like
a married couple . . . get us some supplies."

"Sure, Doc. And you're doing the right thing."

She kissed him once more, then tucked the blankets
around him better and left the room. After supper she
would write a letter—to Anna Kelley. She could mail it
from town. It was only fair to let Anna know that Darryl
was dead.

"Somebody here to see you, Marshal."

Nate turned to look at the aging doctor who had taken
the bullet from his forearm and patched the crease along his
left cheek that had taken a tiny piece from his left ear—a
bullet that had knocked him flat and led people to believe at
first he'd been shot in the head and killed. He was still a
little shaken to think what a difference another half inch
would have made.

"Oh," he answered, buttoning a shirt. "Who's here
now?"

"A very pretty young lady. Want me to send her in?"

Nate grinned. "I'd never turn down that kind of a visitor.
Give me a minute to tuck in my shirt." He quickly but
gingerly tucked in his shirt, wincing with the pain in his
arm. He buckled his belt just before Anna came through the
curtains and into the room. His eyes lit up with pleasure
and astonishment. "Anna! What are you doing here?"

She looked him over, obviously relieved to see him standing up and walking around. Her face reddened at the realization of how much she was giving away by rushing to his
side after hearing he'd been hurt. "I . . . I heard what
happened. The papers made it sound as though you'd die. I
just thought . . . well, I thought maybe you needed to
know people cared. And I didn't want you to die without
. . . I mean, I wanted to see you once more." She smiled,

but felt like crying. "I have apparently made quite a fool of myself. I see you're up and around."

He sensed her embarrassment and stepped closer, taking her hand and squeezing it lightly. "You haven't made a fool of yourself at all. I'm touched, and I'm delighted you came. It was very nice of you. It must have been hard for you—with your busy schedule and all—having to leave the restaurant." He squeezed her hand again. "I'm afraid newspapers have a way of exaggerating things."

She laughed nervously but her eyes were teary. Deep inside, her heart was singing with joy. He was alive! Darryl hadn't killed him. "That's what Agnes told me. I guess she was right."

"Hey, look up here."

She glanced up and he turned his head to show her the still ugly, scabbed crease. "This is why the papers said I was hurt bad. I was out cold for a while, and some folks thought I was dead. I don't need to tell you that another inch would have made them right."

She could not help reaching up to touch his cheek near the wound. "Oh, Nate, so close!"

"He got me twice. This arm is going to keep me awake nights for a while. At least it's my left arm, so I can still shoot." Their eyes held. "Damn, it was nice of you to be so concerned. Don't call yourself a fool, Anna." He searched her eyes, seeing the love there that she could not admit to. "I'm glad you came. I was just leaving the doc's place here, and by God, I'm hungry. There are some real nice restaurants in Topeka. Would you eat with me?"

"Yes, I'd like that. Then I'd better take the next train back to Abilene. It's only a couple of hours' ride. I told Hectar to have Berle and the others take care of things. I wasn't sure how long I'd be gone. I thought it might be several days. But if you're all right, I can go right back and relieve them of having to run the restaurant alone."

He turned and pulled on his vest. "You could stay a day or two anyway, couldn't you? I'd like to take you to meet my brother and sister. Christine lives with my brother Rob and his wife, Marie, right here in Topeka."

Anna thought again about the kind of men who had

wounded his sister and killed his parents. Men like Darryl
. . . Darryl, who had been the one who had hurt Nate,
nearly killed him . . . her own husband. Husband. Yes,
she still had a husband.

"I don't think it would be appropriate right now, Nate."

"Why not? You're a friend, a woman I helped at Centralia. They'd like to meet you. I've already told Rob about
you."

She shook her head. "I'd rather not. I wouldn't feel right
about it. I shouldn't even be here, but I just couldn't help
myself. I wanted to see you, see for myself how badly you
were hurt. Now that I know you're all right, dinner is
enough."

She watched him strap on his gunbelt, wondered how he
could think about going on with his work after being hurt.
She wondered how many other times he had been shot. He
was a good, brave man, who believed in justice and law.
How different he was from Darryl. How her heart ached at
the thought of knowing who had hurt him but not being
able to tell him.

"If you say so." He stepped closer and caught the tears in
her eyes. He reached out and touched her cheek with a big
hand. She could not resist leaning against his chest; then
came the quiet tears. Oh, if only she could explain them.
His strong arms came around her, and it was like being
suddenly wrapped in a heated quilt after being out in freezing rain. Oh, how good it felt to be held, to feel someone
else's strength.

"All these tears just for me," he teased. "I feel honored."
He nearly trembled at the feel of her full breasts against his
chest, at the lilac scent of her hair. The thought of her
caring enough to come to him made him want to grab her
tighter, to plant his mouth over hers and taste her lips, to
tell her right then and there that he loved her. But there
was something in the way, and his name was Darryl Kelley.
How he wished she would hear from the man and have it
over with, before he lost his heart.

"I'm sorry," she said, pulling away and taking a handkerchief from her handbag. She wore a deep blue velvet dress
with a matching fur-lined, velvet jacket. He thought how

beautiful and elegant she was, with so much to give and no one to give it to. How he wished she could give it all to him —her heart, her body. "This is silly, isn't it? It's so strange that I should feel this way about someone I still don't know all that well. I guess the war and the worry over Darryl have left my nerves close to shattered."

"It's all right. I understand."

"I can imagine what you think of me, falling against you like a weak child. This is ridiculous."

He put a hand on her waist. "You aren't a weak child. You're a strong, brave, self-reliant woman who has been through hell and is still there. My God, Anna, if anyone has a right to cry and be upset, it's you. Now you get squared away and we'll go have a nice meal."

"People will see us together. They'll talk."

"Let them. I'm glad you're here and I'm not going to let you go until we at least have a meal together and talk a little more. Promise?"

She smiled as she wiped at her eyes. "Promise. Just let me find a mirror and fix my face."

"Your face is beautiful. It's the most beautiful face I've ever set eyes on."

She looked up at him, her eyes tearing all over again. "I'm so glad you're all right, Nate." *I'm so glad my husband didn't kill you.*

"And I'm glad you came to make sure. And don't you worry. I have a feeling my bullet did a lot more damage to Crazy Doc than his did to me. He might even be dead by now."

She grasped at her stomach and turned away, the words cutting into her like a knife. She wondered if the nightmare would ever end. "How do you know it was the one called Doc?" she asked.

"I remember seeing him at Centralia—he was right in front of us. Somebody there called him Doc. You probably don't remember. But for some reason it stuck in my mind. Of course, I knew he was the one who had been doing a lot of the raiding since then, after breaking off from Anderson and that bunch, because his victims described him. Said he had a big scar on his head and that his men called him Doc.

It was the same with the bank robbery. People heard the name again, and I saw his face again, saw the scar when his hat fell off. It was the same man, all right. He's bad, through and through."

He didn't used to be, she thought, her heart like lead. *He used to be kind. He used to help people. What happened to my Darryl?* She dabbed at her eyes. "Well, I hope you catch him."

"Or that he's dead," Nate added. "Let's go get something to eat. You'll have to walk a little slowly. I'm still shaky on my feet. I lost a lot of blood and I've been down for a couple of days."

She blew her nose and put away her handkerchief. Darryl! Was he dead now? Or was he just hurt? Did he need her? No. Surely not. He had let her know that day at Centralia how he felt. He had chosen a path of destruction she would not follow for any man. He was beyond her help, beyond feelings of tenderness and love. He had stolen, raped, and murdered. If he was lying hurt somewhere, it was a stranger who lay hurt, not Darryl. The eyes she had looked into that day at Centralia were not Darryl's eyes. It was as though he were possessed, and the demons that possessed him were looking at her through those eyes that had once held so much love for her.

"Just lean on me if you need to," she told Nate. She took his arm. He was like the calm eye in the middle of a storm. He was fast becoming her oasis in the desert, her source of hope for what could have been, and yet could be. Just touching him made her feel stronger. She reminded herself as they left to be sure to hide or destroy her pictures of Darryl when she got back to Abilene. Nate had seen his face. If he saw Darryl's pictures, he might recognize him.

Chapter 11

April 1866

Anna wiped sweat from her brow as she finished re-arranging the furniture in the parlor of her new home. Business was picking up fast again at the restaurant, as the year's early arrivals of herds and drovers hit Abilene. Spring had come on early and warm. Anna's house was finished, and she had precious little spare time, which she was using to decorate her home.

She was proud of her success, and of finally having a place of her own, a home she had built with her own money. She knew now that if she never heard from Darryl again and had to go on living in her own secret agony, she at least could take care of herself, much the way Jo was doing up in Montana. The restaurant was already paid for, and now she had enough money to make payments on her home and the new furniture she had purchased for it. It was small, but tidy and fresh.

She stood back and looked around at the dusted hard-wood floors and the lovely brocade rugs that decorated them. A potbellied, wood-burning stove sat in a corner, but it would not be needed today. The gold brocade sofa and loveseat were enhanced by the gold and green flowered curtains at the two windows in the room. Just across the hall was a kitchen and dining room, two rooms she doubted she would use much, especially from spring to early winter, when she would spend most of her time at the restaurant. In the back corner of the house, across from the kitchen, was her bedroom, with a closed-off closet for a chamber pot.

It was a small, square frame house, with just the one floor, and the rooms were small; but Anna was happy. A porch graced the front of the structure, and upon it sat a swinging bench. She hoped to be able to find a little time to sit on that bench and enjoy the evenings, watching and listening to the activity going on in town. One didn't have to be right there to hear the laughter and pianos, the occasional gunshots and rowdy fights. Abilene didn't seem to be getting any tamer, but she was sure it would as more farmers began to settle in western Kansas, permanent residents who preferred law and order. Still, she didn't really want to see the cattlemen leave. They were her best customers.

She turned a plant she had set on the Pembroke table that sat at the end of her sofa, then stepped back to be sure the best side of the plant showed. She smiled with satisfaction and left the room, going to her front door and adjusting the lace curtains at its window before stepping out onto the porch. She hoped Sandra and Berle would get along all right at the restaurant. She had taken a day off to finish getting the house in order.

She sat down wearily on the swinging bench, rocking slowly and letting her thoughts drift back to Nate, wishing he was sitting beside her on the swing. She had left Topeka a month ago, after a very pleasant meal with him. She had been so glad to see he had not been mortally wounded. It would have been bad enough had he been killed; but to have had to live with the knowledge her own husband had killed him would have been devastating.

Her burden had grown worse. Now she had to wonder how badly Darryl had been hurt, if he could be dead. It was unlikely she would ever know, and she had resigned herself to her situation. If Nate Foster was ever to be more than a friend, she had to think about getting a divorce. She worried what Nate would think of such a thing, if it would change his feelings for her. She still hated the thought of it, in spite of her situation, but now there was Nate, and the thought of never being able to share the love she knew she felt for him was almost more frustrating than what she had been through with Darryl.

She decided she had to face the fact that there would be no miracles. To divorce the man Darryl had become would have no bearing on how much she had loved and would have been faithful to the Darryl she had married. She still loved that Darryl and always would. She had to be practical now and forget sentiment. Unless she prompted some kind of end to this hell, she was doomed to being alone forever.

It was obvious Darryl no longer wanted anything to do with her. He had robbed a bank only a day's ride away, and he had still never tried to contact her. It was time to decide either to divorce Darryl, or ask Nate to please not come see her anymore. She already knew that it would be almost impossible now to keep going without seeing Nate.

She put a hand to her head. Sometimes the confusion of it, the right and wrong of it, beat around in her head until it ached. What did she owe Darryl now? She owed her loyalty and love to the Darryl who had left her, but reason told her she owed nothing to the one who had returned. Why? That was the biggest question in her mind. Why had he never bothered to explain anything to her? Even with the head wound, it seemed he could have tried to talk to her. She would almost welcome an explanation, even if he stood and screamed names at her. At least she would know where she stood, if he was even still alive.

Disgraceful as a divorce might be, he could at least have afforded her the choice. Could a woman get a divorce alone, without the man's consent or presence? She would have to see a lawyer and find out.

Her thoughts were interrupted when a wagon approached the house. Anna rose as it came closer, and before it came to a stop she recognized the brown calico dress she had seen before, the plump shape of the woman who wore it. "Claudine!" She hurried to greet the wagon, and the driver grinned as he drew the horses to a halt and put on the brake.

"Brung you a visitor, Mrs. Kelley. Found her lookin' around at the train depot. Had a hard time understandin' her with that funny accent."

Claudine was already climbing down and the two women embraced. "Ah, Anna! *Je me rejouis de te revoir,*" Claudine exclaimed, speaking in French as she did when she was overly excited. *"Ça va, Anna? Ça va?"* The woman stepped back then, looking her over. *"Oh, elle est maigre comme un clou!"*

Anna shook her head, wiping a tear. "Claudine, you know I don't understand French."

The woman put her hands to her cheeks. "I have asked how you are—and now I see you are thin as a rail. This is not good. All that cooking you do, and you surely do not eat any of it." Claudine took hold of her hands, and both women had tears in their eyes. *"Ne vous inquietez pas pour cela.* Claudine will fatten you up. I am here to help you, Anna. I will cook for you at the restaurant so that you can have some time to rest, no? You said in your letter I should come to Abilene if I like, and I decided to come. Like you, there is nothing left for me in Missouri. There is still too much hatred and sorrow there. And many bad things are happening in the South now, I am told. I am afraid to go back to my sister in New Orleans." She put out her hands. "I have no other family. So, here I am."

"Oh, Claudine, it's so good to see you, so good to know at least one old friend still cares."

Claudine's smile faded. *"Oui.* That Francine, she was not a friend. But I have heard from her, Anna, and she sent me a letter to give to you."

Anna frowned, and her heart quickened with the deep suspicion she had tried to convince herself could not be true. "For me?"

"Oui. Help me with my things. We will go inside and I will find it for you."

Anna turned to Luke Cooper, a local rancher who had given Claudine the ride to her house from the depot. He had already unloaded Claudine's luggage. "Thanks, Luke."

"You want me to take them into the house?"

"That would be fine."

The man picked up some of the bags, and Anna and Claudine took the rest. "How do you like the house, Claudine? It's small, but it's all mine. The restaurant is paid for, and I had this built over the winter."

"Oh, such a woman you are—so smart, Anna, and so strong. It is a lovely home. I am so happy for you, the way you have managed to keep going."

Luke set down the bags in the hallway, taking a quick glance around. It was a pretty little house. Like most men in Abilene, he greatly admired Anna Kelley for her fortitude and courage in spite of the sad situation concerning her missing husband. The man bid the two crying, hugging women farewell and left. Anna led Claudine into the parlor. "I'll go put on some water for tea," she told the woman. "It's nearly lunchtime. Would you like a sandwich, Claudine?"

"Oh, that would be fine. I had that man check at your restaurant first. Oh, it is a lovely place, Anna. I cannot believe what you have done on your own. I am so proud of you. They said you had taken a day off to finish decorating your home, and what a fine home it is. And please, I have not come to interfere with your private life. Just help me find a room and I will be out of your way."

"Oh, Claudine, you're not in the way. I'm so happy you came. I would gladly have you stay right here, but I have only the one bedroom. Come, I'll show you and put on the tea. I don't think Hectar has rented my old room at the boarding house yet. We'll go talk to him right away and see if you can have it. The boarding house is the big, two-story house you saw next to mine."

"Oh, then we would be close. That is good."

Anna quickly showed her around, but the news about a letter from Fran nagged at her thoughts. She stoked up the fire in her cook stove and put on the water. "Let's go back into the parlor until it's hot," she said. "It's too warm to stay here in the kitchen with the stove going. I'll open a window and close off the door so the heat doesn't get into the rest of the house." She opened the window and they left the small kitchen. "How long has it been, Claudine? Let's see. I left Columbia a whole year ago already."

"Ah, qu'est-ce que le temps s'envole! I am fast becoming an old woman. And you, child, you are also getting older. It breaks my heart to see you going on alone like this—so beautiful—a woman any man would be proud to call his own. You should be settled with a man and having babies."

Anna sat down on the loveseat and Claudine took the sofa. Claudine's comment stung at her heart. She was twenty-four years old already. Yes, she wanted very much to be settled with a man, to have babies. That had been her dream with Darryl once. "I would like that, Claudine," she said sadly. "But you know my situation." She sighed deeply. "In fact, I've . . . met a man. Actually, I met him that awful day at Centralia." *Oh, Claudine, Darryl was there! He shot down one of those poor boys and laughed about it!* "I think I told you about him—Marshal Foster?"

"Oui, I remember."

"Well, he came to see me in Columbia a few months later, just to check up on me and see how I was doing. Then he happened to come by the restaurant several months after that. He's a good man, kind, caring. If we can't be anything more, we're at least good friends. He was hurt in a shoot-out a month ago—when the bank in Topeka was robbed."

"Ah, yes, that was in the news in Columbia."

"I went to see him. I was afraid his wounds were very bad. But he was all right." She leaned back, toying with a flower embroidered on the skirt of her dress. "At any rate, he would be easy to love, Claudine. And I know he cares about me very much. But my situation hasn't changed. I'm still a married woman. I just don't know if my husband is dead or alive." *He is alive. But he's a murderer and a thief! He's the one who shot Nate. What should I do, Claudine! What should I do! He's my husband!*

"It is too bad you cannot enjoy the feelings you have for this man," Claudine said. "He sounds like a fine man. Perhaps you should finally think about divorcing Darryl Kelley, or have him declared legally dead."

"I don't know if I can do either. I have to contact a lawyer."

"Well, it is time you do *something,* Anna."

Anna thought about the letter again, feeling a cold suspicion she would learn something about Darryl in it. "Where's the letter, Claudine?"

Claudine reached for her handbag and took out the letter. "I have had this for over two weeks. But I was sick and could not come out to you right away. I am sorry I let it sit for so long. Perhaps it was wrong of me. But something inside me—I do not know why, but I felt I should be with you when you read it and not just send it on to you and let you read it alone. Forgive me if I was wrong in waiting."

"It's all right. I just hope you're feeling better now."

"*Oui,* I am fine." Claudine handed the letter to Anna. "God be with you, child. I hope it is not bad news."

Anna took the letter with a shaking hand and carefully opened the envelope. Claudine watched her slowly pale. She remained silent as Anna went back to the beginning of the letter and read it again. She seemed to wither before her eyes. Finally Anna folded the letter and carefully put it back into the envelope, but her hands were shaking badly.

"What is it, *ma chérie?* Has she seen your husband?"

"Could you go see about the tea, Claudine? I want to be alone for a minute."

"*Oui.* I will be in the kitchen." The woman got up and left reluctantly, fearing Anna needed a shoulder to lean on at the moment. As soon as she left the room, Anna gasped in sorrow and horror. Darryl and Fran! Somehow she had suspected but didn't want to face it. Darryl had only added to his list of horrors by blatantly taking up with another woman. Now he had died in that woman's arms instead of her own.

What a cruel letter! Francine gloated about how she was the better woman for Darryl, how Darryl had come back to find Anna had deserted him, and only Francine had remained loyal. As though to be sure this was real and not a nightmare, she scanned the letter again. "We were both lonely," Fran wrote. "We shared a sorrow you never could have shared with him. I know you saw him at Centralia, Anna. He told me. But you didn't. You just ran away from it. You were ashamed, but I wasn't. I was proud. Darryl knew you wouldn't want him. I became his comfort. You know him as an outlaw, but I consider him a proud Southerner who was doing the only thing he could to help him bear the loss of his family. Yes, he lost his family and home, and he had a head injury that gave him terrible headaches and made him drink a lot. But you wouldn't know about those things, because you didn't care."

As she read the words, Anna could almost see the sneer on Fran's face. Apparently Fran had convinced Darryl she had deserted him. But then the woman surely couldn't understand her shame. How could she, when she thought what Darryl did was wonderful? Francine had even given up everything she had to ride off with him, to support his hideous crimes. She was as demented as Darryl had become.

"Now Darryl is dead," the letter went on. "I didn't think at first that you even deserved to know. But I suppose it is best that you do. Now you can go on with your lovely little life and be happy, find yourself a new man to replace the one you didn't want. In case you are not aware, Darryl was the one known to people like you as Crazy Doc. He robbed the bank at Topeka. He shot that Yankee marshal, and you probably read that he got shot in return. You can tell anyone you want now who Crazy Doc really was, because he's dead. He died from his wounds, and his friends and I buried him near our hideout in Missouri.

"You can't say I haven't done you a favor, Anna—an undeserved one at that. You will not hear from me again. I loved Darryl. Yes, I loved him, for the little while that I had him. I was a wife to him—the wife you should have been. Now he's dead, and my heart is more bitter than it has ever been, for I have lost two men that I loved. I am going away with Darryl's friends. I won't tell you where, because you would probably betray me and get all of us caught. I know you left a forwarding address to Abilene, but I am sending this letter to Claudine because I am afraid perhaps you have left Abilene and have gone on to Montana. I know Claudine will make sure you get it and that it will not lie around in some post office never to be delivered.

"I guess this is a final good-bye, Anna. You have your life to lead, and I have mine. You can put your mind to rest now about Darryl. He is dead, and the war is over for him. But for some of us, it will never end."

She felt stunned, empty, totally betrayed. Fran should have contacted her, no matter what her opinion of what she had done. Darryl was her husband. She had a right to talk to him, to find out for herself what had happened, to decide what they should do about their marriage. It was obvious from the letter that Fran had slept with him—slept with a man who had been her own dead husband's best friend. Perhaps they were meant for each other after all. Perhaps there never again could have been anything between her and Darryl, but she had a right to see him, talk to him, explain her side and hear his own.

She wanted to cry, but strangely she could not. For her, Darryl had been dead for a long time. The news was more a relief than a disappointment. At least now she didn't have to worry about her husband going around killing people, raping women. Whatever his personal torture had been, he was finally out of his misery. If he had lived with pain, it was best this way. And if he had been meant to live the outlaw life, he was better off dead. She could only hope to be able to bury her own shame with him.

She heard the rustle of Claudine's dress as the woman came back inside the parlor, carrying a tray. "I . . . found the cups and the tea," she said hesitantly. "I took the liberty of fixing it myself. Are you ready to drink some, or would you like me to leave again?"

Anna rose, walking to a window and looking out at Abilene in the distance. "You can stay. I have something to tell you, Claudine." Her throat ached, and her stomach felt on fire. "Because you knew me and Fran so well and are aware of where this letter came from, I don't have much choice but to tell you. But I need your word you will never tell another living soul, no matter what." She turned to face her, and Claudine was astonished at the hardness in her eyes, the gray look to her skin. "Will you promise me? No one must know—especially Nate Foster."

"*Oui*, you have my promise, *ma chérie*. Come. Have a little tea first. You look very bad, child."

Anna walked over to sit back down, her legs feeling heavy

and tired. It was over. Darryl was dead. It seemed so strange and unreal. She took the tea, adding no sugar. She wanted it strong and stiff. She drank a little, letting the hot brew soothe her as best it could. "Darryl is dead," she said flatly.

Claudine frowned. "It is as I thought. She knew where he was, didn't she? He came to see her and she went off with him."

Anna met her eyes. "You suspected, too?"

"Oui. She was so changed."

Anna closed her eyes. "What you didn't know, Claudine, is that I already knew myself he was alive. I saw him—at Centralia."

The woman's eyes widened, and Anna spilled out the whole ugly story, feeling some relief at sharing it with at least one person. Claudine listened sympathetically, clucking and gasping at what Anna told her.

"J'en suis désolée," she finally said. *"Quelle brute,* that Darryl. It is a terrible thing he did to you."

"I have a feeling he didn't fully understand what he was doing."

"You should not be ashamed, *ma chérie*. It is not your fault."

"I can't help it. And at first I was afraid I'd be arrested or abused if people knew. Now, I've let it go so long. It's going on two years since Centralia. And with Darryl dead, I see no reason to tell Nate, or anyone else. If at all possible, I would like to keep pride connected with the name Kelley. I'd like to keep the memory . . ." Her eyes teared and her throat tightened. "I'd like to remember Darryl the way he was . . . before he went off to war. He was a good man, Claudine . . . handsome, kind, well educated. I suppose in a lot of ways he couldn't help what happened. Now he's dead, and that's the end of it." She quickly sipped some more tea and wiped at her eyes. "I'm not sure yet how I'll tell Nate I found out about his death, but I'll think of something. I just don't want him to know the truth. You must never say a word about it, Claudine."

"If this man, Nate Foster, is the kind of man you say he is, the truth will not change his feelings for you, Anna."

"But it might, and I don't intend to take the chance. I've been robbed of a lot of precious years, Claudine, robbed of a husband and the good life that should have been ours. I can't say what Nate and I have will turn into something permanent, but I don't want to do anything that might jeopardize the tiny bit of happiness I have found in his friendship. He's a lawman, Claudine. A few years ago he lost his parents and a brother to bushwhackers. A sister was crippled for life. I can't tell him my own husband was the kind of man who took part in such raids, let alone that it might be Nate himself who killed Darryl. I just can't." She grimaced at the horror of it. "Oh, Claudine, is it wrong to have deep feelings for the very man who might have killed Darryl?"

Claudine shook her head. "No, Anna. You do not know for certain it *was* the marshal who killed him. You said yourself Marshal Foster told you many men shot at him that day. But even if you knew for certain, you cannot hold it against the man. I understand your fear, child. If your husband was still alive, Anna, I would tell you it is wrong to keep this from your marshal friend. But as long as he is dead, I see no point in telling him the truth. What good would it do now? It is done. It is time to put the past behind you, no?"

Anna nodded. "Yes, it's time."

"You poor child. I am glad now that I am here. You must take another few days off, Anna. I will help at the restaurant."

"Yes, I . . . I suppose I should take a day or two—for appearance's sake. But I find it hard to grieve, Claudine. I've already been grieving, for five years, ever since Darryl first rode off to war. That seems like such a long, long time ago now. All the grief has gone out of me already."

"Will you contact your marshal friend to tell him you have learned your husband is dead?"

Anna sighed deeply, looking down at the letter again. "No. It would seem a bit forward. He'll be around to see me in a few weeks. I'll tell him then."

"You should tell him right away, *ma chérie*. Do you not

think he has a right to know? If his heart is waiting for you, is it not cruel to make him wait longer than necessary, the way Francine did to you? Have you not already made the man wait and wonder long enough?"

Anna wiped at her eyes again. "Perhaps I have. But I still can't rush right out and send him a wire as though I'm happy about it. I don't want to give the wrong impression. I'm *not* happy about it, Claudine. This is a worse grief than if I had simply gotten news he had been killed in the war. Much worse, because I know the kind of man he had become, the awful things he did."

"I know this. But you still owe it to the marshal to tell him. Maybe in two or three days you can wire him, no?"

Anna closed her eyes. She could not imagine anything more welcome right now than having Nate Foster at her side, Nate Foster to lean on. But would it be right? Was it Nate's bullet that killed Darryl? Still, what difference did it make? Darryl had chosen a doomed fate when he chose the outlaw way. And he had chosen to cast away their love and their marriage as though it were nothing. He had lain with another woman, his best friend's wife. What made her interest in a good man like Nate Foster so terrible, considering what Darryl had done to her? She couldn't feel any animosity for Nate, in spite of the incident at Topeka. If not his gun, it would have been someone else's. But her constant wrestling with guilt and indecision was wearing her down to nothing.

"Anna," Claudine said, "you worry too much about what others will think, and not enough about what is good for you. Now it is your turn. You have worried and mourned much too long. Now it is time to look ahead, to enjoy the years of youth you have remaining. No matter what Francine or anyone else thinks, you were a loyal, devoted wife. You waited faithfully for your husband. And what happened to him was beyond your control, Anna. Just because he was your husband does not mean you were obligated to agree with the things he did or to go to him the way Francine did. There is right and wrong, Anna. He chose the wrong way. You could never have gone that way with him, even if he had lived. God has shown you a way out. He has finally taken the burden from you."

Anna managed a half-smile. "Thank you, Claudine. And I know you just got here, but . . . do you mind if I go lie down for a while?"

"Of course not. I will go to the house next door that you told me about and I will introduce myself and see about a room. What is the man's name?"

"Hectar, but he's probably at the restaurant. His wife is Agnes. Agnes White. She'll help you. Just tell her I've learned through a letter you brought that Darryl is dead, but you don't yet know the details. I'll explain later after I've rested a while."

She rose, walking on rubbery legs toward the doorway. Claudine followed, putting a hand to her waist. "Don't you worry about a thing. You take as long as you need, Anna. And you do like I told you—you tell your friend as soon as possible."

Nate! The thought of him always brought her such comfort. Surely that meant something. Perhaps God had led her to him because He knew she would need someone when this day came. It seemed traitorous and outlandish to feel as though she should thank God that her husband was dead; yet she could not help the thought. It was over. Over! The terrible burden had been lifted, but it had left her weak and spent. She went to her bedroom and removed her shoes and dress, then crawled under the blankets, suddenly feeling cold, even though the air was warm.

Darryl was dead. How strange it all seemed, as though her early years with him had been just a distant dream. That part of her life was over, and it was time to put it behind her. She would try to forget the Darryl she had seen at Centralia, the Darryl who had gone off to lie in sin with Fran. She would remember only the Darryl who had made love to her that night five years ago before he left for war, the Darryl who had solemnly promised to come back to her. That was one promise he would not keep.

It wasn't his fault, she told herself. She had to believe it. *It was the war. He's just another casualty of the war.* Now that ugly war was finally over—or was it? She still could not tell

Nate the whole truth. She could only tell him Darryl was dead. That much, at least, was true.

She shivered, pulling the blankets closer around her shoulders.

Chapter 12

Claudine's eyes widened with delighted surprise at the sight of the tall, handsome man who stood in the doorway. His eyes were a gentle gray, his square jawline and high cheekbones graced with skin tanned from the sun, the eyes outlined with dark brows and lashes. He quickly removed his hat and ran a hand through the gentle waves of his thick, dark hair to keep it back from his face.

"I've come to see Anna," he said in a deep voice. "I got the message she wasn't well. I'm Nate Foster."

Claudine glanced at his badge and gun. "Ah, I knew it the moment I opened the door," she said excitedly, but keeping her voice down. *"Entrez! Je suis ravie de vous voir!"*

Nate grinned. "Pardon me?"

Claudine put a hand to her breast and laughed lightly. "I must remember to speak in the English. I said I am very happy to see you. I am glad you got my message." She put out her plump hand. "I am Claudine Marquis. I was a good friend to Anna in Columbia, when we both worked at a restaurant there. I had no work, and Anna, she wrote to me and said I should come here, so, here I am. And I am glad to be with her in this time of mourning."

"Mourning? The message just said Anna was sick, and would I come."

"*Oui, monsieur*. But she is sick since learning her husband is dead." She caught the tiny flicker of relief behind the concern in his eyes.

"When did she learn this?"

"About three days ago. You got here quickly, monsieur. She told me I should not send for you, that she would wait until you happened to come visiting. But then she went to lie down after the news, and for some reason she has been unable to get up again, except for necessities, and then she needs help. She is very weak and is not eating right. I think perhaps it is her nerves, *monsieur*. She has been through so much these last few years. I think the news brought everything to a head, and the worry and suffering has all caught up with her. I thought perhaps seeing you would help. She has spoken very fondly of you, and you are, um, good friends, *oui?*"

Nate hung his hat on a hook in the hallway. "Yes, we are. And I'm glad you went against her wishes and wired me. I've only got a couple of days, but I'll spend them with Anna." He looked around the little house, glancing into the parlor. "She's done well. This is very nice."

"*Oui,* she is a hard-working woman, a good woman, no?"

Nate grinned at her obvious attempt at "selling" Anna to him. "I am very aware of the kind of woman she is, Mrs. Marquis. It *is* Mrs., isn't it?"

"*Oui,* but my husband, he was killed in the revolution in '48 in France. My sister and I, we came to America after that. Oh, but you do not want to hear the rest. You should go to Anna. I know the feeling of losing a husband, but for Anna it is worse, all those years of waiting and wondering. The strain has been too much, and I think working so hard here with her restaurant has worn her down. I am helping the cook at the restaurant. We take turns coming here to watch over Anna."

"Well, now, don't *you* overdo it."

Claudine reddened and laughed. "*Merci, monsieur*. You

are kind to be concerned. I can see why Anna is so fond of you. Come."

He followed her to the door of Anna's bedroom, and Claudine quickly left to let him go inside alone. He walked inside, closing the door and approaching the bed. Vases and baskets of flowers sat all around the room, gifts from friends and restaurant patrons who had extended their sympathies.

Anna looked asleep, and he studied her thin, pale face for a moment. So, Darryl Kelley was dead. He was sorry for the man, sorry for Anna's loss; but he could not help thinking that at least now there was hope of winning Anna Kelley for himself. His heart ached at the circles under her eyes, at how terribly thin she looked.

He quietly took a chair from her dressing table and set it beside the bed, then sat down, deciding to let her wake up on her own. She probably needed the sleep. He enjoyed just looking at her, imagining what it would be like to run his hands through the lustrous, long, golden hair, now in tangles, that was spread out on the pillow. It was obvious she was not eating right, but he surmised she needed more than just physical nourishment. She needed love, and if she would accept it from him, he was going to give her that love, give her his strength, nourish her with attention and affection. For there was one thing he already knew. He was in love with Anna Kelley, and someday, if he had his way, she was going to be his wife.

Anna could hear the guns. She saw the naked bodies falling, young, helpless men. She heard the laugh, the familiar laugh that once belonged to a kind, good-humored man but belonged to someone evil. Darryl? No, it wasn't possible that a man she had once loved and shared her body with could be a murderer. She saw him falling then, falling into a black pit. She reached out for him, trying to grasp his hand. Yes, there it was! She had hold of him. She could pull him out, pull him back to her world where they could be happy. She clung tightly to the hand. "Darryl," she screamed out to him, little realizing the word came out in a murmur as she jumped awake, still clinging to the hand.

"It's not Darryl, Anna," came a familiar voice, as a big, strong hand squeezed her own. "It's me, Nate."

She blinked, allowing herself a moment to orient herself. So, it had been a dream. Darryl had fallen into the pit, and she had not been able to stop him. "He was . . . falling," she said. "I tried . . ." She blinked again, realizing she was in her own bedroom, and Nate Foster was sitting beside her holding her hand. "Nate! What are you doing here?" She put a hand to her hair, wondering how terrible she must look.

"I believe I was asking you that only a month or so ago. You came running to me when I was hurt. I'm just returning the favor. Your friend Claudine sent me a wire. Said you were ill. Now what is a fine, strong woman like you doing in bed?"

She closed her eyes and her arm fell back limply at her side. "I don't know. I just . . . I heard about Darryl . . . and I came in here to lie down—just lie down and rest a while. For some reason, I couldn't get back up."

He ran a thumb over the back of her hand. "It's just all the years of worry and hard work catching up with you. It's time to look to the future now, Anna. All the wondering and agony is finally over for you. I'm sorry about your husband, but at least now you know."

She met his eyes. "Yes." *He was an outlaw, Nate, a murderer. My God, it might have been your own gun that killed him!* What did it matter now? Darryl was dead, and that was all Nate Foster needed to know. She couldn't risk his reaction to the truth. She couldn't bear to see the look in his eyes change to hatred and distrust. Perhaps if she had not been there that awful day at Centralia, if she had not witnessed the bloody massacre that her own husband took part in, if she was not so certain the Darryl Kelley Nate had shot at bore no resemblance to the Darryl Kelley she had married, maybe then her feelings for Nate would be different. Maybe then she could hate him the way she was supposed to.

But, God forgive her, she didn't hate him at all. He was everything she wanted and respected in a man, and more. He had done what needed doing, and a man had died—just a man—not her husband. That outlaw was not the man she had loved.

"I . . . I got a letter from a man who fought by his side," she lied. Oh, how she needed him now. What was the harm in lying about how Darryl died? She thought about her dream, about the black pit. "They were fighting somewhere in Georgia. Darryl got shot down, and his friend was afraid that when the Union soldiers came across the body, they would mutilate it. He said he had seen it happen before. He . . . shoved the body into a nearby abandoned well pit. Then he got captured and sent to prison. That was—" She thought about Centralia. Yes, that was where Darryl had died for her. "Around September of '64. It's strange that it happened about the time I met you at Centralia." *Oh, Nate, how can I tell you the truth? You would not only lose your respect for me, but even if you didn't, you would say it wasn't right to have fond thoughts for a woman whose husband you might have killed.*

She closed her eyes and sighed deeply. "The man . . . remained in prison until the war was over, and after that he was sick for quite a long time. That's why he just now got around to writing me. He said Darryl had told him where his wife was . . . had talked about me." Had he? How soon had he been wounded? Was it then that he started thinking of her as a traitor, stopped loving her? "He feared Darryl's body had never been found and that perhaps I didn't know whether he was alive or dead. That's why he wrote me to explain. At least . . . at least I heard from someone who was with him at the end."

Yes, she certainly had, but it was no war buddy who had written her. It was another woman, one she had once tried to befriend. She put a hand to her aching head. "Five years. It's been five years since Darryl left. Five years out of my life. I don't even have a child. The only photographs I had got lost—I think when we fled Lawrence." *I burned them, Nate, all but one. I couldn't bear to look at them anymore, to see how happy we once were.* "It's almost like he never existed, like we were never married at all. And there's no grave, no last good-byes."

He squeezed her hand. "Anna, I've never been married,

but I can understand the empty feeling of a loved one disappearing from your life. I, uh, I was in love once, and she died."

She looked at him in surprise. "You never mentioned being in love."

He shrugged and smiled with slight embarrassment. "It was just something that never seemed appropriate to bring up. Kind of personal for a man to get into."

"Yes, I suppose. I'm sorry."

"Well, I just mentioned it because I can understand at least a little how you feel. I was pretty young, only twenty-two. Melanie was eighteen. We were going to be married. That was back in '57. She left Topeka to go visit some relatives in Illinois, and she . . . she got sick and died there." He cleared his throat; it was obviously still painful for him to talk about. "She was buried there because that was where her family was from. Her parents came back without her, and it left such an empty feeling inside. Like you, I think it would have been easier if I could have been with her, could have seen her grave. But she just left and never came back. So I do understand." He met her gaze, his eyes watery. "I guess we both have pasts we need to forget. Oh, I don't suppose we can really forget. 'Accept' is a better word. We've got to accept what has happened and get on with our lives. You already know you're special to me. I have to leave day after tomorrow, but until then I'd like to stay with you, help you however I can."

"Just having you here and knowing you care helps. But Claudine shouldn't have sent for you. You're such a busy man."

"Never too busy for you. And the first thing you're going to do is have Claudine come in here and help you clean up and get on a robe. You're going to get out of this bed and on your feet. You lie around too long and your muscles will quit working. Haven't you ever heard that?"

She managed a smile. "I think you're making it up."

"No, it's the truth." He leaned forward, his elbows on his knees, and Anna realized he seemed to fill the whole room with his size and power. "And as soon as you're up, I'll help you into the kitchen. Claudine saved some lunch for us, and

I want you to eat it at the table—and *eat* you will. You're much too thin. It feels like I'm holding a skeleton's hand. There is a lot of food out there. Some of your friends brought food over. You aren't alone in this, Anna. You have a lot of sympathy here in Abilene; you have a lot of friends and admirers. You're quite a woman, you know."

She smiled sadly, and a tear slipped down the side of her face into her ear. "I don't know about that. I've just done what I had to do." *And now I've lied to you, Nate. Please don't hate me for it. I just don't want to risk losing you.*

She felt his big, strong hands at either side of her face and he leaned close. "You've suffered more than anyone should have to suffer. Now it's over, Anna, and you've got to rejoin the world of the living. It's like you said. Five years are gone out of your life, five years when you should have been sharing a home and husband, having children. But you're still young, and now God has given you the opportunity to get on with your life." He leaned down and kissed her forehead. She caught his masculine scent, thought about how badly she needed to be held by someone very, very strong. She reached around his neck, unable to control the tears she had so far kept inside.

"Oh, Nate, just . . . hold me," she wept. "Hold me and don't let go!"

Nate moved to sit on the edge of the bed, embracing her, not noticing that all she wore was her flannel gown. How he wished he could comfort her in more ways than just putting his arms around her. "Go ahead and get it out," he told her, his lips caressing her hair. He enjoyed the feel of that hair brushing against the back of his hands, the feel of her full, young breasts against his chest. He was more than happy to be the one upon whose shoulder she cried, the one to give her the support she needed right now. She was like a little girl in his arms, vulnerable, perhaps a little bit afraid.

It took all the willpower he possessed to keep from moving his lips to her eyes, her mouth. He knew that would only upset her. It was much too soon for such things. She still had some healing to do.

* * *

Summer came on hot and dry, but Anna was not bothered by the heat. She was in love, although the words had not actually been spoken yet. Nate had managed to come and see her at least one weekend a month since her collapse in April. Sometimes she wondered if she would have made it through those terrible first days without him. He had made her eat and walk, let her cry, held her. He had shown himself to be a man of compassion and concern, the kind of man Darryl once was.

It was time to put Darryl and the bad memories behind her now, just like Nate had told her to do. Business was better than ever, as more herds arrived at Abilene than had in previous years. She was forced to add onto the diner in order to accommodate more customers, and Claudine worked for her full-time now. She had hired two more waitresses, and by summer's end her house was paid for. She realized she had risen above the past, that she could not only take care of herself if she had to, but she could finally love again.

She no longer had any doubts about her feelings for Nate Foster. They had shared so much on his visits, had talked for hours. They had both experienced their share of sorrows. Nate was such a supportive, caring man. Now every time he left her, she worried about his safety, always breathing a sigh of relief when he came back to Abilene again in one piece.

He was coming again today. It was September 1866, exactly two years since she had met him at Centralia. The horror of that day would haunt her forever, but she could not help being grateful that at Centralia she had at least met a wonderful man who was now helping her conquer the past and look to the future.

Two years was long enough to know how she felt about him, and considering the time she had been away from Darryl before that, the past five months of seeing Nate since learning of Darryl's death seemed a proper waiting period before allowing her needs and feelings to be reawakened by another man.

In Abilene she was known as "Nate Foster's woman."

Men treated her with respect, and no one gave her trouble. None of them cared to cross Nate Foster, a marshal with a reputation for bravery and skill with a gun. Nate's popularity was growing in Kansas, and Anna often read about him in the newspaper. He had captured many an outlaw and had practically single-handedly put an end to remaining bushwhacker raids in Kansas. He was known as the man who had killed Crazy Doc, even though Nate claimed it might have been one of his deputy's bullets. Word had spread fast through outlaw networks and eventually to the law that Crazy Doc had indeed died of the wounds he suffered at Topeka, only verifying her letter from Francine.

She finished putting a pearl comb in her hair, which she wore swept up at one side of her head. She picked up a straw hat trimmed with pink ribbon that matched her pink gingham dress. She hesitated, staring at herself in the mirror. Crazy Doc. She had been his wife. The more time that went by without her telling Nate the truth, the more impossible it became to tell him. She wondered if her own mind had been altered by the war, like Darryl's, for since her collapse it had become easier to pretend that part of her life had never happened. Was she treading a thin line between what was real and what was not? Between normalcy and insanity?

Yes, she had been married to a doctor named Darryl Kelley. He had been killed in the war, and that was that. The rest of it surely couldn't be true. For months she had been digging her way out of the past, and she was determined to stay above it now, to keep from falling into that black pit with Darryl.

She pinned the hat to the side of her hair that was swept up. What she saw in the mirror now was a new woman, one free of the past, a woman in love again. Joline had found love and had started over again. So could she. All that mattered now was not losing Nate.

There came a knock at the door. Her heart quickened as she took one last look at herself. She hurried out into the hallway and opened the door to see Nate standing there, wearing a white ruffled shirt and a black woolen suit jacket. His face lit up when he saw her. "Hi, Anna."

Her face glowed with love. "Hello, Nate. Did you bring a buggy?"

"I rented one from the livery. It's a little cool, but we can still go for a ride."

She smiled. "I packed a picnic basket. I'll get it." She hurried to the kitchen to get the basket and brought it out to Nate. She took her cape from a hook in the hallway and drew it around her, then followed him out, closing and locking the door. "I made arrangements for Claudine to handle the cooking today. But I will have to go over in the morning and help out. I'll try to get tomorrow afternoon off again if you can stay that long."

Nate put the basket into the back of the buggy and helped her climb up into the seat. "I think I can." He climbed up beside her and picked up the reins, turning to look at her before driving off. "Rumor has it Bill Sharp and his gang of outlaws is back in Kansas. I've got some scouting to do after this visit. I might be gone longer than I would like this time. A judge back in Topeka is preparing some search warrants in order for me to investigate some places where we think Sharp and his men hide out. There has already been a train robbery."

Anna's heart quickened with dread as he slapped the reins against the roan mare that pulled the buggy. "Oh, Nate, I die every time you ride out. Isn't there something else you can do for a living? Something safer?"

"Oh, there are lots of things, but I'm dedicated to this. I've had some folks after me to run for some kind of office—state representative, something like that. But I wouldn't consider it unless—well, unless I had family . . . responsibilities. Then I might think about it." He looked at her and their gazes met. "Where do you want to go?"

She felt her cheeks growing pinker at the thought of going off alone with him. Because of her situation, she had kept their relationship platonic, avoiding being alone with him except for short walks. But they both understood what they wanted the last time he had come, both knew why Anna had suggested the picnic. It was time—time to know the truth of their feelings, time to be open and say what must be said. She knew what Nate really wanted, but she was still so afraid to make that kind of commitment again, to care that much again, to risk getting her heart broken all over again. Yet here she was, going off alone with him, knowing full well that if he drew her into his arms just once she would be unable to say no to anything he wanted.

"There's a nice place by a creek about a mile from town," she told him. "Hectar was telling me about it. He takes Agnes there sometimes. He said it's pretty and quiet—on the north side, away from cattle and drovers."

Nate nodded. "I already know about it. Checked it out on my way out of town last time I was here." He gave her a wink and she reddened more, taking his arm. It was exciting but a little frightening to care this much again. Still, she had lived with ugly memories and horrible realities for too long. She must stop this constant worry. Surely God had brought Nate Foster to her. He wouldn't take away the only chance at happiness she had had in years.

Nate drove the carriage to a grassy spot alongside a creek, where he got down and tied the horse, then took her hand to help her down.

She turned and took the picnic basket from the buggy. Nate watched her, studying the beautiful hair, the slender waist. How he loved her! They moved through setting out a blanket and the basket and food, both of them warm with desire, neither of them really caring about the picnic. Nate filled up on chicken, which he declared was the best he had ever eaten, and Anna poured each of them a glass of wine. He looked into her eyes as they touched glasses.

"To us," Nate said.

Her eyes shone with tears. Could there really be an "us"? Could she really be this happy again? "To us," she replied. They each drank a sip of the wine. Nate set his glass aside then and took hers from her. He leaned closer, putting a big hand on her stomach and gently pressing, laying her back. "Nate—"

Her words were cut off when his mouth covered hers in a warm, searching, passionate kiss that sent her senses reeling and set her heart pounding. It seemed fire moved through her blood as he parted her lips, his tongue tasting and exploring. How long since she had been kissed this way?

Years. And this was Nate, her handsome, brave, daring lawman.

He left her mouth, his lips traveling to her throat. She gasped in the sheer ecstasy of his touch as his hand moved up from her belly and gently ran over her breast.

"Anna," he said again in a gruff whisper, "I love you. You must know that by now." He moved his lips back to her mouth, kissing her more deeply, moving on top of her. He wove his fingers through her hair, running them up into it so that her hat came off, while his tongue searched deep, leaving her breathless. When he left her mouth again he moved one arm under her neck and the other under her back, holding her close and kissing at her neck and ear.

"And I love you, Nate," she whispered in one quick breath, relishing every touch, breathing deeply of his tempting, masculine scent. "But I'm so afraid to care like this again."

He raised up slightly, kissing lightly at her eyes, her nose. "You shouldn't be. You can't spend the rest of your life living in fear, Anna. You can't deny yourself love just because you're afraid of what might happen. You'll end up living alone and lonely, wasting your life away." He raised up slightly, resting on one elbow, again moving his hand to her stomach, massaging it lightly as though he wanted to touch more secret places. His face was flushed, and his gentle, gray eyes were shining with love and desire. "You're so beautiful, Anna, and such a fine, strong woman."

But you don't know, Nate. You don't know! "I keep thinking it's too soon to feel this way."

"Too soon! Anna, you've wasted enough years. I just . . . I couldn't hold back my feelings any longer. I'm tired of all this talk of being close friends. You know it's been more than that for a long time."

"What are you saying, Nate?"

"Just that I think you're wonderful and beautiful," he said, "and I want to marry you." He saw the surprise on her face. "Not right this minute. I know you need a little more time. But I also know you love me. This next time I leave, I might be gone three or four months, Anna, maybe even longer. It isn't just the Sharp gang. There's Indian trouble down on the Kansas border near the Indian Territory."

He sighed deeply, leaning down and kissing her lips lightly then. "I just want to know if you love me enough to marry me, Anna. I want to know you'll think about it while I'm gone. When I come back, I'd like to take you to meet my family in Topeka. I know I have a dangerous job, but I'd think real serious about running for some kind of office if I had a wife and family. I wouldn't let you live in fear all the time. I know being the wife of a marshal would be a living hell. Most lawmen like myself won't marry at all, but I can't stand the thought of never . . . never holding you next to me at night, never giving you the things you've been too long without. I know you can take care of yourself, but there's more to life than having a successful business and proving you can make it alone, Anna. I'm thirty-one years old, and you're twenty-four. If we're going to do something about our feelings for each other, it's got to be soon. I want a family before I'm an old man."

She had known it would lead to this, had wanted it. Yet now that it had, the thought of having and losing a husband again brought a painful fear to her insides. And she had been the wife of an outlaw! An outlaw! Here was a marshal asking her to marry him. She had been so sure, loved him so much. But what if he was killed, or what if he found out the truth after they were married? But how could he? Darryl was dead. Dead.

She looked into his eyes, so soft and pleading, so full of love. How could she send him off on a dangerous mission with the horror of the truth in his mind? He might get careless and get hurt. And how could she send him off without a promise of marriage, which she wanted more than anything in the world, even if she might not feel worthy of him? It was what he wanted, and she did love him so. What was there left for him to discover? Nothing. It was done with. She had decided to live for the future and quit letting the past control her.

Sometimes it seemed as though Darryl was trying to reach out from the grave, grabbing at her and trying to make her life miserable. It was foolish to let herself think that way. Here was a man who could make her a whole woman again, who loved her the way she had once been loved by Darryl, but a man who was stronger than Darryl, a man who knew right from wrong.

"Oh, Nate, it's so hard for me. But I do love you so much. You know I'd like to marry you. But I do need a little more time." She reached up and ran her fingers along his hard jawline. "I just get so afraid. What would I do if I lost you?"

"Would it matter now, Anna, whether we were married or not? Would your heart grieve any more just because I was your husband? Aren't you already committed emotionally?"

She reached up and hugged him around the neck. "Oh, yes, Nate, I know you're right. I've already lost my heart to you. I do love you so much." *I can't lose you, I can't! I can't tell you and see the horror in your eyes. I can't risk losing this. Better to lose you to death than to lose you to the past.* "I'll wait for you, Nate. Surely you knew I would."

He kissed at her neck, then moved his lips to find hers again, wrapping one hand into the hair at the back of her head while he moved the other up to again enjoy the pleasure of feeling her full breast in his hand.

The kiss was groaning and breathless. How he longed to pull her dress away and taste the fruits of her breasts, to make her his woman right here and now. She was vulnerable and willing, he could tell. She had been so long without a man. But he couldn't guarantee he'd make it back. He felt almost cruel for telling her all this before going after the Sharp gang, but he simply could not control his emotions any longer. Still, he loved her too much to try to cajole her into letting him make love to her before leaving. She was too precious, too much of a lady. What if he got her pregnant and never came back? She had suffered too much already.

"Nate," she was whispering, clinging to him.

With great agony he sat up, pulling her up with him. He held her for a moment, letting her head rest against his chest. "I'd better get you back before I do something you'll never forgive me for." He kissed at her hair.

"There would be nothing to forgive," she said weakly. "I love you, Nate."

"I want to do right by you, Anna. You've suffered enough in this life. I know what I needed to know—enough to go and get the job done and get back to you. You can bet I'll be damn careful. I've got something to look forward to now."

She pulled away slightly. "I never meant—"

"It's all right, Anna. We love and want each other, that's all. It's all just natural emotional needs. But we've got to wait until I get back."

She met his eyes and he saw the fear in hers. "I loved another man. He rode away too, promising to come back. But he never did."

He grasped her arms. "I will." He kissed her lightly. "I will. And I won't leave you hanging in wonder. I'll keep in touch. That's a promise."

Her eyes teared. "He promised, too."

"Don't do this, Anna. We've been all through this. We're both over the past now. It's not going to be that way for us. Tell me you believe that. Tell me you trust me and believe me."

She nodded, a tear slipping down her cheek. "I do."

He smiled for her. "You'll be saying that in front of a preacher someday soon."

He kissed her once more, and she ran her fingers into his thick hair, glorying in the wonder of feeling like a woman again, the joy of being held in Nate Foster's strong arms, of knowing he loved her and wanted her to be his wife. She would have a fine husband again, one of whom she could be so proud, as she had once been proud of Darryl. They would have babies, and she would never be alone again. Life would be so good.

Chapter 13

Anna set down her cup and looked across the table at Claudine. The autumn night was quiet, and Claudine had stopped to see Anna before retiring to her own room at the boarding house.

"I am still waiting, *ma chérie,*" she told Anna. "All day I worked at the diner while you were with your marshal friend. Now I see a strange look in your eyes. I cannot tell if it is happy or sad."

Anna smiled. "It's both, I suppose." She sighed. "Nate asked me to marry him."

"This is sad? *C'est splendide!*"

Anna drank some tea. "I agree it's wonderful. I love him very much, Claudine. There's nothing I want more than to be Nate Foster's wife."

"Then what is the problem?"

"You know what the problem is. Darryl is the problem."

"Darryl is dead. Do you doubt it?"

Anna shook her head. "No. What reason would Francine have to lie? If he was alive, she would have told me and gloated about how he was with her instead of with me.

Besides, Nate heard the same thing through a kind of grapevine that moves from outlaws to men like Nate. Word gets around."

"Then I still do not understand why you have doubts about marrying your marshal."

Anna met her eyes. "I have no doubts about marrying him, at least not as far as whether I'd be happy. But the fact remains he doesn't know the truth about Darryl. Now I've waited too long to tell him. I don't want to lose him, Claudine, but I can't help wondering whether it's right to marry the man who probably killed my own husband, let alone not telling him who Crazy Doc really is, or was."

"So, still you dwell on the past. I thought you said you had put it all behind you. God and you know that you waited faithfully for that man, and look what he did. You have done enough, Anna. Now let go. Do not lose this new love. Marry the marshal. Be happy, Anna. Your husband is dead and can cause you no more trouble."

Anna stared at her cup. "Fran could. It worries me that she's out there somewhere, hating me."

"She has turned her back on you and the civilized world. She has gone off with those bad men and I doubt you will ever hear from her again. If she did not intend for you to be out of her life, she would not have sent that awful letter. What did you do with it?"

"I burned it."

"*C'est bien.* It is done. Now you can go on with your life. Stop torturing yourself for something you could not help, Anna. You are putting a noose around your neck on behalf of Darryl Kelley, but you had no part in what became of him. It was the war, Anna, and the war is over. Do you understand? The war is *over*. But I will say this much. I think you could tell Nate the truth, and it would make no difference. You should trust in his love, child."

"I know. But he's been so good to me. Every time I think about telling him, I imagine the worst: disappointment and disgust in his eyes. If I saw that, I would want to die, Claudine. He means everything to me. When he touches me, kisses me, I'm in another world, where everything is beautiful and peaceful and good—a world where there are no bad memories, no ugly pasts, no murdering thieves who once were loved ones. Only Nate and I, alone together, as though there had never been anyone else for either of us before."

"Mmm-hmm. And you have answered your own question, *oui?* You must marry him because it is right for both of you, and because you cannot go on alone, now that you have met him. So, you will marry him and you will be happy."

Anna smiled again. "You make it sound so simple."

"It *is* simple. You will simply do it."

Anna got up and walked to the back door, looking out at near darkness. "Yes. I *will* do it. But first he has to come back from this mission unharmed. I'm so afraid for him, Claudine. It's going to be a long four or five months without him."

Four or five months. It sounded like forever.

Nate halted his buckskin gelding. It was a big, broad-shouldered horse, the kind needed to carry a big man. He dismounted, studying more tracks. "Here's that shoe with the crack in it again," he said. He looked up at the three deputies who rode with him. "Same one we spotted back at that ranch."

The memory of the burned-out ranch still clawed at his gut: a woman raped and murdered, a man with at least twenty bullet holes in him, two little children found cowering in a root cellar. A fourth deputy had been sent back to Topeka with the children. White men, the children had said. Not Indians but white men had done it—stolen food and fresh horses. If it had been Indians, it would be a lot easier to accept, albeit still horrible. But Indians were Indians. They had their way, and many of them still considered whites their enemy. But for a man to do such a thing to his own kind—for a few lousy horses and food . . .

He sighed deeply and rose. "We're sticking to this trail if we have to follow it all the way to Texas or Missouri or wherever they decide to go. Anybody gets tired he can turn back, but I'm not stopping till we get these bastards."

"You think it's the Sharp gang, Nate?"

"Most likely. They're the ones who shot up that little town they first sent us to, and they rode this way. They don't know one of the horses they stole has a cracked shoe. Let's hope they don't notice it for a while. It's an easy track to follow. Let's go."

They rode off again, all of them saddle weary. They were headed southeast, toward the corner where Kansas, Missouri, Arkansas, and Indian Territory came together.

"I've been meanin' to ask you, Nate. You ever ask that woman in Abilene to marry you?" one of his deputies asked. It was Jim Lister, a close friend.

Nate stared ahead when he answered. The thought of Anna always brought an ache to his insides. She wanted him, he had no doubt. He never thought he could love so much again, and he could not imagine more pleasure than reawakening a woman's buried needs and desires. She had gone well over five years without a man, and he had no doubt there had been no others—not for a woman like Anna. Even after all these years she still felt a little guilty for turning to another man. It was no wonder she had had a nervous collapse. She had had no one—until now. He would make up for all the lost love.

"I did," he answered.

Jim grinned. "What did she say?"

Nate grinned a little. "What do you think she said?"

The deputy chuckled. "You must be mighty anxious to get this damn search over with."

"You bet I am. It's been four months too long already. First that Indian trouble in the south, now this."

Jim shook his head. "Sharp and his men are clever, all right. We've hit every outlaw hangout in Kansas and Missouri and back again. Now here we are headed back toward Missouri."

Nate nodded, thinking about the grave they had found in Missouri at an outlaw hideout a prisoner had told them about. The crude engraving on its stone read, "Crazy Doc. Fought for the cause." He wondered if it was his bullet that had killed the man and hoped it was. He was as bad or worse than Bill Sharp. He would not forget the young innocent woman who had been shot down for no reason inside the bank the day Crazy Doc robbed it. And that was just one of many deliberate murders. He remembered seeing the man shoot at the naked soldiers at Centralia, and he wished he could have shot him then and there. At least now he knew the rumors of the man's death were true.

Little did he know the body buried there was that of a traveling preacher who had been shot down by one of Crazy Doc's men and put in the grave so there would be a body there if it was ever dug up.

Nate and his men made camp for a few brief hours of rest before heading out again at dawn. Day after day it was the same thing, but Nate was determined not to give up. After another three weeks of hunting, the tracks Nate and the others followed relentlessly led into a ravine. Nate slowed his horse, putting up his hand for the others to stop. The ravine was banked high on either side. "Something's wrong," Nate said quietly. "All of a sudden it seems as though they're making it too easy for us."

A light crust of snow blanketed the ground, making it even easier to follow the outlaws' trail. Nate looked around, seeming to be literally smelling the air like a wolf. Over the past three weeks the trail had led them to burned-out ranches and dead bodies, Nate and his men always one step behind, never able to quite catch up. For two weeks they had lost the tracks completely, then found them again when they got news of a bank robbery in a small town in northern Arkansas.

"You suspect an ambush?" Jim asked. The early March air was cold, and he could see his breath.

"I don't know. It just doesn't feel right. I have a feeling they're tired of us dogging them. I think we'd—"

A shot rang out, and one of the other deputies cried out and fell from his horse, which reared and ran off with the man's foot still caught in the stirrup.

"Head for cover," Nate yelled to the others. The outlaws were approaching from behind, leaving Nate and his remaining two deputies no place to go but into the wooded ravine. There was no way to stop and fire back until they could find cover. Nate heard another man cry out and saw blood appear on Jim's left shoulder, but the man kept to his horse.

"Hang on, Jim," Nate shouted. He headed for a group of boulders near a creek, grabbing his repeating rifle from its boot before his horse even came to a halt. He quickly dismounted and gave Jim a hand in getting off his horse. "Here!" He dragged Jim down an embankment and into a cave-like washout along the bank, bullets flying around them. He heard a horse whinny in pain and knew the outlaws were shooting at the horses so the lawmen would be unable to ride out.

Jim grunted when Nate shoved him into the washout. With bullets zinging and spraying bark and dirt around him, Nate quickly set aside his rifle and grabbed at the reins of his horse, yanking the animal to the entrance of the washout. He cried out when he felt a sting across the top of his shoulder, but there was no time to see how badly he'd been hurt.

"Sorry, boy. This breaks my heart," he said, before pulling his pistol and shooting his own horse in the head. The animal collapsed at the entrance to the washout, which was just what Nate wanted. The horse created a bullet barrier, but how he and Jim were going to escape this, he had no idea. At least the gear on the horse held some food and water. They could hold out for a while.

Suddenly everything was quiet. Nate looked at Jim, who was breathing hard and holding his left shoulder. "How bad is it, Jim?"

The man flexed his left arm but winced with pain. "Not bad enough to keep me from shooting at those bastards! See if you can find some gauze and just wrap it around me, shirt and all. There's no time for anything fancy."

Nate leaned forward and looked out over his horse, seeing no one. He reached out and untied the gear, yanking it off the animal. "Look through my saddlebag. I'm going to keep my eyes open for a couple of minutes. You think Dan's dead?"

"No doubt in my mind."

"I wonder what happened to Joe. I can't call out to him. If he's just hiding, he'll give away his location if he calls back to me. He's either found a place to hole up, or he's dead, too."

"How about you? There's blood on your jacket up by your neck." Jim managed to wiggle out of his jacket while Nate reached inside his own jacket to feel his wound.

"Must have just cut through the flesh across the top of my shoulder. It will be sore, but I don't think it's too bad."

"If it got a piece of the shoulder bone or collarbone, it's gonna be *real* sore, my friend. You'd better keep moving that arm around. It won't be easy putting a rifle to that shoulder."

"I've got no choice." All the while he spoke, Nate was watching the trees along and above the ravine. "Bastards," he grumbled. "It's going to be mighty cold here tonight. No fire. We can't just sit here like trapped animals, Jim. We've got to think of something." *I've got to get back to Anna,* he thought. *I promised. I can't let her down, not after what she's already been through.* "I should have seen this coming," he said aloud.

He turned and quickly wrapped Jim's shoulder as best he could. "The wound is right through the top here," he commented, "right at the corner. Hard as hell to wrap it right."

"Don't worry about it. Do the best you can." Nate quickly tied it off and helped the man get his jacket back on. "It's a damn good thing we found this washout," Jim commented. "Otherwise we'd be dead ducks right now. How many do you think there are?"

"From the tracks, I'd say about eight. They lost a couple when they robbed that bank."

"You down there," came a gruff voice from somewhere above them. "You might as well give it up! You ain't got a chance!"

Nate moved to the opening above the horse, but kept back out of the light. "That you, Sharp?"

"Yeah, it's me. Who's the sonofabitch been doggin' my trail?"

"U.S. Marshal Nate Foster," Nate shouted back. "You kill me, and you'll have even more come for you, Sharp—maybe even the army!"

The man just laughed. "After all I've done, you think it's

gonna matter whether or not I kill a marshal? I don't pick and choose, Foster. Woman, child, soldier, marshal—makes no difference to me! Besides, I'd be doin' the memory of Crazy Doc an honor by killin' you. Everybody says it's your bullet that killed him."

"It's my bullet that's going to kill you too, Sharp," Nate answered. His reply was a volley of shots that made him duck back. Bullets hit the dirt around the washout and splattered into his horse. He caught the movement of two different men as the shots were being fired.

"Say your prayers, Foster," Sharp yelled. "We aim to get you off our backs. You can come out and get it over with quick, or you can rot in that hole. Makes no difference to me which way you choose. We've got lots of time. Ain't nobody for miles around."

Nate crouched inside the hole and took careful aim. The pain near his collarbone was getting worse, but he forced himself to ignore it. He waited patiently for one of the men he had spotted to move out from behind the tree again. The minute he did, Nate fired. The man cried out and fell and Nate grinned. "Well, I got it down to seven," he told Jim.

"Good work." Jim pulled his pistol. "I didn't have time to grab my rifle, Nate. I can't shoot long-range, but I'll do my best if they get closer."

Nate looked around inside the washout, reaching out and feeling the dirt. In this country it got cold in winter and sometimes snowed, but very seldom did the ground freeze. "You think you're able to do some digging while I keep them busy?" he asked Jim.

The man frowned. "What have you got in mind?"

"They'll be watching the opening to this washout." Nate watched outside again as he spoke. "My guess is they'll come for us at dark, when it will be harder for us to see them. Right now it's too dangerous for them to come at us. We've got good cover. But tonight, they'll do whatever they can to flush us out and gun us down." He looked at Jim. "Only we won't be in here. If you can dig back a ways and almost to the top, come sundown we'll crawl out a few feet back and they'll never know it."

"We'd never get away, Nate. We've got no horses."

"I don't intend to try to get away. I'm not leaving here until Sharp and his men are dead or captured. We can do it, Jim, if we can keep the element of surprise. You with me?"

"Do I have a choice?"

Both men grinned nervously. Nate turned his attention again to what was happening outside their small sanctuary, waiting for more movement.

"Your other two deputies are dead, Foster," Sharp shouted then. "You two ain't got a chance. You want to die slow, it's all right by me. We'll enjoy the wait." There came the sound of several men laughing. Nate caught another movement and again aimed his rifle. He waited. The man moved again, rising up and aiming a rifle at the entrance. Nate thought he must be drunk to do something so foolish. He fired again, and a second man went down.

"You want us to rot in here, Sharp, you'd better tell your men to quit coming at us, or by the time we die, you won't have anybody left yourself."

"You sonofabitch!" Nate heard what sounded like arguing and he grinned.

"I got it down to six," he told Jim, who grimaced with pain as he clawed at the cold, muddy ground with his bare hands.

"Keep it up and we won't need this hole," the man answered.

"Well, trouble is I can't be sure of my numbers. It's just a guess. The bastard might have picked up a few more men."

"Well, I'd better keep diggin' then, huh? You keep shootin' so they don't suspect we're up to somethin' else."

Nate shot off a few rounds at intervals, while Bill Sharp laughed and shouted obscenities at him, telling him what a fool he was to be wasting ammunition. "You won't see me or any more of my men today, Foster. We'll wait till dark. Your hours are numbered, Marshal. Better say your last prayers, like I told you. And we won't kill you quick, either. A man who's gave our kind as much trouble as you have deserves to die slow. We'll use you for an example to others who might try to come after us. Then me and my men will be on our way, and I'll pick up more men. You can't stop us, Foster. Ain't you learned that by now?"

For hours the shouting continued, along with potshots and laughter. Nate's horse was riddled with bullets. Deep inside he wanted to weep over the animal. A good horse was like a close friend, and Nate's had been with him for five years now. In the moments he took to rest, he laid his head down and reached out to touch the horse's neck, grasping at its mane, his heart heavy with grief.

Throughout the afternoon Nate and Jim took turns digging and keeping watch. Jim would dig until his shoulder could take no more pain. Then Nate would do the same.

"Sun's nearly gone," Jim finally told Nate. "Sky was cloudy all day. It will be a dark night."

Nate crawled out from the narrow tunnel. The washout was getting smaller, full of dirt. "Good," he answered, looking down at filthy clothes and hands and muddy fingernails. "A dark night will be to our benefit. I think it's far enough back that we won't be noticed. All we have to do is dig up through the top come dark."

"Dark can't come soon enough far as I'm concerned. I've never been more miserable—cold, wet, bloody. My shoulder feels like somebody's holding a hot iron right on the joint."

"I know the feeling. And I think you were right about that bullet getting a piece of bone. I'm not going to be able to handle a rifle much longer," Nate answered. "We'd both better drink some more water. We're going to feel dizzy enough from loss of blood when we get to our feet. We've got to have our wits about us."

Jim nodded, pulling the canteen to himself and taking off the cap. He held it up. "Here's to us, old friend."

Nate thought about the picnic with Anna, the wine glasses. *Here's to us*, he had told her. He had to get out of this. He had to get back to Anna.

"It's all over now, Marshal," Bill Sharp goaded as he and his men moved in closer. "Go around behind the washout," he said more quietly to two of his men. "Wait till you're behind it to light the torches so they can't see you. Throw them into the washout from above."

The men nodded and darted off into the darkness.

"I'm gonna enjoy watchin' Nate Foster beg for his life," Sharp said with a grin to the remaining three men. "He's gonna lose every finger and every toe and anything else that hangs free before he dies." They all snickered at the words, knowing good and well what Sharp meant. "Any other lawmen who've got a notion to come for us will think twice about it after Foster's body is found."

The two men with torches made their way through the darkness across the creek and around behind the washout, squinting through darkness to try to see their way. Once they were on the other side of the creek, they lit the rags on the end of the torches so they could see better, then made their way to stand just above the washout entrance. "Come on out, Marshal," one of them said. "This is your last chance." They waited a moment, then began scraping up leaves and brush and throwing them down at the entrance.

"We've got the light of torches and our guns aimed right at you, Marshal," Sharp yelled out. "You can't see us, but we see you."

The two men at the entrance leaned over and threw their torches down into the hole, setting fire to the debris they had thrown inside. They quickly scrambled around scooping up more dry pine needles and dead branches, throwing them into the hole to make a bigger fire, while Sharp and the other three men approached the entrance, standing only a few feet away, guns aimed.

"Ouch! Goddammit!" One of the men above the washout swore then.

"What's wrong?" The second man walked farther into the darkness, where the first man had gone to find more dead wood to burn Nate and Jim out of their cover.

"I don't know. There's some kind of hole here," the first man answered. "I stepped in it. Help me up."

In the next instant both men felt the brutal blows to their heads, one from a huge rock, the other from the butt of Nate Foster's rifle. With hardly a sound they both went down, one of them dead from a split skull, the other uncon-scious.

"Let's go," Nate whispered to Jim. Both men kept to the darkness as they moved behind Sharp and the other three men, who waited, laughing and drinking, at the entrance to the washout.

"Won't be long now," Sharp said. "No man can stand that much fire and smoke, even if he knows he's gonna die when he comes out."

"Hold it right there." Nate spoke up then from behind the men. "Drop your guns, all of you."

Sharp looked at his men. "What the—" One of them started to scramble away. Jim's revolver stopped him cold. By then Sharp and the other two were ducking and run-ning. Nate fired twice, catching two of them before they could get out of the light of the fire. He took off after Sharp then, who stumbled and fell before his eyes could adjust from the bright fire to the darkness. Nate heard the man cuss and ran in the direction of his voice. He heard a thrash-ing sound and cussing. He approached slowly, seeing Sharp lying on the ground, tugging at his foot, which was caught in a thick growth of vines. The man suddenly lay stock-still when he heard the cock of a rifle.

"Give it up, Sharp, or you're a dead man. There's nothing I'd like better than to pull this trigger and blow your head apart," Nate said, sneering. "The only thing that keeps me from it is the thought of watching you hang in front of the good citizens of Topeka and the people whose lives you've destroyed."

Sharp gave thought to firing, but he knew Nate Foster would get a shot off, even if he managed to hit him. He'd take his chances on escaping later. He tossed his gun aside. "Crazy Doc should have aimed better that time he shot you," he muttered.

Chapter 14

"Anna, you've got to see the paper," Hectar told her, coming to the kitchen of the restaurant. "And there is a telegram for you, too."

Anna quickly stopped kneading the bread dough and wiped her hands on her apron, her heart quickening with fear for Nate. It had been several weeks since she had received any word from him, months since she had seen him. She opened the paper and read only the headlines at first.

NOTORIOUS SHARP GANG CAPTURED BY MARSHAL NATE FOSTER. In small letters she read "Foster hurt in shoot-out but brings in William Sharp for trial."

"Oh, Hectar, it says he was hurt," she said, her heart filling with dread. She quickly tore open the telegram. It was from Nate. "Am all right. Staying for trial. Will come to you within the month. Stay in Abilene. Don't want Sharp or his men to see you."

She breathed a sigh of relief and smiled inwardly at the last sentence. If by chance the notorious Bill Sharp escaped, Nate didn't want the man to know she was Nate Foster's woman. She could come to harm.

Nate Foster's woman. The thought sent her blood rushing warm. Nate was back and he was all right! "Thank God," she said aloud. She looked at Hectar with tears in her eyes. By then Claudine was standing beside her.

"He is all right?" the woman asked.

"Yes." Anna picked up the paper again and read the rest of the article. "It says here two of Nate's deputies were killed and he and another man were wounded. They were ambushed. 'Marshal Foster and his deputy, Jim Lister, dug their way out of the washout where they had barricaded themselves and escaped after dark,'" she read aloud for them. "'When the outlaws tried to burn them out of the washout, Foster and Lister turned the tables and attacked the men from the rear. Of the eight outlaws who originally bushwhacked Foster and his men, only three survived. They are being held for trial and public hanging, an event which will be much celebrated in these parts.

"'This all but puts an end to some of the worst raiding Kansas has seen since the war ended. Along with . . .'" Anna hesitated, glancing at Claudine. She breathed deeply for courage, not daring to show her sudden shock. "'Along with the death of the notorious . . . Crazy Doc, whose grave was discovered by Foster when he searched an outlaw hideaway in Missouri, the capture of Bill Sharp marks the end of an era of bloodshed, and, we hope, an end to the lingering hatreds left over from the bloody Civil War.'" Her eyes teared and she turned away.

"Well, now, why the tears, Anna?" Hectar said, putting his hand on her shoulder. "Your marshal is fine and I expect he'll be coming soon for you. You had better start planning a wedding, young lady." He patted her shoulder. "I am glad it all worked out. I will go back to my work now. There are customers to be served." He smiled and patted her again before returning to the dining room.

Claudine came up and put a hand to her waist. "Anna, you knew he was dead."

Anna nodded. "It just . . . gives me the shivers . . . brings it all back, having his grave found that way, realizing they're talking about a man who used to be my husband, a man I loved once. Part of me wants to go to the grave,

Claudine, and—" A tear slipped down her cheek. "I don't know. I just feel I should pay some kind of last respects to the man he once was."

"You cannot go. There would be no explaining it to Nate Foster. And the man in that grave is not the Darryl you knew, so there is no need for tears."

"At least I can be even more certain that he's dead."

"*Oui.* And soon Nate will come for you and you will be Anna Foster, not Anna Kelley."

Anna breathed deeply and wiped at her eyes. Claudine took the paper from her and scanned the article herself. "My, my, what a man your Nate Foster is. Look. Here is another article. It says citizens are signing a petition backing him to run for lieutenant governor for Kansas. What do you think of that?"

Anna took the paper from her and read the article for herself. "Oh, Claudine, isn't that wonderful? I hope he'll consider it. He told me he'd quit what he's doing if he got married and had a family. He's already mentioned running for some kind of office. This would be wonderful. I wouldn't have to worry any more about him getting hurt. We could live a nice, peaceful life in Topeka."

"*Oui,* that would be good, *ma chérie.* I hope that is how it will be for you. You deserve a peaceful, normal family life now. You both deserve it."

Anna breathed deeply, wiping at her eyes again. "I'd better finish the bread dough. I'd like to leave early today. I have a lot of planning to do." She put a hand to her chest, excitement running through her at the thought of seeing Nate again. He had kept his promise. This time her man had come back.

May 1867
Anna turned the pie crust and floured it, rolling it out more and hoping the pie that was already baked would be enough for the evening's desserts. She could hardly concentrate on what she was doing, aware that Nate could show up any day now. It had taken only two weeks to try and convict Bill Sharp and the two men who had survived with him. The hanging had taken place four days ago, and it seemed half of

Abilene had gone. They were all back now, and the spring herds were coming in. Out in the dining room all the talk was either about the latest cattle drive, or about the hanging.

Men treated Anna almost like a queen, carrying packages for her, always removing their hats when they greeted her. She was Nate Foster's woman, and Nate Foster was almost a hero in Kansas. A few began asking when the wedding would take place, but Anna had no answer for them.

She placed the pie dough in a pie pan and cut off the excess dough, wrapping that into a new ball of dough and rolling out more. A figure loomed at the screen door at the back of the kitchen, which was very warm. Anna wiped sweat from her brow, getting flour on her face. She glanced at the doorway to see a man standing there watching her. She gasped at first, then realized it was Nate. She quickly set aside her rolling pin and ran to the door, pushing it open. "Nate!"

In the next moment she was swept into his arms, laughing through tears as he nuzzled her neck. "Nate, I've been going crazy waiting."

"I came as soon as I could."

He held her with her feet off the ground as she kissed at his cheek, which was freshly shaven. He quickly found her mouth, and they shared a hungry kiss that told each of them how much they had been missed, and much more. He turned with her, still searching her mouth while he pulled her away from the doorway.

"Anna?" Anna heard Claudine calling for her, but all that mattered was that Nate was here. She could not bring herself to leave his lips or pull away from the wonderful comfort of his arms. "Anna?" She heard the squeak of the screen door. "Ah, *splendide!*" The door banged shut and Nate and Anna began laughing as they kissed when they heard Claudine rattling off excitedly in French, obviously trying to tell the others that Nate was back.

Nate left her mouth and nuzzled at her neck again. "God, you feel good," he told her. "I came to the back door because I wanted to surprise you. Seems like every place I go these days people are stopping me and congratulating me.

It would have taken me a half hour to get to you if I'd come through the front."

"Oh, Nate, are you really all right? Where were you hurt?"

"It wasn't much. You already know how newspapers exaggerate. I lost a little bone off my right collarbone, but it's healed now."

She leaned back as he slowly set her on her feet, and she realized he had flour on his face and vest. "Oh, Nate, I'm covered in flour. I got some on you! I must look a mess and smell like an old kitchen maid."

"You smell wonderful. And there's no way you could ever look anything but beautiful. Pretty soon you'll be baking pies just for me instead of half of Abilene." He sobered slightly. "You *are* still willing to marry me, aren't you?"

Her eyes filled with intense desire. "You know I am, if you still want me."

"Did that kiss say I *didn't* want you?" He kissed her again, a long, slow, sweet kiss that told her how a man like Nate Foster would treat her in bed. As though reading her thoughts, he moved his hands to her hips and pressed her close. Passion surged through her at the feel of his hardened desire against her belly. He left her mouth again, kissing at her cheek, her hair. "I can't wait any longer, Anna. Let's get married right away."

"Right away! But . . . there are things to do, plans to be made." He kissed her again, hungrily, suggestively. "I haven't even met your family in Topeka yet . . ." He kissed her again.

"What plans do we have to make that we couldn't make as man and wife?" he argued. "And I'll take you to meet my family as my wife. They won't care. I'm a grown man. Besides, I already know they'll like you. If they didn't, it wouldn't matter." He kissed her again. "How about tomorrow?"

"Oh, Nate, I've hardly been able to catch my breath. I can't think straight."

"I don't want you to think straight. I want you to be careless and silly and recapture some of those lost years of being a young woman in love. You know better than most how precious time is, Anna. Marry me tomorrow and we'll work out whatever we have to after that. I've got a two-week leave. We'll get married and spend the next two or three days at the house—just you and me and a bed and a little food. Then we'll go to Topeka and meet my family. You can take care of the restaurant and other matters after that."

"You make it sound so easy."

He kissed her again. "It *is* easy. We just do it." He lowered her to her feet again and she rested her head against his chest. "When I was out there in that washout thinking I might not make it back to you after all, I was wishing I had married you before I left. I was afraid I'd never get the chance to hold you again, afraid I wouldn't be able to keep my promise about coming back. I told myself then and there that as soon as I could get back to you, we'd come up with no more excuses about why we can't marry yet."

She hugged him around the middle. "What about your work?"

"I'm committed until December. But I've routed out the worst of them, Anna. I don't think there's anybody else looking for me who's worth worrying about. People are after me to run for lieutenant governor, and I'm seriously considering it, if I can get enough financial support, and I think I can."

She leaned back and looked up at him. "I have the restaurant income, and a considerable amount of money in the bank."

"I won't have you working and I won't live off your money."

"It would be *our* money, Nate Foster. I worked hard for it, and I can't think of any better reward than to use it to help you stop being a marshal and get yourself elected to a state office. I could sell my house, or rent it to Claudine. That would bring even more money. We could find a place in Topeka where I would be closer to you. Claudine and Hectar could manage the restaurant. Please, Nate, let me help."

He smiled, petting her hair. "Lord knows a marshal doesn't make much money for all the chances he takes. But

I'd be making good money as lieutenant governor, and I think I have a good chance, with all this recent publicity. My campaign promise is going to be to keep outlaw raiders out of Kansas."

She sobered slightly. "That could keep you in danger, even if you aren't a marshal."

He sighed, pulling her close again. "Anna, you might as well face the fact that even after I resign, for the first few years there will be men who would like to see me dead. It's part of the package, Anna. Don't let that stop us. Would either of us feel any better if we *didn't* marry, and something happened to one of us? I don't know about you, but I'd rather have you in my bed and share everything with each other for a few days than to have us both live forever and never share ourselves completely. I want you to be my wife, Anna. Don't let anything stop us. You've let too many things get in the way of your happiness in the past."

He ran his hands over her slender back, and his words of sharing bodies and bed were more than she could resist. Could she really keep going without having him that way? She knew the answer.

"All right," she told him. "But how about the day *after* tomorrow? That will give me time to shop for a dress and make some other arrangements." She looked up at him again. "A traveling preacher was just through here this morning and held services. He rode east. I'll let you go and find him while I make my own plans. I'll have Claudine decorate the restaurant and we'll move the tables back and get married right here. The day after tomorrow is a Sunday. I can't think of a better day to get married than a Sunday in May, with birds singing and wildflowers blooming."

"And cattle bellowing and drovers whooping it up."

She laughed. "We won't hear any of it."

Their eyes met, and his glittered with desire. "No, we sure won't." His smile faded. "I'll be good to you, Anna. You've been alone much too long. Life is going to be good now, happy. And before you know it, you'll have a baby to keep you busy. Then you'll *have* to sell the restaurant."

She felt weak at the suggestion, and neither of them could resist another hungry kiss. Oh, yes, she would gladly give Nate Foster a child—lots of children. And how joyfully and passionately they would be conceived!

"Let's go and announce the wedding date," he told her. "I've got to get riding and find that preacher." He walked her toward the back door. Anna hesitated at the entrance and looked up at him. "That Bill Sharp and his men, they're all dead, then?"

"Yes, ma'am, and I gladly watched the hanging, after witnessing some of the things they did. You don't have to worry about them."

She touched his arm. "And is it true . . . you found the grave of the one called . . . Crazy Doc, the one who shot you after the bank robbery?"

He frowned. "It's true. Anna, I want you to quit worrying about those men. They're dead. The worst of them are done with. With men like Quantrill and Anderson gone, there isn't much danger from men like that anymore."

No, I suppose not, she thought, thinking how her own husband had been one of them. "Kiss me once more before we go inside."

He grinned. "Gladly." His mouth covered hers again, and all doubts vanished.

Anna felt as nervous as if this were her first marriage. In a sense this marriage meant much more than the first, for she had only been sixteen when she married Darryl, much less aware of men and what was expected of a wife, much less ready to understand the commitment she was making. She realized now she had been nearly a child when she married Darryl Kelley. A woman was marrying Nate Foster, a woman who had experienced and suffered more in the eight years since that first marriage than most women experience in a lifetime.

Hectar drove the rented carriage toward the restaurant, and Anna's heart quickened at the sight of the crowd that surrounded it. Apparently most of the town had turned out for her wedding to Nate Foster. Men grinned and removed their hats when the carriage approached, and shouts and hoots went up as she disembarked, every man in town deeply envious of Marshal Foster when they set eyes on Anna.

Her hair was swept up at the sides, an array of wildflowers pinned into it, and golden curls brushing the nape of her neck. Her creamy skin was revealed by an ivory-colored dress cut low off her slender shoulders, exposing just enough breast to send a man's imagination spinning. The short sleeves were graced with a fall of lace that draped to the elbows, and the fitted bodice moved into a tight waistline beneath which billowed a full, double skirt of white, lacy tulle that draped diagonally and elegantly over a silk skirt with what seemed hundreds of puffings that were crossed and tied with deep purple ribbon. The hemline of the dress, which Anna carefully picked up to keep from letting it drag over the dusty street, was quilled with the same purple ribbon.

Anna had found the dress on her trip to Topeka the year before, feeling foolish at the time for buying it, sure she would never have occasion to wear anything so elegant. But she had fallen in love with it and could not resist having something so beautiful. She supposed it was living in a dirty cow town that made such a dress especially attractive. If there was one thing Abilene didn't have yet, it was a place of elegance and culture where a woman could wear a dress like this.

But now she had a reason. Her heart quickened as Hectar held her arm and helped her climb the steps to the doorway of the restaurant. Inside a piano had been brought over from one of the saloons, and a man began plunking out the wedding march, while men lined up outside with hats removed. Anna entered the restaurant with Hectar to see Claudine already crying at the sight of her. Prairie flowers decorated the tables and nearly every nook and cranny, and the restaurant was packed with more men and a few women, including Sandra Sloan, who was herself planning to marry a drover soon, and Berle Cotton, who stood watching with her husband and two children.

Then her eyes rested on Nate, who looked back at her worshipfully. Passion surged through her at the sight of him. Nate looked wonderful, standing there in a white ruffled shirt with a small black bow tie and wearing a black waistcoat with tails, the narrow collar faced with black velvet, the edges of the lapel and entire coat trimmed with silk cord. For once she saw him without a gun on his hips. His gray eyes sparkled with love, and the hard lines of his jaw seemed to be flexing with what she knew was repressed desire. It would be a long afternoon for them both, while they went through the necessities of greeting people, opening gifts, and eating some of the wonderful cake Claudine had baked.

Nate wondered if any more beautiful creature existed in the whole world than Annabelle Lynn Barker Kelley. He considered himself the luckiest man on earth, for not only was she beautiful, but she was humble about it; and she was industrious, independent, strong, intelligent, and most of all, loyal. If she had waited so faithfully for a dead man, how much more faithful would she be to one who was alive and there for her? She was everything a man could ask for in a woman, and soon she would belong to him. He told himself that he should not move too quickly tonight. It had been a long time for her. Part of him wanted to be slow and considerate, but his passionate nature and virility made him want to ravish her. He had wanted her for so long.

Hectar walked Anna up the small aisle that had been created for the occasion. Nate and Anna had eyes only for each other, both of them hardly aware now of the presence of anyone else, in spite of the crowded room. In the distance hundreds of cattle bellowed and swished their tails at flies, but inside Nate took Anna's arm and they both stood before the traveling preacher, who raised his Bible. The piano player finished the wedding march and the room, in fact the whole town, was amazingly quiet.

Anna felt reassurance and love in the strong arm that came around her waist as the preacher went through the marriage ritual. She looked at Nate and spoke her vows. For a brief moment she remembered another marriage, another husband.

Darryl! Her voice choked. There was a time when she never dreamed she would be doing this a second time. She swallowed, and tears formed in her eyes. Nate squeezed her hand, seeming to understand her thoughts. She told herself this was here and now. The past was done. Here stood a man who loved her. He was alive, and this was her future.

She finished her vows, and Nate spoke his own with such sincerity that she wanted to throw her arms around him then and there. They slipped plain gold bands on each other's fingers. Nate had already promised her a nicer ring when they got to Topeka, but the gold band was all she wanted. The preacher pronounced them man and wife, and in the next moment Nate was drawing her into a delicious kiss, his arms wrapped around her, while the room erupted in a round of cheers that rippled to those standing outside. In seconds the whole town erupted in shouts and hoots and gunshots. Some of those outside immediately hit the saloons to do their own celebrating, and piano music began to be heard elsewhere in town.

Inside the restaurant and out, many remained to congratulate the newlyweds and wait in line for a piece of Claudine's cake. Claudine was herself awash in tears.

Anna and Nate politely stayed, shaking hands, hugging, accepting gifts, sharing cake and a little wine. Men occupied Nate's time with talk of politics and capturing outlaws. Through the next three hours Anna and Nate kept glancing at each other, both of them anxious to go to the house and consummate the commitment they had just made. Anna felt dizzy with a mixture of anticipation and some apprehension. It had been such a long time since she had lain with a man. What if he wasn't pleased with her? What if she couldn't give him the children he wanted? After all, for some reason she had never gotten pregnant by Darryl. She prayed it was only coincidence, or that it was because something was wrong with Darryl and not with her.

The piano player started up a waltz tune and called out for the newlyweds to dance. Anna smiled as she approached Nate. His arm came around her waist and he took her hand, swirling her around to an admiring audience. He leaned down close to her. "I think it's about time to leave," he whispered into her ear. Her cheeks reddened and a few men gave out whistles, easily guessing what they were talking about.

"Whenever you think it's appropriate," she answered. "It turned out to be a very nice wedding, didn't it?"

His eyes dropped to the tempting bit of bosom that peeked above the low-cut bodice of her dress. He wanted nothing more than to pull the dress the rest of the way off those lovely breasts and taste their pink fruits. He met her eyes again, and Anna felt weak with desire, reading his thoughts. "It was real nice. Now, see? You didn't need a whole lot of time for planning."

"Maybe not. But I think I'm going to sleep all day tomorrow."

"Sleep?" He grinned. "Well, I might let you take a few breaks to get some rest."

She blushed deeply and he laughed. A few other couples joined in the dancing, and the two of them danced a few more times, sometimes with other men and women. Nate finally announced they were leaving. In one quick movement he swept Anna up into his arms, and men cheered and whistled as he carried his blushing bride out of the restaurant and to the waiting carriage. A barrage of suggestive remarks as to how the groom should handle the bride rained down on Anna's ears, and she couldn't bring herself to look at any of the men. Nate set her in the carriage, then whipped the horse into motion and turned the carriage, heading toward Anna's house, which would now be a temporary home for both of them until they moved to Topeka.

More shots were fired into the air as men cheered the newlyweds and the carriage clattered off. In moments they were at the house, and Nate climbed down and tied the horse. "Hectar will come take care of the horse and carriage," he told her, reaching up for her.

Anna leaned out and met his gaze. "You look beautiful, Mrs. Foster," he told her.

She smiled. Mrs. Foster. She could put the name Kelley behind her now. "And you look very handsome, Mr. Foster." She put her hands on his shoulders and he grasped her waist to help her down, then picked her up in his arms again and carried her to the doorway. He kissed her before going inside, a deep, suggestive kiss. She rested her head on his shoulder as his lips moved to her cheek.

"It's going to be all right, Anna. I love you so much."

"And I love you," she whispered. He carried her inside.

Chapter 15

Anna lost all track of time. The night became one of sensuous caresses, heated passions, a reawakening of all that was woman about her. She realized she had not asked or thought about women who might have been in Nate Foster's life since he'd lost the one he had intended to marry. It seemed she was the only one who had meant anything to him since, but she realized a man like Nate surely had not gone all those years without some kind of satisfaction. The thought of him being with other women seemed to bring out a boldness in her she did not know existed, for she wanted to please him in the way the others had, whoever they had been.

From the moment he carried her inside the house, he was in command of her heart, her physical senses, her entire body. His kiss, his touch, wiped away all her inhibitions. He left her breathless and on fire, starting when he carried her into the bedroom and set her on the bed, leaning over on his knees to kiss her tenderly, moving his lips to her throat while he gently pulled her dress down from her shoulders and away from her breasts.

She had planned to change first into a nightgown, but as his lips traced over the fullness of her breasts and found their way to their taut, pink nipples, she didn't want to put off the inevitable any longer than he did.

The feel of his lips and tongue at her breast made her gasp his name, desire pulsing through her almost painfully. She ran her fingers into his hair, grasping his head to her and drinking in the ecstasy of his gentle pull at her breast. It was as though she fed him, as if he took a kind of nourishment from her.

"God, Anna," he groaned, moving his lips back to her throat. "I told myself I would go slower than this." He held her face in his hands and covered her mouth in a warm, delicious kiss, pushing her down onto the bed, moving his hand to her breast and running a thumb over a nipple to bring out its fullness.

"It's all right," she answered when his lips left hers for a moment. Her voice was husky with her own desire. "We've both . . . needed this for a long time."

He moved to cover her mouth again, gently sliding her farther back on the bed. From then on she was lost in him as he moved on top of her, running a hand up under her dress to lightly touch at secret places. The next thing she knew she was helping him remove her clothes, until finally she lay in splendid nakedness under his adoring eyes.

Her whole body felt on fire. She boldly watched him undress, her heart aching at his many scars from old wounds. Two of them, one on his arm and the small white crease that still showed on the left side of his head, were put there by Darryl. No! She shook away the awful thought. She must not think of that now! Not now! And it wasn't Darryl. It was Crazy Doc, a man who was a stranger to her. She must not let him spoil this magic moment.

Her eyes fell to that part of a man she had not seen or touched in years, that part that would give her the most pleasure. He moved under the covers with her, little realizing that part of the reason she was so open and eager was because she was trying to bury a memory he knew nothing about. For the moment it mattered little to him why she responded so readily. In his mind it was simply because she had been so long without. Whatever the reason, Nate Foster was relishing the most exotic woman he had ever known, enjoying the most pleasurable sex he had ever performed or received, so much more wonderful than with the girls he'd paid for a night's pleasure. Here was a woman he possessed completely, a woman who gave herself to him because she loved him totally and loyally.

He took only a moment for preliminaries. He would take longer the second time, show her the slow, delightful, teasing pleasures she deserved. For now she seemed as anxious as he for the final union, for the glory of being one. She gasped and groaned as he again covered a breast with his mouth, while with his fingers he searched deep inside secret places, feeling the warm moistness that told him she was already eager to mate with her new husband. He ran his fingers deep, making her arch up and groan his name. He moved on top of her then, and she opened herself to him. He rested on top of her, studying the beautiful face, the eyes closed, the flowers falling from her hair, the slender throat and the beautiful, full breasts. He reached down and guided himself into her, pushing deep, wanting to experience her depths and give her every inch of himself in return.

He grasped her under the hips, pushing rhythmically now as her slender fingers moved along his powerful arms and dug into his shoulders. She responded in perfect rhythm, and to his frustration and dismay he felt his life pouring into her much too soon, but the glory of that first coupling was much too wonderful to hold back. He moved his arms under her neck and kissed at her eyes.

"Just lie still," he whispered.

She opened her eyes and he kissed her tenderly, both of them flushed, their skin damp. He moved his lips down over her throat again, kissing at her nipples then.

"You're so beautiful, Anna, just the way I pictured you would be. I'll try to be a good husband to you."

She touched his hair. "I know that. And I'll try to be the wife you've been wanting."

He remained inside her, and already she could feel the life coming back to him. Their eyes met, and he grinned. "I think we can continue this little liaison."

She reddened more, smiling a little. "I didn't mean for this to happen quite so fast," she told him. "I . . . had a very lovely gown picked out to wear for you. I hope you don't have doubts about my morals, Nate Foster."

He laughed. "When a wife is with her husband, she doesn't need any morals. That's what keeps it exciting, even after you've been married a while. Promise me you'll always be totally wanton and immoral when we're in bed together."

Her smile began to fade as he began a slight rhythmic movement again. "I promise," she answered, her eyes becoming glazed with desire.

Then he began the ecstasy all over again. This time he raised up on his knees, grasping her hips and moving in ways she never knew a man could move. She felt the glorious, pulsating climax seizing at her insides so that she grabbed his forearms and cried out his name over and over. This time he kept up the wild, wonderful intercourse until she wondered where her next breath would come from, until finally she felt his own throbbing release, heard him groan her name. She enjoyed knowing she had pleased him as much as he pleased her.

He lay down beside her, pulling a blanket over them and letting her nestle into his shoulder. "The sun hasn't even set yet. It's going to be a long, enjoyable night."

She ran a hand over his arm and chest, leaning up to kiss at his chest, daringly kissing his nipple. "I hope it lasts forever."

He kissed at her hair. "I've wanted this almost from the first time I met you. When I came to see you at Liz Tidewell's, the hardest thing I ever did was not to touch you that day, to leave you behind knowing I might *never* get to touch you."

"And it was hard for me to let you go, wondering if I would ever see you again. Or if I did, if I would have to tell you not to come visiting again."

He petted her hair. "I didn't mean to be so impatient about making love, Anna."

She smiled and blushed, kissing his chest again. "You didn't find me objecting."

He tousled her hair, then sighed and moved back against a pillow. "It's been a long day. We'll rest a while, maybe wash up and eat something later. And then, my love, we are coming back to bed. I'll never get my fill of you." He kissed her hair again. "Day after tomorrow we'll go to Topeka and meet my brother and sister, and then we'll do the town. We'll spend a little time looking for a place to live, or maybe we'll have a place built."

"That sounds nice. I'll rent this house to Claudine, and we'll build one a little bigger, with one or two extra bedrooms. After all, we might need them sooner than we think."

He gently cupped a breast in his hand. "We might at that. I hope so. I'm not getting any younger. The sooner we start a family, the better."

"I think we've already made a good start," she answered, sounding sleepy.

Nate began gently rubbing her shoulders and back until the excitement of the day caught up with her and she fell asleep. But neither of them would sleep steadily through the night. Right now there were some things more important than sleep, and both of them felt a need to make up for lost time.

Darryl came staggering out of the bedroom of the small stucco home he shared with Fran, Jerry, and Mink, the only people who knew he was alive. Fran looked up at him from where she sat mending one of his shirts. The tears in her eyes made him scowl. He took another drink of whiskey and plunked down in a chair across from her. "Don't be looking at me that way."

She swallowed. "I gave up everything to come with you, because we shared so much in common, and because I love you," she said quietly. "And you go and sleep with that whore!"

"She's not a whore. I'm the only one she's been with. I bought her fair and square. If her father was willing to sell her, what do you care? I don't love her. I just like a little variety, that's all. A man in my condition needs to know he's still a whole man." He looked toward the bedroom.

"Lana! Get out here and fix us up some chili or something!" He looked at Fran again. "Hell, you got a damn servant out of the deal, and a cook to boot. You should be glad. I told you we'd live like kings down here, didn't I?"

A young, thin Mexican girl came out of the bedroom, buttoning her ragged cotton dress. She looked at Darryl with wide, brown eyes that were full of fear and scurried to the kitchen to make him something to eat.

Fran set aside her mending. "Take me to bed with you tonight, Doc."

He shrugged. "Whatever you want. I've got enough to go around." He smiled and winked, deciding not to tell her he was tired of her, that physically she couldn't hold a candle to Lana . . . or to Anna. He couldn't help wondering if he had been right to just leave without a word and let Anna think he was dead. Fran kept telling him she had probably already had him declared legally dead. In his confused mind he couldn't quite decide if that was right or wrong.

A tiny part of him still loved Anna, but it was a very small bit of the old Darryl that felt that way, the old Darryl he could never be again, the one who had no power over the Darryl he had become, over the demons he was certain had taken control of him after his head wound. He was firmly convinced that when he was first wounded, Satan had managed to send spirits into the open wound to take over his mind and body. But he really didn't mind, as long as the power those demons gave him allowed him to vent his wrath and vengeance on Yankees.

And it seemed lately that nearly everyone north of the Mexican border had become a Yankee. He trusted no one anymore. Sometimes he didn't even trust Fran, but he kept reminding himself Fran was his kind, a Confederate, a woman devoted to the cause, and she was his good friend. She was not a traitor like Anna. Yes, that's what Anna was— a traitor. Was the war really over, or were people just trying to fool him? Other men told him it was over, but Fran, she said the war would never really be over, that the hatred would go on forever and they must always be wary of others if they ever went back home.

But where was home? Certainly not Georgia anymore. He had a home there once, a family. But he remembered how he last saw them—his mother's bloated, naked body full of stab wounds, his father's head missing, their beautiful home burned. That was what Yankees did!

"When are we going back, Doc?" Fran said then, reaching over and grabbing his whiskey from him to take a swallow for herself. "We're getting low on money. There's certainly nothing worth robbing around here, and I'm getting tired of Mexico. I want to go home."

"We've got enough money left for another year."

"A year!"

"Yes, a year," he shouted. "You arguing with me, woman?"

She stiffened, handing back the whiskey. "No. But have you forgotten about that marshal you wanted to kill? Have you forgotten he lived, that his bullet left you with another pain that makes you drink even more?"

He scowled. "I haven't forgotten." He rubbed at his head. "Nate Tucker. See there? I remembered."

"It's Foster. Nate Foster."

"Oh, yeah. What's the difference? I'll pay him back, don't you worry."

"When? It's been a whole year already."

"I've got to think—make plans. Hell, everybody up there thinks I'm dead. We've got it easy for as long as we want."

"Until the money runs out."

"You sure do bitch a lot lately. You want to go back, go back. But just where would you go? What do you call home?"

Her eyes teared and her throat tightened. "I don't know anymore. They robbed us of it, Doc, not just our homes, but our country. It belongs to the Yankees again. The old South we once knew is gone, changed. Mark is dead, my mother is dead." Her voice broke and she sat looking at her lap.

"Anna's not dead," he said then, almost wistfully.

Fran's heart quickened with dread as it always did when he mentioned Anna. "She *should* be. She's a traitor. You remember that. She left you, remember? She left you but I stayed by your side. *I've* been the loyal one, not Anna. She's probably cavorting with some other man by now."

He grinned a little. "I'd sure like to see the look on her face if she saw me now. I ought to go get her and bring her down here and remind her she's still my wife. I expect she'd look at me with fear and disgust, wouldn't she, Miss High and Mighty, looking down on her outlaw husband. I remember how she looked at me that day we shot those soldiers at Centralia."

"You'd better also remember she never told anyone because she was ashamed, ashamed of her own husband. She should have supported you, not turned her back on you. And remember that if she were ever to see you, she'd be afraid enough by now to run right to the law. You stay away from Anna. She'll only get you caught and hanged. Besides, she's probably clear up in Montana by now. Maybe she never got there. Maybe Indians got hold of her a long time ago and some buck is wearing that blond hair on his belt."

He laughed lightly. "Maybe." He thought about that hair. "But I'll bet he had himself a good time before he took that hair." He slugged down some more whiskey, then leaned forward, putting his hand on her knee. "Tell you what we'll do. We'll stay here till the money just about runs out. That Marshal Foster, he'll be resting easy, thinking I'm long gone. Things are probably quieting down up north, everybody thinking the war is over, huh?" He grinned. "Then we'll go back up there and take care of a few things. I'll get even with the marshal. Maybe we'll even hit the bank at Topeka again, something they'd never expect. We'll hit a few farms around Lawrence, too. Those people owe me after kicking me out of town all those years back. We'll just keep collecting loot, and this time we'll head north afterward instead of back to Mexico. They won't expect that. Maybe we'll steal a few horses and cattle along the way, herd them up to Montana, the Dakotas. Before we came down here I heard men were finding gold up there. We could get a good price for the horses and cattle, maybe look for gold. That would be a change from this place, wouldn't it? While we're at it, maybe we can find Anna. I'll show her what happens to a wife who turns traitor on her husband."

Hatred came into Fran's eyes. "Kill her?"

"Maybe. But first I'd remind her whose wife she is."

"You should stay away from her or kill her, Doc. One or the other. Otherwise she'll always mean trouble for you."

"Could be."

She picked up the mending. "We'd need more men to do what you're talking about doing."

"We'll find them. All a person has to do is hit a few small towns, ask around, find out who still has a good, Confederate heart. I expect after the war there's plenty of homeless men with no money who'd be willing to join up for the loot and the excitement." He sighed and leaned back. "That's what we'll do, so I don't want to hear any more bitching. You can help me plan it all, help me find men." He looked her over. "I'll want you to take care of them, Fran, like before, like you do for Jerry and Mink. It's all for the cause, you know. Whatever they need, you give it to them, just like before."

Her stomach tightened at the words. Part of her told her it was wrong, but part of her thought if she could help men whose hearts were devoted to the Confederacy, she would do what she had to do. Yankees had destroyed her happiness. She saved herself now just for Darryl and any men who devoted themselves to him. She met his gaze. "As long as you know I love just you, Darryl. I'll never leave you, never."

"I know that." He gave her a wink. "You come to bed with me tonight. Jerry can have Lana."

She smiled. "I'd like that."

He rubbed at himself, proud that none of his injuries had affected his ability to be a man. That was one thing Fran always made him feel better about. She had a way of letting him know he was appreciated. He doubted the traitorous Anna would ever give herself to him again that way. But he considered how pleasant it would be reminding her how it had once been between them, showing her that sexually he was still the man she had married.

He looked down at his hands. It was the left one that trembled the most. At least with his right hand he could still shoot a gun. But those hands would never again be used to cut into people and save lives. He found it preposterous he had ever led that life, had actually *wanted* to help people. All that education and dedication for nothing—stolen away by the war and the damn Yankees.

Anna awoke to the singing of birds and the smell of food. She sat up, realizing the sun was high enough that it must be at least nine A.M. She quickly got out of bed and pulled on a robe, realizing Nate was not in the bed or in the room. She ran a brush through her hair and went into the kitchen, where Nate stood at the stove wearing only his long johns and turning some bacon.

"Nate Foster!" She hurried around the table to him. *"I'm supposed to be cooking the breakfast!"*

He looked at her and grinned, and renewed desire swept through her at the sight of his broad chest and flat stomach when he turned to face her. To realize she had lain with this splendid specimen of man through the night, had mated with him more times than she could remember, brought a wonderful warmth to her blood and a flush to her cheeks.

"Is there a rule that a man can't cook for his wife once in a while?"

"Well, it just . . . it doesn't seem right. Besides, where did you learn to cook?"

He laughed lightly and pulled her into his arms. "Anna, if a man who's been a bachelor all his life and has spent a good deal of that time alone on the trail doesn't know how to cook, he'd starve to death real fast."

She hugged him around the middle. "Well, it just isn't right—our first morning together and you're out here cooking. I meant to make you a real nice breakfast."

"Well, you were sleeping so soundly I didn't have the heart to wake you. But now that you're up, I'll let you cook the eggs. How's that?"

"It would make me feel a little better."

He rubbed his hands over her back. "How do you feel this morning?" he asked, kissing her hair.

"I feel wonderful. But I must look a mess. I'd appreciate it if you'd go pump a couple of buckets of water and set them on the stove. I'd like to take a bath."

"All right, Mrs. Foster." He drew back a little, pulling open her robe and running the back of his hand over her breasts. "How about if you let me wash you?"

She grasped his wrist and bent down to kiss his palm. "I think I'd like that."

He reached inside her robe, moving his big hands to her bottom as their lips met in another sweet, seductive kiss. "I think I would, too," he told her, kissing her eyes then. "And maybe you could wash me."

"Maybe."

He massaged her bottom. "And maybe we'd end up in bed again and have to take baths all over again."

Their lips met again, and he searched her mouth suggestively. She reached around his neck and he hoisted her up so that she wrapped her legs around his middle while the kiss lingered. He supported her with one arm while with the other he took the bacon off the stove and set it on the table so it would stop cooking. She rested her head on his shoulder while he carried her back to the bedroom.

"No sense wasting that first tub of water," he told her.

"I suppose not." He laid her back on the bed and unbuttoned his long johns. "Sooner or later we've got to stop this and behave like normal adults," she told him then.

"We *are* behaving like normal adults—like adults who haven't enjoyed these things in a long time. I told you we both had a lot of lost time to make up for."

"What about the bacon?"

"I took it off the stove."

"What about breakfast?"

"I'll start my meal here." He moved his lips down to taste her breasts.

"What about the bath?"

"We'll just have more reason to take one now, won't we?" He kissed at her cleavage and moved between her legs. "You just quit asking so many questions, Mrs. Foster."

She took a quick, deep breath as he moved inside her. *What about going to see your family?* she was going to ask; but for now it didn't matter.

Chapter 16

Anna smoothed the skirt of her blue chambray dress. The fitted bodice accented her full bosom and tiny waist, and was decorated with small white buttons that ran from the slightly scooped neckline down the front to the tip of the pointed waistline. White lace trimmed the neckline, the short sleeves, and the hem of the dress. She wore a straw bonnet decorated with blue ribbon.

The weather had turned hot, and she took a handkerchief from her handbag to dab at perspiration on her brow. "Nate, I'm going to be a melted frazzle when I meet your family."

He grinned. "Honestly, Anna, you'd think you were going to meet the king and queen of England. It's just my brother and sister."

"I know, but here we are already married, and they haven't even met me yet. Are you sure I look all right?"

She met his gaze, which was moving over her appreciatively. Her blood warmed even more at the thought of their intimacy over the past three days, and what she knew he was thinking now. He leaned over to kiss her cheek. "Anna, you could make a potato sack look wonderful, and you know it. Now quit worrying."

She sighed deeply, studying his handsome face a moment longer, still finding it hard to believe he was really her husband. He sat beside her on the train, wearing simple blue denim pants and a cotton shirt with a leather vest and knee-high leather boots. He again wore a revolver, never caring to be out in public without it, even though he was still on leave from his duties. "Troublemakers don't take leaves," he had told Anna when he strapped it on. She glanced at the leather strap tied around his thigh and she sighed.

"I'll be glad when you don't have to wear that anymore."

"Oh, I don't know. I'll feel kind of naked without it."

She met his eyes again. "You like being a lawman, don't you?"

He pushed his hat back and shifted in his seat, always finding there was never enough room for his legs between train seats. "It kind of grows on you, Anna. I guess it's mostly just the idea of finding men like the kind who hurt my sister. Some things get in a man's blood." He paused a moment. "Like a beautiful woman." She smiled, but he saw the worry in her eyes. He took her hand. "I have to admit it won't be easy taking off this badge, but I'll do it, for you."

She studied the eyes she had come to love and trust. "I want you to be happy, Nate."

"As long as I have you I'll be happy." The train began to slow down, and it let off a couple of long whistles. "We're coming into Topeka."

Anna's heart quickened as she watched the crowd at the depot. "There's my brother," Nate told her as he leaned across her to look out the window. He pointed to a man who sat on a wagon parked just past the depot. "Apparently he got my wire."

Anna stared at a man who looked very much like Nate, but when he removed his hat to wipe sweat from his face, she saw that his hair was much thinner.

"Rob is about eight years older. Christine is only seventeen. She was the accident baby—you know, the ones that come late in life when you think you can't have any more children."

She looked at him, and both of them felt a flush of passion. "That could happen to us," he told her with a wink. "I don't intend to let age stop me from anything."

She smiled and looked away.

"We'll get a hotel room later. Rob will want us to stay there, but I think we'd better be alone, don't you?"

"Nate," she chided, her face reddening.

He laughed as the train came to a halt. He stood up and took Anna's carpetbag from a rack above, then reached over and took his smaller bag of clothes from an empty seat. "Let's go, Mrs. Foster."

She moved into the aisle and to the platform, hearing Nate's name called out when they stepped into the open. Nate called back to his brother, who climbed down from the wagon. They shook hands, then embraced for a moment, and in those first few seconds Anna could see that Robert Foster was as fine a man as Nate. He was obviously pleased and impressed with Anna, embarrassing her with teasing remarks in much the way Nate could do, exclaiming over how beautiful she was and how lucky Nate was. He put an arm around her waist and led her to the wagon, helping her up into the seat while Nate put their bags in the back of the wagon.

"Anna, I love any woman who can make my brother put down that gun," Rob told her. "I've had to visit him at the doctor's office too many times. I live in fear that one of these times he won't be getting right back up, or maybe will never get up again. We've had enough losses in this family, and he has to go running around after the worst men in the state."

"Well, I have the same worry," she answered. "And he would make a wonderful lieutenant governor, don't you think?"

Nate climbed up and sat beside her on the wooden seat. "All right, you two, you don't need to do all this hinting and plotting. But I'm committed until December, don't forget."

"Six months too long, far as I'm concerned," Rob answered. He sat on the other side of Anna and picked up the reins, turning the wagon and heading out of town. It seemed to Anna that everyone in Topeka knew Nate. People smiled and waved; those who knew he'd gotten married yelled out their congratulations. He was a popular, well-liked man, and Anna had little doubt he could win an election to any office he chose.

"We'd have come to the wedding, Anna," Rob was saying. "But it's hard to travel with Christine like she is. She takes a lot of care and it isn't always easy to find someone to watch over her. Marie—that's my wife—we generally do our shopping and things like that separately so there's always somebody at the house. Our oldest daughter, she's getting big enough to help so that Marie and I can sometimes get away for a while—go out to eat, things like that."

"I'm so sorry about your sister," Anna answered. Darryl had hurt people that way and thought nothing of it. Her lingering guilt over not telling Nate the truth still haunted her at times, but it seemed far too late to be telling him now. She was deliriously happy, more content than she had been in years.

Rob shook his head. "It was a terrible thing. Ma and Pa, they had a little farm east of here. The bushwhackers came at night, surprised Ma and Pa. Me, I wasn't there. I've been married now for fifteen years, living right here in Topeka. I've got a supply store here. At any rate, the bushwhackers set the house on fire. They shot Christine as she ran from the house. Nate, he got a few of them before they rode off with the horses and cattle. But it was too late to try to save Ma and Pa. They died in the fire."

Anna moved her hand to put it over Nate's arm, realizing he had never told her the details of the raid. Perhaps it was too painful for him to talk about. He stared straight ahead, saying nothing.

"That's my store there," Rob was saying. It was obvious that he was more talkative than Nate as he continued to point out various places in Topeka.

"I was here a little over a year ago, when Nate was—" She hesitated. *When Nate was shot by my husband,* she thought. "When he was . . . hurt after that bank robbery."

"Yeah, Nate talked about you way back then. Me and

Marie, we could tell he was in love even then." He leaned slightly forward. "Weren't you, brother?"

Nate grinned and looked over at him, then at Anna. She could see tears in his eyes, and her heart went out to him. She knew it was from talk of the raid. "I've loved her since I first met her two and a half years ago—it'll be three years come September." He placed his big hand over hers and gave her a wink, obviously trying to hide his sorrow. "Stop at the hotel there, Rob. I want to get us a room for tonight."

"Hell, Nate, you don't need to do that. We'll make room."

Nate laughed lightly. "Rob, we've only been married three days. I want to be alone with my wife when we retire."

Rob laughed loudly and Anna blushed. "I guess I've been married too long. All right, I'll stop." He pulled up in front of the hotel and Nate squeezed Anna's hand.

"You wait here. I'll rent us a room and be right back."

She watched him climb down, watched as more people greeted him and shook his hand. She sighed deeply, turning to look at Rob. "It still bothers him a lot, doesn't it—the raid? He had never even told me the details."

Rob sobered, looking out at the busy main street of Topeka. "Yes. I suppose it's worse for him because he was there. He was a real angry man for a long time. Strapped on a gun and a deputy marshal's badge, started going after bushwhackers with such a vengeance and did such a good job of it, he was a full-fledged marshal in no time. I think he felt bad that he couldn't do more that night to help our folks and Christine. In a way I guess he's been trying to make up for it ever since." He paused. "He's good at what he does, Anna. I'm not positive he'll be happy doing something else, but he'll do it for you. And as long as he has you, he'll be all right. Doing what Nate does, it kind of gets in a man's blood."

"That's what Nate told me. I know the world needs men who will stick their necks out like that, but I don't like the fact that it's my husband who's doing it. I do want him to be happy, though."

Rob patted her hand. "Like I said, he'll be fine, long as

he's got you. I know Nate. He's tough on the outside, especially when he's dealing with criminals, but he's soft on the inside. He really wants a home and family, and he'll do whatever it takes to keep those things safe and be there for you. If that means putting down his badge, he'll do it."

Nate came out of the hotel, all smiles again as he climbed up into the seat. "Got us the best room in the hotel," he said, slipping an arm around Anna's waist. "Rob, where do you think the best spot would be to build a house? I've got to get Anna to Topeka permanently where I can see her more often."

"Oh, that little hill near our place is a good spot—grassy, good view, a couple of big cottonwood trees. It's my land, so it wouldn't cost you."

"Oh, yes it would. I'll pay whatever the going price is."

"Oh, yes, we would want to pay for it," Anna put in.

"Forget it," Rob answered. "Consider it a wedding gift. I was going to farm it at one time, but I did so well with the supply store that now the land is just sitting there." He got the horses into motion again. "I hear you own a restaurant and have your own house in Abilene, Anna."

"Yes. When my—" Again, the piercing agony swept through her. "My husband was missing for so long, I knew I had to do something to fend for myself until I found out what had happened to him. I had worked in a restaurant in Columbia." She thought about Fran with bitter resentment. "I saw how well something like that would do in Abilene, with those hundreds of drovers who come to town every summer. So I opened my own place. It's already paid for itself and for my house. I'm going to rent the house and Nate and I will use the money as extra income. I want to keep the restaurant, though. It will help bring in more money while Nate runs for office."

Rob shook his head. "You've picked yourself quite a woman, brother," he told Nate. "Independent, hard-working, even comes with a dowry."

Nate laughed. "I didn't marry her for her dowry. I can take good care of her on my own. Actually, I want her to sell the damn restaurant, but she worked hard to build what she has and I really can't blame her for not wanting to let go of it—at least not yet. Maybe once we have a family she'll change her mind." He gave Anna another wink. "But I agree, she's quite a woman. She's everything I said she was, isn't she?"

"That and more. I envy you."

"Rob Foster, you've got a damn good wife and you know it. I don't know how Marie puts up with you, but I'm glad she does."

Rob laughed. "Yeah, she's a good woman. Lord knows it hasn't been easy for her, raising four kids and looking after Christine. She took Christine in like she was her own."

"I'd be glad to help however I can once Nate and I get settled," Anna told the man. "I can at least relieve you and Marie more often, so you can get away together to shop or go to church and the like. The two of you must need a vacation. If you'd like to take Marie away someplace for a few days, I'd be glad to stay with Christine and your children."

She felt Nate's arm tighten around her in gratitude for her offer.

"Well, that's real nice of you, Anna," Rob was saying. "We just might take you up on that." He headed toward a neat two-story frame house that sat on the outskirts of town. "But you and Nate get everything taken care of first, and enjoy these first few weeks together. You've got a lot to do, what with having property in Abilene and building a house here and all."

He drove up to the house, where a pretty young girl with long, dark hair sat in a wheelchair on the porch. "Marie, they're here," Anna heard the girl call out. An older woman appeared at the door, all smiles. She wiped her hands on an apron and ran out to greet the wagon, followed by four children, the oldest a girl looking about twelve or thirteen, the youngest a tiny girl of perhaps two or three years old.

Marie embraced Nate, then turned to Anna as Nate introduced them. "Oh, Nate, she's so beautiful," the woman exclaimed with a smile. She hugged Anna and welcomed her into the family, and most of Anna's nervousness left her. Marie appeared to be about thirty-five, a slightly plump woman whose once-youthful waistline had been lost through giving birth to six children, two of whom were buried in the town's graveyard. Her blue eyes, lined from the Kansas sun and a life that was not always easy, sparkled with genuine affection, and her dark hair was spiced with gray at the temples where it was drawn back into a bun.

Nate took Anna's arm and led her up the steps to the porch, where Christine sat in a wheelchair. The girl was all smiles as Nate leaned down to give her a hug and kiss her cheek, and Anna noticed she could not even raise her arms to hug him back. Her heart sank at the realization the girl was in worse condition than she had imagined. The sight of her lovely face made it all seem even sadder—a beautiful, budding young woman, shot down before she could even enjoy some of the most basic pleasures of life. Again Anna was overcome with the realization her own husband could have been responsible for similar atrocities, and again she nearly withered at the thought of Nate ever learning the truth about Darryl.

Nate stepped away and introduced Anna, who nodded and smiled to the girl, telling her how happy she was to finally meet her, feeling awkward because she couldn't even reach out and shake the girl's hand.

"Marie is right, Nate," she told her brother. "Your wife is so pretty. We're so glad you've married." She moved her gaze to Anna. "You'll make sure he puts away his badge now, won't you? I get so scared for him."

"I'm trying," Anna answered with a smile.

Christine looked up at Nate, her eyes suddenly tearing in spite of her brave smile. "When he gets hurt, I always feel a little bit responsible." She looked back at Anna. "He does it because of me, and I keep telling him he doesn't have to."

"None of that," Nate said, leaning down and lifting her out of the chair. "I do it so there won't be *others* like you." He carried her thin body inside the modest frame home, while the four children clamored around Anna, spouting off their names: Nora, thirteen; Benny, ten; Paul, six. Marie picked up the youngest one.

"This is my baby, Nancy. She's two," she told Anna.

Anna could see that family was important to Nate and his

brother. She prayed she would be able to give Nate lots of children like Marie had done for Rob.

The house was full of good smells, and Marie excused herself to go to the kitchen. "I was hoping you would get here before dinnertime. I have quite a meal prepared. I just hope it's good enough," she laughed. "Nate tells us you're a wonderful cook, with your own restaurant in Abilene! That sounds so exciting. I admire your ability to be so independent and support yourself that way, Anna. It's so sad that you went so many years not knowing about your husband. You must be a very brave, adventurous woman, going to a place like Abilene and starting your own business."

Anna smiled, putting aside the mention of her husband. "I wasn't being adventurous at all," she answered. "I had decided to try to go to Montana to be with my sister, but the railroad tracks ended at Abilene, and everyone there told me to go any farther would be suicide because of Indian trouble. So I ended up settling in Abilene almost by accident." She looked at Nate, who still held Christine. "But I'm glad I did, or I might never have seen Nate again."

"Well, we're glad, too. You all visit now, and I'll go finish dinner."

"Oh, please let me help. It's what I do best, and you shouldn't have to do all the work."

Marie insisted she didn't need her help, but Nora grabbed Anna's hand. "Let her help, Mother. We can all talk in the kitchen." It was obvious the girl already adored Anna as she half dragged her along. Anna helped with preparations, then through a window she noticed Nate walking into the backyard with Christine. He set her on a swinging bench and sat down beside her to hang on to her while he pushed the bench back and forth.

Anna felt a lump in her throat at the sight. "I never totally understood Nate's commitment until I met Christine," she told Marie.

The woman glanced out the window and smiled sadly. "Yes. Christine was the baby of the family, spoiled by two big brothers. After the raid, well, it was harder on Nate because he was there and saw it all, and he has always felt he should have been able to do something to prevent what happened to Christine. But he couldn't have stopped it. He *did* try, and got hurt. There were just too many of them. We have tried to tell him she was probably lucky to catch the bullet. If she had not been hurt, they would have taken her away with them, to a fate much worse than what she suffers now. But Nate keeps blaming himself. It will go hard on him when she dies."

Anna looked at her in surprise. "Dies?"

Marie breathed deeply and blinked back tears. "Didn't Nate tell you? The doctor says she has maybe another year or two." The woman began slicing some bread. "When Christine was first hurt, it was only her legs that were paralyzed. She has grown gradually worse. As you saw, she can no longer use her arms. The bullet is still in her. The doctor said to remove it would be to kill her instantly. It somehow affected her nerves so that slowly all her muscles will lose their ability to work, including the ones that help her breathe. When that happens . . ." The woman turned and set the bread on the table.

"Does Christine know?" Anna asked her.

"Oh, we haven't actually told her. But I think she knows. You saw how thin she is. It has gotten so she can hardly eat. It is hard for her to swallow. We fear she will die of malnutrition before she stops breathing. But she still has her good days, like today."

Anna felt her own tears wanting to come. *My husband was a bushwhacker, a murdering raider.* Sometimes she wanted to scream it, just get it out and suffer the consequences. "It's so sad," she said aloud. "I'm so sorry. And it's surely been hard on you, taking care of Christine."

"She's a sweet girl, who has taken all of it with amazing grace and courage. She never complains. I think Christine has made peace with God and is ready to go to Him. When she does, we shouldn't be sad. We should be glad for her. She'll be released of her pain and agony, and this cruel, slow death." The woman faced Anna, putting a hand on her arm. "Sometimes I find myself praying He will take her soon, so she will be out of her misery. I pray that she dies quietly, before she loses her breathing muscles. I can't help thinking what a horrible, terrifying death that would be, to have to struggle for breath—a slow suffocation. Do you think it's wrong to pray for someone to die?"

Anna thought of Darryl. She realized there had been times when she had prayed he would die too, although she didn't like to face that fact. "No," she answered. "I don't think it's wrong at all."

Marie took a deep breath. "Well, enough of this sad talk. This is a day to be happy. Nate has a new wife, and we are so glad for him, and so relieved he is going to turn in his badge in December." She turned away. "Nora, is the table all set?"

"Yes, Mama."

"Well, then, let's carry out the food."

Anna helped, and soon everyone was gathered around the table eating food as good as any Anna had tasted. The talk was of building a house in Topeka, questions from the children about what Abilene was like, questions from Marie about the restaurant business. Anna watched Nate helping feed Christine, who took a long time swallowing each bite and who Anna was desperately afraid was going to choke on something. But the girl made it through the meal, although it left her worn out. Nate carried her to her room, which was one of the two downstairs bedrooms. Marie liked to keep her downstairs near hers and Rob's own bedroom so that she could hear the girl in the night if she needed help.

Anna helped clean up the table and helped with dishes, until someone grabbed her from behind, pulling her close and leaning around to kiss her cheek. "How about a walk?" came Nate's voice.

Anna laughed. "Nate, we aren't through with dishes yet."

"Oh, please go with him. Nora will finish helping."

Anna tried to object, but Marie would hear none of it. Nate untied the apron Marie had given Anna and tossed it aside, putting an arm around Anna and leading her out the door. "Tomorrow I'll take you to the courthouse and show you my home base—the place where I get my orders," he was telling her. "Right now, let's try to get an idea where we'd like to put our house."

He led her to a grassy knoll about a hundred yards from his brother's house. They reached a big cottonwood tree at the top of the hill, and he turned and pulled her close, kissing her with great passion. Anna sensed a kind of desperation in the kiss, and she knew he was troubled. He held her tight against himself for a moment, and to her surprise she felt him suddenly tremble, felt a wetness on her cheek. "She'll never know this, Anna," he said, his voice husky. "Never know love, never have children." He swallowed. "She would have made such a sweet mother."

He suddenly released her, turning away and wiping at his eyes. "Jesus, this is a hell of a way to behave in front of a new wife."

Anna put a hand on his back. "Nate, you've got to stop blaming yourself. That's ridiculous," she told him. "Marie said there were far too many of them. And like she said, what happened to her is almost better than if she hadn't been hurt and they had got hold of her."

He took a handkerchief from his pocket and blew his nose. "I know." He threw his head back and breathed deeply. "Did Marie tell you she's slowly dying?" He cleared his throat and shoved the handkerchief back in his pocket, leaning against the tree and staring out at Topeka.

"Yes. Nate, why didn't you tell me how bad it was? I had no idea. I thought it was just her legs, and that would have been bad enough."

He shrugged, moving an arm around her and holding her close. She rested her head on his chest. "I don't know," he answered. "I guess . . . it's just hard for me to talk about, that's all. It's easier to let somebody else like Marie tell you. Marie's a good woman. Rob has a nice family, doesn't he?"

"Yes. I feel right at home already." She hugged him. "I hope I can give you a lot of children like that, Nate."

He ran a hand over her back. "You will. But the important thing is that we're together. I have to admit, when I see Christine, it isn't easy for me to think about putting away my gun. But I realize a man with a family can't be putting his life on the line all the time and most of the men who did the kind of thing that was done to Christine are either dead or in prison now."

Men like Darryl Kelley, she thought bitterly. "I'm so sorry, Nate," she said aloud. "I don't know what else to say."

"There *is* nothing else to say. And I'm sorry to put a damper on things."

"Oh, Nate, it's only natural to feel the way you do. Your compassion is part of what I love about you." She gave him another hug and pulled away, turning and looking out at a view of Topeka on one side of the hill, and a lovely, sprawling view of rolling hills and woods on the other, a small farm and grazing cattle in the distance. "This is a lovely spot, Nate, just as your brother said. I think this would be a wonderful place to build our house, and we'd be close to Christine." She turned to face him. "I don't know about letting Rob just give us the land, though."

He smiled, his love for his brother showing in his eyes. "Well, I don't feel right about it, either. But I know Rob, and he'd be hurt if we insisted on giving him something for it. He mentioned it three or four more times when we were talking back at the house. He really wants us to have it, Anna."

She came closer, and he slipped an arm around her waist. "He's a wonderful man, Nate. You both are. Your parents did a wonderful job with their children."

She felt him stiffen at the words, and knew he was thinking about how his parents had died. "We'll go back to Abilene in a few days and take care of things on that end," he told her. "Before we leave here we'll talk to some builders. We'll make our home in Abilene until our house here is done. I expect I'll be gone again for a couple months at a time anyway until December. The house here will be finished by then and we'll come here to settle."

She turned and looked up at him, her heart aching at the trace of tears still in his eyes. "Nate, I hate the thought of you going away again. Now that we've been together . . ."

He took her face in his hands. "I hate it, too. We'll just have to store up some of that lovemaking by doing more than our share before I leave. And each time I come back, we'll make up for lost time." He gave her a wink and a smile, then leaned down and met her mouth in a long, delicious kiss. Both of them were anxious for night to come, when they could go to their hotel room, neither of them still quite able to satisfy their awakened sexual desires and pleasures in each other. He moved a hand to her bottom, pressing her to him and groaning as he drew out the kiss before finally brushing his lips over her forehead, her hair. "God, I love you, Anna."

"I love you, too," she whispered, feeling the sweet pull at her insides at the thought of taking him into her again. The way she had seen him today, the agony and sorrow in his eyes, the love he showed for his sister, made her love him all the more; and it made her all the more determined that he must never know about Darryl.

Chapter 17

December 1867

The house was two stories high, with sloped walls in the upstairs rooms because of the steeply pitched roof. There were two stained-glass wheel windows upstairs, with dormers over the rest of the windows. Everyone in Topeka admired the lovely new home of Mr. and Mrs. Nate Foster, with its gingerbread trim along the eaves and gable edges, and a porch that ran around the entire lower floor of the house.

Anna was finally living the dream she had once hoped to live with Darryl. Those first several passionate nights with Nate Foster had planted a seed in her that Darryl had failed to do, and she was with child. Finally, a real home, not the lonely little house in Abilene; finally, a loving husband at her side again; and for the first time, a child growing in her belly.

Sometimes she worried that something would happen to spoil this new love and happiness she had found, and she waited anxiously for the next two weeks to pass, for then the long, six months of waiting for Nate to turn in his badge would be over.

For the first four months of their marriage Anna had continued living in Abilene, managing the restaurant, and waiting in constant worry while Nate rode the Kansas plains chasing cattle thieves and outlaws. She saw him only every two or three weeks, each encounter full of joy and hungry lovemaking.

Now, finally, the danger of his work would be over in two more weeks, and since Anna was six months pregnant, Nate was just as anxious as she for him to find an occupation that would mean a normal family life. Soon he would start campaigning for public office. The new home in Topeka was finished, and life would be better than she ever thought possible just a year ago.

Thoughts of Darryl and the last six years of hell since he first rode off to war were becoming more vague. Anna had begun to allow herself only memories of that first year of marriage, when Darryl was a compassionate young doctor. She refused to dwell on memories of the Darryl she had seen at Centralia, the Darryl who had murdered and raped and plundered. He was gone now, and she had nearly convinced herself that he really did die in the war, for the war had killed him just as surely as if that first bullet had taken his life instead of destroying his mind.

Occasionally she still worried that she should have told Nate in the beginning, but fear and shame had kept her from it; and now that they were married and she was carrying his child, it seemed far too late and unnecessary to dredge up the ugly past. Darryl was dead—killed in the war. That part of her life was over, and she had a whole new life now with a wonderful man.

Moving into their new home had been easy, since Nate insisted Anna do nothing at all. He hired men to haul the things she would bring from Abilene. Anna had ordered most of the furniture from St. Louis, and Nate insisted she do no more than stand and tell the help where to place things. He fussed over her pregnancy like a mother hen, and Anna knew he would be a good father.

In mid-December Claudine came to Topeka to see Anna's new home. Anna's faithful friend had stayed in Abilene to manage the restaurant, and she had rented Anna's house there. She was thrilled about Anna's new life, and the woman had faithfully kept the secret about Darryl. On this visit the past and Darryl Kelley had not even been discussed in Anna and Claudine's private conversations. There was talk only of the new and the baby that would be born in the spring.

When Nate and Anna saw Claudine to the train station, Anna felt as though she were waving good-bye to old, painful memories when she waved to Claudine as the train pulled away. When she first went to Abilene, she had been a lonely, heartbroken woman, building the restaurant as a form of survival, convinced her future held no hope, no joy. Little did Nate understand the reason for Anna's quiet tears as the train clattered off to the west.

Nate put an arm around Anna and led her back to the buggy he had recently purchased. "No more crying now," he told her. "Claudine can come visit anytime she wants, and she'll come and stay with you when the baby is born. You'll see her often enough."

She's the only one who knows the truth, Anna wanted to tell him. *Maybe I should have told you, Nate.* He helped her into the buggy and climbed up beside her. She looked into his gentle gray eyes. *What would you think of me if I told you now?* she wondered. She chided herself then for allowing the past to sneak in and interrupt this new happiness she had found. She wiped at her eyes and put on a smile. "It's just that Claudine was so good to me during those awful years back in Columbia," she said aloud.

Nate smiled and leaned over to kiss her cheek. "Christmas is just a few days away," he told her, "our first one as man and wife, and in our new home. How about I give you one of your presents now?"

She met his eyes. "Now?"

An odd sadness came into his eyes. "Now." He reached inside his sheepskin jacket. When he brought his hand out, it held his marshal's badge. "I'll take you home, then I'm going to the courthouse to turn this in."

Their eyes held. "Nate, I—"

"It's all right. It means a lot to me, but not as much as

you and my family. It's time I put some of it behind me, Anna."

"I just want you to be happy in what you do, Nate. A man has to do what is most important to him."

"Right now, *you* are most important to me." He kissed her again. "Come on, I'll take you home."

He drove her to the house, and as he headed back to the courthouse, he glanced back at his pregnant wife standing on the porch of their new home. Yes, that sight told him he was right in giving up the badge, difficult as that was going to be for him.

He reached the courthouse and climbed down from the buggy, staring at the courthouse for a quiet moment. The memory of the horrible event that had first brought him here to volunteer his services flashed through his mind, bringing back the hatred. He could hear the shouting and the gunshots, the squealing horses and screeching, clucking chickens. He could hear his parents screaming, trapped in the fire, see Christine falling to the ground when she ran from the house and was shot. He had been in the barn, tending an ailing horse. He had fallen asleep there.

He shook his head. Fallen asleep! If he had stayed awake —His fist closed around the badge. Oh, he had got a few of them, five or six, in fact. But much too late to help his sister or his parents. *Forget it, you fool,* he told himself. *It was nine years ago. Think about Anna, the baby.* He walked into the courthouse, meeting Jim Lister at the door. He stopped and shook the man's hand.

"You come to turn that badge in?" Lister asked.

Nate sighed, releasing his grip. "I figure it's about time."

They looked at each other, both of them remembering the time they were holed up against Bill Sharp and his men. Jim understood the secret agony Nate suffered over his sister. "You've had a fairly short career for a marshal, Nate, but a damn good one. At least it's ending on a happy note. You're doing the right thing, friend. Me, I've got nobody depending on me, no woman waiting in my bed at night. But if I had what you have now, I'd give this badge up quick enough."

Nate smiled sadly. "I'm not so sure about that. You love it and you know it."

Jim laughed lightly. "Well, I predict you'll get that lieutenant governor job, Nate, and you'll be better off for it. In this work, a man's got to get out while the gettin's good. And that woman of yours makes it all worth it."

Nate nodded. "Yeah, it does at that."

Lister put a hand on Nate's shoulder and led him into Nate's old office. "It's too bad about your sister, Nate, but you've made up for it, by God. You've done a good job."

Nate walked to his desk, a distant look to his eyes. "I'll never make up for what happened to Christine," he answered. "But I've come to terms with it as best I can. I can't change what happened, Jim. That's the hell of it."

"I know, Nate. I know." He adjusted his hat. "Well, I've got to be riding out."

Nate turned and met his eyes. "You be careful, Jim. And be sure to come see us whenever you're in Topeka."

"I'll do that. Good luck, Nate, and I hope your wife has a fine, healthy baby."

"Thanks."

Nate sighed and looked down at his desk again. It seemed strange to have Jim going out on patrol without him. He took the badge from his pocket again and stared at it a moment before laying it on his desk.

There was little time for settling into the new house. Anna insisted on accompanying Nate to cities along the Kansas-Pacific tracks, where he was invited to speak at various church and school functions, or at political meetings, and meetings of clubs and organizations. Nate decided it was none too soon to toss his hat into the ring for the '68 primaries, since several other Republican hopefuls were also voicing their intentions of running for the same office.

These first few months after retiring his badge would be spent hopping from city to city, and Anna realized her husband was still going to be absent often, but at least this would be for good reason. He would not be in the danger he was in as a marshal, and if his campaign was successful, it would lead to a job that would mean he could be home with her.

In February Nate was to speak in Kansas City to a group of Kansas merchants. Anna, in her eighth month of pregnancy, insisted on going with Nate, realizing this was probably the last time she would be able to accompany him until after the baby was born. The Kansas City merchants provided Nate and Anna with a room at one of the best hotels in the city. Their second-floor room was decorated with lovely furnishings imported from Spain, among them a huge mahogany four-poster bed that drew a gasp of delight from Anna when they entered the room. The floor was thickly carpeted, and the bed was made with satin sheets and quilt, a fringed satin canopy gracing the top of the posts.

After resting, Anna dressed for supper. She walked to a window to look down on a city street while she waited for Nate to get ready.

"Oh, Nate, you're going to make it, I just know it. Anyone who is supported by someone wealthy enough to put us up like this—it must mean you have a lot of powerful people pulling for you."

Nate walked up behind her, moving his arms around her, just under her breasts and above her swollen belly. "It's going to be nothing but the best for you, Mrs. Foster," he told her. "Didn't I tell you that?" He moved one hand over her stomach, holding it there for a moment until he felt the baby move. "And nothing but the best for this kid, too."

She smiled. "Are you sure you don't mind if it's a boy or a girl?"

"Just so it's healthy and strong. How are you feeling?"

"I feel wonderful. I'm fine, Nate."

He sighed deeply. "Well, I don't care if you feel like climbing a mountain. This is our last trip together. After this, you go home and take it easy. You only have a month left. I'm not about to get caught having you go into labor on a train between towns, or land in a town without a suitable doctor."

"Oh, Nate, I hate the thought of being apart again. We've had so little time together."

"Well, we have to quit being so selfish about our love and think about the baby. It will be hard for me, too. I hate being away from you." He nuzzled at her neck. "Any traveling I do after this, I'll check every day to make sure you're all right. And if you go into labor, I'll catch the quickest train back to Topeka."

He kissed her hair and let go of her, walking back to a mirror. "After the baby is born, you'll have plenty to keep you occupied so you won't get so lonely. Then I'll be going into some of the more remote towns, the ones away from the K-P. A man can't win an election without getting out to the rural areas. That's the important vote, and I think I have a good chance there because those are the people who appreciate me the most, the ones most vulnerable to outlaw raids."

He combed his hair and adjusted his tie. "We'd better be ready. That Mr. Wilder will be here any minute to take us downstairs to eat."

"Have you actually met him, as a marshal, I mean?"

"No. But he's good friends with Jim Harvey, whom I *have* met. Harvey stands an excellent chance of winning the governor's office. He's hoping I'll be running alongside him for lieutenant governor." He frowned, turning to face her. "My biggest problem is that I'm not sure I'm educated enough for this job, Anna. I mean, I had all the basic education it's possible to get in this state, but no higher learning. Seems like most men who run for these things are teachers or lawyers or something else that takes extra education—or else they're wealthy. I can't boast about either attribute."

"I'm not so sure I'd call being wealthy an attribute," she answered, walking up to him with a smile. "But I know neither education nor wealth would matter where you're concerned. You're a fine, honest, brave man, Nate Foster, and that is what people admire about you. You have risked your life several times over to rid this state of some of its worst human elements." Again came the stabbing reminder of her own past, so that she had to look away from him for a moment. "You stand for law and order," she continued, "and that is what Kansas needs more than anything else right now." She looked back at him and smiled. "You'll do just fine. You're the best man for the job, and everybody knows it."

He smiled and winked at her. "I do believe you're slightly prejudiced, Mrs. Foster." He looked around at the fancy room. "One thing I want you to know, Anna. This room—I'm accepting it only because I want you to be comfortable. I don't like accepting things like this for free. Makes me feel like a man who's been bought off."

"You could never be bought off. Not Nate Foster."

"Yeah, well, this Wilder is a rich man. As long as he simply supports me just the way I am, I appreciate his help. But I'm not going to change my principles or basic pledges for him or any man. I'm just Nate Foster, Anna, a man with a relatively decent education who believes this state can't grow and get itself unified now without law and order. Whether we sympathized with the Union or the Confederacy, we have to be united now under one law that is the same for everybody. Whoever breaks the law gets punished, no matter what their supposed cause. The war is over."

Her heart tightened. *Yes,* she thought. *It's over.* "I suppose for some it will never be over," she said aloud.

His eyes clouded. "That doesn't give them the right to continue their own war against innocent people."

She broke into a smile. "A fine speech, Mr. Foster. Just keep telling that to the people out there in the streets."

He grinned in return. "Sorry about that. I've been talking about this so much, I guess I forget when to get off the soap box."

There came a knock at the door. Anna quickly took a last look at herself in the mirror, wishing there was some way to look more elegant when pregnant. But no matter how fancy the dress, her belly was still huge, although at least she didn't seem to have gained a lot of weight otherwise. Her face and arms looked the same, but her legs were beginning to swell painfully, especially after long days of travel and standing around with Nate.

She adjusted her velvet and taffeta hat. At least her hair was still pretty, if nothing else was. She wore a chocolate-brown taffeta dress that was drawn tightly under her breasts with velvet ribbon, then hung loosely over her round, pregnant middle. She reached for her handbag as Nate greeted a heavyset, bald man at the door. The man held a cigar in one hand as he shook Nate's hand with the other.

"Henry Wilder," he was saying in a hearty voice. "And I'm proud to finally meet you, Marshal Foster. This is quite an honor. Why, I've heard stories about you that came close to growing the hair right back onto my head." He laughed heartily as Nate grinned and reddened a little.

"I'm glad to meet you too, Mr. Wilder, but I have a feeling the stories you heard were somewhat exaggerated. I would like to thank you for these fine accommodations. This fancy room wasn't necessary."

"Only the best for the man I'm supporting to run with Jim Harvey. I'd like to take you and the wife to supper." The man's gaze moved to Anna, admiring her evident beauty in spite of her present condition. "And you must be the missus."

Nate moved an arm around her as she stepped closer. "Mr. Wilder, this is my wife, Anna."

Anna reached out and shook the man's hand, noticing he wore an expensive suit with a gold watch hanging from the vest pocket.

"A pleasure, indeed," he told her. "So, you're the one who managed to get this man to give up his badge. I'm glad you did. We can use him to help *make* the laws instead of going out there after men who break them. He's done such a good job of that, he's made it easier for the ones who'll come after him."

"I agree, Mr. Wilder," Anna answered with a smile. "And I would much rather have him making the laws, too. He's a man who understands what needs to be done."

"Well, there is plenty more to be done out there in the hills," Nate put in. "It still isn't going to be easy for the ones who wear the badges."

Wilder grinned. "Well, you'll be in a position to help *make* it easier for them, Mr. Foster." The man turned. "Follow me, folks. We're going down to the dining room. I've reserved a table for us."

Anna looked up at Nate and they both smiled, realizing Wilder was a man who loved to try to impress people. Nate just shook his head and took Anna's arm, leading her down the stairs to the elegant dining room, where Wilder pulled out a chair for Anna at a candlelit table. Wilder ordered champagne, but Anna refused, preferring only water in her condition.

"You have a beautiful and elegant wife, Nate. May I call you Nate?" Wilder asked.

"Considering your generosity, I'd be pretty rude to tell you you couldn't."

Wilder laughed. "Well, you just call me Henry." The man sobered then, putting a hand on Nate's arm. "Nate, I can read those eyes. They look very wary. You're wondering if I'm after something, or if I'm going to use my money and power to try to sway you in some way. Well, my man, there is nothing to sway. My counterparts and I like you just the way you are. That's why I have invited you here to speak at the meeting of Kansas merchants tomorrow night."

The man poured some champagne into Nate's glass. Nate looked at Anna and she smiled supportively.

"Nate, what you've done is help protect Kansas merchants, helped keep robbers from attacking our supply wagons, helped keep our money safe in the banks where it is held, helped keep our towns peaceful, which makes for better business."

"I didn't do all that alone, Mr. Wilder—I mean, Henry. I'm just one of many."

"Maybe so. But yours is the name that seemed to make it into the news most often. You're the one who captured some of the worst of them—brought in Bill Sharp and his men, killed Crazy Doc."

Anna felt suddenly light-headed as the man went on about Nate's accomplishments. Crazy Doc! It had been so long since that name was actually spoken aloud. To her, the name seemed to stand out as though Wilder had shouted it.

She suddenly wondered what was she doing here, the wife of a lawman who might end up sitting at the right hand of the governor, carrying his child, putting on this visage of the fine, upstanding woman, when her first husband was the very man Wilder and others considered one of the most notorious outlaws of Kansas!

"There's no proof it was my bullet that killed Crazy Doc," Nate was saying.

Anna's stomach tightened. Why hadn't she told him? Why! Oh, it was much too late now. And Darryl was dead. Dead! She had to remember that. It was over. There was no need to tell him now.

"Nevertheless, you're a hero in the eyes of a lot of Kansans, Nate. Jim Harvey realizes that. You're getting all this royal treatment because Jim is a good friend of mine, and I firmly believe he's going to be the next governor of Kansas. I want the best man he can get at his right hand, and I believe that's you. You understand the law, understand the best and most effective punishment for offenders. Our meeting tomorrow night is to express our support. We've raised a lot of money for your campaign, Nate. And the other merchants also wanted a chance to just plain thank you for some of the things you've done for them, even if it was, as you say, somewhat inadvertent. The fact remains, you've cleaned up Kansas. Oh, there will be other problems. I've heard the James brothers who once rode with Quantrill are causing some trouble now, but as long as men like you have rallied people to vote for law and order, their days are numbered."

Nate sipped his champagne. "Well, when I hear about men like Jesse James, knowing he was at Centralia, remembering what my wife and I both saw there, it makes me want to put that badge right back on. I'm not so sure I can be as effective this way, but I have a family to think about now."

"Centralia!" Wilder looked at Anna, who was feeling weaker by the moment as all the talk of outlaws dredged up memories of Darryl. "You were there, Mrs. Foster?"

Anna swallowed, suddenly feeling sweaty. "Yes. I . . . I met Nate that day. That was when . . . when my first husband was still missing, before I learned he was dead. Nate just happened to be sitting next to me on the train and . . . he helped me when we reached Centralia and realized what was happening." *My husband was there! He was one of the horrible outlaws who killed those soldiers!* She met Nate's eyes. "Nate, would you mind terribly if I went back to our room?"

Nate frowned. "What's wrong, Anna? A moment ago you said you felt fine."

"I . . . I don't know. I'm suddenly very tired. The day caught up with me, I guess."

Nate rose and came around beside her, taking her arm. "It's all this talk about Centralia, isn't it?"

"I don't know . . . partly."

Nate helped her up. "I'm afraid the memory of Centralia still haunts her, Henry. That and the long day—well, do you mind if I take her upstairs? I'll be back down in a few minutes."

Wilder rose. "Of course. I'm awfully sorry, Mrs. Foster. We shouldn't be discussing some of these things in front of you."

Anna gave him a weak smile. "It isn't only that. I think it's just . . . my condition. I assure you, Mr. Wilder, I don't usually grow faint so easily."

Nate kept an arm around her. "I'll agree with that, Henry. She's a strong woman who has been through an awful lot and has done well for herself. It's all this travel. I told her this was the last trip. After tomorrow night she's going back to Topeka and staying in bed until this baby comes."

"Well, I hope she'll be all right. You let me know if she needs a doctor. I'll have the best physician in town sent over."

"Thank you," Nate answered. He led Anna away and up the stairs, keeping such a supportive arm around her so that the climb was easy.

"Nate, I'm sorry I spoiled everything. I don't know what came over me."

"I do. All this traveling is too much. This is it, Anna. I had a feeling I should have ended it sooner." He unlocked the door to their room and led her inside, then helped her undress.

"This is ridiculous. I'm fine, Nate. I can finish myself. You go back down with Mr. Wilder. You shouldn't make him wait."

"The day I put a man like Henry Wilder over my own wife is the day I get out of this rat race." He rummaged through her luggage for her gown, then slipped it over her head. He pulled back the covers on the bed and she sat down on the edge of it. He sat down beside her, putting an arm around her and moving his other hand over her belly. "You aren't . . . I mean, if you thought you were going into labor, you'd tell me, wouldn't you?"

She put a hand over his. "Of course I would." *Oh, Nate, it isn't the baby. How can I tell you?* "I'll be all right, honest. I'm just tired. I'll just rest while you eat with Mr. Wilder. Without me there you can talk about anything you want. Maybe it would be better that way." She sighed deeply, meeting his eyes. "You called this a rat race. Do you hate it, Nate?"

He smiled reassuringly. "No, I don't hate it. I just don't know if I can be as effective as I could be if I was out there with a gun on my hip." He kissed her cheek. "I just need a little more time to get used to all this. When you've spent years on the back of a horse, riding the plains, out there alone searching out the worst elements, well, the way I'm living now is quite a change, that's all." He leaned around her and pulled the covers back more. "You climb under these covers. This hotel has piped steam heat. I'll turn it up before I leave. It was awfully cold when we got off that train today. I don't want you getting sick on me."

She crawled under the satin quilt, luxuriating in its splendid warmth and comfort. Now, here in this lovely bed, with Nate leaning over her, she was able to again push aside the ugly memories that had upset her moments before. She had Nate. That was all that mattered. And she was going to have his baby. Everything would be better after the baby. Nate kissed her lightly.

"I love you. I'll come up every hour to make sure you're still all right. Want me to bring up some food later?"

"Maybe just some soup and a roll or something."

He grinned. "I'm at your service, Mrs. Foster." He sobered then. "Are you *sure* you're all right now?"

"I'm sure." How she loved him! If she lost him, she would want to die! He rose from the bed.

"I'll be back in a little while to check on you. I can send a doctor if you want."

"No. I don't need a doctor. I think I just need to sleep."

"If you say so." He watched her a moment longer, then left reluctantly. She watched the door close, and then the tears came. Darryl! Why had he done this to her? Even in death he had a way of coming back to haunt her, and for the first time in months she could see his face vividly again as it was that day at Centralia, hear him screaming the words "Go to hell!"

Nate put a temporary halt to his campaigning the end of March and came home to Topeka, worried that when Anna went into labor he would be too far away to arrive in time for the baby's birth. It was late in the night that the pains came, first in a dream. Anna could see Darryl's face. He was laughing again. He pointed a gun at her and pulled the trigger. A bullet ripped through her belly, bringing a searing pain that made her gasp and wake up. She sat up slightly, panting.

"Anna?" Nate sat up, lighting a lamp. "Anna, what is it?"

She stared at him a moment, reminding herself it was Nate, not Darryl. "I . . . had a nightmare." The pain came again, and she doubled over. "Nate, the baby . . ."

Nate quickly rose and dressed. "Just stay right there in bed, honey. I'll go get Marie and send her over and I'll go rouse the doctor." He buttoned his pants and only half buttoned his shirt. He pulled on some boots over bare feet, then leaned over her and tucked the blankets around her. "You'll be all right, Anna. I'll be right back." He rushed out without even grabbing a jacket.

Anna lay in black pain, suddenly wondering why she had wanted a baby. She was afraid of letting it be born, realizing that birthing it would have to be even more painful than the pains she was already having; and suddenly desperately afraid perhaps the baby would be deformed, as some kind of punishment for not telling Nate the truth about Darryl.

She curled up in the bed, reminding herself this was Nate's baby. Nate was a good, loving family man. God would never mete out her punishment on a man like Nate. He wouldn't give Nate a dead or deformed child. No, the punishment had to come directly on her. The pain seemed only to accentuate fears that for months she had been able to keep buried.

Although it was only minutes, it seemed hours before Marie finally came into the room. She heard Nate's voice again, felt his big hand on her forehead, heard him telling her he was going for the doctor.

The rest of the night was like a strange dream, a mixture of reality and her own past fears. Sometimes she could hear Darryl laughing, but then she would open her eyes and see Nate standing over her.

"You really shouldn't be in here," she heard the doctor saying.

"I have a right to be here. I want to be with her," she heard Nate answer.

Pain ripped through her like witches' claws, and Anna could not help the screams it brought. Sometimes it actually felt good to scream, not just because of the pain, but as a way of purging her emotional agony. How many times had she wanted to just scream and scream until her voice was gone?

For hours the clawing pain continued, until she felt the anxiety in Nate's voice when he asked the doctor if everything was all right.

"Everything is fine," the doctor answered. "The first one is often the hardest, and she's fighting it. She's got to relax and let it come."

The pain started coming again, a deeper, grabbing pain that made her stiffen as muscles contracted. Nate was amazed at the strength he felt as she grabbed onto him and gritted her teeth when the doctor told her to push. Nate urged her to cooperate, coaching her through the pain.

"That's better, Anna," the doctor said. "Help it along and we'll get this over with."

For several more minutes the pain tore at her, but she hung on to Nate's hand. Nate. What would she do without him? This was for him. She could do it for Nate. Suddenly she felt a tremendous relief, and a moment later she heard a kind of squeal, then a hardy bawling.

"It's a girl," someone said.

Anna thought she heard Nate laughing, and then she felt

him kissing her damp cheek. "We've got a little girl, Anna. She's beautiful!" The room seemed full of voices then. She heard Marie say something about cleaning up the baby, and she felt the doctor pushing at her stomach. She cried out with pain. "We've got to make sure we get out the after-birth," the doctor was telling her. "Don't worry. I'll be done shortly and I'll leave you alone for a while. Everything seems fine, Anna. Marie will bring the baby back in soon and you can see her." She felt him washing and packing her, and moments later Nate was back in the room, washing her face and helping the doctor put a clean gown on her. Nate covered her and leaned over her, stroking the hair back from her face.

"She's beautiful, Anna."

Anna opened her eyes to see him grinning from ear to ear, his eyes watery. "Are you happy . . . with a girl?" she asked.

"You know I am. Besides, there will be more, but not for a long time. I know you're the one who suffered the pain, but I'm not sure *I* can go through this again."

Anna was amazed to realize that already she was thinking the pain wasn't all that terrible. Marie had told her once that most women swore with each baby that it would be the last, but that the pain was quickly forgotten, and the joy of the child made her want more.

"We'll have more," she told Nate with a wry smile. "I hate to think of . . . the alternative if we choose . . . not to."

He frowned, then realized what she meant. He laughed lightly then. "Come to think of it, so do I." He leaned down and kissed her lips lightly. "Thank you, Anna."

"Just . . . promise me you'll never leave me."

The frown returned as he petted her hair. "Now why in hell would I ever do that?"

Her eyes teared. "I don't know. I guess . . . I'm just not thinking straight right now. You'd better wire Claudine. She'll want to . . . come stay with me a few days. It's too much for Marie. She needs to watch after Christine."

"I'll do it as soon as the telegraph office opens."

"Nate."

He kissed her cheek. "What is it?"

"Don't go back out campaigning right away. You'll . . . stay a week or two, won't you?"

"I told you I would. You know I'd never let anything about this campaign get in the way of you and my new daughter."

She grasped his wrist and held it tightly. "I need you, Nate. I love you so much."

He attributed the strange fear in her eyes to the ordeal she had just been through. Rob had told him once how women get strange ideas and fears when they were pregnant. Marie brought the baby in and handed her to Nate, who held her awkwardly. She was not even as long as his whole forearm, and her tiny head fit in the palm of his hand.

"My God, Anna, she's so little." He leaned down and laid the baby beside her. Anna managed to turn on her side a little so she could see her. She opened the blanket around the baby and studied her. Perfect—all fingers and toes in place. Her red face was wrinkled up in irritation at being uncovered, and she opened her mouth then and began to squawl.

"Do you think she already . . . wants to eat?" Anna asked, her voice weak.

"That seems to be the first instinct they have," Marie told her. She moved around Nate and propped an extra pillow under Anna's head, then opened her gown for her and helped her position herself to feed her new little girl. "There is a technique to this, but your natural motherly instincts will help you learn quickly enough."

The baby found its mark and was instantly quiet. Marie smiled, turning and putting a hand on Nate's shoulder before leaving the room. Nate watched the baby feed at Anna's breast, and she smiled. "She *is* pretty, isn't she?" she said to Nate.

"She'll be as pretty as her mother."

"She'd be pretty enough if she took after you."

"You saying I'm *pretty?*"

She smiled more. "You know what I mean."

He laughed lightly, but she caught the tears in his eyes. "Well, you've topped the day you said you'd marry me, and the day you told me you were pregnant," he said then. "I thought those were the happiest days of my life. Now it's today, March fifteenth, 1868. You never cease to give me cause for celebration, Anna Foster."

She bent down and kissed her baby's fuzzy head. "The next celebration will come when you win the primaries next August and the final election next November." She met his eyes. "And you *will* win."

He leaned closer, kissing her cheek. "I've already won everything I want in life," he answered. "What do you think we should call her?"

Anna sighed, watching her baby nurse, glorying in the wonderful satisfaction of being a mother. "I was thinking maybe Rebecca, after your mother." She looked at him and saw a mixture of love and pain in his eyes.

"That's a wonderful idea, Anna, and very thoughtful of you. I'd like that just fine. The whole family will."

She smiled. "Then that is what she will be called—Rebecca Joline, after your mother and my sister. I'll have to write Jo as soon as I'm able."

Nate touched her hair, wondering if any man could be as happy as he was at this moment. He looked down at his little girl, vowing her future would be safe from the kind of men who had destroyed Christine's life.

Chapter 18

Anna received almost daily wires from Nate, as he campaigned heavily in remote Kansas towns she had never even heard of. In the newspaper she read about her husband, and his campaign promises to keep Kansas free of men like Bill Sharp and Crazy Doc. Every time she read her first husband's nickname, she shivered and immediately went to pick up Rebecca, holding her close. The baby had become a kind of comfort to her, a very real thing that she could cling to when Nate wasn't there, something that was a part of her and Nate that no one could take away from her, and no haunting memories could destroy.

Little Becky was nearly two months old when Nate came home again at the end of May. Anna waited with the baby at the train station, and her heart raced with joy when Nate disembarked the train and walked to the wagon where Anna and the baby sat with Rob.

Nate was all smiles. Anna handed Becky to Rob and climbed down from the wagon. She was quickly swept up in Nate's arms, where she felt safe and protected. Here, in these arms, all bad memories vanished.

"My God, I missed you," Nate said softly.

"Not as much as I missed you."

"I don't believe that. At least you were home with Becky instead of in a different hotel or boarding house every night."

"Just so you were alone," she teased.

"After being with you, why would I have any desire to be with anybody else?"

"Well, I know how attractive you look to other women."

He grinned, leaning down and kissing her mouth while a few people watched and Anna reddened. He brushed his lips over her hair. "None can hold a candle to you. You in condition to make up for lost time?" he asked quietly in her ear.

"I think so."

They turned and he walked her to the wagon. "What are you holding there, brother?"

"A pretty little girl your wife handed over to me."

Nate threw his baggage into the back of the wagon and helped Anna climb up, then got up into the seat beside her. "Hand her over," he told his brother, reaching out for Becky. He took her into his arms. "She's heavier," he exclaimed.

"She's two months old," Anna reminded him. "The last time you held her she was only one month."

Nate frowned, kissing his daughter's cheek. "Now I *know* I don't like this campaigning. I'm missing my daughter growing up."

"Well, in a few more months you'll be staying in Topeka permanently and the traveling will be over," Rob told him. "Just remember that what you're doing is for her own good."

Rob drove them to the house and Nate kept hold of Rebecca while Rob carried in his baggage for him. "I'll be over later to see Christine and the family," Nate told him. "How is Christine?"

"Oh, she's been a little better lately, got a little feeling back in her arms. But the doctor says it's just temporary. Her prognosis hasn't really changed, Nate."

An expression of pain returned to Nate's eyes. He nodded

and went inside with Becky in his arms. Anna brought in his two large carpetbags, and Nate immediately chastised her for picking them up.

"I'm not an invalid, Mr. Foster," she chided. "I'm fine now and perfectly capable of picking up a couple of bags."

She turned, and old desires swept through them both as he looked her over, noticing she was hardly changed from the Anna he had married. He smiled softly. "Maybe you should lock the door," he told her, his eyes beginning to sparkle.

Anna felt a rush of passion at the words. She bolted the door and took his arm. They walked into the bedroom, where Nate sat down on the bed and began talking baby talk to Becky, exclaiming over her pretty smile.

"Now that she's bigger, I can really see the resemblance, Anna. What a lucky little girl. She's going to look just like her mommy." He kissed her and held her close. "God, I missed her, Anna. I hate being away from her."

"I know. How long can you stay this time?"

"I intend to stay a good two weeks. I've talked Henry Wilder into arranging my travels so that I can come home for a couple of days every two weeks, at least until around July, just before the primaries."

"Oh, I'm glad, Nate." She sat down beside him.

"How are things here?"

"Everything is fine. And Claudine is sending money regularly. I'm so happy with the way things are working out with the restaurant. She must be getting awfully busy about now. I really should go there for a couple of days. Maybe we could both go."

"Fine with me, but not for a few days yet. I want some time alone with you." He frowned. "I still think you'd be better off selling it. I don't like you having the headache of worrying about that place. You've got Becky now, and this house to take care of and all."

"I'm managing just fine. And once you're more settled here in Topeka, we can both take a weekend a month to go to Abilene." She took the baby from him and laid her in a cradle.

How could she explain to Nate the reason she couldn't

bring herself to let go of the restaurant? She couldn't even explain it herself. Somewhere, deep inside, she feared she might need the business again. She still had not quite been able to shake the distant, haunting notion that she could end up alone again, that all this joy and happiness she had found would be taken from her, that somehow her past would catch up with her and destroy this new life.

"Besides," she said aloud, "for now we still need the income. We'll worry about the restaurant after you become lieutenant governor."

"Well, I'll be glad when all this is over. I don't like having to use that money. I'm not a man to live off his wife. It eats at me."

She sighed and rose, turning to face him. "Nate Foster, I am your wife, which means that money belongs to *both* of us. Besides, it's not as though I'm slaving away there while you're out campaigning. I'm living very comfortably right here, and I'm so proud of what you're doing. Everybody understands this is all just temporary—and *necessary.*" She came back to sit down beside him, reaching up to touch his face. "I am perfectly aware of the kind of man you are, more man than most women are lucky enough to have protecting them, or to have in their beds at night. I love you, Nate Foster. I love everything about you, and I love what you're doing. If I can help by keeping the restaurant, what difference does it make? We're together and safe, and life is going to be good."

"You're a hell of a woman, Anna. I've missed you," he said softly. He leaned over and kissed her hungrily. He laid her back on the bed, removing his hat and tossing it aside.

He covered her mouth in a sweet, passionate kiss, the kind of kiss he had not given her since a month before the baby was born, the kind that told her he was a man wanting his woman. It felt wonderful being in his arms this way again.

He raised up on one elbow, putting a hand to the side of her face. "I suppose we should save this for later," he told her.

"I suppose," she answered. "You'll get me all messed up and I'll have to fix my hair all over again before we go over to your brother's. Besides, he'll rib us to death if we take too long."

Nate grinned. "He'd rib us no matter what we did. It doesn't take you that long to fix your hair, does it?"

She laughed lightly. "No." Their eyes held reawakened passion. "I love you so much, Nate. It's so good to have you back."

"Well, at least now when I go away you know it isn't to something dangerous." He began unbuttoning her dress, and she ran her fingers through his hair.

"A handsome man like you, such a heroic figure—I'll bet young women are always batting their eyes at you. Some probably make it pretty evident that they're available."

He grinned. "Oh, there have been a few offers."

"Nate!" She pouted slightly, and he laughed.

"You said it, I didn't. It doesn't matter anyway. There isn't a woman in Kansas who can hold a candle to you. You're my whole world, Anna Foster, you and that little girl in the cradle over there."

He opened her dress, then unlaced her camisole. She reddened a little, afraid he would be offended by the damp gauze she kept inside her camisole because of her milky breasts. But he only kissed at the fullness of her breasts, lightly tasting his daughter's nourishment. A rush of manly urges surged through him then, and he groaned with the desire for her. He moved his mouth to cover hers again, and he gently removed the rest of her clothing.

It felt wonderful to have her old figure back, to have him look at her with the old need in the gray eyes she loved. He sat up, and she helped him undress, opening his shirt and leaning forward to kiss at the hairs of his broad chest. He finished undressing and they moved under the covers. There was nothing to be said. They both had a long-neglected need.

She closed her eyes as his hand moved over her, massaging, feeling every part of her almost as though it were the first time he touched her this way. To Nate she was even more enticing, now that her body was just slightly fuller, her breasts big with milk, milk to feed his pretty daughter.

He met her mouth again, kissing her almost savagely. She

returned the kiss with as much eagerness, each of them sensing that the other did not need to wait for any more foreplay. All Nate wanted was to be inside her, and all she wanted was to take him, to please him and take pleasure in his grand manliness. Her fingers dug into his arms at the first thrust, which brought slight pain. But in moments his gentle, rhythmic movement brought back all the passion and ecstasy she had learned to expect from this man who had become her whole world.

She met him in perfect rhythm then, arching up to him, feeling wanton and daring. He seemed to have a way of bringing out her deepest needs and satisfying every womanly desire. "Anna," he groaned, his face buried in her hair, his hands grasping her bottom. "God, it feels good."

She breathed deeply, overjoyed that having the baby did not seem to have detracted from her ability to give him pleasure this way. Oh, how she loved him. How sweet life had become.

She felt his life spill into her then, hoping the old wives' tale that a nursing woman seldom could get pregnant was true. She wanted more children, but not quite yet. At the moment it didn't matter. All that mattered was sharing Nate Foster's body again and pleasing her husband.

"Welcome home, Mr. Foster," she told him as he sighed and moved to lie beside her.

"Good to be here, Mrs. Foster." He stretched and kissed her lightly, then got up and rummaged through his bags for a clean pair of long johns. He walked into a small, closed-off room at the corner of the bedroom, where they kept a chamber pot and a wash bowl. "You rest and stay here till Becky's next feeding," he told her. "I'll wash and go see Christine. I'll be back in a little while. We'll eat with Rob and the family tonight."

She rolled to her side, pulling the covers over herself and feeling pleasantly satisfied. "And then?" she asked.

He peeked around the doorway at her. "And then later tonight we'll pick up where we left off here."

She smiled and snuggled into a pillow. "How did everything go, Nate?"

"Great. It looks like a sure thing, Anna. People like what

I'm telling them about keeping outlaws out of Kansas. And I think they realize I'm not just making empty promises. I've already proven my dedication to that cause. Trouble is, I think the James gang and others are going to put us to the test. I doubt they like hearing my promises. If they try too hard to test me out, I just might have to get on a horse and help the lawmen in person, show them that just because Nate Foster has been elected to a fancy office doesn't mean he's forgotten how to roust out the no-goods with his own hands."

Her heart tightened. "Nate, you wouldn't really do that, would you?"

He laughed lightly. "I doubt it. That's just the old lawman in me talking. Don't worry your pretty head about it. You just worry about taking care of Becky."

She breathed a sigh of relief, but she knew he was still a lawman at heart, and it worried her. It always bothered him most when he saw Christine again. She thanked God for Becky. The baby would keep him from strapping on a gun. He came out then, wearing the long johns. She studied his god-like build and sighed.

"It's strange, isn't it, how things work out," she said. "That first day I saw you in the telegraph office at Columbia five years ago, I never dreamed we'd end up like this, husband and wife, with a little baby. It's kind of scary realizing we have no idea what life holds in store for us."

He came and leaned over her. "Only good things from now on, Anna. *That's* what life holds for us. Now you rest." He pulled on a pair of denim pants and a plain cotton shirt. "Sure feels good to get out of a suit," he commented. He ran a belt through his pants and buckled it, then ran his hands over the sides of his thighs, as though he seemed to be missing something. He glanced at her and grinned. "I still feel naked without a gun."

"You did what you could, Nate. Now you can do more good sitting in an office in the courthouse."

He smiled almost sadly. "I suppose." He turned and walked out. Anna curled into the blankets, content that he was sincere about leaving his gun behind him for good. She closed her eyes, thinking how sweet it was being able to make love again. She could rest easier now. Nate was home again.

It was late July 1868 when the train rolled into the depot at Lawrence. Elections were coming soon. Fran watched as the handsome former marshal Nate Foster waved to people from the platform of the passenger car. A band started playing, and children raised a banner that read Harvey & Foster, and other banners were raised, some reading Nate Foster for Law and Order; others, Foster for Lieutenant Governor.

Fran smiled. *A dead man can't hold any office,* she thought. No one in Lawrence knew her. It had been easy to come into town and buy a newspaper. Darryl needed to find out where Nate Foster would be so that he could finally get his revenge. It was time now. He had shot Foster down once. He would do it again, only this time the man would not get up.

Darryl and his men had robbed four banks in Texas and a dry-goods store in Arkansas, where they had raked in supplies and new clothes. They had a good hideaway in Indian Territory, where the nine men Darryl had gathered waited for them. She and Darryl had come to Kansas, cleaned up and dressed out like a decent married couple, Darryl careful to keep a hat on his head so his scar wouldn't show. They stayed in a tiny cabin, deep in a thick grove of woods along the Arkansas River, a spot removed from civilization, where they would go and hole up temporarily until the turmoil over Nate Foster's shooting had died down. Then they would join the men in Indian Territory, where they would plan their next robbery, either a train or a bank. But it would take place in Kansas. Darryl Kelley intended to show the world that Kansas was not free of raiding outlaws after all. And after today, there would be no Nate Foster to come after them.

Fran watched the ex-marshal with a feeling of imminent victory, a near sneer on her face. *The high and mighty Nate Foster,* she thought. *You'll get your due, Yankee. And then Crazy Doc will tear Kansas apart. These people will find out no one man can put an end to men like Darryl. The cause still lives, whether you know it or not.*

She had learned through a newspaper that Nate Foster would be in Lawrence to deliver a campaign speech. She and Darryl had decided this was perfect timing and the perfect place, since before the war Darryl had been run out of Lawrence by jayhawkers. He would teach them all a lesson.

She watched then as a beautiful woman emerged from the passenger car, carrying a baby on one arm. The woman smiled and waved to the people, and Fran's smile faded as she watched the woman in near shock.

She moved a little closer. She had to be sure! She was careful not to let herself be seen as she kept her eyes on the woman, who was apparently Nate Foster's wife. He took her arm and helped her down the steps of the passenger car. They walked through the crowd as the band continued to play patriotic songs. The Fosters passed by very close to Fran, close enough for Fran to get a closer look at the woman, who did not notice her.

"Anna!" Fran whispered the word in disbelief. There was no doubt in her mind who it was. Anna Kelley was *married* to Nate Foster! She had had a baby by him! Fran's heart beat with glorious delight. She considered how devastating it would be to Anna to know her first husband was still alive, and the very kind of man her second husband had vowed to crush! And with Darryl still alive, the haughty Anna Kelley was living in sin, a bigamist, her baby illegitimate!

She followed the crowd. This was going to be more enjoyable than she had thought. Not only was Darryl waiting on a rooftop to end Nate Foster's life, but Fran would get to watch the look on Anna's face when she lost a second husband to death. Yes, she thought Darryl was dead. What a wonderful trick she had played on the traitorous Anna Kelley!

All along the way she contemplated the various ways she could use what she knew. Should she tell Darryl? Perhaps not. She had always been jealous of Anna. Darryl might try to take her off with him if he knew she was right here in Kansas. No. She wouldn't tell Darryl, not now anyway. It was Anna who had to suffer, and she would suffer plenty when she watched her new high-and-mighty husband die before her eyes. Later, when the law figured out who had shot Nate Foster, Anna would realize Foster was never legally her husband. She would know Darryl Kelley still lived and that she was right back in the living hell she thought she had left behind.

She wondered if Anna had ever told Foster about Darryl. Surely not! A man like Foster wouldn't marry the wife of an outlaw, even if he believed Darryl to be dead. She wasn't sure which would be more delightful, to have Foster killed, or to have him find out his beautiful wife had once been married to an outlaw who was still alive.

There had to be a way to use this knowledge, but not yet. She would save it for a time when Darryl was threatening to leave her, which he had done more often lately. She had to keep him convinced that he needed her, for she needed him desperately, and, after all, Darryl didn't really know how to take care of himself without her. The knowledge that Anna was Nate Foster's wife might be something she could use later to again convince Darryl to keep her with him.

Besides, it was too late now to change their plans. Darryl was already primed and waiting for his prey. She wondered if he would recognize Anna from his perch and prayed he would not. Anna wore a wide-brimmed hat to protect her lovely skin from the sun. Darryl would not be able to see her face under the brim from where he would be positioned. And his mind had grown so much worse, maybe he wouldn't even recognize her anymore. She threw her head back and laughed. What a wonderful day this was going to be!

The crowd proceeded to a platform in the center of town decorated in red, white, and blue banners. Nate Foster stopped and kissed his wife's cheek, and a couple of well-dressed women led her to a hotel. Fran watched, glad Anna would be out of Darryl's sight. She supposed she was going to find a private place to feed her baby—her *illegitimate* baby. It didn't matter. She would still hear the gunshot. She would know. She watched Anna disappear into the hotel, while the rest of the crowd paraded Nate to the platform, where he took his place behind a podium, continuing to smile and wave as the band played and crowds cheered.

Fran looked up and saw Darryl peek over the false front of a store across the street. There would be so much bedlam after the shooting that Darryl would easily be able to mix into the crowd and casually walk away afterward.

Anna followed her two escorts into the hotel, where she was taken to a lovely room that would be hers and Nate's for the night. She thanked the women, who left her alone to feed Rebecca.

Anna closed the door. A baby's feeding could not wait for its father's speech. She walked over and opened a window so she could hear the crowd below and hear Nate's speech. She pulled a chair over to the window and sat down, opening her dress and putting a fussing four-month-old Rebecca to her breast. This was her first trip with Nate since the baby was born.

The baby sucked contentedly, pinching at her breast with tiny fingers. From the window Anna could see Nate in the street below. He was holding up his hands to quiet the people more so he could give his speech. He opened with the words that brought cheers wherever he went.

"Ladies and gentlemen, it's time to let those who want to break the law know that their outlaw ways will not be tolerated by the citizens of Kansas! It is time to move forward, time to stop looking back and feeding on old rivalries. It is time to look to the future, and to show Washington that Kansas is a state of civilized people—a state that emphasizes education, organized and well-planned cities, a state where our children can get a good education, and where our farmers and settlers in outlying regions no longer have to fear for their lives, their crops, and their possessions—and where law and order will be the *first* order of business!"

The cheers came then, banners waving. The crowd was so loud that at first no one realized the popping sound they heard had been a shot. No one noticed the sudden glint of the sun on a rifle barrel. Even when Nate's body suddenly lurched backward, landing against the men who stood behind him, it took people a moment to realize the awful truth of what had just happened. It even took Anna a moment to understand, but within seconds the nightmare became horribly real.

People watched in stunned confusion, then women began screaming and running for shelter with their children, fearing more gunfire. Anna stared in disbelief as men began hovering over Nate, and someone yelled the dreaded words "Get a doctor!"

"Nate," she whispered. "No," she said louder then. "My God!"

She pulled Becky from her breast and quickly closed her dress, holding the baby close as she ran to the door and down the stairs. Becky began crying at being suddenly deprived of her meal.

Two men stopped Anna as soon as she got outside. "Stay here, Mrs. Foster," one of them told her.

"Nate! What's happened to Nate!" Anna did not notice a dark-haired woman who stood not far away listening. The woman grinned, walking away to join her "husband," who emerged from an alley wearing a fine suit. They walked arm in arm in the direction of the train depot. A man came running toward them.

"What's happened?" he asked.

"I don't know," Darryl answered him. "There's been some kind of shooting, I think. I didn't want my wife around there. Too dangerous."

The man went running off, passing people running the other way in fright. He pushed his way through the crowd to see Nate Foster lying on the speaker's platform, his chest a mass of blood, his wife bent over him sobbing, while her baby squawled in her arms.

Darryl and Fran headed toward waiting horses near the depot. Darryl suddenly pulled her into an alley, laughing like the crazy man that he was. "I did it, Fran! I did it!"

She smiled, embracing him. "Yes, you did. Just don't say it too loudly for now. Let's get out of here, Doc." She led him away, her heart soaring with glee at the memory of the look on Anna's face. Revenge was indeed very sweet.

Claudine walked quietly into the ward where Nate lay looking gray as death. Anna sat in a chair next to the bed, looking little better than Nate, her eyes puffy and outlined with dark circles. Becky was sleeping in her arms. She looked up to see Claudine, and the woman's heart went out to the stricken Anna. She had been through so much, and now this. Claudine knew what it could do to Anna if she lost Nate, and it seemed very likely that she would. "Claudine," Anna said in a pitifully thin voice.

The woman hurried to her side as Anna reached out with one arm. Claudine knelt in front of the chair and embraced her. *"Quelle pitié! Rien ne peut adoucir ta peine!"* She kissed Anna's cheek and the baby's. "I came as quickly as I could. The news must have been wired all over Kansas right away. We got the message in Abilene yesterday just a few hours after it happened. Let me hold the baby."

Anna pulled Becky closer. "No. I . . . I need to hold her, Claudine." Her voice was ragged, and terror was evident in her eyes. Claudine frowned and took her hand. "You have been sitting here for hours, I suppose."

Anna turned to look at Nate. "The bullet is still in him. The doctor said . . . the bullet hit him at an angle, tore through a lot of organs and lodged near his spine. The doctor here is afraid to operate. He's afraid he'd . . . kill him, or paralyze him." She looked at Claudine. "Wouldn't it be ironic if he ended up like his sister? Wouldn't it be cruel and ironic?" Her voice was beginning to shake. Claudine grasped her shoulders.

"It will not happen, Anna. You must believe."

"Somehow, deep inside . . . I knew something like this would happen." Her breathing came faster as the panic began to build again. "Everything . . . was too wonderful. I'm not supposed to be that happy."

"Of *course* you deserve to be happy, and you *will* be. Nate is a strong man. He will not die and he will not be paralyzed."

"It's my fault." Anna squeezed her eyes shut, and tears slipped down her cheeks, following the stained pathways of tears that had come before.

"Your fault! *Allons donc!* Why are you always blaming yourself for things over which you have no control!"

"I made him . . . turn in his badge, give up his gun. I

never thought about . . . all the men out there who . . . might hold a grudge against a man like Nate, the men who wouldn't want a man like Nate in an important position. If he had still been carrying a gun . . . he wouldn't have been as vulnerable. Men were afraid of him then. But when he turned in his badge and gun, he was a natural target for every remaining outlaw and raider in Kansas."

"Anna, he gave those things up willingly, on his own, for you and Becky. He is his own man. If he truly did not want to give them up, he would not have done it."

"How could God . . . let this happen to him! I don't understand!" Anna held Becky close to her breast and rocked in the chair, breathing deeply to keep from screaming, afraid to let the tears come too willingly, afraid that once she let go completely she would lose control and be no use to Becky or to Nate. "His . . . parents, Christine, now Nate. After all he did to stop men like that . . . it's so unfair, so unfair!"

Claudine heard someone closing the curtains around Nate's bed. She turned to see his brother Rob, whose face was as pale and stricken as Anna's. She rose and turned to him, putting a hand on his arm. "The last time I saw you was when I was in Topeka to stay with Anna and the baby. Everyone was so happy then. *Je suis désolée,* Monsieur Foster. It is such a terrible thing. I do not know what to do for Anna."

Rob looked over at Nate. "No one does." He sighed deeply. "Thank you for coming. It will be good for Anna to have you here."

"What will happen, monsieur? Anna says he still carries the bullet."

Rob nodded, leaving her and going to stand on the other side of the bed, touching Nate's arm. "There's a doctor coming from St. Louis tomorrow. He's the best around. He's going to try to take out the bullet. After that, as soon as he says Nate can be moved, we're taking him home." He shook his head. "I thought after our folks and Christine, this kind of horror was over for our family. But a man like Nate makes a lot of enemies."

Claudine walked up to the other side of the bed, reaching

out and touching Nate's forehead. She looked over at Rob. "He will live, and he will recover. I know this in my heart. He will do it for Anna, and for his daughter." She turned and looked at Anna. "Do you hear me, Anna? Somewhere deep in his mind and heart he knows, he remembers. He knows he must get better so he can take care of you and Becky. He wants to watch his daughter grow up, be a father to her. He wants many more children. It is your love that will get him through this, Anna, and you must be strong now, stronger than you have ever been through all the other things you have suffered. Nate Foster is a big, healthy man and a fighter. Do you think he would let the kind of man who shot him get away with this? Not Nate Foster. He would not allow such a thing. He will live and he will be responsible for finding and catching whoever did this to him. And he has many lawmen friends who will help."

The woman bent down and took the baby from Anna's arms before Anna realized what she was doing. Anna looked up at her in surprise. "Have you eaten or slept since this happened?" Claudine asked her.

Anna moved her eyes to look at Nate. "No."

"Then you will go and do both, right now. If you get sick, who will there be to feed Nate Foster's baby girl? Who will there be to stand beside him and encourage him? He needs you, Anna, and you will be no good to him if you collapse from lack of rest and food. You come with me now. We will get something to eat, whether you feel like eating or not, and you will go to your hotel and you will rest."

Anna looked over at Rob. "Do it, Anna. Do it for Nate," Rob said. "I'll be right here. If there's any change, or if he wakes up and calls for you, I'll let you know right away. You get some rest, and when you come back, I'll do the same."

Anna sighed in resignation, slowly rising on legs that were shaky and weak. She leaned over Nate and lightly kissed him on the cheek. She caressed his hair gently, touched his cheek with the back of her hand. Just two nights ago he had made love to her, so vital and strong. Would those arms ever hold her again? Would his lips ever touch her own? Would she know the joy of being with him that way, hear his teasing remarks, ever again share the kind of joy they had known in the fourteen months they had been married?

"I love you, Nate," she said softly. "And Becky needs her papa. You've got to come through this, Nate, for us, for Christine. It would break Christine's heart if you didn't stand up tall and strong again. And *I* need your strength and your love." She kissed him once more, realizing Claudine was right. She had to be strong for him. She just wasn't sure where that strength would come from.

Chapter 19

Anna sat with Claudine in the waiting room of the small hospital, which had only two wards in each wing, each of which held ten patients. There was one operating room. Anna wondered if Nate's chances would be any better if he were in a bigger hospital, perhaps in St. Louis or Chicago. But moving him that far would have been too much of a risk. At least the doctor who had come from St. Louis to operate on him was one of the best.

Nate's horrible groans of pain when he was moved onto a stretcher to take him to the operating room still haunted Anna. She realized that even in his unconscious state, the pain must still be excruciating to cause such pitiful groans.

How she wished she could kill whoever did this to him! Now she understood the bitterness and determination Nate himself had carried after Christine was hurt, the hatred that had made him put on a badge. And she worried about what he would do if he survived this. A man like Nate would not let this go.

Being lieutenant governor would not be enough for him now; and that was a post he had already lost. He was in no condition to run for the office now. And with no guarantee he would ever be healthy enough for such a thing, there was no sense keeping his name on the ballot. Their dreams of a peaceful life in Topeka with Nate behind a desk were finished.

She had bathed the night before and managed to get a little sleep. When she realized how much support there was for Nate, she had gathered more strength. When she reached her hotel room, it was filled with flowers and notes from well-wishers. The hotel owner had told her a special service was being held this morning at which the townspeople would be praying while the doctor operated on Nate. Henry Wilder, who had sent for the specialist from St. Louis, had met the doctor in Kansas City and had come to Lawrence with him. Wilder had offered to help Anna and Nate both in any way he could. He had gone to the church service to pray.

Outside, people who had not gone to the church milled about quietly in the street, waiting to hear any news.

"They don't want too many people inside," Anna heard a nurse telling someone at the door then.

"I'm a Deputy U.S. Marshal and one of Nate's best friends," came the reply. Anna recognized Jim Lister's voice. She quickly rose and went to the door.

"Please let him in," she told the nurse.

The woman stepped aside, and Jim walked in. The pain in his eyes told Anna what devastating news this had been for him. He quietly closed the door and took her arm as he led her back to her chair and sat down beside her.

He rested his elbows on his knees and sighed, turning to meet her eyes then. His face was pale, his blue eyes showing their sorrow and concern.

"I don't know quite what to say, Anna," he told her. "It just doesn't seem like enough to say how sorry I am—" His voice broke and he looked away.

"I understand, Jim," she answered.

Anna had met the tall, hard-toned Lister numerous times now. He had come to visit Nate often. They were good friends; they had come close to dying together when they went after the Sharp gang.

Lister removed his hat, revealing a balding head. "I came soon as I heard. And you can bet I'm gonna try to find out who did this. I'll bring him in if it's the last thing I do."

Anna nodded. "I know you will. I just hope Nate's alive to know about it."

He put a hand on her arm. "He'll be alive, all right. If I know Nate, he'll want to ride *with* me. Between his love for you and that baby, and a burning desire he's gonna have to find out who did this, he'll make it just fine."

She met his eyes again. They were narrow and piercing, but showed only love and concern at the moment. Lister was a hard man, with a sharply defined face, a thin, prominent nose, and a blond mustache. It was obvious he was a good man inside, but a man who would be hard to deal with if a person was on the wrong side of the law. Anna could not think of a better man to be riding at Nate's side on a dangerous mission.

"Was I wrong, Jim, to want Nate to give up his badge?"

He sighed and shook his head. "No, ma'am. Nate did that on his own. But you'd best understand that when he comes out of this, he's gonna want to put that badge and that gun back on."

She pressed Becky closer. "I've already thought of that."

"It's in his blood, Anna. And what's happened, it's just gonna bring it all back for him. He wanted real bad to make this other thing work, to do something that would mean he was safe for you and Becky. But you can see now that just taking off a badge doesn't mean he's out of danger. A man like Nate makes a lot of enemies. In a way, he might be better off wearing that badge and gun. Men know how dangerous he is that way, and Nate himself is just naturally more alert. I guess the last few months, he's just been so happy and contented, he kind of forgot about the enemies he's got left out there. We'd like to think the job is finished, but it ain't, Anna. There's more to do." He looked down at his hat, fidgeting with it absently for a moment. "I'd like to wait here till after the operation, if it's all right with you."

Somehow his presence gave her hope, as though perhaps Nate would know Jim was waiting, ready to ride with him again. "I'd like that," she answered. "His brother is in the operating room helping the doctor however he can."

Jim leaned back and put one booted foot up on his knee, then perched the hat on his bent knee. "How long did the doctor think it would take?"

"He wasn't sure. He said it could be two hours, or eight. It's been four hours already." Anna looked at him. "If . . . if Nate decides to wear a badge again, would he be riding with you most of the time?"

He grinned a little. "I reckon we'd both make a point of gettin' duty together."

She turned away, looking down at Becky. "Good. I trust you, Jim. You'd risk your life for him if you had to. I know that, and I appreciate it. I'd feel better . . . at least knowing you were together."

Jim put a hand on her shoulder. "Anna, Nate knows what he's doing. Like I said, I reckon he'd be better off, maybe even safer, if he put that badge back on."

"I feel like what has happened is partly my fault."

"No, no, what he did was *his* decision. He thought it was the right thing to do. You've just got to let what he does after this *also* be his decision. Whatever it is, you've got to support him."

She stroked Becky's cheek. "I know."

"Let me hold the baby for a while, *ma chérie,*" Claudine said then. "Your arm must be getting tired."

Anna handed the baby to her. "Oh, Claudine, I'm so sorry. I didn't introduce you. This is Jim Lister, the deputy marshal Nate used to ride with, the man who was with Nate when they caught the Sharp gang. Jim, this is Claudine Marquis, a very good friend. She manages my restaurant in Abilene."

Claudine leaned over and smiled and nodded to Jim. "It is good to meet you, *monsieur.* I have heard many things about you, and I thank you for being such a good friend to Anna's husband. He is such a good man. This is a great tragedy."

Jim nodded to her in reply. "Yes, ma'am, it is. But Nate's a fighter, and I expect right now, down deep inside, he's damn mad. Between that and knowin' Anna and the baby need him, he's gonna make it."

"*Oui,* that is what I have been telling Anna."

Anna smoothed her dress and put a hand to her stiff neck. It seemed every muscle was in a knot. How wonderful it would be to go to bed and lie in Nate's arms, let him rub her neck. She leaned forward, resting her head in her hands. "Does anyone have any idea who might have done this, Jim?"

The man ran a hand through his thin hair. "Not yet. It could have been any one of a dozen men. There's been no word through the outlaw grapevine who might have done it. I expect they're waitin' to see if Nate dies. Then they'll start braggin' about bein' the one to kill him. Wouldn't surprise me if more than one man claims he did it. Their problem is, Nate's gonna live, and whoever did this is gonna be shakin' in his boots, wonderin' when Nate will figure it out and come after him."

"Whoever it was will probably get himself clear to Mexico or something. He'll never be caught."

"Oh, I wouldn't say that. I think he'll be curious enough to stick around, proud enough of himself to want to strut his stuff and take the credit. No, I think he'll stay around where he can get news, find out if Nate Foster is gonna live or die."

Live or die. They were such awful-sounding words. Anna wondered how she could go on living herself if Nate died. She would do so only for Becky. Thank God she had her daughter, a part of Nate that would live on.

It was an agonizing seven hours before the doctor and Rob finally came out to talk to Anna. Rob's face was ashen, and he looked ready to pass out.

"He's still alive," he told Anna, his eyes tearing. Anna went to him, and he embraced her. "I never want to go through something like that again. I sure as hell got a lesson in what the inside of a body looks like."

He kept an arm around her as Anna pulled away to face the doctor. "How did it go, Dr. Madison?"

The man folded his arms as Jim and Claudine both rose. "As well as can be expected," he answered. "It's one of the worst cases I've seen, as far as one bullet managing to damage a number of organs. The important thing is that the heart and lungs were missed, by what miracle I can't imagine. But I've repaired his stomach, part of the intestines, a kidney, and I stopped massive internal bleeding from the abdominal aorta. The pancreas was singed, but I don't think major damage was done to it. The stomach and intestines will heal, although he'll have to be on a liquid diet for quite a while. Now, the kidneys have a remarkable ability to heal, but whether this one will is yet to be seen. But he's a big, strong man, and I'm told he's a fighter. If Nate himself has anything to do with this, I think he'll survive it. I've done all that medical science can do at this point. Maybe someday we'll know a lot more about the human body. In some instances I had to literally experiment. This is the biggest test of repairing a man's insides I've ever been asked to take."

The man put a hand on Anna's arm. "The only thing I can't guarantee is whether or not he'll be able to walk." He squeezed her arm when he saw the hope go out of her eyes. "The bullet lodged near the lumbar vertebrae, Mrs. Foster, in the lower back. I was as careful as my skills allow me to be, but there is no way of knowing about nerve damage until he comes around. Don't be alarmed if at first he *does* seem paralyzed. He'll be in a great deal of pain in that area, and any movement will probably bring enough pain to bring him close to passing out. But even nerves can heal, Mrs. Foster. As the back heals, the pain will lessen, and he'll be able to try moving around. For now we've strapped both his legs and his hips and lower back to a special brace so that he *can't* move around. For the next month or so I don't want him moving at all."

Jim turned away, not wanting anyone to notice the tears in his eyes.

"But what if others lift him?" Anna asked. "Can he be taken home? I think he'd recover better in our own house in Topeka. His sister-in-law and brother and I can take care of him."

The doctor nodded. "In about two weeks. I'll stay here four or five days and keep an eye on him. Then I must get back to St. Louis, but I'll leave instructions for the doctor here and your doctor in Topeka. And if there is a sudden change for the worse, send for me. But I really think if he gets through these next few days, he'll be out of danger."

Anna shook his hand. "Thank you for coming. Can I see him?"

"You can go and sit with him, but he will be out from sedation for quite a while. And don't be alarmed if he gets sick when he first wakes up. Patients usually react that way to ether. Watch him closely or he could choke on his own vomit. I'll be nearby. Right now I am going to get something to eat and get a little rest."

"Yes, you should. You deserve it." Anna looked up at Rob. "And so do you. Rob, you look terrible. Are you all right?"

He grinned nervously. "Just a little shaken." He rubbed at his eyes. "I think I'll go send a wire to Marie and get some rest myself. Besides, I'm afraid I've got to get out of this place for a while."

"You go ahead. I'll go sit with Nate."

He searched her eyes. "What about you? You seem awfully strong and calm all of a sudden."

She smiled, her eyes shiny with tears. "I know Nate. If he lived through all of this, he's going to make it. It's like Jim here said a while ago. He's going to be awfully mad, Rob. And that's what he needs right now—to be mad as hell. He's going to want to find out who did this, maybe go after them himself, and I'm not going to stop him. If thoughts of revenge are what it takes to keep him alive and make him walk again, then let him think them. Let him put on a gun and a badge and do what he needs to do."

Rob smiled sadly. "Well, I guess he sure did marry the right woman." He turned away. "Come on, Doc. I'll walk you outside. I expect there are people out there waiting to hear about Nate."

Anna watched them leave, suddenly thinking of another man who had once cared about people and wanted to save lives. Darryl had been a good doctor. She turned and put a hand on Jim's back. "Why don't you go get yourself a drink?" she told him. "I have a feeling you're needing one about now."

He nodded, turning and quickly walking toward the door, putting on his hat. "I'll be back later to see Nate," he told her before going outside.

Claudine walked up to Anna and they embraced, hugging the baby between them. "Come, we will go to be with Nate," Claudine told her. "He needs to hear your voice, needs to hear Becky crying. He needs to hear the sounds of life and love, Anna."

Anna nodded, struggling to remain strong. She realized the next few weeks were going to be the most trying time of her life, nursing a man who was going to be totally helpless and dependent on her. She must never show doubt or discouragement. If Nate Foster was going to believe he would walk again, she must *make* him believe it. She would feed that drive deep within his soul that would make him want to get out of bed and find his assailant. She could not imagine anything more frightening and disappointing than to have him put on a badge again, but she had already vowed to not try to stop him. The need to do so might be all that kept him going through the pain and agony of the next few weeks, perhaps months.

She breathed deeply for courage and headed for Nate's ward, holding back a strong urge to scream when she saw him. What was it about such an injury that seemed to change a person's features? It hardly looked like her Nate lying there, so gray, looking more like a corpse than a breathing man.

"Oh, Nate," she whispered, wishing she could take some of his pain upon herself.

Nothing Anna had experienced could compare to the agony of watching Nate suffer and not being able to do anything to relieve him of his misery. The first few days were filled with wretched sickness and groans of agony that cut into her like a sword. To see such a big, once-vital man lying in such misery, to hear him cry out her name so pitifully tore at her until she too wanted to scream and groan.

A cradle and a cot were brought to the hospital so that

Anna could stay by his side and keep the baby there, for she refused to leave him. Rob finally had no choice but to go home. Marie and Christine needed him. Claudine also had to leave, much to her regret. But Anna insisted on it.

"I'll rest easier knowing other things are being taken care of," she told the woman. "If Nate doesn't recover, I'll need the restaurant, Claudine. I can't afford to have my business fall apart right now. It might be all Becky and I will have." Memories of the survival instincts that had originally led her to Abilene returned to cut into her heart. Would she be twice widowed? "There's nothing more you can do here."

The woman frowned and fussed but knew Anna was right. It tore at Anna's heart to let her go, for emotionally she needed Claudine's support. But life went on, and someone had to tend to the restaurant. It annoyed her that she had to be so practical and think about business at such a time.

Claudine left a week after the operation, and Anna struggled on alone, helping care for Nate, bathing him, trying to get him to eat. But all he could manage those first few days was water, for which he begged almost constantly. He seemed hardly aware of her presence, except for the times when he would call her name and grasp her hand so tightly that it hurt.

Now he seemed to be wasting away from lack of food. Every day his face looked thinner, his eyes more hollow. Anna knew from his screams of pain whenever she and the nurses touched him to clean him that his pain was much greater than they could imagine. Nate Foster was not the kind of man to make a fuss over a wound. But this was not like any wound he had ever had.

It was seven days after the operation before he looked at Anna with any kind of recognition in his eyes. He watched her quietly for a moment as she retucked the sheets around him. Anna looked at him then, realizing he was looking right at her as though he wanted to speak.

"Nate?" She moved closer, touching his face. "Are you truly conscious? Can you talk?" He started to shift in bed, then gasped and shuddered. "Don't try to move, Nate," she told him. "Not yet. You have some healing to do first."

He looked around the room, then back at her, suddenly resembling a confused little boy. "Where . . . am I? What's wrong . . . with me?"

She closed her eyes and quietly thanked God he at least seemed to have his wits about him. It was an improvement, no matter how minor. She leaned closer and kissed his cheek. "We're in Lawrence, Nate. You came here to give a speech, remember? That was over a week ago." She gently smoothed back his hair. "Someone shot you, Nate. A sniper. We don't know yet who it was, but Jim and others are working on it."

She saw the concern and then the bitterness come into his eyes. "Shot me? Why? How . . . bad?"

"Who knows why? We can only guess it was someone who didn't like your stand against outlaws in Kansas. As far as how bad—pretty bad, Nate, but you're going to be all right. The bullet hit a lot of organs. We brought in a specialist from St. Louis, and he's coming back soon to check you over before we leave here and take you home to Topeka. The bullet landed near your spine. That's why you're in so much pain." She took his hand. "Nate, the doctor said for you not to be alarmed if it seems at first you can't move. He said the nerves will heal and you'll be able—"

"Can't move!" His gritted his teeth. "What do you mean . . . can't move?" He tried but cried out with the pain. "My God . . . not like Christine! This . . . will kill her. I *have* to move. I have to get . . . out of this ⸱ . . . goddamn bed, get the sonofabitch . . . who did this!"

"Nate!" She grasped his face in her hands. He was shaking and was suddenly drenched with sweat. "You *will* walk out of here, but not if you try to move too soon! You have to do what the doctor says and give it *time,* Nate. Please just do what he says. Do it for Christine, for me and Becky."

His eyes teared. "Becky," he whispered. "Where's . . . Becky?"

"She's right here beside you in a cradle." She kissed his forehead. "I'll get her. She's all right, Nate." She leaned down to pick up the baby, holding her in the crook of her arm and opening the blanket for him to see. "Here's why you have to get well, Nate. You've already survived a wound that would kill most men. The doctor said if you got this far without a serious infection, you would live. Now all you've got to do is lie still and let your back heal."

His eyes drooped shut. "What if . . . it doesn't? I couldn't . . . be a husband to you, a father to . . . Becky, couldn't go after . . . the man who . . . did this."

"It *will* heal, Nate. The doctor is sure of it," she lied. "But you have to do what he says."

"Anna . . . poor Anna, what hell this must be . . . for you."

She laid Becky back into the cradle. "Don't mind about me, Nate. You're the one going through hell."

A tear slipped down the side of his face and into his ear. "Jim. I want to see . . . Jim . . . you send . . . for him."

"I will, Nate."

"Where's . . . Rob?"

"He was here almost all week. He had to go home to Marie and Christine. Claudine came too, but I sent her back yesterday to take care of the restaurant. I'm here, Nate, and I'm not going anywhere until you're ready to leave with me."

"Something . . . hard . . . on my legs."

"It's a special brace so you don't move the wrong way and reinjure something."

His breathing came quicker then. "Who . . . did this? Who?"

"How I wish we knew." She leaned down and kissed his cheek again. "Don't fret about that now, Nate. Just concentrate on getting well. You've got to start eating, darling. You'll never get well if you don't."

"I'll . . . try." He seemed to be drifting off to sleep again. "What about . . . lieutenant . . . gover . . . nor."

She blinked back tears. "I'm afraid that will have to wait until next term, Nate. But Henry Wilder said to tell you he'll support you again next time if you choose to run again. He said you'd have an even greater chance of winning— maybe even governor."

"No . . . governor . . . just marshal . . . get the man . . . who did this."

She smiled through tears, hating the thought of it but knowing he needed that drive to keep him going. "You will, Nate. You'll get him."

Well-wishers gathered at the train depot as a groaning Nate Foster was carefully carried on board a boxcar where he could lie flat. Rob had come to help, and Jim Lister was also there. The ride in the wagon from the hospital to the train was unbearably painful for Nate, but Anna took hope in the doctor's diagnosis that he was actually greatly improved because he could move his toes.

Nate was still in the brace and was tied securely to a stretcher. As Rob and Jim set it carefully down on a feather mattress inside the boxcar, people outside quietly watched, a few women crying. Many knew Nate Foster, and most could hardly believe the thin, pale, unmoving man on the stretcher could be the same man who had ridden from Kansas nearly to Mexico chasing outlaws.

Anna climbed into the boxcar, and Rob handed Becky up to her, then collected all her baggage.

"Jim," Nate groaned inside the boxcar, his face covered with perspiration.

"I'm right here, Nate." Jim knelt beside him.

"What did you . . . find out?"

"Not much, really. We're working hard on it, Nate. You know the James gang and the Youngers are raising all kinds of hell in Missouri, robbing banks and trains. They're another bunch who are still licking their war wounds. It's pretty well known now that Jesse James was among those men that murdered those soldiers at Centralia. A lot of innocent people have died since then. Some damn newspaper reporter is making them out to be heroes or something, comparing them to Robin Hood. Can you believe that one? They're nothing but damn worthless outlaws who need to be hanged."

"You saying . . . you think one of them did this?"

Jim shook his head. "I just don't know. If not, it was somebody who at least thinks like they do. I haven't heard anything about the Jameses or the Youngers hitting these parts, but then Lawrence isn't all that far from Missouri. Still, this thing smells of revenge, Nate. You've never personally run into any of them boys, except at Centralia. But you didn't do anything against them that day."

"I sure . . . would have liked to. There were . . . just too many. Anna . . . she saved my life that day."

Jim grinned. "You've told me."

Anna's eyes teared when she noticed Nate actually smiled a little. Hope welled up in her soul at the sight.

"What's your own guess, Nate?" Jim asked, hoping to keep the man's thoughts busy and help keep his mind off the pain.

Nate swallowed and licked his lips. "Can't . . . figure it. Anybody who'd really . . . have it in for me is dead. That one called Crazy Doc . . . he'd be a good suspect, if he was alive. And maybe Bill Sharp."

Anna turned away at the mention of Crazy Doc. She sat down on a bale of hay, breathing a sigh of relief to think that at least this was not something in which her first husband had had a part.

"What bothers me," Nate went on, "is the bastard . . . could be right out there in that crowd . . . watching me and smiling about it. And he . . . could hurt Anna . . . or Becky."

"They aren't going to be hurt. And once you get to Topeka, I'm arranging for your house to be watched for a while. Just don't you be worryin' about it right now," Jim said. "You just worry about getting well and getting back on your feet."

Nate breathed deeply. "This is a little worse . . . than that wound I got when we went after Sharp . . . isn't it?"

Jim laughed lightly, but Anna caught the tears in his eyes. "I expect it is. Hell, Nate, you can get yourself out of the worst fix, and you'll get out of this one." He touched Nate's arm. "Don't let them win this one, Nate, you hear me? Don't let those bastards win this one. If you're gonna go down under a man's bullet, do it when you're wearin' your own gun and shootin' back."

"That's . . . how I always . . . figured it."

Jim patted his shoulder and stood up. "I'm goin' to load up my horse, Anna. I'll be back."

"Thanks for being here, Jim," she answered.

"Well, luckily I'm done with my latest run and on my way to Topeka for orders. I'll have a few days when I get there."

"Good. I think having you around is good for him."

The man nodded and left the boxcar. Rob finished throwing baggage inside and climbed aboard, and moments later Jim was back. The train blew off steam and began chugging off.

Anna looked out at waving well-wishers, realizing she would never think fondly of Lawrence again. Eight years ago the people of Lawrence had run her and Darryl out of town. Now her second husband had been shot here. Even Joline didn't want to come back here.

She thought about her sister, missed her. How good it would be to be able to talk to her right now. How many years ago had she visited Joline here in Lawrence? Nearly five now. It was amazing how many things had happened since then: Lawrence was attacked by Quantrill and his men, and Jo had fled to Montana and now was married to the man who had guided her there. Quantrill was dead, and so was Bill Anderson . . . and Crazy Doc.

It had been seven years since she had last seen Darryl Kelley—seven years in Anna's mind, because she didn't count that day four years ago when she saw him as the man he had become, the day she buried his wedding ring at Centralia.

She watched Lawrence disappear, and she vowed to never go back to her hometown again. True, she had been happy here once, so many years ago, when everything was peaceful and happy, before all the prewar hatreds got into peoples' hearts. The war had reared its ugly head again. It had ended more than three years ago, but when she looked at Nate's pale, pain-filled face, she realized it still raged on.

Chapter 20

Weeks turned into months, the first two of which were filled with excruciating pain for Nate and constant, patient, but backbreaking care for Anna. Rob brought Christine over often to visit with Nate, and the girl pleaded with him not to let himself end up like her.

Christine seemed more frail than ever, and as Nate improved, she seemed to grow worse, as though each time she came over and held Nate's hand, some of her strength went into his blood and left her weaker. Anna noticed her breathing was becoming more shallow, but she said nothing to Nate about it. If he noticed, he said nothing to her.

By November of that year Becky was eight months old and sitting up and crawling. Nate was able to bring himself into a sitting position and get himself into a wheelchair, and he had begun eating and gaining back some weight. But the old, teasing personality was missing. Anna could feel a bitterness setting in, a rigid determination even greater than what he had felt when Christine was hurt.

Her heart wilted at the realization of what the shooting was doing to him. He was like a changed man, angry and short-tempered. The bitterness seemed to grow worse in November, when Nate learned that James Harvey had won the election for governor. His dreams of winning lieutenant governor had been dashed, and Anna knew he felt as though he had somehow failed her.

It was close to Christmas when Rob brought over some crutches, specially made to fit Nate's height and build. "Maybe now I can start getting out of this damn chair," Nate grumbled.

Anna walked over to help him up as he grasped the crutches. "Leave me alone," he barked. Her eyes widened in surprise, and her heart tightened into a small, aching organ, while a lump swelled painfully in her throat. She backed away, looking at Rob, who frowned. He also realized how Nate had changed. Nate looked at her and saw the hurt expression on her face. She picked up Becky and took the baby into her bedroom to put her to sleep, saying nothing. Nate sighed and threw the crutches down. "Goddammit," he mumbled.

"Do you realize what that woman has been through for you the last few months?" Rob asked him.

"Of course I realize it. Go on home, Rob. Thanks for the crutches. I'll try them tomorrow. I want to talk to Anna."

Rob sighed and nodded. "You're her whole world, Nate. You've needed her these past few months, but don't forget she needs you, too. Not just your physical presence, you— the Nate Foster she married."

Nate rubbed at his eyes. "I know, I know. Go on."

Rob pressed a hand at his shoulder before going out. Nate glanced toward the bedroom and wheeled himself down the hall, where Anna was changing Becky's diaper. She said nothing, realizing Nate was watching her. She knew that if anything was to be said, Nate had to say it. She was afraid if she spoke first she would say the wrong thing.

She slipped a nightgown over Becky and laid the girl into her small bed, which was kept beside Nate and Anna's bed —a bed Anna had yet to sleep in since coming home. She had slept on the sofa so that she wouldn't disturb Nate and bring him pain.

Anna laid Becky on her tummy and rubbed her back

gently until the baby's eyes closed. She could still feel Nate watching her. "I'm sorry," he finally said.

"You don't have to be. I know what all this is doing to you. I just—" She hesitated. Was she already saying too much? "I just wish I had the old Nate back." She rose and met his eyes. "Not physically. That doesn't bother me at all. It's the Nate inside I can't find." *Please don't change like my first husband did. Don't let me lose you even though you still live, Nate.*

His gaze moved over her, then he ran a hand through his hair and looked away. "Anna, when I get angry, I'm not really angry at you. I just take it out on you, the last one I should hurt. I need to lash out at someone, and you're the closest. I really am sorry, Anna. I just . . . I get so frustrated when I watch how hard you have to work just to take care of me all day. Maybe I'd feel better if you complained a little, I don't know. I just can't stand not being able to be a real husband to you, and I hate the fact that right now it's your money that's supporting us."

"We've been over that subject before, Nate. It's *our* money. For God's sake, where the money comes from right now should be the *least* of your worries. All you should care about is getting well."

She saw the sudden boyish look in his eyes, mixed with great sorrow. "It isn't even the money, Anna. I'm just . . . I keep trying to think up reasons to vent my anger. The biggest problem is . . . dammit, Anna, I want so much to have you beside me at night, but I'm . . . I feel a little embarrassed, I guess. That's a whole new feeling for me."

She frowned. "Embarrassed? About what?"

The anger came back into his eyes. "I shouldn't have to explain that. My God, Anna, here you are a beautiful, vital woman and I can't be a man to you."

She gave out a little gasp, a mixture of despair and a temptation almost to laugh. She sat down on the bed, letting out a long sigh of relief to realize what was really bothering him. "Oh, Nate," she said quietly, meeting his eyes. "How could you think—" She smiled. "Nate, do you have any idea how I've longed every night to feel your arms around me—just feel your arms around me? That's all I need, Nate. It's *you* I need—not the sexual part—just *you*. I just need to know you still love me."

His eyes widened in surprise. "*Love* you? How in God's name could you doubt that? Without you and Becky, without wanting to get better for you, I don't think I could have made it."

She rubbed at her eyes. "I thought the only thing that kept you going was the thought of going after whoever did this—and Christine's support."

He sighed deeply. "Anna . . . my God, Anna, those things have helped. But my biggest drive has been you . . . you and Becky." He rolled his chair closer, reaching out and taking her hand. "I had such big plans for us."

She squeezed his hand. "You'll get well, Nate, and you'll be the husband you want to be. In the meantime, it's enough for me just to have you close and know you're alive."

He studied the blue eyes he loved. "Will you sleep with me tonight? I hate going to bed alone. I think I need to hold you as much as you need to be held, Mrs. Foster."

She looked at him with tear-filled eyes. "I know . . . how awful it's been for you, Nate. I know how you've suffered. But . . . do you have any idea what it was like for me, thinking you were going to die . . . after already losing a husband, and having you for such a little while—"

"I do know," he answered. "This is the reason I almost decided against marrying. I never wanted you to go through this." He rubbed a thumb over the back of her hand. "I guess there are all kinds of suffering when something like this happens. But I'm not dead, Anna, and I can tell by the way I'm getting stronger every day that I'm going to walk again, and I'm going to make love to you again, by God. That's a promise."

She smiled sadly, wiping at tears. "It doesn't matter, as long as I have you emotionally."

"Well, you do. And do you realize we haven't even kissed in months, except for the love pecks you give me when you're doing something for me? I'm talking about a *real* kiss."

She saw a hint of the old sparkle in his eyes. He pulled on

her arm, and she leaned forward and met his lips. He grasped her face between his hands then, and she could feel strength in them. He kissed her deeply, gently, suggesting some of the passion they had shared before all this happened.

He pulled away then, his gaze moving over her again. "Why don't you get ready for bed," he told her. "I like to watch you undress. Do you realize I've watched you nearly every night, longing to touch you again?"

She reddened a little as she pulled away and unbuttoned her shoes. "You can touch me all you want, Nate Foster."

"I just felt bad that I couldn't do more than that, so I just let you go sleep on the sofa."

She sighed and rose, setting her shoes aside and unbuttoning her dress. "Nate, let's not let anything come between us and the love we share—not anything, not even this. What we have is too special. People can love in more ways than sexually. We have each other and we have Becky. That's all that's important."

"I know that." He studied her slender body as she removed everything but her bloomers. Old urges moved through him. Did she know that he had regained all feeling in that part of him necessary to make love to her? If he could just make his legs work. That was what frustrated him. He couldn't move in the right ways.

She pulled a nightgown over her head, then helped him undress. God, how he hated when she had to help him. He realized he had been short with her because that made it easier for him to ignore his own frustrations. Rather than face up to his embarrassment and inadequacy, he made sure he erased any feelings of love and desire. For months she had bathed him, serviced his bedpans, fed him, nursed him like a baby no more able to care for himself than Becky. The poor woman had *two* babies to take care of.

Not any more, he vowed. Now he bathed himself and fed himself and got around fine in the wheelchair. Come tomorrow, he was going to start using his damn legs if it killed him. And after that he was going to be a real husband to Anna.

She stripped him to his long johns and helped him into

bed. She lifted his legs over, then turned down the lamp and climbed in beside him. Nate looked to be sure his rifle was beside the bed in a position where he could grab it. "Did you bolt the doors?" he asked.

"Yes." She pulled the covers over them and moved into his arms. For the moment their thoughts were on the reason he had asked the question. Someone wanted him dead, and he might try again. "Oh, Nate, hold me," she whispered.

His strong arms came around her, and she carefully moved against him. When she touched his chest, she could feel the indentation of one of the several scars left from his operation. But his chest was still broad and solid, and the scars did not matter to her. It felt wonderful to be held again, held in Nate Foster's strong arms. This was all she needed.

"I'm going to walk by Christmas, Anna. That's going to be my Christmas present to you."

She kissed at his chest. "Nate, that's only three weeks away."

"I don't care if it's three days. I'm going to walk by Christmas."

Christmas of '68 was one of mixed blessings. Although the last five months had been filled with pain and heartache, the Foster family was thankful that at least Nate had not died, and that he was now improving at a more rapid pace.

Nate and Anna spent Christmas Eve with Rob and Marie, the children all around, little Becky very willingly handed from one person to another, finding great pleasure in playing with a string of popcorn. It was warm for December, and Nate managed to walk to his brother's house on the crutches, with which he had practiced close to eight hours a day for the past three weeks.

His first attempt was embarrassing and painful, the first several days ones of struggle and determination. His legs were weak and uncoordinated, and he still suffered pain in his back.

Anna had at first wanted to object, seeing the perspiration on his face, which she knew was from pain. She had wanted to run to him and help him, but she realized that to object would only upset him again. He was determined. At least he had not been one to just give up and resign himself to life in a wheelchair. After the first few terrible days, she realized his progress was remarkable, and she kept herself occupied preparing for Christmas while Nate walked up and down the hallway for hours at a time.

It was a happier Christmas than she would have thought possible a few months earlier. Jim Lister, who was a man without a family, was able to join them. And since he had begun walking with the crutches, Nate's spirits had improved considerably.

It was a Foster custom to open presents Christmas Eve, and the children gladly tore into their gifts. Becky humored everyone by shoving most of her presents aside, finding more pleasure in ripping at paper and fingering bows than in the toys inside.

Marie and Anna prepared a late meal that was fit for kings, after which Rob carried Christine to bed for the night. Marie got her own children settled into bed while Anna laid Becky on Rob and Marie's bed. The weary baby fell asleep almost instantly. The women returned to the kitchen then to clean up the dishes, while Nate, Jim, and Rob retired to the parlor for smokes.

"He's so much better, isn't he, Anna?" Marie said. The woman picked the remaining meat off the turkey to save it.

"Yes. The crutches have made a big difference. He's going to be all right, Marie." Anna scrubbed at a plate absent-mindedly. "I just . . . I wish he didn't feel compelled to put a badge back on, but I know he will."

"Yes, he probably will. But it's too important to him to try to force him not to, Anna."

"I know. But it terrifies me, the thought of having him gone for days or weeks at a time, never knowing if he's all right."

"Well, maybe eventually he'll give it up again, especially once he finds out who shot him. And maybe he can request duty that will keep him closer to Topeka."

"I'd like to think—"

"Anna?" She turned to see Nate standing in the doorway,

his eyes holding a kind of teasing glitter, a look she had not seen in them in months. "Stay right there," he told her.

She noticed he did not have his crutches with him. "How did you—"

"I walked. It took me a few minutes, but I got here from the parlor without crutches. Now stay there and I'll walk to you."

"Nate . . ." Her eyes teared. "Maybe it's too much at once."

"I told you what your Christmas present would be. Now stay there like I told you."

He let go of the doorjamb and stood there for a moment to keep his balance, then put one foot in front of him, steadied himself, keeping his arms out as though he were walking a tightrope. He took another step, slowly making his way across the kitchen to Anna. When he reached her, he said with a wink, "You'd better grab me now before I fall."

"Oh, Nate." She put her arms around his middle, and he embraced her. How she enjoyed that embrace! "This is the best present I've ever had."

He kissed her hair. "I can't bend over or kneel yet, but I'll get there. I'll practice this until I'm walking normally, then comes getting on a horse. By spring I'll be the Nate Foster you married."

"Nate, I can't believe my eyes," Marie told him, coming over and leaning up to kiss his cheek. "I can't wait until Christine sees."

"I'll show her in the morning."

"She'll be so happy. I'm so glad she's lived long enough to—" The woman sobered. "To know you've come this far. She was so devastated when she first heard about the shooting."

Nate kept an arm around Anna. "She's worse, isn't she?"

Marie sighed. "She's got so she can't control her . . . her bodily functions. And her breathing is a lot more labored." The woman's eyes teared. "I really don't see how she'll live out the year, Nate." She looked away. "I didn't mean to bring that up today of all days."

"It's all right. I noticed the breathing myself." He put a

hand on Marie's shoulder. "Thank you for all you do for her, Marie. I know it's been hard on you. If it weren't for me getting hurt, Anna would have gladly helped more."

"Oh, I know that." She took a deep breath and put on a smile. "Well, let's not talk about it any more tonight. You're walking. This is a wonderful Christmas." She noticed how Nate looked at Anna and she laughed lightly. "I'll leave you two alone for a minute and go make sure those children aren't sneaking out of bed to play with their new toys."

She left the kitchen, and Anna saw an old, familiar look in Nate's eyes she had not seen in a long time. He leaned down and met her mouth, in a hungry, passionate kiss that sent a rush of desire through her blood she had deliberately kept buried for five months. He moved a hand to her bottom, pressing her close, and she felt the evidence of the manly desires and abilities that were returning to his healing body.

He left her mouth and kissed at her neck, whispering her name. He met her lips again in groaning desire. "I already asked Rob to keep Becky here tonight," he told her softly. "Let's go home. I have to know, Anna. I have to know, or go crazy."

Her face was flushed with passion. "I already know," she told him. "But right now I'm just happy to see the old Nate back in those eyes, to feel him in this embrace and in his kisses."

He kept one arm around her and pushed some hair behind her ear with his other hand. "I heard you talking to Marie about me putting a badge back on. I'm sorry, Anna, but I have to do what I have to do."

She closed her eyes. "I know. I just don't think I could take seeing you hurt again."

"We can only take one day at a time. This is Christmas Eve, and tonight I want to try to give you a better present than seeing me walk. I think I can, Anna, but it scares me a little. Can you believe that one?"

She caught an almost little-boy look in his eyes, and she smiled. "We'll manage."

He smiled and pulled her close again. "God, I love you, Anna. I'm sorry for all the hell you've put up with."

"Well, it wasn't exactly your fault." She pulled back and looked up at him. "I love you too, Nate Foster. And right now you'd better go back and join Jim and Rob and let Marie come back in here so we can finish in the kitchen."

Their eyes filled with renewed love and desire. "Don't take too long. I'm ready to leave." He let go of her and turned, taking slow, faltering steps as he walked back to the parlor. Anna watched, her heart breaking at the thought of how he had suffered, terrified over the prospect that it could happen to him all over again, or that she could lose him to death the next time.

He's safer with a badge and a gun, Jim Lister had told her once.

Yes, she thought. *I suppose he is. May God protect him.* She finished helping Marie, her body tingling at the thought that Nate would try to make love to her tonight. She felt almost as excited as on her wedding day, her whole body tingly with anticipation. She prayed nothing would happen that would destroy Nate's manly pride, which was so delicate right now.

They said their good-byes, and neither Rob nor Marie made any teasing remarks about Nate wanting to leave Becky with them for the night. This was not a time for poking fun. Rob understood without Nate saying a word that this was an important moment for his healing brother. Nate had said nothing more than to ask Rob to keep the baby, and Rob needed no further explanations.

They walked through the cool, crisp night air, saying good-bye to Jim Lister, who thanked them for letting him join them and rode off to return to his hotel room. Nate used his crutches to walk back, since it was uphill. He and Anna nodded to the deputy who had been assigned to watch their house that night.

"Hell, it's Christmas Eve, Luke, and freezing cold," Nate told the man. "Go warm up somewhere."

"I'm supposed to stay right here," the man answered.

"It's all right, Luke. I mean that. I'm well enough to handle a rifle as good as ever, and it's too damn cold tonight even for outlaws to be out prowling around. We'll be okay."

Luke, who was only in his mid-twenties, rose, pushing

back his hat. "I don't know, Nate. I'm supposed to stay right here."

Nate rolled his eyes. "Luke, it's my house, my porch, and my family. Do you think I'd put Anna in any danger? Go on now. I'll take full responsibility. I'll not have you sitting out here freezing on Christmas Eve."

"Well . . . maybe I could just sit inside the door."

Nate grinned. "Not tonight. Now get going."

Luke reddened some, noticing Anna would not meet his eyes. "Oh," he said, the moment suddenly awkward. "Well, if you say so. But if I get in trouble for this—"

"You won't. Go buy yourself a whiskey and warm up your blood."

"Yes, sir. Thanks."

The young man left, and Nate laughed lightly. Anna joined in the laughter as they went inside the house. It was wonderful to hear Nate laugh, to know the old Nate was coming back into the body that was getting stronger every day.

"Oh, Nate, this has been the best Christmas, in spite of all we've been through," she told him, turning to him as he closed and locked the door. "To see you walk on your own . . . I couldn't have asked for a better present."

He leaned down and kissed her forehead. "We'd better stoke up the fire," he told her.

Anna felt flames move through her at the thought of his reason for wanting to keep the house warm. She held his arm as they walked to the potbelly stove that sat in the corner of the parlor. Anna picked up a hot pad and opened the heavy, iron door, helping Nate throw in more wood. She closed the door, and he leaned on her shoulders as they walked into the bedroom. They slept in the downstairs guest bedroom, where Nate had been sleeping since coming home, so that Anna would not have to go up and down stairs to take care of him.

Nate sat down on the bed. He sighed deeply, smiling rather sheepishly then. "You want to know the truth?"

Anna removed her hat and cape. "What's that?"

"Promise not to laugh?"

Her eyes shone with love as she came closer, touching his hair. "I would never laugh," she said softly.

"I feel like a bride on her wedding night."

She smiled softly. "Then I will be the groom."

She stepped back and began undressing, blushing at her own boldness as she gradually revealed her naked body. She reached up and unpinned her hair, letting it fall over her shoulders. "You'd better get undressed for bed, Mr. Foster," she said then.

His eyes moved over her lovely form, a great hunger moving through him at the sight of her taut, pink nipples, the tiny waist and beautifully rounded hips. God, how he wanted her, but he could not make himself move.

Anna again saw the frightened look of a boy in his eyes. She moved closer, kneeling in front of him. She unbuttoned his shirt, opening it to kiss at his chest. She traced her fingers over the scars and closed her eyes against the horror of the day he was shot and the days that followed.

She kissed at the scars, moving her lips over his chest and down his stomach. She pulled off his boots, then unbuttoned his pants and long johns. "Stand up," she told him.

He wanted this, more for her than for himself. He managed to get back up, and she pulled off his pants and long johns. He stepped out of them and she rose, gently caressing that part of him she had not dared to touch for so long because he was not ready. He pulled her close and whispered her name, kissing her hair. "Help me, Anna," he whispered.

She kissed at his chest again, then pulled back the covers and turned down the lamp. She got into bed, holding out the covers for him. Nate managed to lower himself to a sitting position and lay back, using great effort to move his legs under the covers without her help. Anna pulled the covers over them, then put her arms around his neck and kissed him. Nate grasped her hair, returning her kisses with hunger and urgency.

Suddenly, without speaking, they both understood how they could make love these next few weeks without hurting him. It was something she would never ordinarily consider, something Nate had done with the whores he had known before this beautiful lady had come into his life.

With strong arms he gently pulled at her, urging her to move on top of him. Her own needs and passions told her what to do. She guided him into herself, feeling an exhilarating mixture of intense sexual desire and embarrassment. But soon the embarrassment left her when she realized how much her husband needed to know he was still a man. She knew it would be only a matter of time before Nate Foster would make love to her in his own, virile way. But for now, she would make love to him. She would be the active one, she would do the moving. She would show him he was still a man.

It became one of the most pleasurable experiences she had ever known. The feel of his hands at her breasts, the sound of his groans of pleasure instead of pain, the glory of having her man inside of her again, all brought forth such exquisite pleasure that she soon felt the pulsating climax that convinced Nate he had pleased his woman the way he had hoped. Moments later she felt his own surge of life. She stayed on top of him, leaning down to rest her head against his shoulder.

He caressed her hair, and she could feel him trembling, suddenly realizing he was quietly crying. "Thank you, Anna," he whispered.

She pulled the covers closer around them. "Merry Christmas," she whispered in reply. "I guess this was our present to each other."

"The best one," he answered.

Jim Lister swatted at a fly, cursing the heat. He knocked the fly off his desk with a piece of paper, then looked up when a tall figure loomed in the doorway. "Nate!" He rose, putting out his hand. "You're looking great, friend. My God, I never thought I'd see the day." They shook hands vigorously, and Jim grasped Nate's shoulder. "Well, that's a lie, actually. I knew you'd come walking in here someday soon."

Nate smiled rather sadly. "You know why I'm here, Jim."

Jim sobered, letting go of Nate's hand and looking him

over. "I just got back from a long circuit. You were doing damn good when I left. I suppose you're back to normal now."

"As normal as can be expected." Nate took off his hat and wiped at his brow with his shirtsleeve. It was July 1869, and it was hot. "I've been practicing with my gun—see no difference there, and that's where it counts. I can ride and walk just fine, but I get pains in strange places at strange times. They don't stop me, just nag at me. I have a feeling pain will remain a familiar foe for the rest of my life, especially in my back. But it won't stop me from doing my job right."

Jim sighed and walked around behind his desk, sitting down and telling Nate to do the same. "I've got some reports to make up for Judge Hewitt, but I'm too tired to monkey with them right now." The man offered Nate a thin cigar, and Nate took it. Both men lit up, while the air hung silent for a minute or two.

"Well, like I said, I'm not totally surprised to see you here," Jim said then. He watched the smoke from his cigar rise in the lazy, hot air. "This is a far cry from a year ago, isn't it? One year ago you were greeting cheering crowds in Lawrence, a man on his way to governing this state." He looked at Nate. "You still could, Nate. None of that has changed. That Mr. Wilder is still behind you, and Governor Harvey—"

"You can't talk me out of it, Jim. Anna didn't even try. You should know better."

Jim nodded. "I know I should. A friend can try, can't he? Wouldn't be much of a friend if he didn't."

Nate smiled a little. "I suppose not."

Jim leaned forward, putting his elbows on the desk. "The attorney general tried to get me to wear your marshal's badge, but I said no. I told him a long time ago you'd be back wearing it. Up until you got hurt, they couldn't make up their minds who should take your place, other than me, and those first few months I just didn't feel right stepping in. Then you got hurt, and I knew the job was still open." He stuck the cigar in his mouth and talked with it between his teeth. "Oh, I filled in, but I left on the deputy marshal badge. I knew this day would come, and I have no doubt it will be approved with no objection from anyone." He opened a drawer and took out a U.S. marshal badge, tossing it to Nate. Nate caught it in his palm, and Jim grinned. "Just testing your reflexes."

Nate eyed him narrowly. "My reflexes are just fine, especially when it comes to drawing a gun." Nate stared down at the badge, moving his thumb over the lettering. "Now all I need to know is who the hell did this to me."

Jim set his cigar in an ashtray and leaned back in his chair again. "I have a pretty good idea."

Nate shot him a dark, excited look. "Who! You been holding out on me?"

"I've been snooping around. Didn't want to say anything to you till I knew you were really ready, physically. I was afraid you'd go manhunting before you were well and do yourself more harm than good. I've been looking around myself, but he's a slick one—so slick he led us to believe he's been dead these past three years."

Nate frowned. "There are plenty of my old enemies dead now. Which one are you talking about?"

"The one they call Crazy Doc."

Bitterness and revenge came into Nate's eyes. "Crazy Doc! He's alive?"

"That's the rumor. I arrested a pair of horse thieves a couple of weeks ago down near Indian Territory. The man who owned the horses wanted to hang them both right then and there, but I wouldn't let him. We were in Judge Quill's district, though, and both men knew Quill's been known to hang horse thieves, so their chances were runnin' only slightly better than with the rancher. One of them asked me if I'd intervene with the judge if he gave me some important information." He swatted at another fly. "I said it depended on how important it was. He said a few months earlier he'd been ridin' with the one called Crazy Doc, the one the law in Kansas thought was dead." He picked up his cigar and puffed at it again, keeping his eyes on Nate's, seeing the anxiousness and revenge growing.

"You think he was telling the truth?"

Jim nodded. "I do. For one thing, he wasn't dumb enough to make up a story like that and expect anybody to believe it if it *wasn't* true. He said Crazy Doc's been hidin' out in Mexico with just a couple of men who knew who he was. Then he came back north about a year ago—did enough raiding and robbing to build his stash again, gathered some new men, including this one. Then he had them all hole up in some hideout in Indian Territory while him and some woman he's been keepin' got all dandied up and came north. Told them he had some personal business to tend to. Next thing they knew, they heard Marshal Nate Foster had been shot. He told me Crazy Doc used to talk about you, about how he owed you one, called you a Yankee and such. He suspected Doc's the one who shot you, so he lit out before Crazy Doc and this woman ever got back from wherever they had gone. He didn't want to be around the man. Figured what he'd done would bring a lot of trouble, considering your importance. He never saw the man after that."

Nate looked down and pinned on his badge. "He tell you the woman's name or where they hid out in Indian Territory?"

"Said Doc called her Fran. Fran Rogers, I think."

Nate looked up, a frown on his brow. "Fran Rogers?" He ran a hand through his damp hair. "For some reason that name sounds familiar."

"Maybe you'd heard of her those few times you had to go to Columbia, Missouri. This guy heard her mention something once about givin' up her business in Columbia and sacrificin' everything to be with Doc. Mentioned she owned a restaurant once."

Nate's eyebrows arched, and his heart quickened. A restaurant! Now he remembered. "My God," he muttered.

"What is it?"

"I think that's the name of the woman Anna used to work for in Columbia. She mentioned her to me a time or two, said they had some kind of falling out because of the war. This Fran Rogers was a Confederate through and through. That must be why she took up with this Crazy Doc. I wonder if they were seeing each other clear back then. I'll have to ask Anna if the woman ever mentioned seeing a man. Her own husband was supposedly killed in the war." He sighed deeply. "I doubt Anna would know much about it. She and this Fran didn't get along so well. Anna finally left the restaurant because of hard feelings."

"She's gonna be real upset when she hears this Crazy Doc is still alive and probably gunnin' for you. He's plugged you twice, Nate. You can't afford a third time."

"The third time will be *his* turn." Nate rose and paced, tension filling the room. "I'm ready right this minute, Jim. That guy tell you where the hideout was?"

Jim sighed. "That's the bad part. Before I finished talking with him, some goddamn sniper got him *and* his friend. I know good and well it was somebody hired by that goddamn rancher, but I can't prove it. Now they're dead and our best source is gone. Some of these high-and-mighty ranchers think they can take the law into their own hands. I wouldn't let them hang the men, so they shot them down instead. Pisses me off when we put that much time into a job and somebody does something like that. Judge Quill, he believes in hanging horse thieves anyway, so he was no help. He just said if it was the rancher or one of his men, they just saved the state some money."

"Damn," Nate grumbled. "We'll play hell finding the bastard now!"

"Maybe not. He knows by now you lived. We'll have the papers make a big deal about you pinning that badge back on. He'll get wind of it, and the temptation will be more than he can resist. He'll start bragging about how he was the one who shot you—if he's the man. And he'll come for you again, only this time we'll be ready."

Nate grinned, almost wickedly. "We'll be ready, all right. If that man was telling the truth about Crazy Doc being alive, this is the biggest break we've had in figuring out who did this. It all makes sense—the timing, the grudge. I'm not so sure I should wait for him to come to me, though. I don't like being his sitting duck again. We know he must be somewhere down in Indian Territory."

"You know that land, Nate. It's next to impossible to find anybody there. And the Indians and outlaws spread the word like wildfire when the law starts snooping around. This Crazy Doc would get wind of it and he'd disappear into thin air, just like the first time. He's crazy, all right. But like most nuts, he's also very smart. This guy told me he's called Doc because he really was a doctor once."

A quiet, disturbing thought passed through Nate's mind. Anna's first husband had been a doctor. He quickly dismissed the thoughts that fact suddenly conjured.

"You don't want to scare him off, Nate. When he hears you're wearin' that badge again, he'll show his hand. He's bound to. He's gonna make a mistake, Nate. He already did —last July in Lawrence." Their eyes met. Jim was just as anxious to catch the man as Nate. "You gonna tell Anna about this?"

Nate sighed. "In time. Besides, I have to ask her about that Fran Rogers. I think I'd better give her a couple of days to get used to looking at this badge again first before I tell her I think I know who's after me. It always upsets her to hear me talk about some of these men. This has all been so hard on her. I wish I could give it all up and forget it, but I can't. She understands that. I—"

Suddenly eleven-year-old Benny Foster appeared at the doorway, panting and sweating. "Uncle Nate!"

Nate turned, alarmed by the fright in the boy's eyes. "What is it, Benny?"

"It's Aunt Christine. She can't breathe! Pa said to come and get you. Anna and Becky are already at the house."

Nate grabbed his hat. "Talk to you later, Jim." He hurried out and headed for his horse, turning and lifting Benny into the saddle, wincing with pain when he did so. He climbed up behind the boy and rode off toward his brother's house.

Jim walked to a window to watch, realizing that if Nate's sister was dying, Nate would be more ruthless than ever in finding the man they called Crazy Doc, a man who was the same kind as those who had hurt poor Christine.

Chapter 21

It seemed that half the town of Topeka attended Christine Foster's funeral. Anna held sixteen-month-old Becky in her arms, grateful that the child seemed to sense she must be still. Anna wished she knew of a way to comfort Nate. She stood beside him, feeling his hard silence, aching at his efforts not to break down completely.

Christine's death had been harder on him than the others. The old guilt had returned, Anna was sure. He had held her in his arms as she gasped desperately for her last breath, her eyes wide with fear until Nate held her against his chest, rocking her gently until he realized she was gone. It had taken a long time for the rest of them to convince him to let go of her. And now Anna knew how it hurt him to see his pretty sister lowered into a black hole in the ground.

She was better off. Everyone, including Nate, knew it, but that didn't ease the hurt. The service finally ended. People expressed their condolences, but Nate hardly seemed to hear. People began leaving until only Rob and Nate and Anna were left. "We'll all be at the house," Rob finally said. "Folks brought food and such—you know how it goes. I'd better get over there and be with Marie." He put a hand on Nate's arm. "Come on away from here, Nate. Let them cover the grave."

"I'll be along," Nate answered, his voice gravelly.

Rob sighed and left. Anna set a now-wiggling Becky down, and she toddled off after a butterfly. "I don't know what to say, Nate."

"There isn't anything you *can* say." He put a hand to his head. "God, my head aches, Anna."

She put a hand to his back. "It's because you won't let yourself cry. You have every right to weep, Nate. You've got to quit holding it all inside."

"It's men like the ones who put her here who should be in this grave, not Christine. And of all the men I've caught and brought in, I've never found the ones who attacked our farm that night. But I tried. God knows I tried."

"Yes, He does. And for all you know, some of those you *did* bring in had something to do with it. You've done all that could humanly be done."

He looked down at her, his eyes pitifully bloodshot and tired-looking. "I'm not through yet. I might never be through, Anna."

Becky hugged him around the leg, and he bent down and lifted her, giving her a hug and a kiss. He handed her to Anna. "Go on back to the house. Take the buggy. I'll be along. I need the walk, and I want to be alone."

Anna blinked back tears, taking her daughter. "I love you, Nate."

He leaned down and kissed her cheek. "I love you, too," he answered, his voice breaking. He turned away. "Go on."

She turned and left, plunking Becky into some straw in the back of the wagon, then climbing up onto the seat and driving off. She didn't look back. She couldn't bear to see him standing there alone at the grave.

"That sonofabitch is wearing a badge again!" Darryl paced, knocking things every which way.

"Doc, I just cleaned," Fran complained.

He pushed over a small table that had a vase of flowers on it. "What the hell do I care about that right now, woman?"

She sighed and stooped to pick up the pieces of the vase. They lived in a neat little farmhouse in southwest Missouri, in an area where no one knew them. They had purchased the house with stolen money, and other than the stay in Mexico, it was the only time they had lived something that resembled a normal home life in years.

Darryl and the nine men who rode with him had discovered that robbing banks and stagecoaches in southern Missouri and northern Arkansas was lucrative and almost too simple. Most of the robberies and murders they committed were blamed on the Jameses or the Youngers, whose reputations were becoming notorious. Darryl had kept his own name out of the news, but he was tired now of the James boys getting all the publicity. What better publicity than to proclaim it was he who had shot down Marshal Nate Foster, and to declare that he intended to do it all over again—this time pumping enough lead into Foster to use him for a strainer.

"Nobody lives through what I did to Foster. Nobody!"

"Well, he *did* live. Hank showed you the newspaper. It made headlines all over the Midwest. He lived and he's a marshal again, looking for the man who killed him."

"Well, he'll damn well *find* him, because I intend to do the job right next time! It was bad enough he lived at all, let alone he's walking and riding and wearing a badge! What the hell does it take to bring the man down!"

"Just another well-aimed bullet."

"*That* one was well aimed. And now that he's parading around in a badge again, it will be harder to get close to him, but I'll by God find a way!"

Fran thought of Anna. She stacked the pieces of glass. "You sure you want to try again? I thought we agreed we were in the ideal position. The law thinks you're dead. They're probably blaming his shooting on the James boys."

"The *James* boys! There it is again. Well, I'm tired of this anonymity. *I* want some of the credit!" He rubbed at his head, which ached fiercely today. He walked over to a buffet and grabbed a bottle of whiskey, slugging some down. "I want the world to know Crazy Doc is still alive, and that I'm the one who shot down Nate Foster. I want Foster to shake in his boots, wondering when I'll do the same again. I've got to show him up, Fran, make him look like a fool! He's been bragging all this time about being the one who killed Crazy Doc. Wouldn't his face get red if everybody found out I wasn't dead at all? I'd love to announce to all of them that the only thing in that grave back at our old hide-out is a dead preacher." He laughed heartily and drank some more whiskey.

"Don't get careless, Doc. We've got things pretty good now."

"Good and boring. What's the sense in getting your revenge if nobody knows about it? I swear, Fran, you're losing your old gumption. Don't you care about the cause anymore? The James boys and the Youngers still care. Anytime we rob from a Federal bank or rob a payload headed for Federal soldiers, we're making trouble for the Yankees who control this country now. Why make it easy for them? If all you want is to settle down like some old married woman and live a nice peaceful life, you might as well leave us and go find whatever it is you want."

Fran rose and set the pieces of vase on another table. "You'd let me go?" She turned hurt, tear-filled eyes to Darryl. "After all I've done for you? My God, Darryl, I love you. I've always been here for you. How can you say I've lost my interest in the cause, when I've risked life and limb for you, spent my entire life savings to support us when the money ran out? I even slept with your men because you wanted to keep them happy. Do you think that was easy for me? I did it because you asked me to. I've done everything you asked. And when you're sick, or when your mind doesn't want to work the way it ought to, I'm there to protect you, take care of you. You *need* me, Darryl."

"How come all of a sudden you're using my real name? I've told you not to do that."

She put her hands on her hips. "You want true recognition, Darryl? You want the kind of fame the Jameses and the Youngers have?"

He put a hand to his head again, running it through his thick, dark, unwashed hair. "What are you talking about?"

She smiled a little. "Tell me you love me, Darryl. Promise

me it will always be just us, and I can give you the fame you want. And along with it, you'll get the sweetest revenge on Nate Foster you could ever hope to achieve. And you'll do it not as Crazy Doc, but as Darryl Kelley, the name you should start using now. It will help you get that fame and recognition. And it will be the downfall of Nate Foster."

He set the whiskey aside, noticing the glitter of victory in her eyes. Fran was a smart woman. He was fiercely tired of her, yet he realized he could not have survived this long without her. And one thing about her that could not be argued: he could trust her. She knew something, and if she had an idea, it was probably a good one. "Explain yourself, woman."

She folded her arms. "Nate Foster has a wife."

"So what? I already heard that—a wife and a kid."

"But you don't know who his wife is. I do. I saw her that day at Lawrence. I didn't tell you because . . . because I was afraid you'd do something foolish if you knew and get yourself caught. I don't want to lose you, Darryl—not to the law, and not to another woman. I never minded the ones you raped for a thrill, or the little Mexican girls who meant nothing to you. But this one might mean something more."

He turned and picked up the bottle again. "Jesus, woman, will you get to the point? Who the hell is his wife?"

"She's beautiful, and blond . . . and her name is Anna."

Darryl slowly lowered the bottle. He swallowed, color coming into his face as he turned to look at her. "*My* Anna?"

"Not anymore. She's Nate Foster's Anna, or at least she *thinks* she is. Can you imagine her humiliation, the gossip, Nate Foster's devastation and ruined reputation if the whole world finds out that his wife is not really his wife at all—that they're living in sin—that she's a bigamist? And worse than that, the wife of the illustrious, heroic lawman Nate Foster has a first husband who not only is still alive, but is a notorious outlaw?"

She watched him struggle to weigh what she had just told him, realizing it took him longer to digest and figure some things than it took most people.

He scratched at a bristly two-day-old beard. "Anna?" He turned away, pacing for a moment. "I figured she was way up in Montana."

"So did I."

He turned to look at her again. "Why in hell didn't you tell me?"

"I told you why. I didn't think at first it would matter because I figured Foster would die. Anna would be left a widow, for a second time as far as she knew. It served her right. But as a widow she would have been a threat to our relationship, so I didn't say anything. I was . . . I was afraid you'd go and get her. Maybe I was wrong, Darryl. I'm sorry if I was, but I love you and I don't want to lose you. But now, now that I know how badly you want recognition and revenge, I want to help you get it. We have to show Anna up for what she really is, Darryl. I told you she was a traitor. She went and married a Yankee lawman. She's no good, would have turned you in way back when you first came back, just like I said she would. Now after what she's done, she deserves to be humiliated, and so does Foster. Don't you see? It's the perfect revenge on them both."

She smiled more, walking around the spilled flowers, twisting her words just enough to keep him confused and in her control. She had to be sure he wouldn't be angry that she had kept the news from him. She had to be sure he understood her reasons were for his benefit.

"Can't you picture it?" she continued. "Crazy Doc goes to Topeka, holds a gun to Anna Foster's head, uses her as a hostage. I imagine everybody in town knows her. You announce who you really are—your real name—that you're the man who shot Nate Foster, and now you're taking Foster's wife away with you, because she's not his wife at all. She's *your* wife." She laughed lightly. "Oh, what a look Anna will have on her face! And what an embarrassment for Nate Foster—the bank robbed right under his nose, his own wife a part of it, riding off with Crazy Doc, who is really Darryl Kelley, her first husband. Maybe she's never even *told* Foster about you! That would be even better."

Darryl ran a hand through his hair again, trying to get it all straight in his mind. Anna, married to Nate Foster! It seemed incredible. His emotions ran wild, a small part of him remembering another life, another woman. But she had run out on him, hadn't she? Fran told him she had. And she was a traitor! If he could get his hands on her, he'd show her whose wife she was, enjoy the look of shock and horror on her face while he took her. Then he'd wrap his hands around her throat and do what he should have done back at Centralia when he saw her there. Maybe even then she was trying to run away! Prim, proper, Yankee Anna! How could he have married her in the first place? For her beauty? Yes, maybe that was all it was at that. Now Nate Foster had ravished that beautiful body, enjoyed what belonged to Darryl Kelley! Nate Foster had been sleeping with his wife! What better reason for revenge?

"That bastard," he muttered. "That sonofabitching Yankee bastard!" He turned, his gaze resting on Fran. "He *would* come after her, Fran, and that's the best reason to take her! I'd get revenge on Anna, *and* on Foster. He'd come after her, all right, and he'd ride right into my trap! I'd gun him down like a jackrabbit. What better bait than to rob the Topeka bank and make off with his wife? Even if he hated her when he found out the truth, he'd still come after her because that's the kind of man he is. I'd shoot him down, and I'd get my piece of Anna. Kind of a farewell." He smiled through yellowing teeth. "Just for fun, Fran. A man deserves a last fling with his wife, don't you think? Then I'd watch her turn purple and die with my hands pressed against her windpipe. Nate Foster and his wife dead, his wife killed by her outlaw husband who's still alive! That's better than any story that could ever be printed about the Jameses or the Youngers, isn't it?"

Fran smiled. "You bet it is." Her eyes narrowed into slits of hatred. "But you've got to promise to kill her, Darryl. If you can't do it because she used to be your wife . . . *I'll* do it *for* you."

"Oh, I can do it all right."

She stepped closer. "If you're going to have your way with her, then let the others have their share before you kill her. You know what that would do to a woman like Anna. It would be a proper punishment for a Yankee traitor."

He nodded. "Yeah. I expect it would. That's a good idea. Then Foster and his wife would be dead, we'd have the money from that Yankee bank, and more fame than I ever dreamed of."

Fran put her arms around his neck. "You glad I told you, Darryl?"

He grinned. "Real glad, woman. I expect I'll keep you a while longer. You help me think straight."

She threw back her head and laughed with delight. She had wanted to settle into a normal life with him, at least as normal as life could be with a man like Darryl Kelley. But as long as he was unhappy, she had to keep finding ways to make him happy and excited again, ways to make him appreciate her.

He pushed her onto a sofa, giving little care to the fact that one of his men could walk in at any time. Fran didn't mind. She liked being Darryl Kelley's woman. More than that, she liked knowing she could still control him if she was clever enough about it. She had won him over once again. She had waited until just the right time to tell him about Anna. He wasn't angry at all that she hadn't told him before now. It was easy to make him understand her way was the right way. It would surely be even easier to convince him to kill Anna. She realized it was what she had wanted for years.

She laughed lightly, as Darryl opened her dress to celebrate their new idea in a way he always liked to celebrate— with whiskey and sex. She returned his lovemaking with a savagery that matched his own.

Nate kept himself busy doing odd jobs for the court, serving subpoenas, making a train trip to Abilene and one to Lawrence—which gave Anna the chills—but he came home safely.

A month had passed since the funeral, and Nate had been restless and silent ever since. They had made love only once, and that was five days ago, a quick, almost necessary act, as though he had done it only to relieve himself and not for her.

Anna knew he would gradually come around. Their love

was too strong for anything to interrupt that part of it for long. She could not help thinking there was something he was not telling her, something that had nothing to do with Christine. Whenever they went out together, he always seemed on the defense, his eyes darting around like a cat being hunted, and a few times she had caught him staring at her strangely, as though he wanted to ask her something but was afraid to bring it up.

She could not help asking one evening at the supper table. "I can always tell when you're trying not to worry me," she told him as he finished a piece of pie. "But when you do that I get more worried than ever, so you might as well come out with it. I'm better off being prepared. You're keeping something from me, Nate, and I want to know what it is."

She held a spoon out to feed Becky some sweet potatoes. "It has something to do with the man who shot you, doesn't it? You know something and you're not telling me."

Nate frowned, swallowing his last piece of pie and leaning back in his chair. "I've been putting it off, trying to find out some things on my own. I don't like worrying you."

"I just told you that keeping secrets from me worries me more than anything. I'm not a child, Nate. You're wearing a badge again, and I'm well aware of what that means. And I'm certainly aware that you intend to find the man who shot you. If you know something, you might as well tell me."

He laid down his fork, sighing deeply. "I just don't like dredging up old memories from your past. I know how that upsets you."

An odd tremble swept through her, and she hoped the look on her face didn't change too noticeably. Her past? What on earth did he mean by that? She had finally reached the point where she hardly even thought about it anymore, had finally managed to bury Darryl and put the war behind her. What could his shooting have to do with her past?

"Finish feeding Becky and put her to bed. Then we'll talk," Nate was saying.

"All right," she answered, trying to sound cool and steady.

Time suddenly seemed to drag. A sick heaviness began to penetrate her muscles and bones, and her heart beat harder. She told herself it was ridiculous. Whatever he had to say, it couldn't have anything to do with Darryl anymore, so why was she suddenly so shaken? She finished feeding the baby, and Nate left the table to go and read the newspaper. Anna cleaned up the table and left the dishes in the dishpan. She carried Becky upstairs to bed, changing her into her nightie and reading her a story first. But her mind was not on the story at all. Why had Nate mentioned the past?

The old guilt had returned to haunt her again. She should have told him. She *should* have told him. But what difference could it possibly make now? It couldn't have anything to do with Darryl. If only he hadn't said "your" past, as though it were somehow directly related to her.

She called down to Nate to come in and kiss Becky good night. He came upstairs and hugged her and buzzed her neck, making her laugh, just like always. He kissed her again, tucked her in, said a prayer with her, just like always. He didn't seem especially upset about anything as far as home and family were concerned. Surely he didn't know something about her past he wasn't telling her. Maybe all he meant was that he had to bring up the war again, that some former Confederate was the man who was after him. He knew how she hated to talk about those years.

Nate turned down the lantern and they left the room. He kept his arm around her waist as they walked into the parlor, and Anna's tension lessened somewhat. They sat down across from each other in front of the fireplace. The windows were open wide, and a gentle breeze of cooler air blew through the room, relieving them of the days' heat. Nate lit a thin cigar, and Anna nervously picked up some knitting.

"Well, what's the big secret?" she asked.

Nate leaned forward, resting his elbows on his knees. "Anna, you remember a woman called Fran Rogers? I think you worked for a woman by that name back in Columbia, at the restaurant."

Anna's fingers froze. What in God's name could Fran have to do with Nate's shooting! She knew she was paling, knew that while the rest of her face was growing whiter, her cheeks were growing redder. She wished she could control her reactions better, but the question surprised her.

"I don't mean to upset you, Anna, but I need to know if you remember anything about how the woman behaved at the time you left her employment. Jim and I have reason to believe that outlaw Crazy Doc is still alive, and we think Fran Rogers took up with him. If you know anything about where a woman like Fran might hang out, relatives she might have had—" He frowned in alarm as Anna let a knitting needle fall to the floor. Her eyes were wide and showed near terror.

"What do you . . . mean?" she choked out. "Crazy Doc, still alive? That's . . . that's impossible! You . . . you found his grave!"

"We think it was faked. He wanted to lay low for a while, get us off his tail. Jim arrested a man who rode with him just about the time I was shot." He reached out for her but she drew away. "Anna, what the hell is the matter with you? It's not as though the man were standing outside our door. We're on the lookout. I just thought you might know something about this Rogers woman that could help."

Anna felt as though she had just been thrown into deep, dark waters. They were closing in around her, drowning her, filling her lungs so that she couldn't breathe. She stood up on rubbery legs, letting her knitting fall to the floor. She started to stumble away, but Nate grabbed her. "My God, Anna, what's the matter with you?"

She turned and looked up at him. Nate. Her handsome, kind, brave, beloved Nate. So good. So trusting. She should have known it could come to this, should have known she had no right thinking she could leave the past behind her, that she deserved this happiness. Tears were already making their way into her eyes and down her cheeks. She pulled away from Nate, putting a hand to her chest, wondering where her next breath would come from.

"Tell me . . . you aren't sure. Tell me it isn't true about . . . about Crazy Doc."

Nate watched her carefully, an ugly dread moving into his heart. "We're about ninety-five percent sure, Anna. The description the man gave fit, the timing. Crazy Doc had it in for me, always said he'd get me. When I was shot, he and this Fran Rogers took a trip north from where they were hiding out in Indian Territory, all dandied up so nobody would recognize them. I expect with everyone thinking he was dead, if the man cleaned up and kept a hat on to cover his scar, he could move into any crowd and put on an act with the woman as husband and wife, go about anyplace he chose. I'm not sure I'd recognize him myself."

She turned away, grasping the doorjamb. "*I'd* recognize him," she answered. "Oh, my God, what have I done? I've lost you," she groaned.

The heat of the humid night suddenly disappeared for Anna. She shivered as she made her way to the stairs, nearly falling. Nate watched her in astonishment, grabbing her from the fall. "What the hell is wrong, Anna?"

Her mind swirled with the horror of what he had just told her. Alive! Darryl still alive, the man who had shot Nate and put him through all that pain and suffering! At the moment death seemed a better punishment for her secrets and lies than having to tell Nate the truth. She turned and looked up at him. Such a wonderful, caring man he was. To be without him was going to be the worst pain she would ever know. She stared at him, her eyes wide, her face pale. "How much do you love me, Nate, truly love me?"

He frowned, slowly letting go of her. "What kind of a question is that?"

"A necessary one."

He reached out to take her arm then, but she drew away. "Don't touch me, Nate. I couldn't bear for you to . . . touch me lovingly . . . and look at me with hate in your eyes the next moment."

He ran a hand through his hair, beginning to feel strangely numb. No, what he was thinking couldn't be true. There had to be some other reason why she was acting this way. "Why in hell would I hate you, Anna? Dammit, be straight with me."

She slowly sat down on one of the lower steps, taking a deep breath before saying the words she had prayed she would never have to tell him. "The outlaw Fran Rogers runs

with, the one called Crazy Doc . . . is my husband . . .
Darryl Kelley."

There. She had said it. If only she had said it years ago.
She waited, staring past him at the front door. The house
was suddenly so silent it almost hurt her ears. She felt his
eyes on her without even looking up at him. She couldn't
meet those eyes, couldn't bear to see the horror in them.

"I thought he . . . was dead," she groaned. "I thought
I was free . . . to marry you. Fran wrote to tell me he
. . . died. My God, you and I aren't even . . . legally
married. My own husband . . . my real husband . . .
nearly killed you."

She gasped when he grabbed her arm and suddenly jerked
her to her feet. "You aren't making any sense, Anna! What
the hell is all this about? Crazy Doc is your *husband*? You
knew it when he was . . . when we *thought* he was still
alive?"

"I . . . didn't want to tell you. How could I tell you?"
she asked, her voice shaking. "You were so . . . so much
the better man, so against everything Darryl was, so fine
and good and . . . if I had told you, you would have
hated me . . . would have looked at me the way I saw
other men look at the wives of bushwhackers. I might have
even been arrested! Some of those women . . . were
beaten, even raped! And you . . . you hated men like Darryl so much. How could I tell you? Do you know the shame
I suffered? You can't imagine! To have your husband go off
to war . . . a fine, caring, loving doctor, and have him
return . . . a murderer and thief, God knows what else!"

She yanked her arm away and turned to grasp the stair
rail. "He was at Centralia," she gasped. "He was *there*! I saw
him, too, just like you did, but I was watching my own
husband commit those horrors, a man I didn't even know
was back from the war! He never even told me! That's why I
was so shaken that day! That's why I couldn't bear it whenever you talked about Centralia. Witnessing what happened
. . . was bad enough! But to know my own husband was a
part of it was the worst of all!"

She finally turned to face him, and he stepped back. For
the first time his gray eyes were unreadable, except that she

did not see the gentle love that was usually there, even when he was angry about something else. He shook his head and turned away, running a hand through his hair, then throwing his head back and taking deep breaths. Did he want to grab her and beat her? If only Christine hadn't so recently died. It only made all of this so much worse.

"Nate, I thought he was *dead.* I thought it was *over!*"

He turned and put out his hand. "Stop! Stop right there and go back to the beginning." He clenched his fists. "What the hell is going on, Anna! Your husband was at Centralia and you didn't *tell* me? My God, in the beginning, when we were just friends, you could have told me then."

"I was too *ashamed,* and I was scared, Nate. I was scared of what would happen to me. You were a *marshal!* I could have been arrested!"

"You think *I* would have *arrested* you?"

"I didn't know you that well. And I didn't want others to know. A woman in Columbia who was suspected of being the wife of a raiding bushwhacker was attacked and raped by a mob of jayhawkers. Other families were being arrested."

"You could have told me later, when things calmed down, when I asked you to marry me. I had a *right* to know!"

"I was afraid I'd lose you!"

"And you didn't think you'd lose me if we were married a while and *then* you told me?"

"I didn't think it would matter. I thought Darryl was dead and that was the end of it."

He rolled his eyes and turned away again. "Well, at least Jim and I have a name for him now. Darryl Kelley." He snickered. "What a damn mess. How am I going to tell Jim that the man we're after, the hideous outlaw we're after, the man who *shot* me, is my wife's first husband. No, not my wife. She can't be my wife now. She already *has* a husband!"

"Nate, stop it! Please calm down and let me explain. Please try to understand my side. I love you, Nate, more than my own life. I need you. Do you know what it's been like . . . going through all this alone? Claudine is the only one who knows . . . and only because she brought me the letter from Fran. Nate, it was a horrible, cruel, vicious letter. When I got it, I had no idea where Darryl was . . . no idea he had taken up with Fran. In the letter she told me he was dead. That was all I had to go by . . . and you and others told me the same—"

"But everyone believed *I* killed him! As far as you knew, you married the man who killed your own first husband!"

"But the man you killed *wasn't* my husband! He was a *stranger,* Nate! A total stranger! As far as I was concerned, the man I married had already been killed—not *in* the war, but *by* it! The man I thought you had killed was as much a stranger to me as someone I'd never met in my whole life!"

"The fact remains that he was your husband, that you didn't tell me the truth about him—and that he *wasn't* killed! He came back and put me through the worst hell I've ever known!"

"And that wasn't hell for *me?* All those months of loving you, watching you suffer, caring for you? My God, how was I to know it was Darryl who did that!"

"And maybe he knows who I *married!* Maybe *that's* why he shot me. It's a pretty good reason, don't you think? He already had it in for me—then he finds out I'm sleeping with his *wife!*"

The words cut deep. Oh, yes, they had slept together, and they had enjoyed the splendid ecstasy of their love and the sharing of that love. Would he ever hold her that way again, ever look at her with the same devotion and desire in those handsome gray eyes?

"I'll explain it all, Nate, from the very beginning," she said quietly. She turned away. "And then I'll leave, go back to Abilene for a while, visit Claudine. I expect . . . it might be better if you didn't have to look at me for a few days. We both need time . . . to think." She felt herself trembling, swallowed against the ache in her throat. "Just . . . please remember that until I thought he was dead, I never let anything get serious between us. In spite of what he was, what I knew about him, I remained faithful to my wedding vows. I'm not the unfeeling harlot you think I am."

"My God, Anna, I'm not thinking that at all! I'm just

trying to understand why you didn't tell me in the beginning! It wouldn't have changed anything."

"Wouldn't it?" She met his gaze. Still unreadable. Nate! She was losing him!

"Hell, no," he answered. "But to wait—to let me find out this way—"

"I didn't *let* you find out. I would never have *let* you find out! If Darryl had stayed dead . . ." She covered her eyes with her hand. "I should have known," she said wearily. "I was too happy. Everything was too wonderful. All those years of loneliness, the waiting and wondering, praying for and loving the man who left me to go off to war . . . and then seeing the man who had returned. Can't you understand even a little what that was like?"

She lowered her hand and walked to a table in the hall, reaching out to lightly touch a fern that sat on it. She spoke almost absently, as though reliving the incident. "The first time I finally see my husband again, he's dirty and bearded and he's murdering innocent men. His eyes are wild, and I'm afraid of him. He rides up to me and nearly knocks me down, and he throws his wedding ring at me and tells me to go to hell. And then I never see him again. All I get is a letter from a woman I once lived with, his own best friend's wife. The letter says she's been sleeping with him. She calls me a Yankee traitor, tells me how much she hates me . . . tells me my husband died in her arms. My Darryl . . . the man who was once so gentle and caring. Dr. Darryl Kelley, who once had dreams of helping others . . . turned into a murderer and an adulterer . . . calling me a traitor with his last breath, after all the years I waited for him."

She sighed deeply and faced Nate. "All those months I waited alone. And then I met you, and I wanted to be loved again . . . wanted to be a woman again. But you were a lawman, and my husband was the kind of man you hated most. I just couldn't bring myself to tell you. And then, when I was sure Darryl was dead, I didn't see the necessity of telling you at all. I wanted to put it all behind me. But I guess most people aren't allowed that privilege, are they?"

Her eyes looked suddenly sunken, dark circles showing under them. "You've been haunted by the war ever since

Christine. It's been the same for me, Nate, only I've done my suffering secretly. Now Christine is dead, and I've discovered my husband is still alive. Ironic, isn't it? Ironic . . . and cruel. The war still isn't over for us, is it?"

She saw the confusion in his eyes. Part of him was angry with her, maybe even hated her. Another part of him wanted to hold her. Right now the angry part was winning out. She wondered with dread and sorrow if it would ever release its hold.

"Do you have the letter?" he asked.

"I burned it."

"What about a photograph? You have a photograph of Darryl Kelley? He might show up here spruced up and pretending to be Mr. American Citizen. I want to see his face. I want to know what the man who probably intends to try to kill me again looks like."

Her heart fell at the hardness in his voice, his rigid stance. He was not going to allow himself to touch her. His pride had been deeply hurt.

"I kept a picture, from a long, long time ago, when he was a good man, Nate. And he was, or I would never have married him. He suffered some kind of head injury, and it changed him. I never had the chance to talk to him, to find out what happened. If not for Fran, maybe he would have contacted me. He probably went to her first, looking for me. Somehow she turned him against me, probably convinced him I had become a traitor to him."

She turned and slowly climbed the stairs, her body feeling like lead. Each creak of a step almost hurt her ears. She wished he would scream at her more, hit her—anything but his sudden silence. She could feel his eyes drilling into her back as he stood below watching her. She wished he would reach out and tell her everything was all right. But she knew he would not. He needed time. It seemed so ironic that this man she loved more than her own life, this man she had nursed for nearly a year, this man who had fathered her child in such intimate, glorious lovemaking, suddenly seemed such a stranger.

She went into their bedroom, which they had moved back upstairs, and she rummaged through one of her dresser drawers, lifting some paper that lined the bottom of it and taking out a cracked, dulling photograph of her and Darryl, taken at a fair in Lawrence not long after they were married. She turned and came back downstairs, handing the picture to Nate.

"*This* is the man I mourned, Nate. This man died a few months after he left, when a bullet or shrapnel or whatever it was creased his skull and turned him into a different person. I hold no sorrow for the man you supposedly shot and killed, the man who has come back to hunt you again, who did those vile things at Centralia and who ran off with Fran Rogers. I hold no grief for him, and if you kill him for certain this time, to me it will be just like killing any other outlaw. You'll be ridding Kansas of another no-good—a stranger."

Nate took the picture. He studied it, getting a better idea as he looked at the handsome, happy-looking man with Anna. He shook his head. "It's hard to believe this could be the same man."

"If it's hard for you, you can imagine how hard it was for me."

He handed back the picture. "I'm getting out of here for a while," he told her, his voice gravely.

"Where are you going?"

"Just . . . riding, alone. Tomorrow I'll . . . take that damn picture to Jim. I've got to figure out how I'm going to explain all this to him, and to Rob." He turned to the door.

"Will you come back . . . home, I mean?"

He didn't answer right away. Becky made a little laughing sound upstairs in her bed, and he hesitated at the door. "I'll be back," he said quietly, "for Becky's sake, if nothing else."

The words pierced her heart like a sword. She stared after him as he left. Minutes later she heard the sound of his horse as he rode off, and she felt as though he were riding over her heart, back and forth, back and forth, the hooves of his horse battering it into the ground.

Chapter 22

Jim Lister studied the face in the picture. "You think he still looks this way when he's cleaned up?"

Nate stared out a window. "I expect close enough that we would probably recognize him."

Jim sighed, looking at Nate, catching the shadow of beard on the side of his face. "You know, there's no need to tell anyone else about this. If we happen to catch this guy and kill him, nobody will know the difference. No sense dragging Anna's name into it. 'Course, there might not be any way around it. You tell Rob yet?"

Nate rubbed the back of his neck. "No."

Jim rubbed at his dry lips, aching over his friend's trouble. Nate Foster had had his share of heartache. But then so had Anna. "She loves you, you know. I can understand why she did it. She's a good woman, Nate. What she did, she thought she was doin' for your own good. Must have been real hard on her."

"I know that. I just . . . have to get used to it. Before this, her first husband was always this distant, unreal person whom I'd never met and figured I never would. Now, to know he exists . . ." He rubbed at his eyes. "My God, Jim, we aren't even legally husband and wife. I *have* to find this guy, if for no other reason than to let Anna get a legal divorce from him. In the meantime, I shouldn't even be living over there."

"How will you explain it if you don't?"

"I don't know. I'll just keep busy, I guess. Stay away as much as I can, sleep . . . in the guest room when I'm there. It won't matter for the next couple of weeks. She's going to visit Claudine in Abilene."

"You shouldn't let her go, Nate. She could be in danger now that we know this man is still alive."

Nate looked at him in surprise. "My God. I hadn't even taken the time to think of it that way."

"Well, *take* the time. And you shouldn't be giving her the cold shoulder. She needs you now more than she's ever needed you. She was there for you when you were puking and helpless. And if you had never walked again, she would have been right there for you the rest of your life. Now *she's* the one who is injured—maybe not physically, but she's injured. This has to be quite a shock for her, too. And when people begin finding out, which they probably will, she's gonna suffer ridicule. You can't leave it half done like this, and you can't let that bastard ruin what you and Anna have together. Ain't many men find a woman like that."

Nate sighed, his gray eyes bloodshot and shadowed, the lines around his eyes and mouth looking harder. "It's harder for me, Jim. He's the kind of man who killed Christine—he came close to killing *me*. And if I *do* kill him, I'd be killing her *husband*. In the meantime, we had Becky illegally."

"Bullshit! That little girl was conceived out of love. Ain't no piece of paper makes all that much difference. For all intents and purposes Darryl Kelley *was* dead—dead to *Anna*. You think God doesn't understand those things? We'll get him, Nate, and he'll either be shot or hanged. Either way, he *will* be dead, and then you two will just get remarried and you'll never say a word to Becky. That kid never needs to know the difference."

"She will if we stay in Kansas."

"Then *leave* Kansas. This ain't the only place that needs

lawmen. We're gettin' pretty settled now. I hear tell there's a need out in some of them wild mining towns farther west for good lawmen."

Nate sighed, moving toward the door and putting on his hat. "Keep that picture out of sight, will you? I'll be back later." He looked at Jim. "Keep your eyes open. That sonofabitch better show soon."

He went out, and Jim looked at the picture again, noticing how happy both Anna and Darryl looked. He shook his head, his eyes tearing. "Goddamn war," he muttered.

Anna heard the door open and close. She hesitated, then continued packing her carpetbag. Becky sat on the bedroom floor playing. Anna heard Nate's heavy footsteps on the stairs. He had been gone all night, had come back an hour or so earlier, before Becky was up. Anna had waited in the kitchen the first time he returned to the house, but he did not come in to talk to her. She had left Darryl's picture on the table in the hall, and after he quietly left again, she had noticed it was gone. She decided then she would go to Abilene, as she had told him the night before she would do. He apparently did not want to see her for a while.

Now he came into the bedroom. She looked up at him, her heart feeling shattered at the still-unreadable gray eyes.

"You don't have to leave, Anna."

"Yes I do. I'll be back in a few days. Right now we shouldn't even be living in the same house, should we?"

He felt painfully torn. He hated her, loved her. He wanted to hit her, and he wanted to hold her. He wanted her to go away, and he wanted her to stay.

"I knew there was a reason I kept the restaurant," she told him then. "Now I know what it was. I guess I always knew it would come to this someday."

She was stronger today. He could see the old Barker stubbornness taking hold, always the survivor in any situation. He didn't truly want her to have to return to her old, lonely life; she was his wife, yet she wasn't. He still felt the obligation to care for her, protect her, love her, provide for her, yet part of him wanted to hurt her as much as she had hurt him. He looked down at Becky, who looked up at him with

her wide, blue eyes and smiled. She got to her feet and
toddled over to him, reaching up.

Nate leaned down and picked his little girl up in his arms.
He sighed and closed his eyes, kissing his baby's curly,
blond hair. "Please don't go, Anna," he said.

The words were spoken simply, with no anger. The way
he said them erased some of the stubborn hardness that had
come into her heart overnight. She looked at him, her heart
going out to him at the sight of him standing there holding
Becky. He had been through so much, and he was a proud
man. She knew he was doing his best to swallow that pride.
This was as far as he had gotten up to now.

She looked down at the carpetbag. Maybe she should stay
after all. Was she just running away, like when she left Columbia? She sat down wearily on the bed, realizing that was
exactly what she was doing. She loved Nate Foster, no matter what his faults; and God knew she couldn't expect him
to accept all this readily.

"I don't know quite what to do about our situation,
Nate," she told him.

He set Becky back down on the floor, leaning on the
doorjamb then, his gray eyes meeting hers. His big frame
filled the doorway, and she thought what damage he could
do to her if he wanted now. But she felt no fear. She knew
she could hurt Nate Foster in every cruel way a woman
could think of, and he would never lay a hand on her. For a
moment she saw that vulnerable, little-boy look in his eyes
again before he walked to a dresser and picked up a cigarette
paper, then took the lid off a jar that held tobacco.

"I'll find ways to keep busy," he told her, rolling a cigarette. "With my job that's easy enough. We'll just . . .
have to take a day at a time until I find Darryl Kelley and
put an end to this nightmare." He sealed and lit the cigarette, his back still to her. "Part of the reason I don't want
you to leave is concern for your safety. Now that the man
probably knows about us and all, I want you right here in
Topeka where I can keep an eye on you."

She watched him take a deep drag on the cigarette. She
wanted him to make love to her, wanted to show him how
much she loved him in return. How strange that suddenly

the passion they had shared had been turned into something sinful and ugly. "Do you really care if anything happens to me?" she asked.

He turned and looked at her with a frown. "Of course I care. I asked you to stay, didn't I?"

"For my safety—and most likely, more for Becky's. Is that the only reason, Nate? Am I just another citizen under your jurisdiction that you're watching out for?"

He turned away and walked to a window as she spoke the words. "Don't put it that way. Dammit, Anna, this isn't easy for either one of us. I just . . . I don't want to say anything more than we have to right now, because I'm afraid of saying all the wrong things and regretting them later. I know I've got a pride that tends to hurt me and the people around me. But it's there, and I have to deal with it. Just let me do this my own way."

"I just want you to hold me again, Nate." The words came out brokenly, and they tore at his gut; but he couldn't make himself move toward her. He kept looking out the window.

"I can't. Not yet. I'm sorry, Anna."

She bit her lip and breathed deeply. If he was going to be so stubborn, she was not about to break down into desperate tears in front of him.

"Just tell me the whole thing again, in detail, Anna. There might be something I can use. When a man is being hunted, it helps to know something about the hunter."

She leaned down to pick Becky up and set her on the bed. "You probably know more about him right now than I do," she answered. "All I can do is tell you what happened up to the point where we got . . . married." Married. They weren't married at all. What a hideous nightmare this had become!

She told him everything, in as much detail as she could remember. "I wrestled with my conscience night and day for a while," she finished, "when I first . . . fell in love with you. I knew he was alive, yet he was dead to me. I had to decide whether I had the right to love another man, especially the very man who I later knew had shot Darryl. But you were so much more man than he. You represented everything that he was not. And you were there. He wasn't. I . . . needed you so badly. I was so afraid of losing you. I came close . . . so close to telling you so many times. And then I would see the love in your eyes . . . or you would make some comment about men like Darryl, and I would lose my courage. I never meant to deceive you, Nate. I didn't look at it that way at all. I know that's how it looks, but that was the farthest thing from my mind. If I hadn't thought Darryl had been killed, or if I'd had any idea where he was or that you were in such grave danger, I would have told you. I just didn't see the need . . . didn't want to take the risk if I didn't have to."

Nate took a deep drag on the cigarette. "You should have trusted me more than that, Anna."

"Yes, I suppose I should have. But at the time, my nerves were just about finished. I was so confused, so scared, and tired of being alone. I didn't want to do anything that might endanger the sweet love I had found in you. And after getting that letter from Fran, I didn't know who to trust about anything anymore."

She heard a deep sigh. "A lot of things fall into place now. Why you took to your bed when you heard your husband was dead. You made up that story about Darryl being shoved into an abandoned well pit—that was really when you got the letter from Fran, wasn't it?"

"Yes," she answered quietly.

"Jesus. I can't believe I didn't ask to see the letter from the supposed war buddy who wrote and told you he'd witnessed his death. And that night in Kansas City, when we had dinner with Henry Wilder and you got so upset when we talked about Centralia. I think we even mentioned my supposedly killing Crazy Doc. So many things make more sense to me now. I just don't know what to do next, Anna." He put out the cigarette. "I don't even know how I feel right now, except bone tired."

She turned to face him. "I know how *I* feel. I love you, Nate, and that will never change." She wanted desperately to tell him she was going to have another baby, had planned on surprising him with the news after supper last night. She had been waiting for the right time, but then

Christine had died, and now this. Suddenly the fact that she was going to have a baby had turned into a matter of shame. Now she would have *two* illegitimate children. How could she tell him now? The joy of the news had gone out of her, and she was not about to use it as a tool to try to change his feelings. If he was going to love her and want her again, it had to be for her, not for a baby.

He rubbed at the back of his neck, walking toward the door, then turned to face her. "I've got two different people wrestling around inside me right now, Anna. One of them is real angry—not so much at you, but at the idea that something like this could happen at all—angry at the men who caused the damn war and the ones who want to keep it going—angry that a woman like you should feel she has to lie and suffer quietly to keep the man she loves."

"And *has* she kept him?" she asked.

He searched the blue eyes in which he had so often gotten lost. Suddenly he wanted her more than ever, but he couldn't have her now. "Part of him," he answered. "The real question is, does she have a right to him, and he to her? There's another man we have to find first, Anna. This has to be settled, and by the time it is, maybe our lives will be too ruined to pick up the pieces. It won't change the part of me that married you, or the reasons why I did. But I guess in a way we'll have to start all over again, won't we?"

"Yes, I suppose we will."

He rubbed at his eyes and turned away. "I've got to sleep. I'm going down to the guest bedroom. I'll start sleeping there till this is over. Nobody has to know what we do in our own house, and right now nobody but Jim knows about this."

That's right, she thought. *Nobody has to know. You could still sleep with me, Nate, and it wouldn't matter. I don't care about a piece of paper. In my heart you're still my husband. I'm carrying our second child.*

He started out the door. "Nate." He stopped and waited. "I've hurt you deeply. I never meant to. You must know that."

He turned to look at her, suddenly looking much older.

"I know it. And I don't mean to hurt you back. Sometimes we just can't help ourselves, can we?"

He left the room and she watched after him, feeling as though her heart were being squeezed in a vise. He still loved her, but something was different now. It was obvious his whole being would be occupied with one thing now—finding Darryl Kelley. They would never be able to get their lives back to normal until her first marriage was ended—and Darryl dead.

"How's the home life, Nate?" Jim asked. He poured himself a cup of coffee, offering another one to Nate.

Nate eyed him narrowly as he took the cup. "Strained, but not really your business."

Jim grinned. "It's my business when it makes you testy." He sipped some of his coffee. "And it's especially my business when I think it might affect your work—and your ability to be as alert as you should be. The way we've splashed it all over the papers that Marshal Nate Foster knows who shot him and is daring the man to try it again, Darryl Kelley is gonna show his hand pretty soon, friend. And you just might be so full of thoughts of Anna that you're off guard."

"I can handle that sonofabitch any day of the week."

Jim drank some more coffee. "Personally, I think you should be handling your wife the way you *want* to handle her down deep inside."

"Leave it alone, Jim. Technically, she's not my wife. God only knows how this will end. Why lay claim to something that hasn't legally been declared mine?"

"You already own her and you know it."

Nate guzzled the rest of his coffee and slammed down the cup. "Well, it's a pretty big blow to *think* you own something and then find out you don't. Everything is distorted. I look at her and I see his face. The bastard has come between us the same as if he were standing there in person."

"I think it's more than that. I think it's *you* that has come between you."

Nate took out his gun and checked the chamber. "What the hell is that supposed to mean?"

"Means you've got one big flaw, friend. Good a man as

you are, and much as you love Anna Foster, you take honesty to the hilt. You're so damn honest yourself that you can't tolerate dishonesty in another person, and that's how you look at what Anna did—as dishonesty. But it wasn't meant that way, and you've got to understand that or you might as well move out altogether and hang it all up."

"She doesn't have a dishonest bone in her body."

"That's right. Part of you believes that, and that other part of you, that unforgiving part, reminds you she lied to you. There's all kinds of lyin', Nate. Some kinds are done for love. Don't let your personal vendettas against scum like Darryl Kelley get all twisted and turned against good people."

Nate shoved his gun back into its holster and walked to a window. "I just wish something would happen. We can't just sit around here forever. Judge Hewitt won't allow it. We've got duties to perform, cattle thieves to hunt, a hundred other things to do. He won't let us keep hanging around here waiting for something we don't even know will take place. It's hard on Anna too, having men always keeping watch on the house. I can't be sure that bastard won't try to get at me through Anna and Becky."

"The only strain on her is you. Did you hear anything I just told you?"

"I heard you. And I know you're right. I'm trying, Jim, that's all I can tell you. It just takes time. You said once she'd been injured, just like me. And as with my physical injury, it will take both of us a while to recover." He grabbed his hat and looked at Jim. "Sometimes I look at her and I see the love and need in those big, blue eyes, and I feel like I'm going crazy. I see the hurt too, and I know I put it there. I want to reach out to her—but there he is again, reminding me she doesn't belong to me; reminding me that while I loved her and slept with her, she knew he was the one who shot me that first time, knew it when she came to see me; she knew he was at Centralia, knew he never died in the war." He put on his hat. "Let's go make the rounds. If Darryl Kelley is around, I won't draw him out by sitting in here all day."

Jim sighed, finishing his own coffee and putting on his

hat. He opened the door and looked back at Nate. "You still love her?"

Nate smiled sadly. "That's the hell of it."

"Then tell her. That's all she needs to know right now."

Nate lost his smile. "Since when did you give up being a deputy marshal and begin counseling married folks?"

Jim's eyebrows arched. "Since I started watching my best friend let his marriage to the best woman in Kansas go sour."

"You've never even *been* married. Why should I listen to you?"

"If I could find a woman like Anna, I *would* be married. You better watch out, old friend, or I'll take serious that bullshit about the two of you not really being married. I'll take that to mean Anna is a free woman again." He saw the hint of jealousy in Nate's eyes, then laughed lightly. "Just what I thought. You'd better make up your mind, friend. Either she belongs to you or she doesn't. Like I said, a piece of paper and a long-lost husband don't make a whit of difference. You've owned her longer than anybody, and that little girl of yours comes from your seed, not Darryl Kelley's. You remember that. What's that saying the lawyers have for it—possession is nine tenths of the law? Something like that. Come on."

Nate followed the man out, realizing Jim was right. He had to do something about this dull ache to his insides, this constant preoccupation with Anna and how he felt about her, or Darryl Kelley would have easy pickings. After what he and Anna had shared, it seemed preposterous that he had been sleeping in another bed, and sometimes on a cot at the jailhouse, the last two weeks.

Jim walked off to serve some papers on a man being sued for assault, and Nate began his rounds, his eyes catching every shadow, every glint of the sun on steel, watching every stranger closely. He walked right past Doc Long, the local physician. The man turned and called out to Nate, interrupting his thoughts. Nate turned. "Oh, hello, Doc," he said.

"Say, I just wanted to congratulate you, Marshal," the

man answered. "You must be real proud and happy. Maybe this time you'll get that son you wanted."

Nate frowned. "What?"

The doctor's eyebrows arched. "You mean the missus didn't tell you yet? I hope I haven't spoiled the surprise. I thought you knew she was expecting again."

Nate stepped closer, a mixture of surprise and chagrin in his eyes. "Anna's going to have a baby?"

The doctor laughed. "Sure is, in about six months. I expect she's going to be upset with me for spilling the beans. Sorry about that."

Nate shook his hand. "Don't be sorry at all." Nate turned and ran back to the courthouse, where he mounted his horse and rode out, heading for his house.

Anna heard a horse approaching the house at a gallop. Her first thought was that something had happened to Nate, and she hurried to the door, rushing outside to see it was Nate himself approaching. Why was he in such a hurry? Had he heard something about Darryl?

He quickly dismounted and tied his horse, coming up onto the porch. "You scared me to death, riding up here like that," she told him. "I thought it was someone coming to tell me something had happened to you." Her voice broke on the words. Stubborn and remote as he had been, she still wondered what she would do if he wasn't there at all.

"Anna."

She saw a look in his eyes that had not been there for a long time, and to her astonishment he grabbed her close, wrapping his arms around her.

"My God, Anna, you should have told me," he groaned.

How she relished the warm strength she took from his embrace. How her heart soared with love and joy! This was the Nate she had married. "Told you what?"

He kissed her hair. "I ran into Doc Long today."

She stiffened slightly, pulling away. She looked up at him, shaking her head. "I didn't want to use that to win back your love." She turned away.

"My God, Anna, you never *lost* my love. I just let things get in the way of it." He put his hands on her shoulders.

"Anna, listen to me. I can be a damn proud, stubborn ass, and I know it. That's what I've been the last couple of weeks. All this time I've been looking at you with resentment and condemnation, it's *you* who should have been looking at *me* that way, for not understanding what you went through, for turning away from you when you needed me most."

She moved away from him, going to stand against a porch post.

"Dammit, Anna, I'm a little new at this. I mean, I've been struggling to understand that things aren't always all black and all white. I've lived strictly by the law, and I've seen so much of men like Darryl Kelley that I—I couldn't stand the thought of you being with him. I wasn't letting myself understand what a good man he must have been then, otherwise a woman like you would never have married him. And today, today I realized how strong you are, how you're letting yourself suffer alone again by keeping the news of the baby from me. I've been a complete ass in all of this."

She wanted to be angry with him, but always finding it impossible. He stepped closer, grasping her shoulders again. "Anna, I didn't come riding up here just because of the baby. It was because you didn't *tell* me. I realized then the kind of woman I was letting slip through my fingers. Other women would have wept and carried on and used their pregnancy to have their way, or they would have bitterly thrown it in my face. You didn't do either one." He turned her and took her face in his hands. "I'm not going to let you suffer silently like you did all those months when we first met, Anna, like you've been doing ever since we got married. You're not going to carry the weight of this alone. Neither one of us is. We'll share it, like we've shared everything else. You talk about sharing your money, but that's nothing. I want you to share your *sorrow*, your *burdens*. God knows I shared mine with you, what with Christine, and all those months I was sick."

She searched his eyes, a tiny part of her wanting to tell him it was too late, just for spite. But it wasn't too late. It would never be too late for Nate Foster. She reached around his neck, and in the next moment his mouth covered her own, searching deep in a groaning kiss that lingered on, growing hotter, more savage, as though he couldn't get enough of her.

He embraced her so tightly she could hardly breathe, moving his lips to her hair then. "When Doc Long told me," he said, his voice shaking, his body trembling, "I knew, Anna. I knew that a piece of paper didn't matter. Becky, the baby you're carrying now, they're *mine*—Nate Foster's. I don't care what outsiders might think. You're my wife, and the fact that Darryl Kelley is still alive doesn't make a damn bit of difference."

He picked her up and carried her inside, kicking shut the door. "Where's Becky?" he asked.

"Taking a nap," she answered.

"Good." He carried her into the guest room and laid her on the bed, quickly unbuckling his gunbelt and tossing it aside. Their gazes met in heated passion as he moved onto the bed beside her, leaning down to smother her with kisses.

"I've got to . . . get ready to go to the bank, Nate," she told him between each wild kiss. "You know I go . . . every Wednesday."

He kissed at her eyes. "And I'm supposed to be going to talk to a bartender who says somebody stole some money from his cash box." He ran a strong, searching hand under her dress. "Right now I don't give a damn."

She breathed deeply and closed her eyes as he moved his hand inside her bloomers. "I love you, Nate. Nothing could ever change that for me."

"For me, either," he answered. "It just took me longer to realize it." He covered her mouth again, running his tongue deep, suggesting what both knew they must do to keep their sanity. There was nothing more to say, and neither cared about preliminaries. Nate Foster needed to prove that this woman belonged to him, no matter what the legal system might have to say about it. Neither of them stopped to undress, except for what was necessary.

In the next moment he was burying himself inside of her. She gasped at the eager way he took her, arching up to him in return, grasping at his leather vest. Nate! He was back in her arms, back in her heart, joined with her again. No one would ever convince her this was wrong. A little girl lay sleeping upstairs who belonged to Nate Foster. The life in her belly was his, too. Darryl couldn't change that, no matter what he did. And as long as she had Nate, she could bear whatever was to come.

The tears of relief came then, and she wept as they made love wildly. He licked at her tears, all the while moving rhythmically, forcefully, as though to brand her. He pushed hard and deep, until he could no longer hold back the ecstasy she never failed to bring to him. He groaned as his life spilled into her.

He sank down beside her then, pulling her into his arms. "Tell me you forgive me, Anna. I should have been more understanding."

"There is nothing to forgive. I should have told you. I wasn't being fair to you."

"It doesn't matter now. Somehow this whole thing will get solved, and we'll find a way to get back to a normal life."

Someone knocked on the door then. Nate quickly got up and tucked his shirt into his pants, buttoning himself up. "Just a minute," he called out. He strapped on his gun and hurried out and down the hall.

Anna lay listening to voices. She sat up, pulling on her bloomers, wondering what a mess she must be. She would have to take a bath before going to the bank. Right now it didn't matter. Nate was back. They were going to get through this—together. She wanted to cry again out of sheer joy.

Nate came back to the bedroom, and some of that joy vanished when she saw the look on his face. She slowly rose, pushing some hair behind her ear. "You've heard something about Darryl," she said. It was more a statement than a question.

He nodded. "That was Jim. Somebody told him they had seen me ride up here. He just got a telegraph message that a Federal payroll was robbed from a stagecoach between here and Lawrence. A couple of men are dead. Jim and I are heading out to catch whatever fresh tracks we can. One of

the passengers claims one of the robbers was called Doc."
He saw the pain in her eyes. "You have anything I can pack
for food? I'll go wash up a little and get my saddlebags."

She closed her eyes, praying for strength, realizing the
danger into which he was riding. But this would always be a
part of his life, and she had to be strong. He didn't need her
begging him not to go, because he would go no matter
what. "I'll see what I have. You'd better go see Becky for a
couple of minutes."

He caught her arm as she started out of the room. "I love
you, Anna."

She looked up at him, reaching up to touch his face.
"Just get this over with, Nate." She turned away and walked
to the kitchen. Nate hurried upstairs to wash and change
his shirt and long johns. He stood over Becky for a moment, touching her golden hair, praying he would be alive
to see her again when this was over.

He leaned down and kissed his baby girl, then went
downstairs and to the kitchen, watching Anna go to the
cupboard and take out some potatoes. He studied her small
form, realizing she had lost weight. She was as beautiful as
ever, and he hated himself for putting her through hell the
past two weeks.

She put a few potatoes into his saddlebag and handed it
to him. "Potatoes, dried beans, and some fresh biscuits and
a jar of jelly," she told him. "I also gave you a little lard and
flour and some jerked meat." She held her chin high as he
took the saddlebags. "I don't suppose I need to tell you to
be careful. He's already proven what he wants. This could
be some kind of trick, Nate."

"I realize that." He touched her face. "You're the one
who has to be careful. In fact, I want you to go stay with
Rob and Marie while I'm gone."

She nodded. "I will. I'll take Becky over as soon as I clean
up."

"I'll send somebody over here to watch the house until
you're ready to leave."

Her eyes glistened. "Come back to me, Nate. Promise
me, like you did when you went after the Sharp gang."

He gave her a sad smile. "I'll come back. We'll have some

decisions to make when I do, but we'll make them together."

She smiled, her eyes brimming with tears. Nate leaned down and kissed her gently. "I'm glad I came up here, Anna," he said then. "I'm glad we had a chance to make up for things a little."

"I just hope we have the rest of our lives to make up for it," she answered. "You be careful and make sure we do."

"You do the same. Remember what you told me. Darryl Kelley isn't the same man you married. He's a stranger—and he's crazy, Anna, a man who can't be reasoned with anymore." He stepped back, slinging the saddlebags over his shoulder. "I might have to kill him, Anna."

She closed her eyes. "I know," she whispered. "I didn't hold it against you the first time. Why would I now?"

He kissed her once more, his gray eyes shining with love. "Bye, Anna."

He turned and headed out. She walked with him out onto the porch, watched him rig his saddlebags and mount up. He looked down at her for a moment.

"I love you," he repeated.

"And I love you."

Both knew the gravity of the situation, and there was nothing more either could say. He turned his horse and rode off.

Minutes later in town, a neatly dressed man and woman stood in the doorway of a shoe store and watched Nate Foster ride up to another man. "We'll take the train, get there a lot quicker," the other man told Nate. Nate nodded, and they rode off. The couple near the shoe store looked at each other, and the man took a cigar from his mouth. "There they go," he said.

Fran Rogers smiled. "You see? Don't I plan things well? What would you do without me, Darryl?"

He looked her over, wondering if she realized how sick he was of her. But she was right. Her plan seemed to be working, and this was going to be an event to put him in the history books. "You sure she goes to the bank every Wednesday?"

Fran's mouth moved into a sneer. "You'd be surprised

how easy it is to get the old biddy gossips of this town to talk. They love to talk about the lovely Mrs. Nate Foster. They dote on Nate and Anna both. I found out enough about them to know when they visit the outhouse. At any rate, Anna makes weekly trips to the bank to check on deposits sent there from her restaurant in Abilene. She'll be coming, all right."

She watched after Nate and Jim. "Look at how they're hurrying. Our men must have pulled off the payroll robbery. Marshal Nate Foster and his right-hand man are going off on a wild-goose chase. By the time they get back, Mrs. Foster and a lot of money from the Topeka bank will be in our hands. Within a couple of days, Nate Foster himself will ride right into our trap, and you'll have both of them at your mercy."

Darryl put the cigar back into his mouth, looking around to be sure his men were at their posts. The town was peaceful this morning, no one expecting what was to come, especially not Anna Kelley. That was how he still thought of her. Anna was still his wife. She'd learn that soon enough.

Chapter 23

Anna dressed Becky and packed their bags. After watering her plants and checking everything over, she walked out, locking the door. "Let's go, Lonnie." She climbed up into the buggy brought over by a young deputy named Lonnie Gates, whom Nate had sent over for her. Lonnie drove Anna over to Rob's house, where she delivered Becky and the baggage.

"Nate's heard something about the man who shot him," she told Rob when she went inside. "He thinks he was involved in a robbery near Big Springs, and he's gone there with Jim to meet a posse. He told me to stay with you until he gets back."

Rob frowned, taking the baby from her. "I wish to hell he'd have stopped by first."

"There wasn't time. He was anxious to get going."

Rob handed Becky to Marie. "I don't like this. I don't like it at all. But then I guess it's good they've finally got some kind of break. Maybe they'll finally catch this guy so we won't have to worry about him bringing harm to Nate or you and Becky anymore."

Anna saw the concern in his eyes. Rob was a good man, in his own way a more forgiving man than Nate. But then he had not been through quite the same pain as Nate. "Rob," she said. "There is something you and Marie should know. Nate has been trying to avoid telling you, but you're family, and . . . I think you have a right to know. It's about . . . about the man who shot Nate. I'd like to talk to both of you when I get back from the bank."

Rob folded his arms. "I've been meaning to talk to Nate myself," he answered. "He's been acting awfully strange lately. When I try to get him to talk about it, he just clams up. Something's very wrong, Anna, I've noticed that—and it's more than just Christine dying."

"You're right. It *is* more than that. But Nate and I are going to get through this together, and I don't think we should keep it from you any longer."

Rob frowned in confusion. "Keep what from me? What's this all about, Anna? All Nate said was that he found out who tried to kill him, but he wouldn't tell me any more about it."

An ache welled up in Anna's throat. They should know, in case something went wrong, or in case Nate brought Darryl back alive. "I'll . . . I'll explain when I get back from the bank. Thanks for watching Becky. I'll be back in about a half hour."

"You watch yourself, Anna. I don't feel right about any of this. You want me to go with you?"

She put a hand on his arm. "No. I've got Lonnie. Everything will be all right, Rob. I'll be back in a little bit." She leaned up and kissed his cheek, then kissed Becky and turned to leave. She climbed into the buggy beside Lonnie. Rob turned to Marie as the buggy clattered away. "Something's wrong about this whole day, Marie. I don't like this feeling I have."

"You just like to worry too much. Nate's got Jim with him, and other men. He's a smart man and he knows perfectly well what he has to watch out for."

"He's sure been acting strange—him and Anna both. I've noticed a real strain between them the last couple of weeks. It doesn't make any sense."

"Well, she said she'd explain, and she will."

Rob watched through the screen door as the buggy rounded a curve and headed for town. "I'll just be glad when all this is over for them."

The wagon moved into town, and Anna waved to Mrs. Flannagan, wife of the bank president. She and Nate had dined at their home. Pain moved through her heart at the thought of how these same people might treat her and Nate if they discovered the truth about Darryl. She felt responsible for ruining his career, but comforted by his parting words, still warm from his lovemaking.

She put a hand to her belly. Children. That would help repair the damage that had been done. She was glad for the new baby, glad Nate had found out after all. She felt a flutter of warm pleasure at the thought of how this baby had been conceived, in these past few months since Nate had fully regained his strength and movement. Here was a sign that her husband was indeed healed.

Now their hearts had to heal, and that could not happen until the source of the poison was eradicated. Darryl Kelley had to be found and dealt with. Her heart tightened at the thought of possibly having to face the man after all these lost years. Then again, he might be brought back in a wooden box.

Lonnie pulled up in front of the bank and she climbed down. Lonnie did the same, tying the horse and giving only a brief glance at several horses tied outside the bank. A man sat on one, his arm folded under his coat, another stood nonchalantly at the corner of the bank. He wore a gun, but he looked at Lonnie and grinned in a friendly way.

Lonnie walked inside with Anna, who walked to a teller's window and waited behind a man in a neat hat and suit. The man glanced over at a dark-haired woman standing at the next window. Anna followed his eyes, and her heart nearly stopped beating when she recognized Fran Rogers.

Anna felt nearly faint, instantly realizing what was happening when Fran smiled wickedly at her and the man in front of her turned around, shoving a pistol against her throat.

"Hello, Anna," came a familiar voice.

"What the—" The words had come from Lonnie. Darryl moved his six-gun for only a second. A shot rang out, exploding in Anna's ears and making her scream. Lonnie slumped to the floor, a bloody hole in his side.

"Bring the money, Duke," Darryl called out. His wild eyes turned back to Anna. "You're as pretty as ever, Mrs. Kelley."

There was no time to notice people had been herded into the bank vault and that Mr. Flannagan lay slumped in a corner, his head split open by the barrel of a gun. Anna stared wide-eyed at Darryl, needing no explanation now for the stagecoach robbery. It had all been set up to get Nate out of town. Fear ripped through her like a bullet as Darryl told her to turn around. He wrenched an arm up behind her back and led her to the front door, four men and Fran following behind him. He stopped and looked at a woman who sat in a chair, rigid with fear.

"You remember what I told you, old lady. You tell your fancy Marshal Foster that Darryl Kelley's got his wife—not Foster's wife—my wife! You tell him if he wants her and the money, he'd better come after them right quick—alone! Can you remember that? Darryl Kelley, alias Crazy Doc! You tell him I'm the one who shot him. Tell him he'd better be a good tracker, because I've got Anna. The longer she's with me, the worse it will be for her. Remember, he's to come alone."

The woman nodded, tears in her eyes when she looked at Anna. Anna recognized her as Mrs. Lovejoy, who owned a women's apparel shop farther up the street.

Darryl shoved Anna outside toward a horse. "Hey," someone called out. Darryl turned and shot, and Anna whimpered at the sight of Clyde Benson, owner of the hat store next to the bank, falling to the boardwalk.

People began screaming and running out of the way then as Darryl and his men began shooting wildly to keep them back. "Get up on that horse," Darryl ordered Anna. She could hardly make her hands and legs work as she reached up and grasped the saddle horn. Darryl put his hand on her rear in a sickeningly familiar gesture and gave her a shove, then mounted up behind her. His horse reared and whirled at all the shooting. Darryl kicked the animal's sides and took off at a gallop, and Anna hung on for dear life. They were quickly out of town, Fran and nine men riding beside them, all of them hooting and yipping like wild men, including Fran.

"We did it, Fran," Darryl called out. He laughed like the crazy man that he was, a shrieking, wicked laugh that made Anna's skin crawl. For the moment she told herself to just be glad Becky and Rob had not been with her. She struggled to reconcile herself to the reality of what had just happened. This maniac who had just murdered two innocent men was Darryl. He was here. He had finally come for her, just as she had once feared he would do.

He holstered his gun and moved a hand to her breast. "We got some years to make up for, Mrs. Kelley," he told her, laughing again. "And I got me a marshal to kill when he comes for you."

She pushed his hand away, feeling ill at his touch. *And he will come,* she thought, her heart heavy with sorrow. *I've killed him, just as surely as if I had put a gun to his head.* Darryl had given orders that Nate should come alone. She knew Nate. If he thought her life was at stake, he would do just that.

Nate and Jim arrived at Big Springs within two hours after getting the news of the stage robbery that had occurred earlier that morning. They were met by a posse of local men and Paul Bailey, a deputy marshal who had taken a train west from Lawrence. They talked to a survivor of the robbery, John Powers, who seemed badly shaken but remembered there were three men, all masked.

"They kept calling one of them Doc—over and over," the man told them. "Like they wanted to be sure the name was remembered. And they said something about heading south. And that's exactly which way they went—south."

Nate looked at Jim. "They're setting you up, Nate."

"As long as we realize that, there's no problem," Nate answered. He looked at the local sheriff. "How much did they get?"

"About six thousand dollars."

"If you head out to where it happened now, you can get a good start after them," Powers told them. "You Nate Foster?"

"I am."

"I've heard of you. And one of them mentioned you—said something about how this ought to bring you out of the woodwork. I had a feeling they left me alive to be sure there was somebody to tell that this guy named Doc was in on it. Like I said, they headed directly south. I bet they'd be easy to track if you went after them right now. You can't let them get away, Marshal. They killed the driver and the man riding shotgun in cold blood—killed the other passenger, too. I think they left me alive so's I could tell you about it—like they *wanted* you to know." He shook his head. "I just thank God I'm alive."

They all stood around Powers, who sat on the steps in front of the stage station, wiping his brow nervously. "I sure could use a drink," he said then.

"We'll see you get one," a local citizen told the man. "That was smart thinkin' and brave too, the way you picked up them men who was shot and got them and the coach back to town. Too bad there wasn't nothin' the doc could do for them."

Nate watched the man. Something didn't feel right about the robbery, about the whole day as far as he was concerned. He questioned Powers about where the robbery had taken place, then looked at Jim. "Let's get out to the site." They mounted up, the extra men following Jim and Nate's lead as they headed south, leaving Powers behind. The man was helped up and led to a nearby saloon, where he guzzled down a glass of whiskey, paid for by a local citizen who felt sorry for him.

It took over a half hour to reach the site of the robbery. Nate and Jim dismounted, walking around the area. Blood had dried hard into the heated ground where the dead men had fallen. The bodies were gone, taken into Big Springs on the stage by Powers. They could see marks where the bodies had been dragged to the coach. Nothing was left but the blood and the tracks of the robbers, headed south. A light rain the night before had left the ground soft enough that it was easy to spot them.

"Let's head out," Nate said. He mounted up again and they followed at a light trot. "They've only got a few hours on us," Nate told Jim.

"Somethin's not right, Nate. This is too easy."

"I'm thinking the same thing. I know Kelley wants me to come to him, but this smells real bad. I've got a real uneasy feeling."

After nearly an hour of tracking, the tracks veered west rather than south. Nate reined his horse to a halt and looked toward the setting sun. "This smells worse all the time," he said, looking at Jim.

"Want to know what I'm thinking?"

"Of course I do."

Jim rubbed at his lips again, a nervous habit. "I'm thinking maybe we weren't the ones bein' set up. This feels like some kind of decoy, Nate. The more I think about it, the more I realize that Powers fella seemed awful quick and sure-headed for a common citizen who had been through what he had—stopping to pick up the bodies, getting that stage back to Big Springs right away like that. He made an awful big point about which way the men headed afterward, like he wanted to be sure we headed south ourselves. Now these tracks are headin' west. Whoever these men are, I expect they intend to join up with somebody else farther west. And the next town to the west is Topeka."

Their gazes met and Jim saw horror in Nate's. "Anna," he said in a near whisper.

"I hate to say it, but could be. I think we should say to hell with the six thousand dollars and head straight back toward the K-P—hook a ride on a train back to Topeka. We can always come back and track these bastards if my hunch is wrong. Either way, we're still headed west."

Nate removed his hat, wiping his forehead with his shirt-sleeve, suddenly much too warm. His head swam with the dread of what it could mean if Jim was right. Anna! Just as he had begun to make things right again, something might have happened to her. A fierce ache gripped at his throat so that he had to clear it and swallow a few times before he could talk. He turned to the others. "Paul, you keep following this trail—and be damn careful. It could be a trap. Jim and I suspect maybe this is just a decoy. My wife and family back in Topeka could be in danger. We're going back to Big Springs and then head back to Topeka. If these tracks lead there, just check in when you reach Topeka."

"Yes, sir. I hope your hunch is wrong, Marshal."

Fury stormed through Nate's blood like a mighty army. "So do I, Paul." He looked at Jim. "We can wire Topeka from Big Springs and see if everything is all right. If nothing has happened, we can tell them to keep a special guard on Anna and on Rob's house. Bring in more guards than just Lonnie. Before we leave Big Springs I want to have a talk with that supposed survivor of the stage robbery. If something has happened to Anna, we can—his voice caught in his throat—we can catch a train right back to Topeka."

Jim nodded. "Let's go." They whipped their horses into a hard gallop.

Powers looked up from the table in the saloon where he still sat accepting free drinks. He had been telling stories of how frightening and horrible the robbery was, bragging about how he had reacted quickly and got right back to Big Springs so the law could get after the men who had committed the terrible crime. People were smiling and slapping him on the back, and Powers lapped up the attention, until he noticed Nate Foster standing in the doorway of the saloon. He suddenly sobered and paled.

"Marshal! What are you doing here?" he said, quickly trying to put on a friendly, innocent look. "You aren't going to let those bastards get away, are you?"

Nate stepped closer, and the look on his face made the others step back. "I want the truth, Powers, and I want it now," he growled.

The man slowly set down a glass of whiskey. "I don't know what you're talking about."

"Don't you? Those tracks we followed that were supposed to head south suddenly veered west. My partner and I got to thinking—about how quickly you got that stage back here, about how everybody was killed except you."

"But . . . I told you why that was."

Nate leaned over the table, his big hands gripping either side of it. "It was all too easy and smooth, Powers. We've already checked with Topeka! There's been a bank robbery there, mister, and the one called Crazy Doc was in on it— the one *you* said was in on *this* robbery—and they took my *wife!* Where is she, Powers?"

"I . . ." The man began shaking his head as people mumbled and stepped farther back. "I don't know what—"

Nate saw his arm move. In an instant he tipped the table down. A shot went off, splintering a hole in the table. Nate rammed the table hard against Powers, knocking the man over backward. Saloon women screamed and men cowered as Nate tossed the table aside and grabbed Powers up by the lapels. His nose was already bleeding profusely. Nate rammed a big fist into the man's belly three times, then landed a blow to his ear. Powers flew across the room, and Jim picked him up, wrenching his arms behind his back while Nate stormed up to him. He grasped Powers by the hair and jerked his head up.

"Where is she, Powers! Where did Darryl Kelley take Anna!"

"I . . . I don't—"

Nate grabbed him between the legs and squeezed hard. Powers screamed while Nate kept hold of him, grabbing him by the shirt neck with the other hand and throwing the man across the room. Powers tumbled over tables and chairs, landing with a thud and curling up, still screaming. Nate marched back to him, while women turned away and covered their faces. He jerked Powers to his feet and the man could barely stand.

"This is my *wife* we're talking about, Powers! I wouldn't stop short of killing you to find out where she is. I know how to beat a man without knocking him out, and I can keep this up for a long time, if that's what you want!"

Powers grasped Nate's shirt with one hand, keeping his other hand over the front of himself, trying to draw up his legs. He choked on blood and gasped for breath. "All . . . right," he sputtered. "Let me . . . get my . . . breath."

Nate let him drop to the floor, where he curled up on his

knees. "Pawnee Hills . . ." he finally muttered. "About
. . . thirty miles . . . west of Topeka. You're . . . supposed to go in alone. They can see for miles . . . to the
east from there . . . tell if you've got men with you. Doc
said . . . if you come in with men . . . he'll blow your
wife's head off before you get to her. You're the one he
really wants. If he can kill you . . . she'll live. He just
. . . wants to humiliate her for turning on him . . .
wants her to see you killed . . . wants her to go back to
Topeka . . . everybody knowin' he was her first husband."
He managed to sit up a little straighter as people stared in
wonder. First husband? Nate Foster's wife was married to an
outlaw?

Powers grinned. "He got you good . . . this time, Foster. He'll punish her . . . for marryin' a Yankee. He said
how pretty she is. I expect Doc . . . will want to make up
for lost time . . . seein' as how she still legally . . . belongs to him."

Nate slammed a heavy boot into the man's face and people gasped as Powers fell silent. Nate looked around the
room. If ever there was such a thing as a walking volcano, it
would be a fitting description for Nate Foster at that moment. His gray eyes were steely, not soft, as he gazed at the
staring crowd. He knew there was no time to explain to any
of them. He simply turned and looked at Jim, who caught
the desperate fear behind the wild revenge in his eyes.

"Let's get goin', Nate. We'll figure out how to get both of
you out of this."

Nate flexed bloody knuckles, suddenly realizing that if
he opened his mouth right now he would fall to pieces. He
couldn't think about Anna right now. He didn't dare. He
could only think about Darryl Kelley and how to find the
man without getting himself killed. Right now he had to
stay mad, or he would scream and weep and be no use to
anyone. On his way out he grabbed another table and
tossed it aside. Beer glasses went flying and a woman
screamed. He kicked a chair out of the way and slammed
through the swinging doors.

Jim looked at the bartender. "Make sure that man gets
taken to jail. We'll be back for him in a few days."

"Yes, sir."

"Sorry about the mess. Send the bill to the marshal's office at Topeka." He walked out and caught Nate grasping at his middle for a moment before he mounted his horse.

"You all right, Nate?" Jim asked. "You aren't in any shape to—"

"I'm in good enough shape to kill Darryl Kelley and get Anna back," he growled, mounting up. "I should have seen it, goddamm it! I should have realized!"

"Maybe so. But it's done now, and you've got to keep a cool head or you'll *both* wind up dead! We'll figure out a way, Nate. We always have before."

Nate jerked the reins of his horse so that the animal turned in a circle, feeling its master's restlessness and anger. "No one I cared about personally was ever *involved* before! God only knows what he'll do to her."

Jim reached out and grasped the bridle of Nate's horse. "She was his wife once, Nate, and she's a strong, smart woman. She'll figure out a way to take care of herself. We've just got to hope that somewhere deep down inside the man still has enough feelings for her to keep her from harm."

"You heard what Powers said."

"That was for you. Kelley *wants* to get you upset, don't you see? The more upset you are, the more reckless you'll be. That gives him the edge. The man is crazy, I agree, but he's also smart. Don't let him win this one on emotions, Nate. You've got to handle this like you'd handle it if total strangers were involved."

Nate closed his eyes and nodded. "I know." He breathed deeply for self-control. "Let's go catch that train to Topeka. We'd better close our eyes a minute while we're on it. It might be the last rest we get for days."

They headed for the depot.

Darryl and his men rode for hours. Anna had not ridden a horse for very long at a time in years, and she ached everywhere. She could hardly bear the feel of Darryl's arm around her middle, yet she knew if he withdrew it she'd fall from the horse. She told herself she was on her own now.

There was no Nate to help her, and if he came for her, he would surely die.

She tried to concentrate on anything she had going in her favor. Her baby was safe. Nate had been gone, so he had not been involved in the shoot-out. He would at least have time to plan how to get her out of this, if that was possible. But she had to figure a way to stay safe and healthy until then.

Her only hope was Darryl himself. Darryl. Her long-lost first husband, the gentle, caring doctor she had loved so very much, was sitting right behind her, after all these horrible years. Nausea gripped her stomach at the realization of what the war and his wound had done to him, for she really hardly knew the seedy character who had kidnapped her. Was there any hope of appealing to the Darryl she had once known? Was there even a tiny bit of that man left buried in the confused, injured brain of the man who held her now?

She realized that Fran would try to thwart any attempt Anna might make to get through to the man. The love Darryl had once held for her was Anna's only hope, but Fran would surely never allow Darryl to dredge up old emotions. Then again, perhaps there was some way she could use Fran's certain jealousy to her own benefit, if she could just stir some feelings in Darryl, hideous as such a task might be.

Anna had cast Fran an occasional glance. The woman rode beside Darryl, sitting tall and proud on her horse, casting haughty, victorious looks at Anna. She reminded Anna of a witch, with her long, dark hair flying in the wind, her dark eyes drilling into her. She could almost picture her sitting on a broom instead of a horse.

Whatever happened, even if Nate was killed over this, she realized she had to find a way to stay alive, for Becky, for the baby she carried in her belly now. That baby could turn out to be the last living legacy of Nate Foster. Strangely, what suddenly hurt the most about the thought of Nate being killed was the memory of all the suffering he had gone through to stay alive the past year. All that agony, only to turn around and be shot down again. If only there was a way to save him.

They finally stopped at a water hole to give the horses a rest. Darryl dismounted and yanked Anna from the horse. Her legs were numb and burning, and they crumpled under her. Darryl pushed her onto her back and straddled her.

"You were right, Doc. She's a looker," one of the men said with a laugh, coming to stand over them. "We're gonna have us a time tonight."

Darryl stared into her blue eyes, keeping hold of her wrists. "Maybe," he said. "She belongs to me, Trace. You remember that. It's my decision whether she gets handed over to the rest of you."

"That was part of the deal."

"Shut up!" Darryl let go of one of her wrists and pulled his pistol, aiming it at the man. "I never said it was part of the deal! I said I *might* share the woman. I never said for certain! Now go water my horse. We've got to get moving again. Ben and the others will make it to Pawnee Hills soon with the stagecoach money. They're already on their way."

The man backed away, taking the reins of Darryl's horse. Darryl looked back down at Anna, shoving his gun into its holster. He reached out and touched her cheek, and she turned her head sideways, trying to get away from his touch. "It's been a long time, Anna."

She met his eyes boldly then, still finding it hard to face the astonishing truth that she had loved this man once, had given her virginity to him so willingly and with such passion. "That was *your* choice," she answered. "I waited for you—for months and months, wondering, worrying. You could have come to me, Darryl. I would have helped you. You didn't have to turn to this!"

He grasped both her wrists again, leaning down, staying on top of her so she couldn't move. "Yes, I *did* have to turn to this," he growled. His breath reeked of whiskey. He shook his head and knocked off his hat, revealing the ugly scar across the top of his head. "They destroyed all of it, Anna! They burned out my folks's plantation, raped and murdered my mother, chopped off my father's head! They put this bullet through my skull that left me with headaches that would make most men end their lives! Without whiskey and laudanum, I can't even *function!* I lost the use of my hands for surgery, and I lost all feelings. I've got *no* feelings now, woman, except *revenge*—revenge against men like your high-toting Nate Foster! He might have lived through those first couple of bullets. But he won't live through what I'll do to him *this* time!"

He laughed, a high-pitched, wicked laugh, his eyes showing nothing but insanity. "It's going to be so easy! I've got his *wife*—only you're not his wife at all, are you? You're still legally *my* wife! And I can do whatever I want with you!" He leaned down and she turned her face sideways again. His whiskers were starting to stubble out from a morning shave, and they scratched at her cheek and neck as he nuzzled her throat.

"Darryl, please," Anna groaned. "You must have some shred of feelings left. We loved each other. I waited and waited for you."

He raised up, jerking her to a sitting position, then slapped her so hard she saw nothing but blackness for a moment, and her ears rang painfully. "Waited," he growled. His voice seemed suddenly distant. "You ran off! You ran off and married that Yankee lawman!"

"I never ran off. I only . . . went to Abilene, to get away from painful memories. I had to find a way . . . to survive until you were all right again and you came to me."

"Keep your mouth shut," he shouted, hitting her again. She could hardly breathe then when he stretched his weight out on top of her. She felt suddenly sick at the sensation of his hardness pressing against her.

"The men told me you said you weren't going to share her," she heard Fran's voice saying then. Darryl raised up again, sitting on Anna's legs, which were pressed painfully against small rocks.

"Hand me that canteen and quit looking at me that way," she heard Darryl telling Fran. There came a sudden splash to her face. Someone pushed at her jaws painfully, making her open her mouth, then poured water into it until she began choking. "Got to keep you alive for a while, sweetheart," Darryl told her.

"Darryl, you promised them." She heard Fran's voice again. "And you promised me she didn't mean anything to you. This was only to get Nate Foster to come to us. You said you'd take her once for the fun of it and turn her over to the others."

"Quit bitching! That's all you do anymore!"

There was a moment of silence, while Anna focused her eyes and tried to gather her thoughts. She heard something that sounded like a woman crying then. "This was . . . my idea, Darryl. You said . . . you said it was a good one. You loved me for it, remember? She's no good, Darryl. If you keep her, she'll bring you trouble . . . get you caught. It's always been you and me, Darryl, since we were kids. That's the way . . . it should always be."

"I told you to keep quiet! I'll decide what to do with her." Darryl looked down at her, grinning, running a hand over her breasts. Anna grasped at his hand and pushed it away. Darryl only laughed and hit her again. "You have to admit, she's still the prettiest thing west of the Mississippi," he said then. "A hell of a lot prettier than you, Fran. Maybe if you didn't bitch so much, you'd *seem* prettier."

"Damn you," Fran answered. "You and your 'pretty little things'! You lied to me, Darryl!"

He looked up at the woman, his eyes blazing. "Now that we've done what we planned, I might not need you anymore. You remember that. The more you bitch, the less I'll be needing you."

"You *do* need me, and you know it!" Fran's tears had stopped. Her face was nearly black with rage, and at the moment Anna thought her more frightening than Darryl. "Without me you never would have survived this long. I sacrificed *everything* for you, Darryl Kelley, and I love you more than she ever did!"

Anna saw her opportunity. She had quickly surmised that for the time being she had to be as cold and calculating as everyone else here, and she had to stay one step ahead of Fran if she hoped to live through this.

"That isn't true," she told Darryl. "No one loved you more than I did. I still could. She's . . . lying about me. I never . . . deserted you, Darryl. I was never a traitor to you." She could hardly feel her mouth as she spoke, and her ears rang so loudly she could hardly hear her own voice. "I never married . . . or went near another man until I thought you were dead and . . . there was no hope of you returning."

"Don't listen to that whiny Yankee bitch," Fran told him. "We've got to get going, Darryl! Nate Foster will be on our tail in no time. We've got to get to Pawnee Hills."

Darryl finally got up off Anna's legs and jerked her up with him. "We left a good trail, didn't we? He'll follow."

"You bet he'll follow," Fran answered. "And you remember *why* he'll follow. Because you've got Anna—and that's all thanks to *me*. What better proof of who has been most loyal to you? She's been sleeping with Nate Foster all these years, Darryl—probably before she even knew if you were dead!"

"That's not true," Anna told him, looking him straight in the eyes.

Darryl watched her closely. For a brief moment Anna saw a flicker of someone else—a man who used to love her. In that little moment, she saw a hint of feelings, a desire to believe her.

"She's no good," Fran hissed, bringing her face close to them both. "If she could turn you in right now and watch you hang, she'd do it! She's got to *suffer*, Darryl! She's got to suffer like *you've* suffered all these years while she lay in Nate Foster's bed!"

Anna did not take her eyes off Darryl. She watched his eyes change again, to the wild eyes of a stranger. He grinned again. "Yes," he answered.

"You promised the men, Darryl. They've been loyal to you, too—just like me. Don't you listen to Anna. She's just bait, and when she's served her purpose, she's fair game, even for me!"

Anna frowned, looking at Fran and realizing the woman was as demented as Darryl. Fran smiled. "I'm going to kill you, Anna Foster. Or should I say Anna Kelley?"

Anna's eyes narrowed, as she deliberately slid an arm

around Darryl. "Why don't you ask Darryl? If he still wants me, then it's Kelley."

She watched the whites of Fran's eyes take on a red cast, and Anna was more certain she had found the key that could keep her alive.

Fran suddenly lunged for her, grabbing her around the throat and squeezing with the strength of a man. Anna struggled for breath, but quickly everything started fading to gray, then black, until finally several of the men managed to pull Fran off and air began to seep through Anna's larnyx and back into her lungs.

Anna rolled to her knees and coughed and gagged for several minutes, vaguely aware that in the background a woman was screaming. She heard several loud slaps and punches, the word "bitch" shouted several times. The screaming finally stopped, and Anna felt herself being lifted. Someone helped her get back up on a horse, and a man mounted up behind her. She sensed it was Darryl.

"Everything will be all right once we get to where we're going," she heard him saying, his arm coming around her again. "We'll make up for lost time, Anna. Don't you worry about Fran. I won't let her hurt you." He rubbed a hand over her belly. "It will just be you and me, like old times. We'll refresh our memories while we wait for Nate Foster. Then you can show him which one of us you prefer. Maybe we can even make love in front of him. Oh, what sweet revenge that would be, wouldn't it?" She felt the horse begin to move. "Let's go, boys!"

"Yahoo," someone shouted. "We're rich again, Doc!"

"And we'll be famous after we kill Nate Foster. More famous than the James boys or the Youngers," came another voice.

"Hang on to Fran there," Darryl called out to someone. "She's not in much condition to ride alone."

Anna heard laughter. The horses galloped away, and Anna tried to concentrate on sweet, good things, like Becky, and lying in Nate's arms. Would she ever see her little girl again, feel Nate's arms around her again? *Stay alert, Anna,* she told herself. *Don't give it up. Part of the old Darryl is there. You saw it in his eyes. His mind is confused. Fran's been manipulating him. You can, too. You have a bigger hold on him. Use it.*

It was so hard to concentrate. Nate. She had to hang on for Nate, for Becky.

Chapter 24

Nate was met at the Topeka train depot by a crowd of people, most of them concerned about Anna and feeling sorry for Nate; many curious about the rumor that had spread like wildfire through the town—the outlaw who had robbed the Topeka bank and had taken Nate Foster's wife had said she was *his* wife.

"What's going on?" one man asked. "You know those killers, Marshal?"

"Is it true that murderer was married to Mrs. Foster?"

"Whose wife is she, Marshal, yours or his?"

Nate walked straight to the boxcar that carried his horse, saying nothing, his face hard and determined. He kept telling himself he could be grateful for one thing: the wire had said Becky was not with her mother at the time of the robbery and abduction. At least his little girl was safe.

"All of you shut up," Jim shouted at the crowd. "You'll get your questions answered after we find Mrs. Foster and catch Darryl Kelley."

"Don't you kill him, Marshal," someone else shouted. "You bring him back to Topeka! He killed Clyde Benson, just standing in the street. Killed your deputy, Lonnie Gates, too."

The crowd noise grew, and fists went into the air. "Bring him back! We want to watch him hang," most voices raved.

"Maybe his wife was in on it," Nate heard some say.

At those words Nate stopped short and whirled around, immediately able to tell who had said it by the way the man cringed. He stormed up to the man, grabbing him by the shirtfront.

"What was that you said, mister?"

The man swallowed, his eyes wide. "I . . . it was just a thought—"

"Nate!" Jim grabbed his arm before he could punch the bystander. "Don't do it."

Nate gave the man a shove so hard that he fell against some others. "I'll say this once," he shouted at them. "Darryl Kelley was my wife's first husband. The fact that he turned outlaw is something Anna couldn't help. The next man who makes a remark suggesting she's a part of this is going to answer to me, even if it costs me my badge!"

A man lowered a ramp and brought down the horses. Nate and Jim mounted up. Seventeen-year-old Jimmie Flannagan ran up to Nate then, his eyes bloodshot from crying. "Marshal!" Nate looked down at him. "They killed my pa, Marshal. You gotta catch them."

"We will, Jimmie."

"Can I do anything to help?"

Nate rubbed at his eyes. "Yes. You can go to the telegraph office and send a wire to Abilene to a Claudine Marquis. Tell her to come right away, that Anna Foster will need her. She's probably already heard about this anyway, but go ahead and send the wire. She's a good friend of Anna's."

"Yes, sir. Claudine Marquis in Abilene. I'll do it right now."

The boy ran off, and Nate and Jim headed for the courthouse, where a posse was already gathering. Nate noticed Rob was among them. He dismounted and looked at his brother angrily as Rob approached him. "What the hell are you doing here?"

"I want to help," Rob answered. "This isn't just anybody, it's Anna."

"You stay out of it! There's been enough tragedy in this family. You've got three kids of your own, and for all anyone knows when this is over Becky will need a mother *and* a father."

Rob could see the terror behind Nate's fury. "Before she left for the bank," he said more quietly, "she said there was something we should know. Something she was going to tell us when she got back. It had something to do with this Darryl Kelley, didn't it?"

Nate swallowed, again struggling to stay in control. "I know how bad you want to help, Rob. But please just go home. Do it for me. It will be easier on me knowing Becky will have you in case anything happens. Don't put Marie through this. If you really want to help, stay here."

Rob sighed, putting a hand on his arm. "I don't understand all this yet, but you know we're behind you and Anna both. Just bring her back, Nate. You love her enough to work out anything that's gone wrong, if you can just get her back here."

Nate handed the reins of his horse to Jim, who tied it for him. "She's carrying, Rob. God only knows what this will do to her—what *he'll* do to her."

"Don't think about it. You can't right now. Just think like the marshal you are. Keep a cool head and get this guy."

Nate sighed deeply and nodded, heading up the courthouse steps. The crowd of men followed, including Rob, who decided at least to listen in on what was happening so far. Three deputy marshals were among the men who made up the posse. The rest were angry townsmen who wanted their money back and who were furious at the senseless murders and the fact that a woman had been taken. Most understood it was most certainly against Anna's will but were curious about the words Darryl Kelley had shouted before he left—that Anna Foster was really *his* wife.

At the top of the steps Nate turned to them, scanning them carefully. "You had all better understand the kind of men we're going after. They're cold-blooded murderers. Some of you have no experience with that at all, and I don't want you along." He began naming names, singling out close to thirty of the fifty or so men who had gathered and telling them to go home. They grumbled and argued, but Nate would have none of it. "I'd rather have ten men who are good at this than fifty who haven't fired a gun in ten years." He named some of the others who he knew did a lot of hunting and were good with a rifle.

When he was through choosing his posse, there were eight men left besides the three deputies, himself and Jim. Rob followed as Nate led them inside the court building and into the office he shared with Jim, closing the door so he could not be heard by anyone outside. He wanted no slipups. "Are all of you outfitted good? Good horses, food, plenty of ammunition?"

They mumbled and nodded. Nate glanced at Rob. "I have a right to know how you're going to handle this," Rob told him. "I'll rest easier knowing you've got some kind of plan."

Nate removed his hat, wiping sweat from his brow with his shirtsleeve again. "As a matter of fact, I do. Whether or not it works is yet to be seen." He scanned the men. "You all know the problem. Kelley said I have to come in alone, and it's pretty obvious what he intends to do. I'm not going to risk my wife's life by storming after him with a posse—at least not one he can see."

"You gonna paint us invisible, Nate?" one man asked.

They all snickered, needing the release. Even Nate smiled a little. "I wish I could." He sighed deeply. "We figured out the robbery we investigated at Big Springs was a decoy so we wouldn't be in town when this happened. The lone survivor of that robbery turned out to be one of Kelley's men. When I got through with him, he told me where Kelley would be."

There were a few more snickers as they imagined how Nate got the confession out of the man. "He still alive?" one of them asked.

Nate rubbed at the back of his neck. "Oh, he'll survive. Trouble is, I found out this body isn't quite ready for so much ruckus." He moved his hand to his side, and Jim knew he was in pain but was not about to let it stop him.

Rob frowned with worry for his brother. "Knowing exactly where Kelley will be is a big plus," Nate went on. "He figures I'll have to track him, which means I'll *have* to come in alone. He also figures it will take me two or three days to get to him, so he won't even be watching for me right off. He's at Pawnee Hills. A man can see for miles from that perch, no matter what direction we come in from. But knowing his location gave me an idea."

He moved around behind his desk and opened a drawer, taking out a bottle of whiskey. "For medicinal purposes," he told them, "and right now I need some medicine."

There were more nervous snickers. They all realized what Nate Foster was suffering, not just physically, but emotionally. Nate took a swallow of the whiskey. *Anna, what has he done to you?* he screamed inside. *I'm so sorry about the way I acted. I just got you back. Now this. What a damn fool I was.* He handed out the bottle. "One swig each to whoever wants one. No more. I want your aim to be steady."

One man took the bottle while Nate looked them over. "Now, for those of you left, I've got one more thing to say before I tell you what we're going to do. If there is any man here who holds ill feelings toward my wife because of rumors, I want him out of here."

He watched their eyes, seeing no animosity in any of them as they passed around the bottle.

"Darryl Kelley was my wife's first husband," he explained. Rob listened curiously, his heart aching for Anna and Nate both. "Before the war he was a good man, a doctor. That's how he got the nickname Crazy Doc. He took a head wound in the war and it affected his mind. I don't know what all else happened to him—he had family in Georgia. At any rate, the war changed him. There is hardly anyone here who doesn't know someone who was either physically or emotionally affected by the war. Kelley is one of them. Anna thought he was dead when she married me. Not one thing that has happened has been her fault." He took the bottle back from one of the men and put it in the drawer. "Now, I'm going to talk to Judge Hewitt and get permission to wire ahead to Fort Riley for help. The fort is to the west of Pawnee Hills. We could commandeer a train to take us there at top speed where we would join up with some Pawnee scouts."

"How's that going to help?" one of the men asked. "That just means even more men."

Nate grinned a little. "We need the Indians—the authentic ones. The rest of us will take a quick lesson in painting ourselves up. If anybody looks too white from never taking off his shirt in the sun, you paint yourself so much there's no white showing. I don't want any mistakes. And I hope all of you can ride a horse with just a blanket on its back."

Several of them frowned, still confused.

"There are always Indians around Pawnee Hills, mostly Pawnee," Nate explained. "Most of the Pawnee are peaceful now, but not all of them. They're still wild enough that Kelley and his men would think twice about getting into a ruckus with any of them. I don't care how many men Kelley has, they won't want to start trouble with Indians way out there. While they're waiting for me to track them down, they're going to get a visit from a band of Pawnee. A few of them—the *real* Pawnee—will go in first to do a little trading with Kelley and his men. They'll see Anna and demand she be included in the trade."

They grinned and shook their heads. "How in hell did you think of that one?" one of them asked.

Nate remained sober. "The rest of us will move in a little closer so they know we mean business," he continued. "I'm hoping Kelley will hand her over. He'll expect that I'm still tracking him and that I wouldn't know if he still has her or not, so it won't matter. All he really wants is me, and then he can be on his merry way with the money. Once he hands her over, the Pawnee man who takes her will ride back to us. Once Anna is out of range, we move in and take Kelley and his men."

"What if he *doesn't* give her to us?" one of them asked.

Nate glanced at Rob, then at Jim, suddenly having trouble finding his voice at the thought of Anna getting hurt.

"If the Indian is persistent, I think he'll get her," Jim answered for Nate. "Like Nate said, Kelley ain't gonna want to risk a battle with Indians. Anna's not that important to him. She's just bait to get Nate out there, only the Indians will get there first."

"It's our only chance of getting close to them," Nate put in. "We know we can't approach from any direction as white men. And we've got to be sure we fool them. The minute Kelley suspects a trick, my wife will be dead."

The room hung silent for several seconds. Nate moved from behind his desk. "I'm going to talk to the judge now. I'll be back in a few minutes. Link, you go over to the depot and make sure they hold up that train we rode in on."

"Yes, sir." Link Headley, one of the deputies, headed toward the door. Jim called out his name and the man turned. "Don't breathe a word of what we've got planned to anybody," Jim told him.

"No, sir, I won't."

The man left, and Nate walked out. Rob followed. Jim turned to the others. "I hope to hell this works. If it doesn't, it's gonna go real hard on Nate. Real hard."

Outside the office Rob grasped Nate's arm. "We'll all be praying for both of you," he told his brother. He saw the tears in Nate's eyes as he nodded in appreciation.

"If things go right, I'll be back in a couple of days—with Anna," he answered. He walked off to talk to the judge. Rob left reluctantly, wishing he could go along, but knowing Nate was right. He and Marie might be all the family Becky had if Nate's plan failed.

It was nearly dark by the time Darryl and his men arrived at Pawnee Hills with Anna. She had heard of this place, a kind of landmark for travelers and a place where Pawnee Indians used to like to camp because it was one of the few high places in Kansas from where one could see his enemy coming.

"Pitch a couple of tents," Darryl ordered as he dismounted. Anna's stomach churned at the thought of what he might try to do inside one of those tents. He yanked her from his horse, and again she could not stand on her legs at first. Darryl left her lying where she fell as he hobbled his horse and removed its saddle and supplies so it could rest.

Anna grimaced as she got to a sitting position. "Somebody ride down to that stand of cottonwoods and gather some wood," Darryl ordered. "We need a fire."

"Doc, a fire can be seen for miles out here," someone complained.

"So what?" Darryl answered. "We *want* Foster to find us, remember? But after that wild-goose chase we sent him on, it's going to take him a while to find out what happened and track us here. We've got nothing to worry about tonight. Maybe not even tomorrow night. Just rest easy. Ben and the other two will be here sometime tomorrow morning and you can spend your time counting all the money we got. Between the bank and the stage robbery, we'll have a bundle."

Everyone chuckled, and one man broke out a whiskey bottle while others pitched a couple of tents.

"What about the woman, Doc?" someone said then. "You make up your mind yet?"

Anna watched and listened. Darryl grabbed a bottle of whiskey from one of the men and drank some down.

"Not yet. She was my wife once. I've got to think about it." There seemed to be a note of warning in his voice. "When she married Foster, she thought I was dead." He looked over at Anna with contempt. "Not that she cared." He looked back at his men. "Now she's mine again."

The men looked over at her hungrily. "You promised us a piece of the marshal's woman," one of them said, his voice gravely. "That was part of the spoils of this job. We take Nate Foster's wife, get the money and a turn at her. Get Foster to come here alone if he wants her alive."

"You're exactly right about all of it—except about getting a piece of the woman. She's my property," Darryl told them.

Anna didn't know whether to be glad or upset. At least he was apparently going to try to keep the others away from her. Was it out of purely selfish lust, or were there some feelings left somewhere deep in that demented mind?

"That's not the way it was supposed to be," one man objected. "You said—"

"I said I intended to capture Foster's wife," Darryl interrupted. "I never said you'd all get a piece of her. You just supposed that. I told you she belongs to me. When I'm through with her, I'll decide whether or not the rest of you get a turn. I just might keep her with me once we knock off Nate Foster."

"You can't!" The words came from Fran, who stumbled up to the fire. Anna cringed quietly in the shadows, deciding not to move or say anything for the moment. She had to gauge everything she did and said, had to remember Darryl's mind didn't work like an ordinary man's. Her eyes widened when Fran stepped closer. It was not fully dark yet, and Anna could see horrible bruises and swelling on Fran's face. She had not seen the woman since she heard Darryl's punches and Fran's screams back at the watering hole. Since then Darryl had ordered the men to keep Fran behind him. "I don't want to look at her," he had told one of the other men. Anna wondered if this was the first time Darryl had ever hit her, or if beatings were common.

"This isn't the way you said it would be, Darryl," the woman told him, her words slurred through swollen lips. "All of this was *my* idea, and it all worked. Foster will come soon, and you'll get to kill him. You were supposed to kill Anna, too."

"I'll do whatever I want. As far as the men go, the important thing is the money." He looked around at his men. "We'll divide it up when Ben gets here, and if some of you want to leave then, that's fine with me. Any of you who wants to stay and put a piece of lead into Nate Foster is welcome to that, too. But what I do with Anna Kelley is my decision. It's that simple. Anybody touches her without my say-so is a dead man." His eyes drilled into Fran. "Or woman," he added.

Fran's eyes widened with surprise and indignation. "This isn't fair, Darryl, especially not to me. How could you beat me? You've never hurt me before. Why, Darryl?"

Darryl looked at her scathingly. "Because I'm tired of your bitching, especially about Anna. This was your idea. You can live with it and shut up, or feel my fist again." He looked at the others, while Fran's dark eyes fired hatred and murder at Anna. "Any of you object to a man wanting his woman back?" he asked.

"Reckon not," one man said.

"She's a looker," another said, hunger in his voice. "We was lookin' forward to rubbin' Foster's nose in the dirt by havin' a piece of her."

"You got first rights, Doc. You decide what to do with her," another man put in.

Anna noticed Darryl's hand had been resting on his gun through most of the conversation. The men were obviously afraid of him and respected his authority. She had that much going for her, *if* Darryl decided to keep her for himself. Still, that meant he intended to have his own way with her, to take advantage of what he considered his husbandly rights. It seemed ironic that although he truly was her husband, if he tried to force himself on her it would be rape. The thought made her shudder, yet she realized she had to stay on his good side if she didn't want to be turned over to the rest of the men.

There was also Fran to think about. All these years the woman had apparently had a strong influence on Darryl, until now. Her biggest task for the moment was to keep a wedge between Darryl and Fran. If Fran had her way, she would talk Darryl into turning the rest of the men loose on her and into letting Fran kill her. Just the way the woman looked at her made Anna feel as though a knife were being shoved into her middle.

"Hurry up and get a fire going," Darryl was saying. "Fran will fix some food. Everybody can get some rest tonight. There's nothing to watch out for till tomorrow."

"You think Foster will come alone like you told him?" someone asked.

"Sure he will," Darryl answered. "I've got his woman. If he doesn't come alone, the fact that she's mine won't matter. I'll shoot her down right in front of his eyes, and he's still a dead man. There's no way Foster can approach us here with a posse without us seeing him coming. He's got no choice but to come alone."

There were a few chuckles. "You had one hell of an idea this time, Doc."

"*My* idea," Fran nearly growled.

Men began unloading horses and preparing to cook

something to eat. "It was *my* idea," Fran repeated, going up to one of them and grabbing his arm.

"Let go of me, bitch," the man told her. "I'm new to this bunch. I don't give a damn *whose* idea it was, long as I get my money."

Fran turned and walked up to Darryl. "Darryl, you can't do this."

"I already showed you what I think about your bitching," he answered. "Quit whining."

"Darryl, this is *me, Fran.* I'm the one who nursed you back to health, gave up everything to help you when you first got back home, supported you, loved you. We've known each other since we were six years old, and that's how long I've loved you! How can you say you might keep Anna with you?"

He lowered his whiskey bottle and looked her over. "For one thing, she's a whole lot better looking. For another, she's still legally my wife."

"She's a *Yankee!* A *traitor!* She ran off on you, remember? She never even waited to see if you were all right, if you were coming back from the war."

"That isn't true, Darryl," Anna said. She felt nauseated and weak, and it was difficult to talk at all. Her voice would hardly come, and her throat ached fiercely from Fran's choking her. "I *did* wait."

She managed to get to her feet, the left side of her face throbbing from Darryl's earlier blows. She staggered closer to him, ignoring the agonizing pain in her jaw and throat as she spoke.

"Even after I saw you at Centralia I waited. I . . . hoped you would come to me with some kind of an explanation. Then I got scared, because wives of outlaws . . . were being abused and arrested. And I . . . I thought you didn't want me anymore, because you threw your wedding ring at me. Fran hated me because she was jealous. I left the restaurant . . . had to support myself so I opened a restaurant of my own . . . in Abilene. I left a forwarding address at Columbia . . . so you'd know where to find me if you wanted to."

"That's a lie," Fran said, sneering. "You ran out on him!

You started sneaking around with Nate Foster when you knew poor Darryl was still alive!"

Anna shook her head. "No. I left an address . . . and I waited." She kept her eyes on Darryl. "I got a letter from Fran . . . telling me you were dead. It wasn't until after that . . . that I started seeing . . . Nate. And I never told him about you, Darryl. When you were still alive I never told him. I could have tricked you. I could have tried harder to find you . . . led you into a trap so Nate could arrest you. But I didn't. I didn't want anything to happen to you . . . because you were still my husband. And I *did* wait for you. But then Fran wrote and said you were dead. I was never untrue to you . . . while you were alive, Darryl."

"You lying bitch!" Fran headed in Anna's direction, and Darryl grabbed her arm.

"You want more of what I gave you back at that watering hole?" he asked.

The rest of the men watched and listened, none of them daring to say a word.

Fran glared at Darryl. "You're going to keep her, aren't you?" She stood there in her torn dress, her dark hair hanging in strings, looking ugly and threatening, her lips swollen, her dark eyes spitting hatred. "You've always wanted her back, in spite of what she did to you."

"What's this about a letter telling her I was dead? And how come you told me you didn't know where she was, didn't know how to get hold of her? When I first came to Columbia, I asked you to find Anna. I told you I wanted to talk to her, but you told me she ran off, was probably clear up in Montana. You lied, Fran! You knew where she was all the time! You knew because you wrote her a letter to tell her I was dead! Why'd you do that, Fran?"

The woman seemed to be withering. "I did it because *I* love you, Darryl. She's no good for you. She doesn't share the same dreams like we do. She's a *Yankee,* Darryl."

"I'm not a Yankee . . . *or* a Confederate," Anna argued. "I just wanted the war to be over. I wanted my husband to come back to me alive . . . no matter what side he fought on. When I learned the truth . . . I could have turned him in . . . but I didn't!"

Fran grasped Darryl's jacket. "Darryl, *think!* Think what all I've done for you! I even slept with your men to keep them happy. I gave you all my money, comforted you, kept house for you, helped you with the robberies, put up with the other women—"

His hand tightened on her arm. "You lied, Fran," he growled. He tossed aside the whiskey bottle. "You, of all people, the one person I thought I could trust." Anna gasped when without warning he punched the woman hard in the side of the head. Anna's eyes widened in horror as Fran fell to the ground. Darryl picked her up and punched her again, square in the face, sending her flying backward.

Anna covered her face. Was what Fran felt really love, or just grasping at anything that made her feel pretty, wanted? Was her devotion to the Confederacy nothing more than a need to belong to something, to someone? She had slept with Darryl's men. At Darryl's orders? Who was in control of whom? Fran had apparently been able to manipulate his mind, but she could go only so far without stepping on Darryl Kelley's need to be superior, to be in charge.

"You men can do what you want with that one," Darryl was telling the others. "Some of you have never been with Fran before. She's not much to look at, but she's good in bed. Any of you needing a woman can have her for the night. She knows her place and what's expected of her."

"Ain't no fun bein' with a woman who's out cold," one of them joked. He uncorked a canteen and poured it over her face. Fran sputtered and coughed and the man jerked her up and dragged her off into the darkness. Anna watched in horror, folding her arms over her stomach and bending over, sure she was going to be sick. Someone grabbed her hair and jerked her head back, and she looked into Darryl's dark, wild eyes.

"Let's go to my tent," he said with a sadistic smile. "We've got some things to catch up on, *Mrs. Kelley.*" He shoved her toward a tent while the other men gave hoots and whistles and said he should let them know when he tired of her.

Anna thought of Nate, wondered where he was, knew he would come. But that would mean his death. If she could save him by convincing Darryl not to kill him and by riding off with Darryl, she knew she would have to do it. But it could mean never seeing Nate again, or Becky, her precious, sweet Becky.

Darryl tossed her to the ground inside the tent and lit a lantern, and she forced herself not to think about Nate or Becky for the moment. Right now she had to deal with this half-crazed man who was once her husband. She had to pray for a way to reach him, a way to avoid the horror he had planned for her, a way to bide her time until Nate came. But what good would that do, if he came alone? What chance did he have? It all seemed hopeless.

Chapter 25

Anna scooted into a corner of the tent while Darryl unstrapped his gunbelt and removed his jacket. "I like women now—all women—you know that? I mean, ever since this injury, I've got this insatiable appetite." He grinned, moving closer to her. "Fran knew how to satisfy me. A lot of other women *learned* how to satisfy me, whether they wanted to or not. Which way is it going to be for you, Anna? You can make it easy on yourself and enjoy it, or you can fight it and get hurt more than you already have been."

Anna breathed deeply for courage, watching him carefully. "Maybe your problem was that you wanted all those women to be me," she answered him.

He stopped what he was doing and stared at her strangely. "What?"

"I'm not like those . . . other women," she told him, straining to find her voice. "This is me, Darryl. Anna—your wife. Before you left for the war . . . you were tender and gentle, Darryl. You made love to me . . . because you loved and honored me . . . not out of animal instinct. If you try to force me now . . . I won't scream and fight like

you want . . . nor will I be your whore. I'll just lie here
. . . and I'll feel nothing but *pity* for you, because that is
the only feeling I have left . . . for the kind of man my
once caring, loving husband used to be . . . a man with a
wonderful future ahead of him, a man with . . . so much
promise."

His eyes narrowed, and he held out his hands. "Promise?
Look at these hands! I could never be a doctor again,
Anna!"

"That shaking is just as much . . . from too much whiskey as anything else!"

"I *have* to drink whiskey, or go crazy from the pain in my
head! I lived with it every day, Anna—constant headaches.
Do you know what that's like?"

"No. But I can imagine, Darryl . . . and I'm sorry. You
still could have come home to me. I would have . . .
helped you all I could." To talk was painful, but she could
think of no other way to stall him, and she hoped that
maybe she could find a way to get through to him. If she
got nothing else out of this, she hoped at least to get some
answers to all the questions that had plagued her over the
years. If only he had come to her in the first place, explained all of this to her. "Please . . . tell me about it,
Darryl. Tell me what happened. Why didn't you come to
me . . . and let me help you?"

There was the look of a wary cat in his eyes, as though he
felt he couldn't trust her. She could tell he was trying to
figure out if she really cared, or if she was just buying time.
She tried to keep a sincere look on her face, sensing she was
better off if she didn't show the fear he expected. She remembered Nate saying once that if a man stood right up to
a wild animal and faced it down, it would often back away.
That was what Darryl was now—a wild animal.

He looked down at his hands again. "By the time I got
back here, I was *beyond* help," he hissed. "I had already
found my mother and father. My mother lying naked, raped
and murdered—my father with his head cut off! The plantation was burned—house, outbuildings, crops—*everything!*
From the bodies I could tell that if I had got there just a

couple of days sooner, I might have been able to help them. But I was too late!"

He rubbed his hands on his knees to steady them. "Not long after that, our regiment got all split up. Mark and I were taken prisoners, but we escaped. I guess the army never really knew what happened to us, because we never got reported as prisoners. We were on our way back to—"

He rubbed at his head, and Anna cringed at the sight of the ugly scar. He hesitated, as though trying to remember something. "Back to—I can't remember. It doesn't matter. We never made it. Union snipers fired at us—cut Mark down right off."

He drank down some more whiskey. "They left me for dead. When I came to I didn't even know who I was at first. Some people helped me. After that I just left to make war my own way. Somebody must have found Mark, so he got reported dead. But nobody ever knew what happened to me, and I don't suppose anybody cared."

Anna watched him, trying to picture the Darryl she had once known. There was little resemblance. "*I* cared, Darryl. It's the life you've led since then that has turned people against you."

His gaze moved over her. "Like hell you cared! The South lost, and I expect you were happy enough about that!"

"I wasn't happy about any of it. I just . . . wanted you to come home."

"Home? To what? My real home was gone, Mark was gone, and I was useless. You don't understand the hatred in me, Anna, the need for vengeance that has never been satisfied and never will be! I joined up with Bill Anderson, and it felt *good* to shoot down the people responsible for my pain! I didn't care if they were women, children, old men—what does it matter? When you're in pain like I am, *nothing* matters! That's exactly how I felt at Centralia. I enjoyed watching those bastards die! But then I saw you there, and I thought later maybe I ought to find you. I went to Columbia, and after I saw Fran, I knew she could help me. She told me how you ran off on me . . . how you didn't care."

"She lied because she's always wanted you for herself."

"No! Fran understood." He rubbed at his head again. "It doesn't matter anymore. She's turned into a bitch. I'm getting tired of listening to her constant whining."

His talk was astonishing when she considered how caring he used to be. Anna continued to meet his gaze boldly. "It's too bad you . . . listened to her, Darryl. You should have come to *me* first."

"With that much hatred inside me for Yankees? I needed to kill, Anna." His eyes widened wildly again. "Kill and kill and *kill!* You were as Yankee as the rest of them." His face began to redden and he grabbed her wrist. "I had a Yankee wife," he snarled. "Maybe I was afraid I'd kill you! Then after a while I didn't care one way or another. I remembered how you looked at me that day at Centralia! I could see by your eyes what you thought of me, and I knew Fran was right. I *couldn't* come to you. And now any feeling I had left for you is gone. I stole you away for one reason—to remind you of the husband you've betrayed, and to lure that marshal you married right into my gun sight!"

"I don't believe you," she told him, her voice growing more husky from the damage Fran had done. "You still love me, Darryl Kelley. You already said you were afraid . . . to come to me at first . . . because you might kill me. Why did you care?"

"Shut your mouth!"

"No! Somewhere down deep inside that angry, hateful soul you remember how it used to be for us, don't you?"

He suddenly backhanded her, the blow coming so quickly and unexpectedly that she gasped and fell sideways. She felt his heated breath on her neck then. "It doesn't matter how it *used* to be," he hissed. "I feel only vengeance now, Anna. You've been sleeping with another man—a man I hate—a man who stands against everything I believe in. I'm going to get my revenge in the best way a man can get it: by taking that man's woman and letting him go crazy with the thought that you were *my* woman first!"

His voice sounded far away. She felt a hand on her breast, and through blurred vision she saw his face, a bristly beard showing from going a full day without a shave. He ripped the front of her dress partway open. She grasped his wrist, struggling to think straight through ringing ears.

"I'm not like the others, Darryl," she managed to say, forcing her voice to work. "I . . . loved you. Everything Fran told you . . . was a lie. I waited for you. I prayed you'd come to me . . . with an explanation . . . that maybe somehow I could help you . . . and we'd go off somewhere together and . . . start over."

She felt him stiffen. Suddenly he sat up. "Damn you," he growled.

Anna quickly pulled her dress over herself, watching him like a cornered animal. "I . . . loved you for *you,*" she said carefully. She realized it was easy to send his mind spinning, to keep him confused. "It didn't matter if you were . . . a Yankee or a Confederate. I loved you *before* all that."

She secretly prayed God would help her find the right words. How would she face Nate if she was forced to submit to this man? "Fran never really loved you, Darryl. She needs to think . . . that you care about her, because of her unhappy childhood. You were just . . . someone from her past who had befriended her when no one else would. And you both . . . thought alike . . . both wanted to keep the war going. Fran was just reaching out for an old friend. But I *loved* you, Darryl, in a gentle . . . devoted way she isn't capable of loving anyone. Her past is too full of hurt and violence."

She put a hand to her throat, feeling it swelling inside.

"The war is *over,* Darryl. You've got . . . to let it be over for you."

"Shut up!"

"You . . . know I'm right." It made her sick to see him this way. How she wished with terrible guilt that he truly had died. "If you . . . had just come straight to me in the beginning," she said, "before you got into all this murdering and thieving. We might . . . have been able to find some . . . help for you . . . might have been able to save our marriage—"

"I said shut up!" He tossed his whiskey bottle aside and grasped her shoulders, pushing her down. "Lies, all lies! You're trying to talk your way out of this, and it won't work! You're my woman, and I'm going to take what I've got coming! Soon Nate Foster will die, and you're coming with me. And when I'm tired of you, my men will gladly take up where I leave off!"

He ripped at her dress more, moving on top of her. The tent had become terribly stuffy, and her head reeled from his body smell and the whiskey smell, combined with the heat inside the tent. "Darryl, please don't do this," she asked. "This is me, *Anna!* I'm going to have a baby, and I don't want to lose it."

He raised up, and she tried to read his dark eyes, but they seemed to constantly change from crazed to sane, from angry to a look of near tenderness. He began breathing deeply, his nostrils flaring. "A baby! Nate *Foster's* baby!"

"Yes." She gasped for breath, feeling as though her throat were closing up on her. "Darryl, please, I . . . need some water. My throat . . ." Her voice was growing weaker.

He grabbed a canteen and hit her in the chest with it. "Here!"

She uncorked it with a shaking hand and swallowed some water, breaking out in a sweat from the unbearable heat. "We . . . already have a little girl," she told him. *Keep talking,* she told herself. *It's all you've got.* "Don't you see . . . how wrong this is? I have a little girl . . . waiting for me, Darryl. I've never done anything against you. I waited for you, and when I thought you were dead . . . I had to go on with my life. But that doesn't change the fact that I loved you once . . . and you loved me. I don't think you really want to hurt me . . . the way you've hurt other women."

He grasped her hair at the top of her head and jerked her closer. "A baby! How come you never gave *me* a baby!"

"I don't know, Darryl. It just . . . never happened."

"You saying Nate Foster is more man than I am?"

"No . . . I—"

Darryl looked at her strangely then, touching her throat almost gently. "The necklace, Anna. Where is the necklace?"

Her eyes widened. "I . . . I had to sell it. I needed the money."

He suddenly started slapping her, a series of quick, stinging blows that finally made her push at him and try to strike back, while he called her every name in the book.

"*Sold* it," he screamed. "Bitch! Traitor!"

He grasped her wrists, pushing her arms up over her head while he put his weight on her. "Nate Foster is going to die, Anna. Die! You'll come with me and you'll learn quick enough who's the better man. Maybe you don't love me anymore, but I don't give a damn."

She felt his lips at her throat, and she argued with herself whether to fight him, realizing that if he meant to have his way, he would, no matter what she did. Fighting him could only mean losing the precious baby she was carrying; and it only seemed to whet his appetite.

There was apparently no reasoning with him at all. He truly was a crazy man. The only thing that seemed to slow him was to voice her affection, and she tried it again, forcing herself not to cry like a child from the pain of his blows. She stopped straining against him, and she turned her lips to his cheek.

"I love you, Darryl," she said softly. "I never stopped. It's just that I thought . . . you were dead. That's Fran's fault. Please . . . forgive me. I'm sorry . . . about the necklace. I had no choice."

Again he hesitated, and she knew she had found her only weapon—love and gentleness, willing submission. It confused him, ate at what little sense of honor he had left somewhere deep inside his crazed mind. He slowly raised up, and to her surprise he moved off her.

It was then they heard shouts outside. Suddenly the entrance flap of the tent was jerked aside and Fran ducked inside, brandishing a gun. Her eyes were wild and dark, her hair a tangled mess, her dress torn. In the light of the lantern Anna could see her face was more bruised than she realized, swollen so much that she would be almost unrecognizable if Anna didn't already know who she was.

"You betrayed me, Darryl," she screamed. "I'm going to kill both of you!"

Darryl moved quickly away as she shot wildly at him. Anna tried to scream, but her voice was fast leaving her.

Darryl dove at Fran as she aimed the gun at Anna. The gun went off, a bullet spraying dirt into Anna's face as it hit the earth beside her. At the same time Darryl was tackling Fran's legs. He knocked her back out of the tent, breaking the support pole at the tent opening so that the tent partially collapsed and quickly caught fire when part of it rested on top of the lantern inside. Anna scrambled frantically to find the entrance, hearing a gunshot but too terrified now of burning to death to care about who had shot whom.

"Anna!" She heard Darryl shouting her name. Suddenly she felt hands pulling her. He yanked her out of the tent and dragged her away from it, collapsing beside her. Anna rolled to her side coughing, the cough tearing at her injured throat. Finally she sat up and looked the tent, which was already consumed in flames. She turned to Darryl, who was grasping at his leg where a bullet from Fran's gun had grazed it.

Anna reached over to touch his leg, but he knocked her hand away. "It's just a flesh wound."

Anna looked around in the bright fire, then spotted Fran's body lying not far away. "Fran!" She started toward her, but Darryl grabbed her arm.

"I shot her," he growled. "I was getting tired of the damn bitch anyway!"

Anna gasped, looking at the body again. Fran lay sprawled on her back, an ugly, gaping hole in her chest. She didn't know how to feel. Darryl had just saved her life— from Fran's bullet and from the fire. When he pulled her from the fire, he had called her name almost frantically, like a husband would call for a wife with true concern. Yet he had shot Fran with apparently no feelings of regret whatsoever, someone he had known since childhood, a woman with whom he had lived for years, from whom he had accepted help and money. In spite of what Fran had just tried to do, there was a side of Anna that felt sorry for the woman.

Darryl was like two men—one crazy and cruel, a thief, rapist, and murderer. The other man, the Darryl she had known, was still there, deep inside, trying so hard to get out but unable to do so.

Darryl got up and limped over to the campfire, and Anna lay down in the grass, letting the tears come quietly. Everything hurt, and she was afraid now of losing the baby. She felt humiliated, confused, terrified, realizing she couldn't keep appealing to the Darryl deep inside. That Darryl wasn't strong enough to come out and conquer the crazed Darryl. Ugly memories and an ugly wound prevented that. She realized she could be grateful to Fran for one thing. She had interrupted Darryl's intentions and had hurt him enough that he would likely leave her alone for the rest of the night.

"Bury the bitch," he growled to someone. "And any man that lays a hand on my wife tonight won't live to see the sun rise."

The night passed like a strange, ugly dream. Anna's feelings for Darryl were torn between terror and revulsion, and just plain pity. She realized what hell it had to be to live with constant headaches, but the man was demented and dangerous. He had shot Fran with no more feeling than if he had shot a rabbit. It was not just self-defense. He was tired of her. Was that how she would end up if he took her away with him and then got "tired" of her?

She realized he was beyond hope, a man incapable of grasping and hanging on to feelings and reality any longer. The real Darryl could only peek out from behind this demented creature who had taken over his body. Anna knew that the way he treated her, in fact her very life, depended on how she handled both men. For now, he wanted her for himself, whether willingly or by force. That was all that kept the other men away from her. And his wound and the burned tent were all that kept him from finishing what he had started. She knew she would never survive another night with him.

By morning the men were getting much more restless. It had been an eventful, nearly sleepless night, and Anna groaned with pain when someone jerked at her, waking her from a sleep that had done little to comfort her. She had fallen asleep out of sheer exhaustion, waking up constantly from discomfort. Soreness from the long ride the day before and pain from Darryl's beating only added to the agony of sleeping on the cool, damp ground, with only one light blanket to comfort her. Her face was covered with mosquito bites.

She sat up, groaning from aching bones and sore muscles. She could tell her lip and one eye were swollen, and her throat hurt worse than ever. She could barely move her head from side to side.

"Fix us some grub," one of Darryl's men told her. "We ain't got Fran to do it for us anymore."

Anna looked around. A few of the men were still sleeping on bedrolls. Others were up, pacing around and brandishing rifles, watching the horizon. Watching . . . for Nate. Anna could not imagine how Nate could get her or himself out of this mess. From their vantage point, Darryl and his men could see for miles. She moved her eyes to the tent, which lay in ashes. Not far away was a pile of dirt where Fran lay buried.

Anna shivered at the thought of how the woman's life had ended, and she wondered how all their lives might have turned out if there had never been a war. She looked over at Darryl, who lay near the fire, his leg bandaged and blood showing through the white gauze. One of his men was putting more wood on the fire.

Darryl glanced at her and drank down some whiskey. "Do like Trace says," he told her. "He got out the supply packs with pans and food. You're the restaurant owner. Fix us something to eat."

Anna grimaced as she managed to get to her feet. "I have to . . . tend to a personal matter first." She could barely get out the words, realizing when she tried to speak that her voice was almost completely gone now.

Darryl laughed and the others grinned. "Go right ahead. The boys might as well see what they're getting," Darryl told her.

Anna's cheeks reddened beneath the bruises, and she mustered as much strength to her voice as possible. "I thought I was to belong only to you. I'm your wife, remember?"

His eyes moved over her. "You didn't much act like it last night."

"That wasn't my fault. Fran ruined it."

He watched her eyes, and she hoped he believed she had intended to let him have her. She kept her eyes fixed directly on him. "You either find a way . . . for me to do this privately . . . or I'll do it right where I stand," she told him. "Then you can all put up with the smell of me, if that's what you want."

Darryl snickered. "Yeah, you'd do it, too. You always were the independent sort, weren't you?" He gave a nod of his head. "Go over there behind the other tent." He raised his voice then. "You boys over there get over here by the fire till my wife finishes her business. Anybody looks, he's a dead man."

A few men grumbled as they came to stand by the fire. Anna hurriedly took care of personal matters behind the tent, wondering just how much longer Darryl's authority was going to last, realizing what would happen to her if his men decided they no longer needed to listen to him. After all, part of that authority, a great deal of the decision-making, came from Fran before. Now she was gone.

When she rose, she took a quick inventory. There were at least ten of them, including Darryl. She knew from talk that at least three more were on their way. She looked around and realized there was no direction from which Nate could come after them without being seen. He would have to come alone if he wanted to save her life, but she knew that was a vacant promise anyway. Nate would be killed and Darryl would not free her. He would take her with him, abuse her as he wished, turn her over to his men, then probably kill her. She did not know how to control him the way Fran did.

Her fate seemed sealed, and her only comfort was knowing Becky was safe with Rob and Marie. She walked on shaky, sore legs back to the campfire and made breakfast, wanting nothing more than to bathe and sleep, to sleep forever. But for now she had to go on her survival instincts, stay alert to Darryl's moods, watch for Nate.

"I don't like this waitin'," one man complained over a piece of pork. "We're sittin' ducks."

"It's Nate Foster who'll be the sitting duck," Darryl answered. He glanced at Anna. "You get to watch your illegal husband die, Mrs. Kelley."

"You've already found out . . . he doesn't die easily," she answered in a near whisper. She sat on the ground, holding a tin cup of hot coffee in her hand. She looked slyly at the others. "This is Nate Foster you men are dealing with . . . not just the average man. You'd be smart . . . to be on your way and forget about this vendetta . . . once you get your money."

"You shut up," Darryl warned her. "I'll shut that mouth *for* you if you don't. And if you're so anxious to send these men on their way, maybe you'd like it if I gave them a little farewell present from you!"

"I'm only giving you fair warning," she told him. "Forget about Nate, Darryl . . . Take your money and me . . . if you're so determined . . . and get out of here."

He just chuckled, looking at the others. "She just doesn't want anything to happen to her lover. They've got a kid, and she's carrying another one. There's no way Nate Foster can get to us up here without dying—and he'll come alone because of his wife. Don't let her put ideas in your heads. We don't have a thing to worry about."

The men looked around at each other. "We're not so sure about any of this," the one called Trace said. "Nate Foster ain't a man to mess with. And this thing with his wife—hell, if she's carryin' besides, he's gonna be even more hell-bent on gettin' her back."

Darryl eyed the man closely. "Some of the new ones can leave, Trace. But I thought I could depend on you. I'm waiting for Foster, and that's all there is to it." He moved a hand to his gun again, eyeing the rest of them. "Every man who waits with me and helps me gets part of my share of the money. That's a promise."

They all looked around at each other again.

"What are you afraid of?" Darryl asked. "There's no way Foster can approach with a posse without them all getting killed. Don't let a woman's voice and pretty eyes steer you from what we came here for. She's just trying to save Foster's hide, can't you see that?"

Trace swallowed, his eyes on the gun. He glanced at

Anna then. "Yeah, I suppose." He looked back at Darryl. "How much longer do you think we have to wait?"

Darryl slowly moved his hand away from the gun. "I figure he'll come riding in about midday tomorrow. If he followed Ben and the others south out of Big Springs, he wasted quite a few hours there. They circled up to Topeka. By the time he followed them there, he would find out then about the robbery and about his wife. He might wait till nighttime, thinking the darkness will help. We'll keep plenty of guards out tomorrow night." He looked at Anna. "Stick with me, and when this is over we'll hit Abilene next and clean out my wife's savings and the cash at her restaurant. Once Nate Foster is dead, Kansas will be ours."

He drank down some more whiskey, and Anna said nothing. Like the others, she began watching the eastern horizon, looking for a lone figure on a horse. She cleaned up from breakfast, avoiding getting any nearer any of the men than necessary, closing her ears to some of their remarks.

Before noon three more riders came in. It was the one called Ben and two others, whom Darryl had talked about earlier. Everyone celebrated and guzzled more whiskey when they learned the stage robbery had gone well, and they joked about Nate going on a wild-goose chase. They opened a saddlebag full of money and talked about killing the stage driver and a passenger as though it were all in a day's work.

"We left good tracks all the way to Topeka," Ben told Darryl. "Foster will track us there, all right. We got there about eight last night. I expect he didn't even manage to track us to Topeka till this morning because of the dark. There's no way he can trace the rest of you here till late tonight or tomorrow morning."

The man glanced at Anna, his eyes moving over her hungrily. "You were right, boss. If she was my woman, I'd come after her, too."

"Well, she was *my* woman first, and she's still my woman," Darryl answered. "Foster is going to learn that the hard way."

They laughed, and Anna turned away. Morning slowly moved into afternoon, and she fixed another meal, almost glad for something to do in spite of being so tired. The sun rose high and hot, and men grumbled about the fact that there was no shade on the hill where they waited. Tempers were growing shorter. One man went around to the horses, pouring water from a canteen into a hat for them to drink.

"One more day is all we *can* wait," he told Darryl. "We have got to get these horses to water."

"Today is all we need. He'll be here come morning," Darryl answered. "Just keep your eyes to the east."

Anna cleaned up again, then poured some coffee for one of the men. As she did so, she glanced past him to the west. It was then she saw them—riders—coming from the west instead of the east! Her heart pounded, and at first she gave no indication she had seen anything. Could it be Nate? But how? He could only this morning have discovered she had been taken. He couldn't possibly get clear out here so quickly, and certainly not from the opposite side of Pawnee Hills. And he wouldn't come with a whole posse. She wiped at sweat that ran into her eyes.

"Hey, Doc, look," one of the men shouted. Anna's heart fell. It couldn't be Nate. Even if it was, he had been seen.

"What the hell is that?" someone asked.

Darryl stood up, grimacing at the pain from his sore leg. Anna walked quietly behind the rest of them.

"Couldn't be Foster—not this soon—and not from that direction," Darryl was saying.

Trace squinted. "It's goddamn Indians—looks like Pawnee."

"Damn," someone else muttered. "That's all we need."

"The Pawnee are peaceful," Darryl put in.

"Not all of them," Trace said. "You can bet they've already seen us. If they come up here wanting to trade, you'd better trade with them, Doc. Indians are like ants. Where you see a few, there's a hundred more waitin' behind them. I'm not gettin' in any ruckus with Indians, not out here in the open where they can come at us from all sides."

"Don't get all dandered up," Darryl told him. "Wait and see what they want. Maybe they'll ride on by and leave us alone."

"Sure. And maybe the sun won't set tonight, either. There ain't no chance they'll ride on by."

"A fine time for Indians to come along," someone else grumbled. He removed his hat and wiped sweat from his brow. "We should have left here and said to hell with Nate Foster. We've got his woman and all that money. I tell you, Doc, the longer we sit around here, the more trouble we're gonna have."

"And I told you there's nothing to worry about. As far as those Indians go, we've got plenty of supplies. We'll give them a little tobacco and they'll be on their way."

Anna watched, her heart pounding. Indians! All the Plains Indians had been making trouble lately because of the railroad. In all her years in this land, she had always lived in the more civilized areas. She was as afraid of Indians as a greenhorn from the East; and she was just as full of horror stories about what they could do. She was the only woman among thirteen men. If Darryl and the others didn't have enough to satisfy the approaching painted warriors, how far would they go to save their necks? She had no doubt as to the answer.

From where she stood, she counted at least twenty-five. Approximately ten of them, their straight, black hair hanging past their shoulders, began riding cautiously up the hill while the others held back. They were heavily armed, their dark skin unaffected by the hot Kansas sun. Some were nearly naked, others wore white man's pants and calico shirts, headbands and hats.

She watched the others below, wondering why they didn't all come up. Perhaps they were ready to charge in case of trouble. One of them seemed to sit taller in his saddle than the others. His horse snorted and shook its mane, turning sideways for a moment. It was then Anna recognized the brown and white Appaloosa, with one big spot on its left rump. It was Nate's horse!

Chapter 26

Darryl and his men stood with rifles ready as the ten Pawnee Indians rode up close, their dark eyes watching the outlaws cautiously. One of the Indians rode forward, eyeing Anna, who stepped back. She realized that if the horse she had seen waiting below belonged to Nate, this was some kind of plan to get her away. She had better appear frightened to keep Darryl from becoming suspicious.

It was not difficult to act afraid of the dark-skinned, wild-looking man who eyed her at the moment. And she could only pray she was right that this was some kind of rescue attempt. The Indian who had ridden forward finally moved his attention from her to scan Darryl and his men. "Who is your leader?" he asked.

Darryl squared his shoulders and stepped forward. "I am," he replied. "Most call me Crazy Doc."

The Indian looked him over. "I have heard some white men speak of you."

Darryl grinned, looking back at some of his men. "Hear that? We're famous, boys." He looked back at the Indian.

"What is it you want? We're just camping here long enough to rest our horses. Then we'll be on our way."

The Indian glanced at Anna again before speaking. "I am called White Eagle. We need tobacco, whiskey. We also need food. The railroad men have killed the buffalo, so many that we now have to ride far from our reservation to find meat."

Darryl put on a friendly smile. "Well, we've got a little extra to spare of everything you mentioned." He turned to his men. "Pete, gather up a couple bottles of whiskey and a few plugs of tobacco. And give him some of those biscuits Anna baked earlier."

White Eagle backed up his horse a little, while the rest of those with him sat silently watching. Pete collected the things as ordered, shoving them into a potato sack and handing them up to White Eagle. Anna shivered at the tense situation, unsure what to expect, what she should do. Every man carried a gun, including the Indians, and, she was sure, every man below, including Nate. Her biggest fear was that Nate could get hurt again.

White Eagle handed the sack back to one of the others, but he did not move. His dark eyes settled on Anna again. "What about the woman?" he asked.

Darryl's smile faded. "What about her?"

White Eagle met his eyes. "She is a captive? She is worth something to the white men?"

"She's no captive. She's my wife."

White Eagle frowned. "Look at her. She is beaten and dirty. I think you lie. I see fear in her eyes. You have stolen her. You will sell her to the slave traders."

"No. She's my wife. She's bruised up because she didn't mind her place. You know how it is. Haven't you ever given your woman a little lesson once in a while?"

White Eagle looked down at him proudly. "No," he said, sneering. His nostrils flared in an anger and determination so real that Anna truly was becoming more afraid. "I want the white woman! I think she is worth much to some white man. We can trade her back to soldiers for food and blankets."

Darryl looked back at Anna, then up at White Eagle.

"You can't have her. I'm telling you she's mine, and I'm not turning her over to any Indians!"

The statement surprised Anna, who expected Darryl would give in easily to the demand to save his own neck. He and his men were far outnumbered.

"Give her to him," Ben growled. "She's not worth dyin' for!"

"Shut up," Darryl barked. "I'm not giving Anna over to savages. I just got her back for *myself!* I want her here when Nate Foster shows up!"

"To hell with Foster," Trace argued. "We won't be here to greet him at all if you make trouble with these Indians."

White Eagle rode closer to Anna, who watched him carefully, waiting for some sign of what to do.

"You stay away from her," Darryl warned. "You can have all the food and whiskey and tobacco you want. You can even have some of our guns. And money, we've got a lot of money here. You can have that too, but you can't have the woman."

White Eagle raised his arm and made a circular motion. It seemed only an instant later that Anna heard the soft, whirring sound, then the thud. Trace suddenly crumpled to the ground, an arrow in his chest. Anna stared wide-eyed at the sight, as did the others, who for the moment were taken by surprise.

White Eagle took advantage of the situation. He kicked out at Darryl, catching him under the chin and sending him sprawling. The big Indian reached out for Anna then. She quickly grabbed at the mane of his horse while White Eagle swept her into one strong arm and rode off with her, heading back down the hill.

Hardly more than five seconds passed from the moment the arrow hit Trace until Anna was halfway down the hill, held only by White Eagle's strong arm. Already she could hear gunshots, and the men below were heading uphill. Nate's horse galloped past White Eagle, Nate glancing at Anna just long enough to see she was alive and all right. He was so painted up that she only knew by his horse and his own size that it was Nate. She tried to call out his name, but her voice was down to a near whisper now, and the gunfire was deafening.

White Eagle deposited Anna below the hill. "Stay," he ordered. He headed his horse back uphill, and Anna crouched down, watching the battle above in terror. Some of the Indians were yipping and calling as though it were their own attack.

Suddenly Anna saw Darryl. He had somehow managed to get to his horse, which he had not had time to saddle. He rode the animal bareback down the hill at a hard gallop, headed straight for Anna. She got up and started to run, then turned to see Nate right behind Darryl and gaining fast.

Darryl pulled a gun and aimed it at Anna. "If I can't have you, nobody will," he screamed at her.

She ducked and rolled, and at the same time Nate's gun was fired. The motion of his horse caused the bullet to miss Darryl, but it hit the rump of his horse, causing the animal to go down. Darryl was thrown off, and his gun flew out of his hand.

Darryl got up and started running. Nate fired at him, but in the battle above, he had used all the bullets in his six-gun. He threw the gun aside and rode down on Darryl, leaping from his horse and tackling him to the ground.

"Nate," Anna whispered. She ran to where she had seen Darryl's gun fall, and she picked it up, staggering over to where Nate and Darryl rolled on the ground. Nate jerked Darryl up, venting his fury with his fists in well-aimed blows that Darryl didn't have a chance of returning. Darryl's face began to split open and bleed. Anna stood there, her feelings painfully torn into a thousand emotions.

"Bastard," Nate roared. "What have you done to her!"

Nate did not see Darryl pick up a fist-size rock. Suddenly Darryl slammed the rock against the side of Nate's head, and Nate went sprawling sideways, rolling onto his stomach. Darryl quickly scrambled on hands and knees over to where Nate's pistol lay. He grasped it and cocked it. Anna had no idea the gun held no bullets.

"No," she tried to scream. But her voice would not work. She raised Darryl's gun and fired wildly. Darryl grunted and his body jerked and whirled. He landed on his back, then rolled to his knees, pulling the trigger of Nate's gun as it hung limply in his hand. The gun only clicked.

Darryl grasped at his right arm, blood already pouring down and running off his hand. The bullet Anna had fired had torn through his right shoulder. He turned, still on his knees, and looked in shock at Anna, who stood watching him with terrified eyes, still holding his gun.

"Bitch," he roared. "Goddamn you! You *are* a traitor! Fran was right, you Yankee bitch! Your own husband! You shot your own husband!"

Anna dropped the gun, just as Jim came riding down the hill, wearing buckskins and warpaint. "Hold it right there," he yelled out to Darryl, holding a gun on the man. He dismounted as Darryl dropped the gun he held. Jim hurried over to handcuff the man, while Anna stumbled over to Nate, who by then was getting to his feet. Blood poured down the side of his head. Anna grasped his arm, and in the next moment both his arms were around her.

"Anna," he groaned.

"Bitch," Darryl yelled again. "You should have *killed* me, Anna! You should have *killed* me! Now everybody in Kansas is going to know about us! I'll make *sure* they know! I might hang, but I'll have my day in court, and so will you!"

"Get him out of here," Nate growled to Jim.

Two more men had ridden up, and Anna just then realized that the gunfire had stopped. Anna felt suddenly faint, the trauma and her injuries overcoming her.

"Take Kelley back, right now," Jim was shouting to someone. "Get him out of earshot of Mrs. Foster."

The men obeyed, helping Darryl onto a horse, then tying his ankles and securing his wrists to the pommel of the saddle.

Anna saw none of it. She felt herself being lifted in strong arms. Nate. Here she was safe. He had found a way to get her back. Here was the man to whom she belonged now for the rest of her life. The nightmare was over, and there didn't have to be any more secrets.

"Get a blanket," she heard Nate telling someone. A moment later he was laying her down in some shade. "What's the damage?" Nate asked.

"The one called Two Legs got killed," she heard Jim saying. "Bob Lassiter took a bullet in the leg, but he'll be all right. I figure about six of Kelley's men are dead. A couple more are wounded. We found the stolen money." There was a pause, and Anna felt a big hand at the side of her face. "You sure messed up Kelley's face," Jim said.

"I didn't do what I would have *liked* to do," Nate answered, his voice sounding very close. "By the time I got a shot at him, my gun was empty."

"Well, your wife did it for you. He was fixing to shoot you, but she got him first. 'Course, she didn't know the gun he was using wasn't loaded, but that doesn't make much difference."

"My God, Anna," Nate said softly. He gently stroked the hair back from her face. "Look at her. Look at what he did to her!"

"Nate, at least we got her back. Your idea worked just like you hoped it would."

"Maybe so, but look at how she suffered. Kelley was right. She *should* have killed him. She had every right. The sad part is, this isn't over yet."

"You're right. All hell's gonna break loose when we hit Topeka. It's gonna be awful hard for me to keep from finishin' that bastard off before we get there. I hope he tries to escape."

"Take Kelley and his men to Fort Riley first. Pick up our gear and all, and make sure White Eagle and his scouts are properly commended for their help. Leave me some extra water and supplies. I'll take Anna back separately. I don't want her anywhere near Darryl Kelley."

"I understand. You'd better tend to that cut on your head, Nate."

"I will."

Anna slowly opened her eyes to see Nate bent over her, blood clotting on the side of his face. Jim put a hand on his shoulder. "We'll make it a quick trial and get this thing over with," he told Nate.

Nate watched her eyes. "Sometimes I wonder if it will ever be over, especially for Anna."

Jim sighed and turned. "I'll leave you an extra horse."

The man walked off, and Anna reached up to touch Nate's face. "You're hurt," she whispered.

He took her hand and held it tightly, lightly touching the bruises at her neck with his other hand. "My God, Anna, what did he do?"

"Fran . . . she tried to kill me . . . choke me. Darryl . . . killed her. He hit me . . . said he'd kill you." Her eyes teared as the horror of the past day and a half sank in. She had forced herself to stay calm and brave during the ordeal. Now that it was over, she could let go of the terror.

The past had finally caught up with her, but her present and her future was kneeling beside her, his face caked with blood and war paint. He had come for her, risked his life for her, and he still loved her. She saw the agony in his gray eyes, and she knew what he was wondering.

"He didn't . . . touch me that way," she told him.

He closed his eyes, putting her hand to his lips.

"He . . . tried," she told him. "Fran stopped him . . . tried to kill me. He saved me . . . from her. Wouldn't let the Indians . . . take me. I don't understand him . . . so cruel one minute . . . then sometimes he acted like he wanted to . . . protect me."

Nate squeezed her hand. "Don't try to tell me all of it right now, Anna. First we've got to get you back home and into bed. What about the baby?"

"I . . . don't know . . . can't tell."

He leaned closer, pulling her up into his arms. She breathed in his familiar scent. "Forgive me, Anna," he groaned. "I waited until the last minute to realize how much I love and need you . . . and then when I heard he'd taken you off with him . . . when I realized I might lose you . . . I couldn't live without you, Anna."

"I want to go home . . . to Becky."

"We will, as soon as you think you can ride." He gently laid her back down. "I brought one of your dresses along. I had Rob bring me some of your clothes before we left To-peka. I'll wash you up and you can change. You'll feel better." He touched her stomach gently. "I just hope to God you don't lose the baby over this. I'd never forgive myself. I should have suspected sooner that stage robbery might be a setup."

She touched his arm. "You couldn't . . . have known." She raised up to a sitting position. "I need . . . some water."

Nate hurried to his horse to retrieve his canteen and saddlebags. He brought them back beside her and uncorked the canteen, helping her drink.

"He's like . . . two people, Nate. He beat me . . . tried to force himself . . . on me. And then . . . sometimes I'd catch a glimpse . . . of the Darryl I once knew. And he saved me from Fran . . . and from a tent fire."

He took a rag from his saddlebags and poured some water on it, gently touching its cool wetness to her bruised, perspiring face. "You can't let yourself feel sorry for him, Anna, not anymore."

She closed her eyes as Jim and the others rode off with Darryl, who cursed her again as they rode past. Tears slipped down her cheeks. "Oh, Nate," she whispered. "It's so . . . hard to believe. If only . . . you had known him . . . before. It hurts so much . . . to remember. I shot him. I . . . shot Darryl . . . and I wanted to kill him . . . a man I once loved."

"Anna, you were right when you told me that man isn't your husband. Your husband died the minute that shrapnel or bullet or whatever it was creased his skull. That man over there is a stranger, and you only did what you had to do. You thought he was going to kill me."

"It's all so . . . ugly. Fran . . . he beat her so bad . . . then shot her. He shot her to protect me . . . but then it . . . didn't even bother him. He said he was . . . tired of her. He . . . felt no grief . . . at all."

"And that's just one example of why you can't feel sorry for him. His mind is gone, Anna. He's more animal than human. You might have caught a hint of the old Darryl Kelley in his eyes, but that's as close as you'll ever get to the man who rode off to war."

She leaned forward, resting against his chest, and he

wrapped his arms around her. "How did you . . . get here so . . . fast?"

"It's a long story. We'll talk more when you're better. Right now let's get you cleaned up. Then you rest and we'll get back to Topeka and let a doctor look at you."

She touched his leather vest with her hands, feeling his badge against one palm. "I love you, Nate. I'm so . . . sorry. So sorry."

He brushed her hair with his hand. "Don't be sorry, Anna. The war did this . . . to you, to me and Christine . . . to Darryl Kelley and women like Fran. Maybe now we can truly put the damn war behind us."

Nate kept his arm around Anna as they walked past the crowds of people outside the courthouse. He had not allowed Anna to read a paper since he brought her back to Topeka a week ago. The headlines were as full of rumors as the words that passed among the people who stared, but most shouted words of support.

"You should have let us hang him and saved your wife a lot of trouble, Marshal," one man shouted.

Anna's hand tightened on Nate's arm. She realized the hell he had been through the past week, listening to Darryl's spiteful lies whenever he had to be inside the jail; having to protect and defend the very man who had shot him and put him through months of misery, against mobs that formed nearly every night, wanting to drag Darryl from jail and hang him without a trial. Anna knew that Nate would like nothing better than to hang the man himself, but he was a lawman first, and his job was to protect the prisoners.

Just up the street a gallows had already been erected in the expectation that Darryl and all or at least most of his men would be hanged within another two or three days. Rob and Marie followed behind Nate and Anna. Claudine had stayed at their house with the children, fussing over not being able to be with Anna.

They entered the cool courthouse building, where Nate led her over polished wooden floors into the courtroom, which was packed to the rafters, people practically spilling out over the balcony railing. Anna clung even tighter to

Nate's arm as he led her forward. She caught sight of Darryl and six of his men sitting at the front of the courtroom, to her left. She refused to look directly at him, but she felt his gaze on her as she sat down with Nate. Rob and Marie sat down next to them.

People mumbled and stared, then gasped and quieted when Darryl suddenly rose, his wrists cuffed together. "You ought to come sit with me—support your *husband*," he jeered at Anna. "Not your lover."

Jim Lister hit him across the top of the shoulder with the barrel of the rifle he had readied for all of them. "Sit down and shut up," he told Darryl, while people began mumbling and whispering again. Jim stood behind all the prisoners, while two more deputies sat on either end of the line of six men and even more deputies kept guard at the doors to the courtroom in case of trouble.

Anna sat rigid, staring straight ahead, her cheeks crimson from Darryl's shouted remark. Her face and neck still showed heavy bruises. She wore a pale yellow, short-sleeved summer dress of light cotton, with an organdy overskirt and deeper yellow ruffles around the bottom of the full skirt and a yellow satin sash that tied in a bow at the back of her slender waist. Her hair was pulled back at the neck and tied with a yellow bow.

The courtroom was already getting too warm from so many bodies, and Anna felt light-headed, wondering how she would get through this day, until Nate's hand came around her own. She looked at him with apologetic eyes and he gave her a soft smile.

"Nothing they do or say can keep us apart or keep us from loving each other," he had told her that very morning. He had not touched her sexually since her return. Anna had been ordered total bed rest by the doctor, but it was more than her injuries that kept them physically apart. Darryl's presence and the constant publicity since their return had put too much of a strain on that part of their life. Both knew they could not return to a normal married life now until all of this was over.

Judge Michael Hewitt, a federal judge who was also the man who gave Nate his orders, stepped up to the bench and pounded his gavel in an order for everyone to quiet down. His dark eyes studied Darryl and the six men with him. "We all know why you men are here," the man said to the hushed courtroom. "You will be tried before a jury and then you will be sentenced by me. You all have the right to speak up for yourselves, but I will not tolerate free outbursts and uncivil accusations. You will speak when it is your *turn* to speak. Is that understood?"

"Yes, Your Honor," Darryl's court-appointed attorney replied. A few people hissed and booed, and the man's face reddened slightly. He was no more happy than the spectators about having to defend Darryl Kelley and his men. The judge banged his gavel again to quiet the crowd. He looked at the prosecutor. "Mr. Miller, let's get this over with."

Nate leaned close to Anna. "I'm not crazy about Ben Miller. He and I have had our run-ins."

Miller rose and read off a list of accusations, singling out each man and accusing each one of the same murders.

"You can't do that," Darryl protested before his attorney could speak. "We can't all be accused of killing the same men. You have to have witnesses saying which one of us killed which person. I bet nobody can say for sure. And I don't like your attitude, Judge Hewitt."

The judge banged his gavel again, and Jim shoved Darryl back down. "Under the law, Mr. Kelley," he said, his anger evident, "when several people participate in a crime, all bear the same accusation and punishment, even if only one of them did any shooting. And I don't care whether you like my attitude or not."

Everyone in the courtroom cheered, and again the gavel came down several times to quiet them.

"Where's your witnesses? Who can say for sure it was us?" Darryl shouted.

"Be still, Mr. Kelley, or I'll have you taken out of this room," the judge warned.

"We have plenty of witnesses," Miller answered. He looked at the judge. "And not just from the recent robbery in Topeka, but from other robberies, from the robbery in Topeka three years ago when Nate Foster was shot the first time by Darryl Kelley, better known as . . ." He turned and looked at Anna. "Crazy Doc. On that note I would like to call my first witness, *Mrs.* Darryl Kelley," the man finished.

Anna felt as though the blood were being drained from her body. The courtroom burst into mumbles and Nate rose. "You promised you'd call Anna to the stand only if absolutely necessary," he growled at Miller. "You've got plenty of witnesses who can get these men hanged without questioning my wife."

The judge was again pounding his gavel. "She is *not* your wife, Nate. Everyone already knows that. And it *is* absolutely necessary that I question her *first,* so that we can establish a definite identity."

The judge kept pounding, and Darryl threw his head back and laughed. "This is better than killing you after all, Foster," he shouted.

"Shut that man up," the judge ordered. He pounded his gavel harder while Jim untied a bandana around his neck and stuffed it into Darryl's mouth, then borrowed another bandana to tie around his mouth and behind his head. "That should keep you quiet," he growled at the man.

"Nate, sit down," the judge was ordering.

Nate just glared at Miller. "I won't forget this, Miller!"

Miller adjusted his bow tie nervously, holding his chin high, sweat breaking out all over his face. He had wanted to get on the ballot for lieutenant governor when Nate was running and had lost out to him. He had always been of the opinion that only educated men should run for such offices, not men who knew more about horses and guns than the law. He reasoned that this final bit of shame for Nate Foster and his illegal wife would be enough to ruin the man. He suppressed an urge to grin as Anna rose.

"It's all right, Nate," Anna said quietly, touching his arm. "We knew it could happen."

"Not this way," he hissed.

"Nate. It's all right. I *want* to help."

He looked down at her, his jaw flexing in anger. He squeezed her shoulder, moving to let her out. Anna walked on shaking legs to the witness stand and was sworn in. The courtroom quieted, and she felt a thousand eyes on her. She looked boldly at the prosecutor. "Since I am Darryl Kelley's wife, I don't have to testify against him if I don't want to. I think most people in this courtroom know how difficult this is for me, so perhaps they will understand how important it is to me that the man called Darryl Kelley be put away or put to death. I will gladly and fully volunteer any information that will help do so."

"It would help if you could speak a little louder, Mrs. Kelley," Miller told her.

"This is as loud as I can speak. A woman who rode with Darryl's gang tried to choke me when I was kidnapped. I am having trouble with my voice."

Miller looked at the jury. "Can you hear?"

They all nodded and Miller paced a moment. "You admit, then, that the man sitting over there, the one with the scar on his scalp, and who is known to most as Crazy Doc, is indeed Darryl Kelley, and that you are *Mrs.* Darryl Kelley?"

Nate's fists clenched, his heart bleeding for Anna. But she seemed calm and sure. "Yes," she answered. "I married Darryl in Lawrence, Kansas, in 1859." She looked at Darryl. "I was only seventeen. He was twenty-seven. He came from a wealthy family in Georgia. He was a doctor, just getting started. He had come to Lawrence because there were so few doctors on the frontier."

She looked back at the prosecutor. "At that time Darryl was a good man, with a promising future. But because he was from the South, the jayhawkers in Lawrence ran us out of town. We moved to Columbia, Missouri, where some friends of Darryl's lived. Later Darryl and his friend went off to war, to fight for the Confederacy. That was the last I saw of him for three years. He . . . stopped writing. I had no idea what had happened to him until . . ."

She looked back at Darryl, swallowing back tears. "Until I saw him at Centralia." She put a hand to her throat. "I need some water, please."

People whispered as a bailiff got her the water. Anna looked at Nate, remembering how she had met him on the train to Centralia. She could see the love and support mirrored in his eyes, almost wanted to smile at the look on his face, for he most certainly wanted to strangle the prosecutor. She drank some water.

"And what happened at Centralia?" Miller asked.

"Everyone knows what happened at Centralia. The town was raided by Bill Anderson and his men. They murdered Union soldiers." She looked at Darryl again. "I call it murder because they were unarmed, ordered to strip—some were even wounded. They were on their way home on leave."

"And was your husband among those who murdered soldiers?"

Anna looked into Darryl's eyes, struggling to see some remnant of the man she once knew. But the eyes that looked back at her were dark and fiery and full of vengeance. "Yes."

People mumbled again and the judge pounded his gavel.

"And why didn't you tell someone you had seen your husband there, Mrs. Kelley?"

She looked at Miller. "Because I was ashamed, and in shock. I didn't even know he was back. He was just as surprised to see me as I was to see him. He just . . . laughed and told me to go to . . . to hell."

She touched her sore throat as people again mumbled.

"He threw his wedding ring at me and rode off," she continued. "I didn't know what to do. All I felt was great shame—and I was afraid, too. I knew some wives and families of outlaws had been arrested and abused. So I said nothing, hoping Darryl would get in touch with me, explain to me, maybe change his ways. But I never heard from him. I left Columbia and moved to Abilene, where I opened my own restaurant, which I still own. I had to find a way to support myself, and a way to bide my time until I knew what had happened to Darryl."

"And is that when you started seeing Nate Foster?"

Anna frowned. "No. We . . . were just friends. Nate was also at Centralia. He happened to be sitting near me on the train when all the commotion started. He helped me. He even got hurt trying to protect me. It was months afterward when he called on me just to see how I was doing. That was all there was to it."

"And you didn't have contact with your husband during this time? You weren't in some kind of collusion with him?"

"What?"

"Mrs. Kelley, your husband was an *outlaw*. A *murderer*. Nate Foster, as you put it, was a good friend, yet you never told him about Darryl Kelley. You must have had *some* idea where Kelley might be. Why on earth didn't you tell the marshal? After all, you might have saved his getting shot. Were you trying to protect your husband, at the expense of Nate Foster?"

"That's enough," Nate roared, rising again. He headed for Miller and several men quickly grabbed him, pulling him back but having trouble hanging on to him. "You bastard," Nate snarled. "That statement wasn't necessary, and you know it! If you've got something against me, then take it out on *me*, not Anna!"

The judge pounded his gavel again. "Settle down, Nate, or I'll have you evicted from this courtroom."

"He's deliberately rubbing in the dirt to malign my name! He's worried I'll run against him for office again! You know that was an unnecessary statement, Judge!"

"I agree it seemed a bit uncalled for. Sit down, Nate." The judge looked at Miller. "Get on with it, Ben. And be careful how you pose your questions. You know that Mrs. Foster—I mean Mrs. Kelley, has been through a trying experience. You have no call to upset her unduly."

"It's all right. I'll answer the question," Anna said.

The judge pounded his gavel once more, and Anna looked straight at Nate, who had plunked back down into his bench unwillingly. The courtroom again quieted.

"If I had had any idea where Darryl was, if I had thought for one moment I could aid in his capture, I would have felt compelled to tell Nate Foster," Anna said. People strained to hear her. "But Darryl had not contacted me at all. And as I said before, I was ashamed. At the same time, I knew I was falling in love with Marshal Foster. I did not allow him to know my feelings, because I considered myself a married woman. But I respected Nate's position, his honesty. I knew how he felt about men like Darryl. I was afraid if I told him the truth, perhaps he would look at me in a different light or lose his respect for me. I had no idea he was in any danger himself from Darryl until the first robbery in Topeka, when he described who shot him. I was even more devastated then, because Darryl had brought harm to Nate. It just . . . it became harder and harder to tell him. Nate said he had shot Crazy Doc. There were rumors he was dead, so I decided it wasn't necessary to tell Nate after all. Then I got a letter."

She tore her eyes from Nate's and looked back at Miller. "The letter was from Fran Rogers. She was the wife of the friend Darryl had gone off to war with, and after the men left, I stayed on and worked in the restaurant Fran and her husband owned. Fran had been a childhood friend of Darryl's and she was a devout Confederate, a fanatic. When her husband was killed, she only got worse. She considered me a Yankee, and she made life miserable for me. I finally couldn't take any more of her verbal abuse. That's when I left and went to Abilene. I later learned she sold the restaurant and disappeared."

She stopped to drink some more water, and the courtroom remained hushed. "I learned what had happened when I got the letter. It was . . . a very cruel letter. She told me she had run off with Darryl. That he had come back, but for her, not for me. She said she had been living with him, helping him financially, giving him the . . . the love and attention I had denied him. She said all kinds of accusatory things, and then she finished by telling me that Darryl was dead—that he had died in her arms, the arms of a woman who truly loved him. She had apparently led Darryl to believe I had deserted him. She probably told him I had cheated on him." She looked at Darryl. "But I never did. I waited, faithfully, hoping for the impossible. I didn't start seeing Nate Foster seriously until I was convinced Darryl was dead. Even Nate believed it. He said he had found Darryl's grave. Now we know it was apparently faked."

She looked at the jury and around the courtroom. "I married Nate, thinking Darryl was dead. I did not knowingly commit bigamy." She looked at Nate. "And in my heart, I am married to Nate now, not Darryl Kelley. A piece of paper can't change feelings, or alter the fact that I took

Nate Foster as a husband and that we have a little girl, born out of love." She looked straight at Miller. "Or change the fact that I am carrying another child, fathered by Nate Foster." She ignored the whispers. "I did nothing wrong, and I refuse to show shame, because I feel none. Finding out Darryl Kelley was alive was a shock to us both. And I think it is obvious by the bruises on my face and neck and arms that I did not go with Darryl willingly the day he robbed the bank here. I can attest that he murdered at least one of the soldiers that day at Centralia. And I can attest that he murdered Francine Rogers while I was being held captive. I also saw him murder Clyde Benson and Lonnie Gates. I am sure you have witnesses to other murders." She met Darryl's eyes. "That should be enough to get a man hanged."

Mumbles were heard throughout the courtroom again as Anna stared at Darryl. Yes, she could say it now. What was the use of living in the past, of hoping to find some sign of the man she had married ten years ago? The man she looked at now was a menace to society and deserved to die.

"Thank you, Mrs. Kelley," Miller told her. "You may step down."

Anna looked at him, slowly rising. "Don't call me Mrs. Kelley. The man I married died for me a long time ago. The war did this. The war destroyed him, like so many others. The man who returned from that war is a complete stranger to me. I am Mrs. Nate Foster."

People quietly stared in pity and respect as she moved off the stand. Nate walked up to help her. "Let's go home," she told him. He led her out of the room and outside the courthouse building, and Anna breathed deeply of the fresh air while bystanders watched.

"I don't know how you did it," Nate told her. "I'm proud of you, Anna, the way you answered Miller without a flinch. That bastard didn't need to call you at all and he knew it."

She rested her head against his chest. "Maybe it was better that he did. Now people know. It's done, Nate. Take me home."

Rob and Marie came outside to join them. "I'll have to

have Rob take you home," he told her. "I'll be needed for more testimony."

She drew back, looking up at him. "I'm so sorry."

He grasped her shoulders. "For what? For loving me? Don't ever apologize for that, Anna, or for things you couldn't help. You go on with Rob now. There's no sense in you sitting in that stuffy courtroom listening to the grisly details of Darryl Kelley's actions. This will all be over soon, and our lives will get back to normal."

"Will they?" She searched his eyes. "Can it be the same again, Nate?"

He leaned close, kissing her cheek, not caring who was looking. "You know it can. We proved that to each other before this happened."

She smiled through tears. "I love you so much, Nate. Thank you for being with me today—for standing up for me."

"How could I have done anything else? Go on now. I'll be home soon."

She nodded, wiping at tears. She turned and left with Rob and Marie, feeling as though a thousand pounds had been lifted from her shoulders. She had told the truth, and people could like it or not. She still had Nate's love, and that was all that mattered.

As she climbed into the wagon seat, she heard the pounding of nails and glanced up the street at the gallows being prepared for Darryl and his men. She realized the horror was not over yet. In a day or two there would be a hanging.

Chapter 27

Anna was amazed at the crowds in the street as Rob drove her toward the jailhouse. The trial and sentencing had been swift. Darryl and two of his men would be hanged today, just two days since the trial had ended—two long, lonely, painful days during which Anna had not seen Nate at all. For the last two nights he had slept at the jailhouse because of mobs and threats to the prisoners.

"You would think a circus had come to town," she mentioned to Rob.

"That's what it is for some of these people. Nate told me it's almost always like this for hangings. I've never seen one myself. Nate said people come for miles around, make a picnic out of it—want their kids to see the hanging as a lesson to be good. I expect for some it's just an excuse to get out and see people, especially the settlers who live miles from town."

Anna put a hand to her stomach. "I can't imagine watching a hanging and then picnicking afterward."

"Maybe that's because you know one of the men being hanged. You sure you want to do this, Anna?"

"Yes. It's probably useless, but I'll feel better."

"I don't like the way some of these people look at you. What do they know about what you've been through?"

"It's all right, Rob. I expected it. Some have been kind. Mrs. Flannagan brought over a cake yesterday. I feel more sorry for Nate. It tears at me to think what a good man he is and that my past has come along to give him so much trouble."

"Nate can handle it." Rob stopped in front of the jailhouse and climbed down.

"You come to watch your own husband hang?" a man asked Anna. She felt Rob's grip on her arm tighten, and she knew he was tempted to land a fist into the man. She touched his hand and pulled away, walking up to the man who had made the remark. Surprised, he lost his smile.

"I came to say good-bye to a man who was once my husband," she said calmly. "The man they hang will not be the one I married. They will be hanging a criminal who deserves to die." She turned away, and Rob glowered at the man before following her inside the jailhouse.

Nate rose from behind a desk when Anna came inside. "Anna, what are you doing here?"

Her heart ached at the sight of his tired eyes. Oh, how she had missed him, and how she longed for things to be normal between them again. "I . . . I came to say good-bye to Darryl."

Nate frowned, coming around the desk. "There's no sense in that, Anna. He'll just upset you."

Her eyes teared. "I *have* to, Nate. No matter what he says or thinks, I feel a responsibility to talk to him before he dies. Please understand."

Nate glanced at Rob, who raised his eyebrows. "I tried to talk her out of it."

Nate looked back at Anna with a frown, then turned to take the keys from a hook on the wall. "I'll only let you into the cell room, but not into the cell. And stay back from the bars. He could reach through and hurt you." He scowled as he unlocked a heavy wooden door and ushered her into a room full of cells. "He's on the upper floor." He took her arm and led her to the stairs. She turned just inside the stairwell, where the prisoners could not see them.

"I've missed you," she said quietly. "This past week, it seems like we've been so far apart, Nate."

He put a hand to her face. "I've missed you, too. When this is all over, we'll find a way to pick up the pieces." He pulled her close, and she breathed deeply of his familiar scent, relished the comfort of his arms. "The other day in the courtroom, I was proud and touched, the way you held your head up and said you weren't ashamed of our love. I saw a strong, brave woman on that stand, a woman I wouldn't want to live without. Soon as this is over, we're going to see a preacher, Anna, and very quietly and privately make our marriage legal."

"Becky will have to be told someday."

"Maybe. But she's ours, Anna. And if she's anywhere near as strong as her mother, she'll be able to handle it."

She smiled sadly, leaning back and looking up at him. "If she's strong, it will be because of you."

He touched her bruised face and looked up the stairs. "You sure about seeing him?"

"Yes. It's the only right thing to do." She saw the distant jealousy in his eyes and she pressed his arm. "It will ease my own conscience, Nate. The man is going to die, and he's still legally my husband. The least I can do is tell him good-bye."

He sighed. "All right. He's the only one up there. I'll wait on the stairs here. You give a yell if there's a problem. And stay back from him like I told you."

"Yes, Marshal Foster."

He frowned and followed her up the stairs, then sat down on the steps before reaching the top. Anna's heart pounded with a mixture of dread and deep sorrow as she climbed to the top and turned, walking to the cell where Darryl lay on a cot, a hand over his eyes. "Darryl?"

He opened his eyes and looked at her. "What the hell do you want? You come to rub it in? Your stud lover got the best of me. I never should have listened to that bitch Fran. I never should have come for you, you goddamn Yankee traitor!" He sat up, holding his head. "They won't even let me have any whiskey. Nobody understands how bad my head hurts."

Her eyes teared at the sight of him, such a far cry from Dr. Darryl Kelley. "I'm so sorry, Darryl, for what happened to you in the war. I truly am. But a lot of people suffered, Darryl. It didn't turn them into outlaws."

He glared at her with dark, defiant eyes. "Well, hooray for them! We're all different, Anna, and when you know you're going to live with pain the rest of your life, it does something to you—makes it so you don't give a damn about anything except getting back at the people who put you in that pain."

"The people you hurt had nothing to do with what happened to you. But I didn't come here to preach about what you've done. I came to . . . to tell you I love you—I still love the Darryl Kelley I married. I'll have a nice headstone put at your grave, and I intend for it to simply give your name and birth date, and I will put M.D. after your name— and that you gave your life for the Confederate cause."

He slowly rose, walking to the bars and clasping his hands around two of them. "Why would you do that?"

"Because it's true. The war did this to you. You simply never let that war end." A lump rose in her throat. "I testified against you because the man you have become needs to be punished. It had nothing to do with how I once felt about you. I loved you, Darryl. I don't know if it means anything to you or not, but I want you to know that I will truly mourn your death. I will mourn for the Darryl who left me one day to go off to war." A tear slipped down her cheek. "And I was hoping . . . to get at least a glimpse of that man, before . . . before he's gone from my life forever."

He just stared at her a moment. "You mean it, don't you?"

More tears came. "Yes."

He smiled strangely, and an odd shine came into his eyes. He reached out his hand. "Well, here he is. You get him for ten seconds."

She hesitated, but something in his eyes told her it was all right. She reached out, and he grasped her hand. "If I had thought you could really help, Anna, I might have come to you. I was going to—once. Fran talked me out of it. I thought about you a lot of times, and that's the truth. But I was done for, and I knew it. When I kidnapped you, that was the part of me I can't control. I thought I could force you, make it all work. But I get spells where I can't control myself, where I want to lash out at everything and everybody, hurt people as much as I can—even the ones I love." He let go of her hand. "I'll tell you something, Anna. I didn't throw that ring at you that day because I hated you. It was just the opposite. I figured if I didn't contact you, if I was mean to you when I did see you, you'd hate me, and that would make everything easier. I didn't want you—but I didn't want anybody else to have you, either. When Fran told me about you and Nate Foster, that's when I decided to try to take you back."

She stepped closer, unable to control her tears. "Darryl—"

"Go on, get out of here. You've got a new man and a kid and another one on the way."

"I did love you, Darryl. I waited for you—"

"I said to get out now!" His eyes were changing again. He grinned. "I've been thinking. Being hanged won't be so bad. At least I won't have any more of these damn headaches." He laughed. "You can rest easy, Anna. I *want* to die, don't you see? Every time I went on a raid I was hoping somebody's bullet would find me. But I was never that lucky, and I was always too much of a coward to do it myself. Now I'll finally be at peace and out of pain. Go on now. Get out of here."

He turned away. She watched him a moment longer, choking back tears, then moved to leave. For one little moment she had had the real Darryl Kelley back again, and it gave her a sense of relief, a way to touch the past, the ability to close doors that needed closing. Her husband had finally come home from the war. She walked to the top of the stairs and an instant later was in Nate's arms, a place where she knew for certain she belonged now. He walked her down the stairs and out to Rob. "Get her out of here," he told his brother.

"No. I want to stay for the hanging."

"What! Anna, I won't have it."

"You have to let me stay." She looked up at Nate, her cheeks wet with tears. "He should know I'm here, that at least one person in the whole world cares."

Nate's eyebrows arched in astonishment. *"Cares?"*

"Of course I care. Nate, don't you see? I need this. My husband went off to war and never came back. There was this terrible, empty void in my life. For one brief moment up there the real Darryl looked at me, touched my hand. That's the Darryl I have to support now, the one I will mourn. It has nothing to do with how much I love you, Nate, surely you know that. It's just a part of my past I have to put to rest, and I can only accomplish that by doing what I feel is right now. That's my husband up there, much as we both hate to face that fact. He's going to die today. I can't let him die alone, no more than I could let that happen to you. Please try to understand."

Nate turned away, running a hand through his hair and sighing with frustration.

"I'll stay with her, Nate," Rob told him.

Nate clenched his fists and turned. "Dammit, Anna, you've never watched a hanging, let alone someone you know!"

"I have no choice, Nate. It's my duty. I want him to see me before you cover his face. And I promised him a decent headstone, one that speaks only of the man he was before he left. He's a war casualty, Nate, just the same as if a bullet had struck him down in battle. I understand what he did to you, to both of us. But that wasn't the Darryl I married, the one I just spoke to. *That* Darryl deserves for me to be near him when he dies, and *that* Darryl deserves a decent burial. I'm going to see to both."

Her eyes held a challenge. Nate met her gaze, then glanced at Rob. "Take her across the street to the hotel and let her stand on the balcony so she won't have to stand in the middle of the crowd and listen to their remarks. The balcony is right across from the gallows." He looked down at Anna. "I'll tell him where you'll be so he'll know where to look, if he wants. I just hope he doesn't shout out something to humiliate you." He turned and hung up the keys. "You'd better get going. Jim and the other deputies will be coming by to get them in about ten minutes."

Anna watched him lovingly. "Thank you, Nate. I love you."

He just sighed and sat down behind his desk, his eyes moving over her with a chastising look. "I love you, too. That's why I don't agree with this. Just get going, and stay with Rob. I can't think straight till this is over."

She wiped at more tears and turned away, going outside with Rob, feeling more stares. "She's been crying," someone muttered to another.

"Probably got problems with Foster," someone else said. "She couldn't be crying over that bastard who's gonna hang today."

Anna paid no attention. She walked with Rob to the hotel, where Rob checked with the clerk to see about an empty room from which they could go out onto the balcony.

"We're full up," the clerk answered. "Big day, you know." He reddened a little at the sight of Anna's tear-stained face. "Come on up. I'll knock and get you in the room that has a door to the balcony. There's already others up there, you know."

"We're aware of that," Rob answered. "It will still be better than the crowds down here."

They followed the clerk upstairs and through a crowded hotel room. People quieted when they entered, stared as the clerk ushered Rob and Anna out onto the balcony, where more people stood. They also stopped their conversations when they saw Anna. A small boy looked up at Anna, then at his mother. "How come she's crying?" he asked the woman.

The embarrassed mother pulled him away. "That's the wife of one of the outlaws," the woman told him quietly.

The little boy frowned, gawking at Anna again. "How come you married a bad man?" he blurted out to Anna, with the honesty and curiosity of a child.

"Dennis! You shouldn't ask her that," his mother chided.

Anna turned to look at them both, her gaze falling on the boy. "He wasn't a bad man when I married him," she answered. "Bad things happened to him that changed him. He was in the war, and he got wounded in the head. He couldn't really help some of the things he did." She looked at the mother defiantly. "He was a good man," she told the woman. "A doctor."

She turned away then, watching the crowds below while the little boy stuck a piece of peppermint candy into his mouth. Voices grew louder and people actually cheered when Jim and the other deputies arrived and went inside. Anna felt a hand on her arm and turned to see the mother of the little boy to whom she had just spoken. "I'm sorry," the woman told her sincerely.

Anna swallowed back a lump in her throat. "Thank you." She turned away, her eyes riveted on the entrance to the jail. Minutes later the men came out, leading the outlaws. Darryl looked up, and Anna loved Nate more than ever for telling him where she would be. Darryl kept staring at her as he was led to the gallows by Nate himself. He climbed the steps and took his place under a noose, Nate standing behind him. Jim and two other deputies led the other three men up beside Darryl, each deputy taking his place behind his man.

The crowd quieted, and Nate glanced up at Anna. She clung to the railing, trying to tell him with her eyes how much she loved him. A preacher began reading from the Bible, and one of the outlaws began to cry. But Darryl made no sounds. The preacher led the crowd in singing a hymn and in saying a prayer for the men about to die. He asked each man if he had any last words. The man who was crying simply shook his head. The next man said for them to go ahead and get it over with. The third man asked for a smoke, and Jim lit a thin cigar and stuck it in his mouth.

Next came Darryl. He looked up at Anna. "I'm . . ." His voice broke. "I'm sorry, Anna," he shouted.

Great sobs of grief welled up inside of her. She managed to hold on until Nate slipped a black hood over Darryl's head. Then she turned to weep bitterly against Rob's chest. Jim took the cigar from his man and covered his head. The other heads were covered, and each deputy slipped nooses around the outlaws' necks.

Nate and the others stepped down from the platform then, as the hangman checked all the ropes and knots. He also stepped down and walked to the end of the gallows, where the lever waited to be pulled that would drop the outlaws and put an end to their crimes.

Anna remained turned away. She heard the thud of the lever, heard the crowd gasp "Oh!" almost in unison. Her fists tightened into Rob's jacket and he put an arm around her.

"It's done, Anna."

He led her off the balcony, and before she reached the stairs in the hallway, Nate was there. In the next moment she was in his arms, and he held her so tightly she could barely breathe. She wept pitifully into his shoulder, crying the tears of grief she had needed to cry for so many years.

Anna placed a bouquet of flowers on the grave and rose, reading the headstone. HERE LIES DARRYL WAYNE KELLEY, M.D., BORN JUNE 20, 1832, ATLANTA, GEORGIA. DIED AUGUST 2, 1869, TOPEKA, KANSAS. SERVED AS A MEDIC FOR THE CONFEDERATE ARMY IN THE WAR BETWEEN THE STATES. HE WILL BE REMEMBERED BY HIS LOVING WIFE, ANNA.

A hot Kansas wind blew at Anna's green checked dress and loosened a few strands of her hair from the upsweep of curls into which she had fashioned it. "Graves always seem so lonely to me," she told Nate.

He came up behind her, slipping one arm around her waist and the other across the front of her, pulling her close, her back to him. "I know. I feel the same way about Christine's grave."

She put a hand on his strong arm. "Thank you, Nate, for being there through all of it."

He sighed deeply. It had been two weeks since the hanging, and Anna had come to see the new headstone that had finally been delivered. She and Nate were legally married two days after the hanging, but it was not until just last night that they had overcome their ordeal enough to relax and consummate their new vows.

"Anna, I've been thinking," Nate told her then. "There

are a lot of painful memories here now. How would you like to go see your sister in Montana?"

Her eyes widened in surprise, and she turned to face him. "Joline? Oh, Nate, I would love to see her! But how could we? You have your work."

"Well, there's a hitch." He grasped her shoulders. "I've been looking into it, Jim and I both. There's, uh, there's a need for lawmen up in Wyoming Territory, Montana too, what with more and more people going there to settle, the gold strikes and such. The Union Pacific goes all the way to California now, right through southern Wyoming. The place is growing like crazy. I just thought maybe it would be good for both of us to go someplace new. And you'd be closer to Joline. We could go see her first, then decide what to do. You could sell the restaurant and Claudine could come up and join us if she wanted, or she could keep running the place in Abilene if she prefers."

She reached up and touched his badge. "You're determined to keep wearing this, aren't you?"

He studied her lovingly. "It's in my blood, Anna."

"I know." She rested her head against his chest. "What about Rob and Marie?"

"Well, Rob kind of feels the same way, about bad memories around here and all. And there's lots of need up in Wyoming for suppliers. He'd have no trouble transferring his business. But even if they didn't join us, the Kansas-Pacific is linked up to the Denver and Rio Grande, and that goes right up to Cheyenne and the Union-Pacific. It wouldn't be that difficult for them to come visit, or for us to do the same. What do you think?"

She looked intrigued. "Maybe I could go into business up there myself. If you're going to be off gallivanting after outlaws half the time, I'll need some kind of diversion to keep from going crazy with worry."

He smiled softly. "Still can't quite get over thinking you'll need your own way of survival, can you?"

"Not as long as you insist on leading such a dangerous life."

"It isn't just that, Anna Foster. You're just one of those strange, independent women who loves the challenge of being in business for herself." He leaned down and kissed her lips lightly. "But that's part of what I love about you. You're not like any woman I've ever known, and you've got grit, Anna. Have your damn restaurant, or whatever. But you might end up too busy with a brood of little ones to even consider it."

Her eyes shone with love. "I suppose that's possible." She reached up to touch his face. "Maybe you're right. Maybe we do need to start over someplace new. And I guess you wouldn't be you without this badge." She sighed deeply. "Yes. I'd like to see Joline, very much."

She reached around his neck, her new wedding ring catching in the collar of his shirt, reminding her she was truly Mrs. Nate Foster now. Their lips met in a sweet kiss of renewed vows.

"I love you," he said softly.

She gently pulled away. "And I love you."

She turned from him then and looked back down at the grave. "I won't come here anymore after today," she said. "I've got to let go, Nate."

She knelt down to touch an additional stone she had had placed into the ground on top of the grave. It bore an inscription she had composed herself.

"I'll be at the buggy," Nate told her. He left her alone, and she studied the poem cut into the stone, old memories welling up in her soul for one last time as she read the poem.

> I'll remember you the way you were
> Before our hearts were ravaged, dear,
> By war's cruel sword that cuts so deep,
> And leaves but embers, and a tear.

A tear of her own dripped onto the stone. "Good-bye, Darryl. May God understand and forgive," she whispered.

She rose, turning to walk back to Nate. "Let's go to Wyoming," she said. He smiled sadly, helping her into the buggy. The war was finally over for Darryl Kelley, and for Anna and Nate Foster.

A Note From the Author

I hope you have enjoyed my story. If you would like to read about Anna's sister, Joline, be sure to ask for my book *Montana Woman,* published by Bantam Books. Also, I will be glad to send you a newsletter about other books I have written. Feel free to write to me at 6013-A North Road, Coloma, Michigan 49038, and include a letter-size, self-addressed, stamped envelope.

Rosanne Bittner

To my readers . . .

The following is an excerpt from my next Bantam book, *City of Gold*, to be published in the spring of 1991. The publisher and I offer this preview because we are proud and excited about this sweeping saga about the birth and growth of Denver, Colorado. The novel covers approximately fifty years, and I personally put a lot of research into this novel, both in study and in visiting Denver.

There are many reasons why *City of Gold* was both a challenge and a pleasure for me to write. It is my first novel about the very wealthy. The real pleasure came in writing about a place I love with great passion: Colorado. *City of Gold* is a book I have wanted to write for many years. It portrays a big cast of characters whose lives are wrapped up in Denver's colorful history and, inevitably though not deliberately, intertwined with each other.

City of Gold involves a family dynasty (with a skeleton in their closet), power struggles, a marriage of convenience, an ethnic love story, Indian history, Colorado gold fever, the cattle barons, the railroad empire, love affairs, and family treachery. It portrays the heights that can be reached by one woman determined to build a family empire and the depths of personal despair that often and sadly comes to the very wealthy.

City of Gold is packed with real history. Although the main characters are fictitious, people just like them most certainly did exist. It has a vast array of characters from all walks of life who had one goal in mind—to make Denver, Colorado, the greatest city in the country; people who caused Denver to be nicknamed the Queen City of the West. This novel depicts the romantic visions of common settlers who went west to build on dreams, and who became the wealthy founders of places like Denver and San Francisco. Some became shining stars who live in history books; some lost everything.

City of Gold is, above all, a touching love story. Its central character is the half-breed daughter of David Kirkland, who is adopted by David's wife, Beatrice, and is never told she has Indian blood. It is only through personal tragedy that she learns the truth. The following excerpt is from an early chapter in the novel, which explains how David and Beatrice Kirkland make a marriage of convenience. Although these two people never find sincere love in each other's arms, they are forced by secret vows to remain together, feigning happiness in public, often pretending love in their own bedroom. Beatrice evolves from a young woman who dreams of having nice things into a fortress of strength and determination. It is on Bea's shoulders the Kirkland empire is built, an empire that nearly destroys her husband and children and has a painful effect on her adopted half-breed daughter, Irene; yet this same empire becomes a cornerstone for the Queen City of Colorado.

I have no doubts that all of my readers who like a Bittner book will thoroughly enjoy *City of Gold*, as will a vast new audience of readers who are attracted to big novels about the American West, set in one of this country's most exciting eras. Read the following excerpt, and let your imagination stir up all the possibilities that lie ahead for these two people and their daughter; then look for *City of Gold* in 1991.

Bea set the last plate in place, using an oil lamp to see. Voices and piano music from a nearby saloon filtered into the store, and she dreaded going outside to walk home; but she had already decided she would show no fear once she got there. She had upset "poor Cynthia," and her uncle Jake wanted her to suffer for it. She knew that making her walk home alone was his way of causing her anguish, a proper punishment on top of a sixteen-hour work day. She was tired and hungry, but she was determined not to give her uncle the satisfaction of returning home upset. She would walk into the house looking undaunted.

She carried the lantern into the back room, where she brushed dust from her dress and washed her face and hands. She opened a jar of cream that she had taken from a shelf in the store, not caring whether her uncle would be angry about it. After sixteen hours he could afford to let her use some cream, and she decided she certainly deserved it. It was a small enough luxury.

As she worked the cream into her skin, she closed her eyes and pretended she was a beautiful, rich woman who could afford all the creams and perfumes she desired. Her dress was not a dull brown, but a beautiful pink like Cynthia's. Her hair was piled in curls on top of her head, and her cheeks were pink with rouge. Soon a fancy carriage would come for her and whisk her away to her mansion.

She sighed, opening her eyes to stare at the plain face in the mirror. She set the jar of cream aside and picked up the lantern, going into the main store and checking the china display once more before picking up the keys and going to the door. She blew out the lamp and set it down, then went out, making sure the CLOSED sign was turned the right way. Using the light from a nearby street lantern to see, she carefully locked the doors, unaware at first that a man sat on a bench nearby. She slipped the keys into her pocket and turned, then gasped when the man rose. His presence was so tall and commanding that Bea stepped back at first, afraid.

"Miss Beatrice," he said. "Do you remember me? My name's David Kirkland. I was here about a year ago— bought a rifle from the owner—I think he said at the time you were his niece."

Bea looked around to see if anyone was close by in case she needed to scream for help.

"I don't mean you any harm, ma'am. I, uh, I don't remember your last name, but I came here to talk to you. You'll probably give me a kick and send me off, but I wish you'd at least hear me out.

There was a sincerity in his voice that caught her attention. She looked him over, her heart beating a little faster. David Kirkland! Yes, she remembered him, the tall, handsome mountain man in buckskins whom she had met nearly a year ago. She remembered how he had looked at her, thought he might come back to see her again, but he never had . . . until now. "I . . . what on earth do you want, Mr. Kirkland? and why are you here at this hour?"

"I came earlier, but you looked awful busy." He looked around. "You alone?"

"Yes. I had some extra work to do before I could go home."

He frowned. "And your uncle let you stay here alone? He's letting you walk home alone?"

She felt her cheeks coloring, embarrassed for him to know the kind of man her uncle was. "I'm afraid my uncle considers me somewhat of a burden. it's all right. I plan on getting out on my own soon."

"There's no reason for him to make you work this late and walk home alone. I'll walk you."

She felt suddenly weak and nervous. "You . . . don't have to do that."

"Of course I do. Somebody ought to give that uncle of yours what for."

She smiled nervously. "Mr. Kirkland, you haven't said why you're here. You said you had to talk to me."

He removed his hat. "Yes, ma'am. Let's walk farther down the street, away from the noise of the saloon."

She hesitated, then decided there was nothing to fear. He seemed genuinely concerned for her welfare, and his handsome blue eyes brought a flutter to her heart. She nearly trembled when he took her arm, and she walked on shaking legs past other closed shops, heading up the street toward the Ritter home. he stopped at a bench in a quieter section of town and sat down again, urging her to sit beside him. Bea obeyed, wondering if she was being too careless and foolish.

He studied her in the dim light of the street lantern. "Most just call me Kirk," he said. "What was your last name again?"

"Ritter," she answered. "Beatrice Ritter. You may call me Bea."

He nodded, turning and leaning forward to rest his elbows on his knees. "Well, Bea . . ." He cleared his throat, seeming to suddenly be nervous. "I, uh, the fact is, I never quite forgot about you after I left here last year."

Bea's heart beat faster. She put a hand to her chest, feeling suddenly beautiful. She worked too many hours every day to give men much thought, but this one had often been in her thoughts since she first met him. Would it seem too bold to tell him so? After all, he had admitted the same to her. She swallowed before answering. "I have thought about you often, too, Mr. Kirkland."

"Kirk," he reminded her. He turned his head to meet her eyes. "That true?"

She felt herself blushing again, and she dropped her eyes. "Yes."

He looked out at the dark street. "Bea, where I come from, things aren't done the conventional way. I mean, a man does what he has to do to survive. Folks do what's necessary to look out for each other. Why, I've seen men and women marry who are practically strangers. A woman with several kids loses a husband along the trail west, and some single man or some widower hooks up with her so he'll have a woman to tend to him, and she'll have a man to protect her and provide for her and the kids."

Bea frowned, unsure of what he was trying to tell her.

Kirk shrugged, nervously fingering his hat in his hands,

still staring out in the street. "I, uh . . . I came here with a need, Bea. I need a wife, and you were the first woman who came to mind."

Her eyes widened in shock. "What?" She could hardly believe her ears. It was true she had been attracted to this man, but that had almost been a whole year ago, and they had hardly said two words to each other! She started to rise. "Mr. Kirkland, I can't—"

"Please hear me out," he interrupted, grasping her arm and turning to face her. "Please sit back down and listen to me."

Bea slowly sank back onto the bench, staring at him in wonder. His eyes took on a pleading look. "I've got a child," he told her, "a little baby girl. Her mother was Cheyenne, and her people wouldn't let her keep the baby. She came to me at Bent's Fort about a month ago and said I had to take the baby—made me promise to take care of it."

He let go of her arm and looked away again. "I thought about trying to give her to somebody else, but once I held her and all . . ." He shrugged. "She's mine, my little girl."

His eyes met hers again. "She's beautiful, Bea, the most perfect child you'd ever want to see; and she doesn't even look Indian. She's got my hair and my eyes."

Bea tried to think straight. "You . . . you want *me* to be a mother to your little girl?"

His eyes moved over her. "I, uh . . . I thought you might consider it, unless, of course, you're already spoken for. I mean, if I'm going to take care of her proper, she's got to have a mother. I had a hell of a time traveling with her. Why, I had to bring along a stupid goat for milk and special rags for diapers. A lady at Bent's Fort showed me how to change her and how to feed her with one of those contraptions with a nipple on the end." He stopped short, realizing he had embarrassed her with the word *nipple*.

Bea looked away, her cheeks feeling hot. She knew what was expected of a wife, and although she was attracted to David Kirkland and flattered that he had remembered her, she was not ready to be a wife to any man. "I . . . I don't know what to say, Mr. . . . I mean, Kirk. It's all so strange." She met his eyes. "You mean you traveled all the way from Bent's Fort with a little baby?"

"Yes, ma'am. And I'll tell you right now, I'm full attached to that child. Nothing could make me give her up now. If you won't marry me, I'll just have to find somebody else. I just thought maybe you'd consider it. I mean, last time I was here, I got the impression you weren't very happy. It looked like your uncle worked you hard, and he . . ." His eyes moved over plain dress, and she felt embarrassed again. "He doesn't seem to take very good care of you, leaving you alone to lock up and walk home like this. I asked about you when I was here last, and he told me your folks were dead."

He rose, turned to face her, and leaned against a post. "I'll say it out, Bea. I need a mother for my baby girl, and since I'd thought a lot about you over the past year, I figured I'd come to you first. I know it's not a very romantic way to approach a woman, but where I come from there isn't always time for romance. I know you don't love me— yet— and I don't, well, I have to get to know you better, too. But you're a handsome woman and a hard worker, and you need somebody to take care of you. You have my word that I wouldn't . . . well, I wouldn't expect you to be a wife to me in all ways—not right off. I'm not an animal, ma'am, and I've never hurt a woman. I've never lived a settled life, but I'd do it for you—whatever you wanted."

Bea looked at her lap, shivering with a mixture of excitement and fear. "I'm flattered, Kirk. But this is such a surprise." She put a hand to her hair, wishing she weren't so tired and dirty. "I'll have to think about what you've told me." She looked up at him. "Where is the baby?"

"She's at Sadie's place, the other end of town." He saw the shock come into her eyes, and he put out his hand. "Now don't get all lathered. I know what somebody like you might think of a woman like Sadie Blake, but she's a good woman, and she and the other women there are taking real good care of Morning Star."

Bea slowly rose. "Morning Star? That's her name?"

He nodded, searching her dark eyes hopefully. Bea Ritter was not beautiful, but she had fine, clear skin and solid features, with a fine shape to her, except for being a little tall and big-boned. Compared to the kind of women to whom he was accustomed, Bea was beautiful, and he sensed a certain strength beneath the vulnerable look she had. He attributed the vulnerability to her youth and the loneliness she must feel after losing her parents and living with an uncle who practically worked her to death.

"She shouldn't be over there," Bea told him then.

"I know, but I've got no choice for now."

Their eyes held. "I'd be a good husband, Bea. I wouldn't even touch you at first. All I want is for you to love my little girl—not just take care of her, but really love her, like your own. A kid knows when it isn't loved. I know the feeling myself, and I reckon you do, too." He stepped closer. "You and I . . . we're a lot alike in some ways, Bea. I lost my own parents when I was real young, and I was raised in an orphanage. I ran off when I was only about twelve. I took up with a mountain man, and that's the only life I've lived since then. I'm twenty-five now. Could I ask how old you are?"

She swallowed, wondering if she wanted to belong to such a big man who could break her in half if he chose to do so. Still, he seemed like a good man. Surely a man who willingly took his baby daughter to care for had to have a lot of good in him. "I'm sixteen," she told him.

He nodded. "Well, we both understand how it feels to be homeless and unloved, don't we? I don't want that for my little girl."

She searched his blue eyes, feeling a spark that she knew could turn into love if only she had more time to think. "I would never make a child feel the way my aunt and uncle make me feel," she answered. "That much I could promise you. But . . . I need time to think about this, Kirk It's all so . . . so unreal . . . such a surprise."

"I understand." He took her arm. "I'll walk you home. I ought to talk to your uncle."

"No, I . . . I don't want my uncle to see you or know what you want to do."

He frowned. "Why not?"

"I just . . . he wouldn't care one way or another. And I'm afraid he'd try to stop me from doing what I want. It's not that he cares what happens to me, but he wouldn't want to lose my help at the store; and it seems like he and my aunt always find a way to ruin any happiness I find." She held her chin higher. "I have a right to make my own decision, don't you think?"

"I expect so."

She stopped walking, looking up at him. "If I accept your offer, we can do it my way?"

"Your way? What do you mean?"

"I . . . I'm not sure yet. I just want to know that if I promise to love the baby and raise her as my own, I can make certain conditions, certain requests that will be honored."

He watched her closely for a moment. "All right. Long as you say them out up front, before we see a preacher."

"Fine."

"You'll do it then?"

She turned away. "I don't know yet. Meet me outside the store again tomorrow night and I'll tell you. Wait until my uncle leaves."

"Whatever you say, but I still think he should know."

Bea stiffened. "He doesn't deserve to know, not until after it's too late." She looked up at him again. "I'd better get home. You can watch out for me, but don't walk beside me. I don't wany anyone to see us and tell my uncle, or he might not let me leave the house tomorrow. He and Aunt Marlene are afraid I'll be courted and get married before their precious daughter, Cynthia. Uncle Jake doesn't let me see men."

Kirk smiled lightly. "Well, I'm kind of glad. I always figured if I ever took a wife, I'd want her to be just mine, if you know what I mean."

Her cheeks flushed hot again, and she turned away. "Good night, Kirk." She hurried off, feeling a surprising jealousy at the thought of the man going back to Sadie's place tonight. Would he sleep with the woman?

She walked faster, deciding that what David Kirkland did tonight was the least of her worries for the moment. Out of the clear blue sky the man had come back to Kansas City to ask her to be his wife! She realized he didn't really love her, not now, anyway. All he wanted was a woman to take care of his baby. But marrying him would open whole new avenues for her. It could be her way to find some of her own dreams, and it was certainly a way to get out from under Uncle Jake and Aunt Marlene.

She realized that marriage was not a pathway to independence for most women, but to her it spelled a certain freedom. Was she a fool to consider David Kirkland's outrageous offer? She turned to look at him walking some distance behind her. He was a big, handsome, honest man. She believed him when he said he would make no demands on her; but how much future was there for her with a mountain man who had never held a normal job or settled in one place? Still, he seemed willing to settle for her sake.

She felt suddenly beautiful, desired, needed. Perhaps he didn't love her, but people could learn to love each other, couldn't they? Like Kirk had said, out in the great West where he came from, sometimes total strangers got married. She realized his offer seemed perfectly sane and acceptable for him, for he came from a world far different from her own, and that fascinated her.

She looked back at him once more, feeling protected and safe. One thing was sure, David Kirkland was a man who knew how to take care of himself and protect his own. That was a good feeling. She reached the house, then turned and nodded to him before going inside.

Kirk gave her a little wave. He had already decided not tell her about his son. It was enough of a shock to bring her a baby girl and propose marriage and motherhood both at the same time. He would never know his Indian son, and the thought brought a heaviness to his heart, more painful because he would never be able to share the ache of it with anyone else. Only Red McKinley knew about the twin brother, and it was not likely he would ever see Red again. If Beatrice Ritter accepted his offer, his whole life would change forever, He had no choice. He had a beautiful little daughter who needed him, and he would do what was necessary to raise her properly.

* * *

Night seemed a long time in coming. Bea was hardly aware of her daily chores, mechanically moving through dusting, taking inventory, waiting on customers, and thinking with secret excitement and a feeling of victory that no one knew what she would do tonight. It was difficult to add up costs and count out pieces of candy, or to measure accurately bolts of cloth, for her mind was not on her work.

There was nothing logical about her decision. It was dangerous, foolish, risky, yet no argument she posed could change her mind. The thought of getting out of her uncle's house overshadowed all warnings.

No one had asked why she wore one of her better dresses today, not that it was anything overly fancy. Cynthia had half sneered at her at the breakfast table, looking her over as though she were some lowly servant. Bea guessed that Cynthia thought she had worn her pink flowered muslin just to try to look prettier after seeing Cynthia's new dress the day before.

Bea didn't care what she or anyone else thought. At least no questions had been asked. She had bathed before coming to the store, and she had sprinkled on lilac water. She had twisted her dark hair into one thick braid down the back, which she thought looked nicer than a bun, and she had smuggled extra clothes into the store under the skirt of her dress. She didn't have enough in the way of personal possession to bother packing bags; what she needed after tonight, David Kirkland would have to buy for her later.

The time finally came when Jake Ritter turned the CLOSED sign on the door. Her uncle had hardly talked to her all day, still angry with her for upsetting Cynthia the day before. Bea offered to stay and finish inventory, apologizing again for seeming "ungrateful" and telling him she wanted to make up for it.

Jake gladly obliged and left, and Bea pulled the shades down over the door windows. She waited until it was fully dark, then went to the back room and gently applied to her face more of the cream that she had used the night before. She pinched her cheeks to bring some color into them, wishing again that her skin was lighter.

She smoothed her dress and breathed deeply for courage, then walked to the front doors and opened one, stepping outside onto the boardwalk. The streets seemed quieter than usual. She look up and down the street, then she saw him, David Kirkland, walking toward the store. He had kept his promise.

She quickly stepped back inside the building, and when he came close to the doorway, she quietly told him to go around back, then closed and locked the front door. She carried a lantern to the back room, then set it aside and opened the door, letting Kirk inside.

He removed his hat, and Bea looked up at him, sudden doubts again filling her at the realization of what a big man he was. The small back room only accentuated his size. She noticed he had shaved his beard but had left a mustache, and he had gotten a haircut. He wore cotton pants and shirt instead of buckskins, and she smelled the pleasant scent of a man's toilet water. His blond hair hung in the neat waves to his shirt collar, and his eyes seemed even bluer in the lamplight.

Whether the man was worth much as a provider was yet to be seen, but one thing could not be denied: he was indeed handsome. She reminded herself he must be good or he wouldn't have kept his baby girl and willed himself to settle for her sake.

"You, uh . . . you make up your mind, Bea?" he asked.

Her blood rushed with a mixture of anticipation and fear. "Yes," she answered. "I'll marry you, David Kirkland, and I'll be a mother to your little girl, but I have certain conditions."

He nodded. "What are they?"

She wondered where she got her courage. Perhaps it was the deep hurt she had suffered at the hands of her aunt and uncle and Cynthia that drove her to do something so daring and outrageous. She took a deep breath, holding his eyes boldly.

"We'll leave tonight," she answered, watching the surprise in his eyes. "I don't intend to tell my uncle until we're far from here and we're married. Otherwise he might try to stop us."

He frowned. "If you think that's best."

"I do." She folded her arms. "I want to go to St. Louis. I've never seen St. Louis, and I hear tell it's a pretty big city. You could find work there."

Kirk refused to express his aversion to such a move. Farther east. The thought brought an ache to his insides. What about his beautiful mountains? Still, he knew he would have to find work. St. Louis was probably as good a place as any, and he was not a man to take to farming; but living in a city would not be an easy thing for him.

"I want a home," Bea was saying, "a real home—a house of my own that I can fix my own way and live like a proper wife. I want nice things. I don't mean that I expect to live fancy like my aunt and uncle, but I don't want to live like poor folks either. You've go to work like a proper husband, and in return I'll make a nice home for you. I'm a good cook and I'm clean. I'll love your little girl like my own, that you can count on. But I want folks to think she's ours. I don't ever want to tell anyone she isn't. I don't want folks thinking you only married me to be a mother to her, even if it's true."

His eyes moved over her, and he swallowed. "It wouldn't be the complete truth, Bea," he answered, making her cheeks feel hot. "I mean, if I didn't already have fond thoughts of you, I wouldn't have asked."

Her blood tingled and she suddenly felt too warm. She dropped her eyes. "Another reason I don't want anyone to know the truth about your little girl is because some folks aren't very nice to people with Indian blood. It will be better for her not know herself." She met his eyes again. "I think she should think we're her real parents. As long as she doesn't look Indian, like you say, why should she be burdened with knowing she's got Indian blood? She'll feel more loved if she thinks I'm her real mother, and she won't ever feel she has reason to be ashamed."

Kirk frowned, turning away from her and looking around the little room while he seemed to be thinking things over. "I never connected being Indian with being ashamed," he finally said, his back to her. "Where I come from, white men and Indians mix like blood brothers. I lived with

Morning Star's mother for over a year." He turned to face her, seeing a hint of jealousy in her dark eyes. "She was a good woman." He sighed deeply. "What I'm saying is some of my best friends have been Indians, Bea, and I'll never talk against them; and I don't like what I can see is going to happen to them as more whites settle out west. But at the same time I think I understand what you're trying to tell me. In places like this, and cities like St. Louis, people think different. My little girl might get teased and abused. I wouldn't want that." He rubbed at his eyes. "Maybe you're right. She ought to think we're her parents. The only thing about her that's dark is her skin, but it's not near as dark as a full-blood Indian's, and you're dark. With my light hair and blue eyes, I don't see why we can't pass her off as our own."

Bea nodded. "No one needs to know when we got married. We'll go to St. Louis and tell people we've already been married a while. When we get there, I'll write my uncle and tell him where I am and that I'm fine. He doesn't much care about me, anyway. He won't bother coming to find me once I'm married and he knows I'm all right."

"You sure?"

A look of deep hurt came into her eyes. I'm positive. And I don't care if I never see my aunt and uncle and cousin Cynthia again." She held her chin proudly. "I brought some clothes with me. I want to leave tonight. I'll let my uncle wonder for a while what happened to me. It will serve him right to worry for a few days. We'll be married as soon as possible, and I'll be a wife to you." She felt her face reddening again. "I just want your promise that you won't be—that you aren't a man who would abuse a woman, hit a woman."

He shook his head. "No, ma'am. I'm not that kind. And I'll wait as long as you need—"

"No. If I'm going to marry you, I'll be a proper wife right off." She felt herself trembling, and she took another deep breath, keeping her courage up. "If my uncle *should* decide to come after me, I want the marriage to already be properly consummated so that it cannot be annulled. I want us to be a real husband and wife. Maybe in time we'll even be able to say we . . . we love each other."

He stepped closer, and she prayed her legs would not give way. "I don't think that would be too hard," he told her gently. "Feelings like that don't come easy to a man like me, Bea, but since I've had Morning Star with me, I've begun to learn what the feeling is all about." He touched her arm hesitantly. "And I already love you some just for what you're doing for me and my baby girl."

She read only sincerity in his eyes, and she stood rigid as he leaned down and gently kissed her cheek. He was so handsome and manly. She wanted to love him, to release the strange passion he stirred deep inside. But he was a near stranger, and she knew so little of men. She wished she could give herself to him with total abandon, like Morning Star's mother probably had; but she knew that would be impossible for her, at least at first. She would just have to be brave and let the man do whatever must be done.

"I would like to rename Morning Star," she told him as he straightened. "I want to rename her Irene, after my mother. Irene Louise."

He let go of her arm. "That's a fine name."

She swallowed. "It's settled then. I've wrapped my things into a blanket. I'll lock up and leave the keys inside for my uncle. He has another set. We'll take the back way to wherever Morning Star—I mean, Irene—is being kept and we'll leave tonight. Don't tell the woman taking care of her where you're going, and tell her not to say a word to my uncle."

"She won't."

She turned and picked up her little bundle of belongings. "Let's go then. I've already locked the front door and laid the keys on the counter. The back door will lock when we close it. Take that cape from the hook there and put it around my shoulders, will you?"

Kirk obeyed, patting her shoulder reassuringly when he did so. Bea felt numb. For the moment nothing seemed real. She blew out the lamp, and they walked outside. She stopped and looked up at him in the moonlight. "Remember, I want a real home," she repeated.

"You'll have it."

"I don't want you running off on me. You're not much of a settling man, David Kirkland."

"I won't run off, Bea. I'll never leave my little girl, and I'd never abandon you after what you've done. I'll provide for you the best I can."

She took another deep breath, shivering. Whether it was the chilly night air or the realization that she was running off with this strange mountain man, she couldn't be sure.

Kirk put a hand to her waist and led her away. She smiled at the thought of how worried and confused her aunt and uncle would be by morning, and suddenly the thought of never seeing them or the store again made her want to laugh. She did not look back. There was nothing in Kansas City she would miss.